Under an Evil Moon

THE ENCARTHA CHRONICLES
BOOK ONE

J. KALEB WEEKES

CONTENTS

Aella	7
Silver	15
1. Vernal	21
2. Memories	33
3. Imogene	47
4. Chaos	56
5. The Woman in White	65
6. The Outpost	80
7. A Conversation	95
8. The Path	111
9. On the Bank	122
10. The Incident	132
11. Choices	146
12. Pursuit	156
13. Decisions	171
14. Majesty	187
15. Kenichi	198
16. Escalante	212
17. Lookout	225
18. The City in the Lake	236
19. Ilendrin	250
20. The Dryad	261
21. Captain	274
22. Glen Canyon	284
23. North Rim	294
24. Race to Encartha	310
Epilogue - Encartha	322

To those I've loved, to those I've lost, and to those with whom I may yet associate. May this simple tale bring you joy, and if it should not, may you be filled with charity for the one wielding the pen and his eccentricities.

AELLA

"She's close," the woman said, a broad smile sneaking across her thin lips. "Can you feel it?" Aella Meyssika glanced down to where her small companion crept wraith-like through the darkness near her feet. She couldn't help but envy his size at times like this, it was so much easier to move through the thick trees and creeping vines when one's body wasn't much bigger than a cat's.

She stepped over the fallen trunk of a large tree and grinned as her companion struggled, trying to lift his round body over it.

He glared at her. Not always easier, she supposed.

The little man cursed, there was a popping sound, and he disappeared momentarily only to reappear on the other side of her. He was grumbling something unintelligible under his breath.

She shook her head wryly at him. She envied his ability to ride the ether, to skip from place to place through the invisible currents. It was so convenient! Unfortunately, he could only take that which he could physically carry, so she had to get places through more conventional means.

"I'vnt felt nutin this whole year," Fen said, his pointed beard and long eyebrows waggling in the cool, humid breeze. "H'vnt we searched all t' spaces what can be sorted? We's wastin' da times! We must get to the one!" The gnome's voice was anxious, almost desperate. "We needs him! Spring Queen demands it!"

"We need them all," Aella said firmly, her dark eyes set. She breathed in deeply, savoring the sweet intermingling smells of water and azaleas, then sighed. There was much she didn't know about the Spring Queen's plans, but this much she was certain of. "Besides, we can't be sure who he is. If it even is a *he*."

The little gnome stared back up at her, his thigh-high boots creaking as he positioned himself in a low crouch behind a bush. They stood in a spot of dense undergrowth in the Carolinas somewhere outside one of the Ciegos towns. She didn't know its name, what was the point? A tiny sliver of moon shone silvery in the sky, she looked up at it wondering if the people in the area even noticed it. If they did, they'd probably think it was a moon like any other, unaware of what was approaching. But Aella knew better, the moon was about to change everything.

"Can't we skip um?" Fen complained, breaking her reverie.

"They all count, Fen. You know I'm right." The corners of her mouth tugged upward as the little figure grimaced and shook his head. Aella's smile grew wider as she watched him.

He was always so dramatic! But that wasn't the only reason for her smile, she admitted to herself. It had been a long time since she'd felt this light. This, hopeful? It wasn't right. Now of all times she should be afraid, even despairing with what she knew was coming. She gasped and looked down. Her foot was partially submerged in a small creek that she was sure hadn't been there only a moment before.

The Spring Queen, she thought, shaking her head. *I might have known.* She lifted her foot and felt the light feeling subside.

"I should have known you'd be here," Aella said. "Now please stop toying with my emotions."

"I do not toy with emotions child," the voice of the Spring Queen swam through Aella's mind like a cool breeze across the water. "I only help you see the truth. There is hope yet, reasons to believe. Reasons for faith."

Aella sighed and then nodded. "I believe you," she said. "If I didn't, I wouldn't be here."

"I know child, but everyone needs a little encouragement from time to time."

"Thank you, blessed, but I am unworthy of your help."

"You are worthy," the Spring Queen told her, "and so is Medvenah, though he will also not believe it."

"Is the Medvenah a *he* then?" Aella probed, thoughtful.

"Medvenah is an office, Aella. You know this."

Aella grunted. It seemed like ages since the Spring Queen had given her people the task of finding talented Ciegos and bringing them back to their home among the cliffs. It was fulfilling in its way, a job worth doing, even if the Ciegos were know-nothing children. Still, they were *valuable* know-nothing children— and Aella had played her part well. Of all Encartha's finders, she'd been the most successful. This final group, these few, would be the last she'd ever track, her final quarry. The task was nearly finished, and just in time, the foretold was upon them.

ElKing send that it would be enough.

"Thank you, blessed." Aella said and felt the Spring Queen's response before the demigod's presence faded.

She looked again at the little man, who fidgeted nervously, practically crawling in his skin.

"Where?" she asked.

"Far to the west," he said, a longing born of desperation seeping into his voice, "by the river of old bones."

"I need the American or Encarthan name if you please," Aella said, a touch of exasperation coloring her tone.

"I's not knowing those names."

"Then describe it!" Aella took a deep breath to center herself. Her emotions were all over the place.

"West." Fen said and extended a small hand pointing into the darkness behind them.

"You said that. How far, which state?"

"I's not knowing states."

Aella sighed, exasperated. "Really, Fen, I didn't know the names of the states when we started either, and yet here we are, I know them all, and you know nothing. You simply refuse to learn."

The little man pulled down on his long, pointed ears and frowned stubbornly. "You's not be learning gnome names. Ciego names not be mattering soon."

She shrugged. He had a point. Over the millennia, places in the area currently known as the United States had been named many times. First by the Encarthans, then by the peoples now referred to as Native Americans, and finally by European settlers.

Would people go back to using the original Encarthan names after the event? Would new names be created? It was hard to say. It depended on who won, she supposed. The war was certain, but the outcome was in question.

"How far?" she pressed.

"'Bout seven hundred league."

"Nearly two thousand miles," she whispered to herself.

Much farther than she'd realized. She grunted. "Most likely somewhere in Utah or Colorado then."

She paused tapping a finger to her lips in thought.

"Or Arizona," she amended.

She glanced up at the moon, wondering how much time she had left. A week? A month? It certainly wasn't much. She could almost feel the object approaching, like a stranger moving silently behind her in the dark, intent on mischief.

"Let's split up," she said, resignedly. "I'll take the girl here and the two in the northeast, you get those in the northwest. Have Min gather the two in Mexico, and then we'll meet wherever this strong one is."

"Bu' mistress, you'll be needing' ol' Fen wit' all 'em blasted wolves e'rwhere." The little gnome pulled on his long, pointed ears until they wrapped around his jaw. His face was an affected mask of sadness so convincing she could almost have believed it was genuine.

"They're popping up e'rywhere's, like big hairy turnips they are. Up from the grounds they is comin!" he said in a plaintive, high voice.

"Don't pretend you're not glad to be going for the easy ones," Aella said wryly. "I know you too well. Besides, I can take care of myself. I've fought skin-walkers for more than five decades."

The little man frowned dramatically, his shoulders slumping in mock sadness that she didn't buy for an instant.

"Now don' be sayin' such things, mistress. Fen's been doin' such good work he has. You's said so yerself you 'as."

"You have been very good, Fen," she said earnestly, crouching to put a gentle hand on a small bony shoulder. "Better than good, you've been amazing, and we're almost done! After this group, the foretold will have come, and it will be too late to look for more. Still, we must find these last few and get them safely to Encartha."

"Will 'e truly be free, mistress? Black hex on 'es name!"

"Yes," she said simply, though the truth of it made her insides twist. "When the foretold arrives, the barrier won't last long."

She paused to look back to the dark sky. "We have seen nothing thus far, Fen. When the barrier is gone, your hairy turnips will be everywhere." She winked at him.

The little man glanced up at her, met her eyes, and gulped audibly; a thin whimper escaped his trembling lips.

"Shh, Fen," Aella admonished in a stage whisper. "You don't want the Ciegos to see you, do you? They'll put you in a circus!"

"Won' matter at all if I'm in a circus. If he be free, all is done, all is gone!"

Aella gently squeezed the gnome's small shoulder.

"Trust in the ElKing and his Medvenah," she said. "The prophecy foretells victory, the ElKing wills it so. He's set the Spring Queen in motion."

She gestured, laying her right palm over her heart and placing the first two fingers of her left hand to her lips in reverence.

The little man repeated the gesture. "We must be off," Aella said. "Let us make haste. The time is nearly spent, and we have work to do."

She nodded and stood as Fen put a palm to his forehead, the gnome gesture of fealty, and disappeared with a little popping sound.

She felt another little stab of jealousy at how easy it was for gnomes to travel—one moment he was here, and the next, she felt him go far to the north. He would find her once he had completed his task, Fen could find Aella so much easier than she could find him, or the gifted ones that they sought.

She fingered the charms that hung from the silver bracelet on her left wrist and selected one with a circular design. She pinched it between two fingers and held it firmly. Her sense of direction intensified, a tugging sensation blossoming in her chest leading to her right. The charm Fen had given her allowed her to sense the gifted, at least the general direction of any gifted who was not shrouded and had not yet formed a full-bodied manifestation. It was a poor substitute for Fen's ability, but it got the job done.

She took a deep breath. She was on her own now. She had to gather the three they had identified, find them before one of the packs did, take them to the meeting place where Fen and the rest of their little group would wait, and finally make sure they reached Encartha. She moved, heading through the woods toward a neighborhood in the distance.

She fingered the charms, turning them one at a time until she found the lithe, feminine shape of the charm she needed. She gripped it tightly and concentrated. Her clothes rippled, shifting and distorting from her half-robe and secha of rank to a pair of blue jeans and a long sleeve white t-shirt. Her head tingled as long silvery blond hair replaced her natural black locks. She wasn't sure why Fen had added that detail; plenty of Ciegos had black hair, but she liked it. She'd have to remember to ask him someday.

Aella crouched and waited, pressing herself next to a large tree and watching the house, peering to see inside. Minutes passed, and her legs had just begun to cramp when an upstairs light flicked on. A slender teenage girl with long blond hair stepped into view. The girl stopped to look at herself in a mirror and tossed her golden locks over her shoulder. The bauble on Aella's wrist seemed to hum, making the hair on her arm stand up.

Her first target.

Aella still couldn't see the girl's face. She stood and slipped from the cover of the trees to peer over the fence. Quickly she scanned the immaculately trimmed grass.

No dog.

She crouched deeply and leapt, propelling herself up and over the eight-foot fence to land lightly on the grass then slipped across the dark yard to the back door. She grasped the handle and focused, summoning the tendrils. They slid silently out of her palm and into the lock. A moment later it clicked, and she turned the handle.

Child's play, she thought, grinning wickedly. *I'll miss this.* The thought came with an unexpected wistfulness. *Focus on the task at hand.*

She would have them in a few days; three, maybe four. She glanced at the moon.

I hope I have that much time.

She slipped inside, closing the door quietly behind her, and padded to the stairs. The pull emanated from above, and Aella ghosted forward, up the stairs, then down the hall to the second door. Light streamed from under it. Aella turned the handle and looked inside.

The girl gasped, wide blue eyes met Aella's, and the girl grabbed the discarded shirt from her bed and pulled it up to cover herself.

"Good evening," Aella said, a broad friendly smile coming to her lips.

SILVER

Silver tasted blood. He rolled the metallic liquid around in his mouth, savoring its warmth on his long tongue. He swallowed and tore another hunk of flesh from the she-cub's leg.

She'd been young and talented, though not very strong, probably too young for the power to have properly manifested in her. She might not have even known she was different, special. Her essence sang on his tongue, filling him in a way mundane blood never could.

One of the wolves behind him whined softly and was joined by a chorus of whimpers from the pack. A few of the higher-ranking members paced, noses low to the ground, tongues lapping the air in anticipation.

Silver would have to let them feed eventually, but for now, he would keep them waiting. It was his privilege as alpha.

He noted the group of lower-ranking members sitting far in the distance. This kill was too small; they would have to suffice with a rabbit or other more mundane prey.

Weaklings. Silver pitied and despised them in equal measure. Maybe he should do them a favor and put them out of their misery. He felt a momentary pressure at the back of his mind, an almost pain as the compulsion pressed on his thoughts, pushing his mind from the idea. He had been commanded to expand his pack, not to diminish it.

A deep growl rumbled behind Silver, and he turned. A huge shaggy wolf with long black fur and a single white streak below his left eye glared back at him. Silver's hackles rose, his growl rumbled in response to the slight, and his lips curled to expose his gleaming fangs. Rictus stalked closer. Silver turned to face the big black wolf and snapped his jaws in warning. He would brook no dissent tonight.

Rictus hesitated, his golden eyes calculating as he stared back at his alpha. Finally, he paced backward and sat on his haunches, cowed by the warning, for now. Silver knew that Rictus would challenge him soon; he was growing restless in Silver's shadow.

Silver settled down to the meal, taking longer than he had to, his eyes staring down his second. Rictus hesitated then looked away.

Silver ate, slowly savoring the meal for a long moment before finally relenting, raising his muzzle from the corpse and stalking a few strides from the kill. The pack shifted in anticipation, and wolves began inching cautiously toward the carcass, their muzzles scenting hopefully. Silver stood on his back feet, his thickly muscled body stretching out in an almost human pose. He licked some blood from his long, clawed fingers, before turning his attention across the desert. The land was dark, the tiny sliver of a new moon providing little enough light, even for werewolves.

The she-child had been young, small, and not nearly

enough sustenance for a pack as large as Silver's. He would need to find more gifted people to hunt, and soon. If he failed, even he would be forced to eat the lifeless, tasteless flesh of common humans. He turned his nose up at the thought; he might as well eat mud.

Silver settled down and laid his huge head on the ground. His thoughts turned to the next hunt. Talented humans had become increasingly rare over the years. All magical creatures had. Even werewolves. But it wouldn't last. Not after the barrier fell.

His life before his change was so far gone that Silver could barely recall any part of it. What he did remember was hazy and confusing, littered with irrelevant emotions and foolish ideas like love, justice, and friendship. *Ridiculous.*

By the time he was finished grooming, the once-girl had been reduced to a small pile of bones, picked clean, cracked, and empty. Not even her marrow had escaped the pack's hunger. Silver yawned and closed his eyes.

He didn't enjoy the feel of the sun on his skin. It was uncomfortable, hot, and slightly painful. But dawn was still hours away, so he had time for a quick nap before they found shelter for the day.

A sudden powerful prickling in the back of his mind brought Silver up, his ears perking forward. The prickling call hummed in his mind like a trumpet blast from the west.

One of the gifted was out there, someone strong, *very* strong. He scented the wind, and he could almost taste the resonance of power. Around him, Silver's pack had become alert, pacing, pawing, and yipping in excitement at the instinctual need to hunt the gifted.

Silver growled low in his chest, showing his teeth, and the pack responded in kind. The hunt was on. Like a bullet Silver sprang into the night racing westward, his once-human mind now focused with inhuman instinct. The instinct to hunt and kill the gifted.

The pack ran, streaming across the desert in a long line. Silver, the fastest and strongest, led the group at the front, and Omega, the youngest and weakest, fell far behind. In the back of his mind, the instinct called Silver, driving him forward with a call more powerful than the urge to mate. Then as suddenly as it began, the call stopped. It winked out of existence like the light of a candle someone had just blown out. Silver stopped and raised his nose to the wind. The scent was gone.

Silver waited, his senses straining to pick up the lost scent. He glanced back toward his pack. His subordinates were gathering, some beginning to sit, others whining in displeasure. Rictus glared at him. A low growl sounded from Rictus' thick chest, and he bared his gleaming fangs. Silver answered the growl with one of his own and snapped his jaws at the upstart. Rictus retreated. Silver would have to deal with the wolf soon and put him firmly in his place.

Suddenly, there was a disturbance. Yowling and snapping sounded from the back of the pack. Silver turned and trotted to where Omega stood bristling, teeth bared as Red Tooth slowly advanced toward him. Silver sat, watching as things developed.

Omega was young, only a couple of decades old. He was smaller than Red Tooth and held a much lower position in the pack. Red Tooth had been tormenting him, asserting his authority over the younger wolf at every opportunity. Omega's eyes flitted back and forth between Silver and Red Tooth.

Silver's impassive chuckle sounded almost human as he met Omega's eyes. They were striking, mismatched eyes, one gray, one blue. Silver would not intervene. The pack had only one law, one foundational principle—the strongest rule.

Red Tooth moved in, his hackles up as Omega retreated. Red Tooth lunged forward, snapping at the smaller wolf and driving him slowly back toward a nearby cliff face. The young wolf showed his teeth but retreated. The rest of the pack moved closer, watching as the drama unfolded.

Finally, there was nowhere left for Omega to go, with only open air behind him. He bared his teeth, hackles raised, trying to make himself look bigger. Red Tooth moved in closer, paused, and then lunged forward. Omega leapt at the bigger wolf.

The beasts collided in a fury of snapping teeth and slashing claws. The combatants darted in and out in an almost elegant dance. Red Tooth slashed Omega's side, drawing blood. Red Tooth rushed at the younger wolf again and the dance became a melee. There was a yelp, and Red Tooth lurched away, his back leg dragging behind him. Omega charged after him, slashing and biting. Red Tooth yelped and cowered. Omega bit and slashed, opening large gashes in the older wolf's hide. Finally, Red Tooth relented, lay on his side, and showed his belly in defeat. Omega stood over him showing his teeth and growling. Then he raised his muzzle and howled.

It was over. There was a new order in the pack. Red Tooth was now omega; he'd lost his name tonight. Now, the wolf formerly known as Omega needed a new name. Silver considered, meeting the smaller wolf's eyes. White Eye, he decided. That would be his name from now on.

Silver acknowledged the new ranking and declared White Eye's new name to the pack in a series of guttural, feral-sounding words that were as much snarl as speech.

This done, he turned and began loping west. There was blood out there, powerful blood. Whoever it belonged to had made a huge mistake in revealing their presence. Old One had charged Silver millennia ago with hunting down the fledglings.

An eternity of service, but truth be told, Silver had never found it to be a burden. He delighted in the task, the killing of the fledglings, in cutting them down screaming, in the taste of their blood. He couldn't imagine anything else for himself.

There was blood out there, and Silver would find it.

CHAPTER 1
VERNAL

Morgan Foster de la Vega was on his best behavior. "Don't put anything in!" the woman barked. Morgan sighed and stepped back from the Cadillac. The crone shuffled glacially toward the open trunk, then waved him forward with a shriveled arm. "Come over here, you fool!" she snapped, yanking down the side of one of the paper bags as she peered mole-like inside. She rummaged with a bony hand, pushing aside various items.

"There," she croaked, gesturing to a spot in the middle of the trunk. Morgan set his burden inside.

"Not there!" she barked. "There!" She pointed at a spot right roughly an inch from where he'd set the bag.

Morgan repressed a sigh and shifted the bag.

She nodded and began rummaging through the next bag. After what felt like an hour, but was probably only a few minutes, the woman finished painstakingly arranging the bags into the desired pattern and shooed Morgan away by waving a hand at him like he was an overgrown fly buzzing around her head.

He wished the old woman an insincere good afternoon and slunk away, silently congratulating himself on having not been yelled at more this time. He'd had it much worse during some of the woman's previous visits to the grocery store where he worked. She had developed something of a reputation among the baggers. When they saw her coming to the front of the store, they vanished from their normal positions by the check stands like mirages in the desert.

Morgan walked the cart to the return area, gathering additional carts on his way. When he reached the cart return, he stopped, staring down. A small fluttering movement had caught his eye. He squatted and tugged a piece of paper free of the metal railing, unfolded it, and stared in surprise at a weathered fifty-dollar bill.

He looked around, holding the bill in his hand, his heart thumping like he was sprinting. Nervousness and adrenaline poured into him in equal measure.

The rest of the lot was nearly empty, a few older model cars sat abandoned at the far end, vehicles belonging not to customers but to other employees. Morgan licked his lips unconsciously as he held the bill pinched between his fingers. To him, fifty dollars, especially fifty dollars that Eric Steadman, his foster caretaker, didn't know about was practically a fortune.

He thought of his sister, Imogene and bit his lip; and surreptitiously shoved the bill into his pocket. He strode quickly, pushing a line of carts to the entryway of the store, his mind racing through possibilities. He'd avoided a verbal berating, and now this! It must be his lucky day!

He paused as he entered through the front doors and approached the only register that was currently occupied. Jenny Meyers stood behind the counter with one arm crossed over her stomach and the other playing with a strand of her long blonde hair. Nearby Abby, a red-haired and slightly pudgy bagger, yammered on in a run-on sentence that seemed never to pause, not even for breath.

Morgan hardly noticed Abby or her interminable diatribe. His eyes fixed on Jenny. She was tall with blue eyes and a quick bright smile, the kind of girl you never quite expected to see in a town as small as Vernal—and who was lovelier for the lack of expectation. A desert rose among the cacti and sage.

"Did you hear about the asteroid?" Abby said brightly, the change in subject finally breaking Morgan's focus.

He grunted a no, and Jenny shook her head.

"Well, so there's this asteroid that's like, really close. It's supposed to pass by in the next few days."

"Really?" Jenny's tone was flat and uninterested, a forced smile adorning her lips.

"Yeah, it's close. First the dinosaurs, then us," Abby continued, grinning widely. Morgan frowned at the joke. Vernal was a town best known for fossil remains.

Jenny frowned. "How close?" she asked as she pulled a lock of hair into the corner of her mouth and bit down on it.

Abby was in heaven. She preened as she went on with the story in a tone like she was telling a juicy secret.

"It's like almost here. They don't think it will be a big deal though, just a fly-by or something," Abby went on, shaking her head and rolling her eyes, an exaggerated unconcern written on her face.

The creases at the corners of Jenny's eyes relaxed.

"They said it might get close to the moon, but it's too far away to make us into sausages."

"That's good," Jenny said, casting a sideways glance toward the back of the store.

"Better than hitting us. I heard on the news that if it hits the moon, the impact isn't supposed to do anything except maybe look cool and leave another big crater or something. A few of us are going to watch it. We're going to get some rafts and watch it from the river. Want to come?"

"Maybe," Jenny muttered.

"You should come," Abby said excitedly. "We're going to meet down by River Runners storage shed. It's out by where the highway crosses the Green River. Ten o'clock." Abby turned and looked at Morgan. He turned his eyes away, feeling his face flushing.

"Yeah, OK, maybe," Jenny's eyes fixed on Morgan. He swallowed and looked back at her, the corner of his mouth tugging upward in a hesitant grin. He stared into her eyes, searching his mind for something interesting to say.

"How often do you get to see something like this?" Abby continued. The spell was broken, and Jenny turned back toward the other bagger. Morgan groaned internally. Why couldn't he manage to say anything clever? Or funny?

"It's going to be amazing!" Abby finished.

"Ten bucks says it splits the moon in half," a deep voice said from the other side of the check stand. Morgan glanced up to see Todd, the muscular, square-jawed twenty-something that worked as the frozen foods manager. He winked at Jenny, and she lit up. Morgan frowned, his hands gripping the edge of the check stand with finger whitening intensity.

"No chance," Abby droned, "my money wouldn't be worth much if the moon was split in half. We'd probably all be dead anyway."

Todd laughed, his head tipping back, his large Adam's apple protruding like a second chin.

"See that's the beauty of it, Abby," the big man said. "We make the bet, I spend your ten bucks tonight taking Jenny to dinner, and then if you're right, I just stiff you. Either way, I win." Morgan noticed the blush on Jenny's face, and he looked away.

A movement drew Morgan's eyes toward the end of a nearby aisle. A thin woman stood partially obscured by a display of cereal boxes. She was tall, with long silvery blonde hair and a smooth, pretty face. She was wearing a tight pair of blue jeans and a white t-shirt. She was staring at Morgan. When he met her eyes, she grinned and winked.

Morgan started, blushing as the girl slipped down the aisle and out of view. He leaned, trying to see down the aisle after her.

"Ugh, you're such a douche," Abby spat and walked away, shaking her head.

"Who was that?" Morgan said.

"Who was who?" Jenny said.

Morgan looked up at her and hesitated.

"I thought I saw," he started and then thought better of it. "Nothing," he said. "Never mind."

He looked up at Todd, who was staring appreciatively at Jenny. Morgan met his eyes, and Todd winked at him and grinned before turning to his work. Jenny picked up a book from the shelf and began thumbing through its pages.

Morgan's stomach rumbled, and he glanced at a clock in the front of the store. 11:30. "Dotty," he said to his front-end manager, a sixty-year-old woman with a gray bun and rectangular glasses. She stood behind a counter at the front of the store and looked up from a pile of papers she had been absorbed in.

"Can I take my lunch?" he asked, already making his way toward the break room.

"Sure thing, Hun," she said, returning to the papers hardly noticing him.

Morgan purchased a loaf of French bread, a liter of Mountain Dew, and headed to the break room. He paused at the door of the small, dark room. Steve, a bald forty-something store manager, looked over his shoulder from where he sat talking to Jack, one of the dairymen at the store.

Steve nodded to Morgan as he slid into a chair at the table and tore open the bag.

Steam rose from the loaf of warm French bread inside, and Morgan inhaled deeply. An unconscious small smile stole across his face.

"What happened to 'em?" Steve said.

Morgan tore off a large piece of bread and stuffed it into his mouth as Jack nodded importantly.

"Don't know," Jack said, talking around a mouth crammed to overflowing with hamburger. "We just found 'em out there. They's all tore up, half-eaten, blood everywhere." He took another bite of the dripping burger without bothering to finish the previous one.

"Just like that? How many of 'em?" Steve popped a tater tot in his mouth and began to chew, a far-off look in his eye.

"Four heifers and his best bull," Jack slurred. "The heifers are bad enough, but the bull is the real killer. Blue-ribbon winner, got good stud fees, Jack's other bull isn't mature yet, so now he'll be the one payin'." He shook his head somberly and gulped. "Things were bad before, now this. Might be he'll have to sell land to make do."

Steve grunted his sympathy. The old-timers hated to sell land if they could help it. The saying around these parts was that when a man sold his land, his soul was soon to follow.

Morgan hunched over his food, not wanting to intrude on the conversation but without a good way to distract himself. Not for the first time, he wished that he had a cell phone. Headphones would be like a whole new world, a world where Morgan could pretend he did not live in Vernal.

"Feel bad about the dogs too," Jack continued. "Roy loved those damn dogs. Real shame what happened to them."

Steve furrowed his brow. "Damn, the dogs too? What happened to 'em?"

"Just like the heifers," Jack said. "Found 'em in the field. Like I say, whatever attacked 'em was vicious, nearly tore ol' Pepper's head clean off. Skaggs had a slash in his side about that wide." He held up his hand, thumb, and finger several inches apart. "We couldn't even find most of Curly, just one of the 'is back legs. Poor devil." Jack's eyes were haunted, his head shaking somberly as he described the scene.

"Never seen Roy cry like that before," he went on, "and I've known him since we was kids. I never once seen 'im cry. Not once. Not even when Betty-Joe Wilder dumped 'im for Jeremy Winter in front of everyone when we was juniors in high school. Damned shame." Jack shook his head and took another bite of his burger.

"And nobody saw anything?" Steve asked.

Morgan looked up from his bread, his interest peaked despite himself. He'd lived in Vernal for five years and he'd never heard of this type of attack.

"Not a damn thing. They weren't home at the time. They'd gone fer a late supper, and when they got back, the dogs didn't come out to meet them like normal. After a while, Bill wondered what they was about and went out looking for 'em. That's when he found the cattle. The dogs were nearby, just up the hill a bit. At first, he thought the dogs and cattle had somehow done it to each other, but then he looked closer. No way those dogs could have done that much damage, and the way they were mangled—" He shook his head. "A bear coulda done somep'n like that, maybe."

"I mean, it had to be a bear, right?" Steve asked through another bite of food. "Or a cougar."

"Ain't nobody seen any bears around these parts in I don't know how long," Jack said, shaking his head. "Some figure it must have been them aliens. You know like people out to Skin-walker Ranch is always going on about? Aliens or skin-walkers."

Steve snorted. "Them people under-cooked their whisky. Got a bad case of the crazies as a result."

"What's a skin-walker?" Morgan asked, then clamped his mouth closed. The question had just slipped out.

Jack turned to him and nodded. "I forget sometimes you ain't from 'round here. The natives called them that, skin-walkers. Their legends talk of men—evil men, shamans and the like—that can take on the form of animals. Transform themselves into monsters."

"Do they like, turn into a wolf or a bear or—" Morgan cut off as Jack shook his head.

"Nah, that's too normal," he said seriously. "These things are monsters, boy, like I say. Huge, hideous beasts, part man, part animal. You might call 'em werewolves, but they're not like what you've heard, with the full moon and silver bullets and whatnot."

"So, what do they do?" Morgan said.

"How in hell am I supposed to know?" Steve said, grinning to take the sting out of his words. "They're legends, boy!"

"They ain't. I seen one," Jack said.

Morgan and Steve turned to him. His face was set and pale. He bit his lip and stared back at them.

"You're pullin' my leg," Steve said.

Jack shook his head. "No, I ain't. I tell you, I seen one. Big and hairy, must have been almost ten feet tall, and it looked almost human. Almost human, but it had a snout and fangs. It was dark, and pretty far away, but I've never been so scared in all my life." His tone was firm, adamant.

"When?" Steve said with a skeptical chuckle. "When you were on a bender?" He laughed. "When you'd been burnin' the wrong field? One of the Richter's *special* fields?" He grinned and turned to wink at Morgan. Morgan offered a hesitant half-smile in return.

"Long time ago." Jack's eyes were distant, unfocused. "It was back when Henry—" He paused, his eyes turning glassy and locking onto Steve's. Steve stood and stared back at him, neither of them saying a word for a long time.

"Who's Henry?" Morgan ventured, his eyes flitting between the two men.

"I best be getting back," Jack said, standing suddenly and balling up the remnants of his lunch. "Got a load of milk coming in any time. Best make room in the fridge 'fore it does." He strode toward the door without looking at Morgan.

Steve sat back down, staring in silence at the rest of his food. After a minute he pushed the rest of it away, stood, and walked quickly out of the break room.

Morgan sat in silence for a moment, puzzling over the conversation and the men's sudden departure. He looked at the clock, realizing he still had ten minutes before he had to return to work. His mind began to wander from the grizzly scene Jack was describing. He slipped his hand into his pocket, fingering the paper inside. He thought about Imogene. How much would a prepaid cell phone be? A hundred dollars? Two hundred?

He stood, disposed of the remnants of his lunch, and exited the break room and headed towards the check stands.

"There you are." The sniveling voice came from behind Morgan. He stopped in his tracks, repressed a shudder, and turned.

Eric Steadman was standing by the doors, scowling at him. Eric was a short man with squinting black eyes, greasy gray-black hair, and stained teeth. He wore a pair of brown checkered pants and a thin short-sleeved shirt. His square, out-of-fashion glasses sat crookedly on his pocked nose.

"What do you want?" Morgan grated.

Eric grinned nastily. "You know what I want," he said. "It's time to earn your keep."

"The state pays you for my care."

"Well, they don't pay enough to put up with your nonsense!" Eric said, his face twisting in anger. "Don't forget our agreement," he warned, shaking a grimy finger at Morgan. "I'm the one that made this little work arrangement happen for you, and I can end it at any time."

"It's not against the law for teenagers to work," Morgan said, his face heating.

Eric laughed. "It is at fifteen. At your age, you need my permission! I can withdraw that permission at any time. Is that what you want?"

Morgan gritted his teeth. "No." He managed to spit out.

"Go get it." Eric prodded.

Morgan hesitated, glaring back at the man. Finally, his shoulders slumped, and he turned, walking to the customer service desk at the front of the store.

"Hey, Dotty," he said dispiritedly to the old woman behind the counter. "Can I get my check?" She looked up and took in Morgan's demeanor, then glanced behind him to where Eric stood.

She paused, frowning and looking back and forth between Morgan and his foster parent.

"Sure thing, sweetie," she said slowly, opening a locked drawer behind the counter. She withdrew a stack of checks and thumbed through them. She pulled out a check with Morgan's name on it and handed it to him. He reached to take it, but she held onto it with surprisingly strong fingers.

"You know you can have this direct deposited," she whispered looking over his shoulder at Eric, a fierce scowl on her face.

"I don't have a bank account," Morgan said. He looked into the older woman's soft eyes, willing her to understand. "Please don't make a big deal of this," he whispered.

"It's not right." Dotty hissed, glaring past Morgan to his state-appointed guardian. "It's not right what he does." She released the check.

"It's OK, Dotty," Morgan said with a small smile. "Thanks though." He nodded and turned, keeping his eyes down so that neither Dotty nor Eric could see his expression. He walked to where Eric waited, grubby hands practically itching with anticipation and held it out to him.

Eric snatched the check out of Morgan's hand and read the amount. He looked up at Morgan, his red-rimmed eyes glaring.

"Fewer hours this time," Eric complained. "You'll need to do better! Do I make myself clear?" He gave the check back to Morgan. "Sign it." He clicked the tip of a pen and handed it to him.

Morgan took the pen and signed *Morgan de la Vega Foster* before handing the check back to Eric.

"I'll leave your half on your dresser," Eric said and turned.

"I'd be shocked if it were half," Morgan whispered under his breath as the man strode away. It was usually less than a quarter.

Morgan headed back towards Jenny's check stand. When he looked up the woman in white was looking at him, her eyes catching him with a piercing stare. She lifted a folded piece of paper and waved it in his face as she passed. He turned as she walked to the door, shook the paper in the air once more, then lifted a potted plant that sat nearby, and slid the paper underneath it. She met his eyes, nodded at the plant, turned, and walked out.

Morgan stared after her in bewilderment. He didn't even know her. He looked around. None of the other employees appeared to have noticed the exchange. Deciding, he moved quickly toward the door and retrieved the slip of paper. He unfolded the note and read it.

"They're hunting you" was written in a neatly flowing script. Morgan frowned. He turned the note over. The rest of the page was blank. He looked out the glass door to the empty parking lot. The woman was gone.

CHAPTER 2
MEMORIES

The old BMX dirt bike creaked under Morgan as he pedaled slowly down the highway that ran east to west through Vernal Utah. The darkening sky was filled with the brilliant reds, ceruleans, and golds of an early summer sunset. He glanced over his shoulder where the tiny crescent scimitar of a moon was beginning to rise over the jagged peaks in the distance.

A black pickup pouring acrid black exhaust from a comically large exhaust pipe roared past him, its wide tires running over the painted edge of the lane and scattering dust and gravel into the air.

Morgan cursed as he pulled his bike to a stop, coughing on the detritus of the road. He lifted the collar of his shirt to cover his face until the dust settled. He looked at his now filthy red-and-black grocery store uniform. "Redneck!" he shouted vainly as the truck crested a distant hill and disappeared from view.

He brushed off his clothing, remounted the bike, and began to pedal, cursing under his breath and adding "too many rednecks" to his mental tally of reasons that he hated Vernal.

After a few more minutes of riding, he turned into the Walmart parking lot, parked his bike, and walked inside. He made his way to the electronics section, and he wandered up and down the aisles until he located a small section of prepaid cell phones that hung from small metal racks near the abandoned electronics counter.

He didn't need a phone with a lot of features. He wouldn't be downloading apps or even perusing the internet or sending out DMs. He just needed something he could talk on—or text. He found a flip-style phone with a price tag that said $44.99. He glanced above and located a prepaid phone card for an additional $30.

Morgan bit his lip, excitement surging within him. He didn't have that much on him, but with the money from his check and the cash he'd found, it might be enough. He turned and strode to the front of the store, shoving his hands into his pockets and arguing with himself about whether or not his caseworker would give him Imogene's new number. Just as important was the question of whether or not his sister would pick up a call from a number she didn't recognize. He doubted it, but he'd have to try. He'd given his mother a promise, and he wouldn't let her down. Not again.

A half hour later Morgan pedaled down a lonely road on the outskirts of Vernal. He turned toward the small, lonely brick house that stood near where the pavement ended, and the road became a rocky 4-wheel drive trail that faded into the sagebrush.

A single yellow bulb hung over the cracked cement steps of the building, shining down on a weed-infested front yard that Morgan imagined had once held grass. A beleaguered Chevrolet Cavalier sat rusting in the yard on two tires that were pressurized, one that was not, and a single bare rim propped on a log.

Morgan dropped his bike and stared at the door. He couldn't bring himself to go inside. Instead, he took a steadying breathe and strode into the darkness behind the house. He picked his way through a minefield of rusty machinery and derelict farming equipment, crested a small rise, and took a final look back toward the Steadman's home. He'd have to go in eventually, but he could spend a few more minutes alone before slinking inside and finding a corner to hide in.

He moved deeper into the darkness until he reached a tall clump of sagebrush nearly his height. He looked cautiously around then slipped through the wall of brush. After a dozen feet, he emerged into a natural depression where he'd painstakingly removed the jagged rocks and scraggly desert plants to create a smooth bowl-shaped opening a dozen feet across.

Morgan took off his work shirt and carefully laid it over a nearby bush, then strode into the circle rolling his head slowly from side to side. Next, he worked his shoulders, stretching each arm. Then he extended each leg in turn and leaned into a deep stretch. He focused, following the customary pattern of deep breaths and muscle memory, allowing his mind to clear as he shook his arms and legs to loosen the muscles. When he finally felt warm, he settled into a low pose and held it briefly while staring straight ahead. He took one more deep breath and began to move.

He flowed into the forms; their names lost in the pages of his childhood memory. He kicked, turned, ducked, punched, blocked invisible strikes, and struck snake-like at imaginary foes. He danced across the desert like a ghost, flowing and striking, weaving and dodging.

Time slipped by as he wove through the familiar patterns,

his heart rate accelerating. Sweat formed on his face and neck and began running down his bare chest.

Panting from the exertion, he crouched into the final pose, his legs bent wide below him, his right hand held out before him his fingers curled into a rough semblance of a tiger's paw. He held the pose briefly then stood, bowed to the desert, and straightened, taking deep calming breaths.

Morgan stood in the darkness for several minutes, relishing the cool breeze on his damp skin, the smell of sagebrush, and the endorphins his exertions had created, taking time to just breathe and enjoy the brief moment of freedom. Reluctantly he pulled his shirt over his head and headed to the house. He crossed the yard and strode up the chipped stairs to the faded wooden door. On the landing, he paused to look back toward the small dark valley, his secret dojo, to buy himself a few more seconds, then sighed and walked in.

Patrick Steadman, a wiry boy with uncombed brown hair and blue eyes, sat on a stained brown couch playing a game on his cell phone. He glanced up as Morgan approached.

"Hey Morgan," he said, then returned to his game.

"Pat," Morgan said. "Did I get any mail?"

"Nope."

Why didn't she write back, he wondered in frustration. How many letters had he sent in the last several months? Seven? Eight? It had to be at least six, he knew that for certain. And yet Imogene still hadn't responded. Had she even gotten the letters?

He headed down the hall to the door with the dented knob and slipped inside, strode to a battered wardrobe and opened it. On a shelf in the middle sat a small stack of bills, he picked them up and counted them.

Thirty-eight dollars. Morgan's teeth clenched in frustration. Eric had left him far less than half of his check. He wondered what excuse Steadman would give this time. More important however was the fact that even with the money he'd found, it wouldn't be enough to pay for the phone, a calling card, and the tax. He would have to wait until he got paid again in two more weeks. He cursed under his breath.

On another shelf, next to folded socks and a worn pair of soccer cleats, lay a small wooden cigar box. He pulled the box free, sat it on the bed, and reverently opened the lid. Inside lay a small blue notebook and a necklace with a medallion on a leather cord. He fingered the medallion. He'd worn it every day until last week, but he just couldn't bring himself to wear his father's gift any longer.

Morgan picked up the notebook and opened it, flipping to the back cover. Glued inside was a small paper pocket. He opened the pocket, slid the cash from the dresser and the fifty inside, then reached to replace the notebook.

He glanced into the corner of the shelf where an old comic book sat. Hesitating, he put the notebook back in the cigar box and moved to the shelf. He reverently slid the comic book to the side, exposing a worn envelope that sat beneath it.

He picked it up and opened it, cautious not to do any damage to the paper that was already beginning to wear thin and yellow. He opened the letter and reread the familiar words:

Morgan,

I want you to know that things are really good for me here. I'm happy. Don't worry about me. I hope everything is good with you.

Take care of yourself. I love you. Goodbye.

Imogene

Morgan wondered again what had happened. He'd been close to Imogene once. They'd spent hours talking about what they'd do when they were finally old enough to get themselves out of the system. They'd get an apartment together, figure out how to go to college, start living their lives free of the imposition of the state.

Then everything had changed. Imogene grew quiet, distant, no longer interested in talking about their future. He'd assumed it was a phase, a temporary melancholy, that it would pass as quickly as it had come. But one fall afternoon he had returned home from school to find Imogene gone, her room empty and everything she owned missing.

The social worker had come, picked her up, and taken her away, leaving Morgan to wonder what had happened. He knew the state didn't like to separate siblings, not unless there was a reason, unless one of them asked for it. Immy wouldn't have asked for that would she have? Three weeks later he'd gotten the letter with the simple message in Imogene's neat handwriting.

Ten months had passed since he'd received the note. He'd heard nothing more from her. No letters, no phone calls, not even an email to his school address. It was like she had fallen off the face of the planet. A familiar ache filled his chest, and he forced back the traitorous liquid forming in the corners of his eyes.

He thought longingly of the cell phone that Pat had been playing on when Morgan had come in. What would happen if he brought one home? Would Eric let him keep it?

He doubted it. He'd have to keep it secret, smuggle it inside, keep it hidden, only bring it out when he was alone. He wondered how often Eric searched his things. He'd found too many things out of place, too many items disturbed while he was away to doubt that. He'd need a good hiding place, somewhere Eric wouldn't think to search.

With a sigh, he dismissed the problem for later, then refolded the letter, and slid it back below the comic book. He replaced the notebook and cigar box and closed the dresser. He exited the room and sat next to Pat on the couch just as Eric sauntered in.

Morgan pointedly did not look at the man as Eric switched on the TV and plopped himself onto the couch. "Dinner, boy," he snapped at Morgan and pointed toward the kitchen.

Without a word Morgan gritted his teeth and headed to the kitchen while Eric watched TV and Patrick rotted his brain. As he pulled out a saucepan from a cupboard by the stove, Eric turned the channel to the news. A sad sounding weatherman was muttering something about the lack of rain. Eric turned up the volume as Morgan started water to boil.

"Utter bunk!" Eric opined loudly a few minutes later in response to something the news anchor was saying. Morgan dropped a handful of spaghetti noodles into the pot and leaned sideways to see the screen, giving the broadcast his attention. Anything Eric didn't like was sure to be worthwhile.

"Scientists say that the meteor poses no threat to the earth itself. With more, here is Stacey King, our science correspondent."

"Thanks, Jim. I have with me Bill Williamson, professor of astrophysics at Cal-Tech. Professor Williamson, what can we expect with this impact?" The anchor pushed a microphone into the face of a disheveled portly man with unkempt gray hair and a red nose.

"I heard about this!" Morgan said. "At work, there was this girl—"

"Shut it!" Eric roared back at him. Morgan's face flushed, and he stopped talking.

"Oh, I should think it will be fairly spectacular. We can perhaps expect a bright flash that should be visible, maybe even with the naked eye for those in the northern hemisphere," the professor said enthusiastically while the reporter nodded with feigned interest so obvious Morgan wondered if she was even listening to what the man was saying.

"Just a bright flash? Is there anything else that people might expect to see?"

"We believe it will just be the impact flash. Given the estimated size and speed of the object at the time of impact, it should cause an impact similar to that of a hydrogen bomb. Fortunately, because it's out of our atmosphere and quite distant from us, it shouldn't cause any problems down here. People will likely even be able to look at it directly without any adverse side effects."

"Fascinating, professor. What time can we expect an impact?"

"We estimate that it will impact around 10:38 pm Mountain Standard Time tonight."

"Thank you, professor. Well, there you have it, Jim." The anchor looked directly into the camera. "It should be an interesting night."

"Thank you, Stacey. I know I'll definitely be watching, what about you, Suzie?"

Eric flipped the channel and stopped at a baseball game. "Said it before, and I'll say it again. Utter bunk." he muttered.

After dinner, Morgan cleaned the kitchen while Patrick and Eric watched a movie on Netflix. When they were finished, Eric disappeared down the hall to his bedroom leaving the two boys alone. Morgan used this opportunity to slip out the door of the house and make his way to the detached garage. He pulled open the door, yanked the cord attached to the single light bulb, and grabbed a step stool that stood nearby. He set the stool at the foot of a group of wooden shelves that lined the inside of the space. He climbed the steps, selected a long cardboard box, and opened it.

He hadn't been able to keep many of his possessions after

his mother's death, and even fewer of those items had fit into the small dresser he kept his clothes in. The rest remained in the garage or had been thrown away.

He opened the dust-covered box and retrieved an inexpensive red telescope. His father had given it to him for his tenth birthday, just days before he had left them and Morgan, his mother, and sister had moved from Philadelphia to rural Utah. Morgan stared down at a relic of his former life, the life that had existed before the world he'd known had ended in a hospital bed.

He slid the telescope out of the box, stepped down from the ladder, and carried his old treasure to his secret dojo. He set the telescope on its rickety stand, positioning it so that it pointed toward the moon, then pulled up a tattered camp chair and sat, nothing left to do but wait.

He looked at the cheap watch on his wrist. It read 9:32. Assuming the professor was right in his estimation, he had about an hour to go before the impact occurred. He shifted deeper into the chair, pulled the telescope stand closer, and put his eye on the small opening. He adjusted it until the moon shone clearly in the lens then sat back staring into the sky wondering if he'd be able to see the meteor before impact.

After a while, Morgan's mind began to wander, he thought of Imogene, wondering where she was and what she was doing with her new family. Then back to the promise he'd made.

* * *

"Stay here," Morgan said, pointing to the bench that sat in the waiting room. Imogene looked up at him, her eyes wide and liquid. "It will be OK," he said, patting her shoulder. "I'll be back in a minute, and then you can come to see her."

Imogene nodded and sat on the cushion. Morgan smiled gently at her and followed the nurse down the hallway and into the room. The hospital room was full of equipment and smelled in a way that

Morgan didn't like. He walked across the room and looked down at his mother's thin face and sunken eyes. Gingerly he picked up a skeletal hand and held it between his own.

"Mom," he whispered. "Can you hear me?"

Her eyes moved below her eyelids, but they did not open. "Mom," he repeated. "It's Morgan. Can you hear me?" He searched her face for several moments, but she didn't wake. Finally, he walked to the corner of the room and slid a chair to the edge of the bed. Their caseworker wouldn't be back for at least an hour, so he could give her a few minutes to come around.

He picked up his mother's hand again and lifted it, holding its thin warmth up to his face. He kissed it gently and held it, his fingers wrapped gently around hers.

"Morgan?" a rattling voice said from the bed.

"I'm here," he said, sitting up quickly and looking over the rail to meet her gaze. Tears gathered at the edge of her sunken eyes, and she offered him a frail smile.

"Morgan," she said. "I need you to do something for me. Can you do something for me?" He nodded, holding tight to her fingers, not trusting his voice to say the words around the large lump that had formed in his throat.

"You have to—" She cut off, coughing and grimacing in pain.

Tears formed at the corners of Morgan's eyes as he looked down at her.

"Morgan, take care of your sister." Her voice rattled as she spoke, making it difficult for him to understand her. He inched closer, trying to catch every word. "Take care of your sister. You're all she has. Make sure to take care of your sister—she's my baby, my little girl."

His mother's hands gripped his and shook violently as she sucked in a pain-ridden breath. "Promise me, Morgan. Promise me," she gasped.

Morgan nodded, tears sliding down his face.

"I—promise," he choked out. His mother's face seemed to relax, a peaceful expression settling over her.

"Thank you, Morgan," she whispered in a voice so low he could barely hear her. "Thank you, I love bo—" Her voice cut out in a rush of outward breath, and the machine in the corner started wailing.

"Mom?" Morgan shouted, jumping to his feet. "Mom?" he called, frantically shaking her arm, trying to rouse her. "Mom?" The ringing noise was deafening as a strong pair of hands grabbed him by the shoulders and pulled him away from her and out the door. "Mom?" he called back over his shoulder as the nurse pulled him away.

Someone was saying his name, but he couldn't understand the words as hospital staff rushed past him, tense voices sounding above the alarms.

* * *

Morgan shook the memory away and stared up at the moon. He wiped his eyes, gulped down the familiar lump in his throat, and rubbed his arms against the chilly night breeze. He looked back at the watch, 10:27. He took a deep breath, trying to push away the sick feeling the memory always filled him with, and looked into the night sky. He stared. A bright light streaked across the sky from west to east as it swept across the heavens to smash silently into the moon.

Belatedly he pressed his eye to the eyepiece.

A bright bloom of light raced outward across the lunar surface like rings of water rippling in a pond. Day momentarily reclaimed the sky. Ripples of light in exotic shades of red, yellow, and green chased across the surface of the planetoid in swirling arcs. A hazy cloud of light poured from the surface as matter streamed into space from the impact zone. Blue and silver arcs, like a strange form of lightning, crackled from the impact zone to race outward around the surface.

Slowly the light from the impact began to fade.

"Wow," Morgan gasped, amazed.

Circular halos of light raced in succession from the far side of the moon in a repeating pattern. The pattern accelerated, each pulse coming faster than the previous, the lightning-like patterns becoming more frequent until the entire surface of the moon shone like a miniature sun. What had once been a silver crescent, was now a rippling, glowing orb of silver and blue that cast ghostly beams over the surface of the earth. The new light brightened and steadied as wave upon wave of blue and silver arcs raced across its surface.

He watched, waiting for the lunar storm to end, for its light to fade, flicker, and disappear. Five minutes went by, then ten, then half an hour, and the lunar storm remained. It became steady, shining like a giant blue-silver star in the southern sky. A chill went down Morgan's spine as he stared in fascination.

"What you just witnessed," Morgan stumbled upright and spun. A feminine form stood at the edge of the clearing behind him—" was the end of the world." She had silvery blonde hair and wore a white t-shirt and blue jeans; he recognized her immediately.

"You! You were at the store."

She nodded.

"Who are you? How did you find me?" His heart raced. He hadn't noticed her following him home. He stared, suddenly realizing that she was on the wrong side of the clearing for her to have followed him from the house.

"I'm not the only one who can sense you," she said, her voice gentle.

"Sense me?" Morgan shivered and took an unconscious step backward.

She nodded. "They'll be here soon. Tonight. You must come with me."

"Where?" He took another step toward the house.

"To safety. To Encartha," she said, cocking her hip and raising an eyebrow.

Morgan frowned at the strange woman. His mind was racing, and his mouth felt dry. The woman must have been having some sort of episode or had him confused with someone else.

"Encartha is a city," she prompted gently.

"I've never heard of it," Morgan said, his voice coming out unsteadily. He felt his face flush in embarrassment at the sound.

The odd woman laughed. "Of course, you haven't. We work hard to keep it from Ciegos, but I'm afraid the time for secrecy has passed. What you see up there"—she gestured toward the strange light of the moon— "is the death of your world. We needn't keep our secret any longer."

He frowned at her. "My world?"

"Come with me," she repeated, leaving his question unanswered. "Come to Encartha. You'll be safe there."

"Safe from what?"

"From what's coming."

He hesitated, his eyes shifting back and forth between the moon and the odd stranger. "I'm not going anywhere," he said firmly before turning and striding toward the house.

"I'm afraid your only choices are to come or to die," she called from behind him.

He stopped, turning to look back over his shoulder at her. His heart was racing. There was something about the woman that he couldn't quite place. She took a step toward him, and he retreated. Something about the way she moved unsettled him.

"Are you threatening me?" He said, trying to sound nonchalant.

"I'm not talking about myself," she said, "I'm talking about the things that are hunting you."

"People don't hunt other people," Morgan said. "Not in the normal world."

"I never said they were human, and the world you think you know is a thing of the past."

"I see," he said, now quite convinced of her insanity. "Listen—" he paused, realizing that he didn't know her name.

"Aella," she supplied.

He nodded. "Nice to meet you, Aella, I'm not interested," he said and strode toward the house. When he glanced back over his shoulder, Aella was standing with her arms crossed, watching him go. She looked angry.

CHAPTER 3
IMOGENE

"Hey, Imogene!"

Imogene turned to see Jason Parker, a tall muscular boy with long dark hair and blue eyes jogging toward her. She stared back at him dumbly, then belatedly returned the smile. She shifted her weight and fidgeted with her backpack strap as he approached.

What does he want?

Jason was handsome, popular, and well-connected. Imogene was not. Her adoptive mom—Imogene still struggled to think of her that way—had told her she would fit in well in Park City, but so far that hadn't been her experience. A nervous shiver traveled up her spine.

"Jason, hi," she said, steeling herself and fighting the need to fidget as he approached. "What's up?" She finished lamely.

"I was just on my way to practice." He was the captain of the basketball team at Ecker Hill Middle School in Park City, Utah. Imogene nodded, waiting for him to get on with it.

"I wanted to talk to you," he said before glancing over his shoulder to where two of his friends, both popular boys, stood watching the interaction. "I was wondering," he paused momentarily before continuing, "if you were coming to my party on Friday?"

Immy's stomach lurched, and her pulse began to race. "You're having a party?" she said as coolly as she could manage. She knew about the party, of course—every middle schooler in town had heard about it—but she hadn't received an invitation. Only the cool kids would, and everyone knew it.

"Yeah," he said, chuckling. "I hoped you might—" he began.

"I'm not sure—" she interjected, cutting him off.

Jason's face fell, his mouth opening in surprise.

"I'm not sure I was invited," she finished, biting her lip. She glanced around, unable to resist the impulse to see if others were watching. Around her, teens were walking around in small groups, laughing and talking to each other as they made their way to nearby cars, climbed onto waiting buses, or crossed the busy street.

"What do you mean? Of course, you were invited," Jason said with an assuring nod.

She made a skeptical face and shook her head.

"Yes, you were!" he said a bit too loudly, his face flushed as he looked around at people standing nearby. A few heads turned their way, and Imogene felt her own face flush. She shrugged and took a step toward the bus that was pulling up in front of her.

"I would really like it if you came," he said hopefully.

Imogene paused and bit her lip. Her heart was thumping in her chest, and she could feel herself starting to sweat. *Could he be serious?* she wondered. Slowly she turned around.

"I don't know. I mean I didn't get an invitation," she said tentatively. "I'd hate to show up if I'm not invited. That would be so embarrassing."

"It's word of mouth," he said, a tentative smile returning to his face. "There weren't any invitations."

She fidgeted with her backpack strap and looked around. Her bus came to a stop nearby, and the door opened. A group of students began moving toward the open doors as the gray-haired bus driver glared down at her. Imogene held up a single finger. The driver raised a silver eyebrow, her head shaking slowly.

"Hmm, I guess we'll see," Immy said, trying to sound aloof and noncommittal, as she started toward the bus at a brisk walk.

"Imogene!" Jason said hurriedly.

She paused and looked back at him, giving him her best smile.

"Do you know where I live?"

Imogene shook her head. It was a lie. She knew where he lived; everyone did. But somehow, she couldn't bring herself to tell him the truth.

"The corner of Crestline Drive and Alpine," he said a little too quickly to sound cool. "You'll see the house when you get there, it will be the one where the party is happening."

She put on her best smile and nodded. The bus driver made an impatient sound, and Imogene moved toward the open door. She offered a small wave to Jason as she climbed onto the bus, mumbled an apology to the driver, then strode down the aisle and slid into an empty seat. She scooted close to the window and looked down into her lap, hoping that Jason would think she was composed and occupied with something of great importance.

The bus started to move, and Imogene bit her lip as she risked a quick glance out the window. Jason still stood where he'd been, looking up at her bus as she passed. He was smiling and staring back at her. She fought to keep her breath even and stop an excited squeal from escaping.

Jason Parker invited me to his party! By personal invitation! He wants to see me there!

Her hands kept clenching and unclenching in her lap of their own accord.

Jason Parker invited me to his party!

She pulled out her phone and started typing.

"JASON PARKER JUST ASKED ME TO COME TO HIS PARTY ON FRIDAY!!!" She sent the text to her best friend Carol and looked around to make sure no one was watching her. The typing icon popped up, and Imogene bit her lip, waiting for the response. Finally, the message came through.

"OMG! R U SERIOUS!?"

Imogene forcibly kept her body still though she wanted to dance. "I am TOTALLY SERIOUS! I can't believe it! He came running up to talk to me at the bus station. I can't believe it!"

"WOW! You little ho, I hate you!"

"HAHA! Jealous much?"

"I'm SOOOO jealous! What are you going to wear?"

"I have no idea!?? I hadn't even thought about it!"

Imogene's mind raced. She hadn't even asked what they were doing at the party. *Dumb move, Imogene,* she scolded herself. She wondered if she should dress up or if the party would be more casual. She had no idea. She'd have to find out from someone, but she had no idea who she could ask. Who would know, and even more importantly, who could she get that information from without them relaying her questions back to Jason?

Carol's text interrupted her thoughts.

"Maybe you can make out afterwards!"

"Whatev's I wouldn't do that— Too many other people around! HAHA!"

"Probably, but still. JASON PARKER! I hate you so much right now!" Carol sent her an animated GIF of a woman extending her middle finger.

"Luv u too!" Imogene sent an unconscious smile creeping across her face.

"Call me tonight so we can plan! 😊"

"I'll try. Got homework. I'll def call you tomorrow. XOXO!"

Imogene put the phone into the pocket of her backpack and stared out the window, daydreaming of the event and what it would mean for her social life. She'd lived in Park City for less than a year, since she'd been adopted by a wealthy family, the Judges. They were good to her, gave her all the things that her birth parents never could have, and she liked them. They were fun. She felt a twinge of guilt as a thought of her brother, Morgan, crept into her mind uninvited. She pushed it away.

The next thing she knew the bus was pulling up to the stop near her house. She stood, slung the bag over her shoulder, and stepped out onto the street. She turned up a sloping street toward the big brick house that sat at the end of a cul-de-sac.

My house, she thought. It seemed so strange that she'd come to think of it as her house in such a short time. She'd lived in several places since her mother's death, but this was the first time she'd considered it to be hers. It was the first time that the situation felt permanent. It *was* permanent this time. She'd been adopted and was no longer a ward of the state, no longer a foster kid. She exulted. It felt good to *belong* somewhere, to have a family, to know that she never had to leave.

She couldn't help but feel a bit guilty about Morgan's situation. It wasn't his fault after all, not entirely his fault at least. He was older and a boy. It was hard enough to be adopted at 13 as a girl, let alone for a boy at 15.

Morgan had certainly tried to keep up their relationship—

he wrote her letters and talked to his caseworker about her. He asked about visitation and generally pestered the poor woman until Imogene thought she might snap. But Immy had no intention of seeing him, at least not now. Maybe someday, right now she didn't feel up to it.

What could she say to him? *I'm sorry I told the social worker I wanted to be separated from you to improve my chances of being adopted?* She hadn't been able to think of a way to answer the questions she was sure he'd ask, so she'd spurned his attempts to communicate. She knew it was irrational, but part of her was afraid that if she was in touch with him, she'd lose all that she'd gained. It was stupid and unkind, but she couldn't help it. She liked her new life.

Besides, when they'd last talked, he'd gone on about them leaving their situation to be a family together in some little apartment somewhere. When she was younger Immy had loved the idea. The dream of being on their own, independent, with no parents or caseworkers to tell them what to do, just a little family of their own, she'd wanted that more than anything. But now it just sounded depressing.

Immy thought about her adoptive parents as she approached the door. They were wholly unlike her birth parents: wealthy, respected, living. Her adoptive father was a partner at a large tech firm he'd helped found in the valley. In the almost year since they'd taken her in, she'd been to Paris, Sydney, and Rome. She had a closet full of name-brand clothes, the newest iPhone, and an allowance that rivaled her birth mother's full-time income.

She squared her shoulders, forcing the thoughts of her biological family away. They were in her past, and she intended to keep it that way. She had friends, and the most popular boy in school had just invited her to a party at his house. She was finally happy. Morgan wouldn't want to take that away from her, would he? He should be happy for her, glad that her life had finally taken a good turn. She shook her head and pushed open the front door.

The house was large, with tall ceilings, expensive woodwork, and a series of broad windows that looked out on the slopes of the ski resort. The hills were green now, but the lifts still ran, carrying people with mountain bikes to the top where trails were open to them.

"Anyone home?" she called. The house was silent.

Patrice must be shopping. Her new mom loved to shop and frequently checked Imogene out of school to go with her. Gary, her adoptive father, would still be at work. She climbed the steps and went to her room.

She spent the next few hours trying to do her math homework, but her mind kept slipping stubbornly away from the topic.

I can't believe Jason invited me. Did he invite any other girls? Obviously, there will be other girls there, but if he didn't personally invite them, if he invited me as a date, then it's different.

Imogene wondered if she could invite Carol to come with her, she didn't want to go alone. You never look cool at a party if you're alone. She put down her math book and looked out the window. Darkness had already fallen, and Imogene's attention shifted to her lamp by reflex. It read 8:45. Gary and Patrice should have been home by now. Imogene got up and headed downstairs, flipping on light switches as she went.

Where could they be? She picked up her phone, thumbed to the last text labeled "Mom," and began to type. "Hey, haven't seen anyone all afternoon. Are you going to be home soon?"

She sent the text, pulled open the fridge, took out her Chinese leftovers from the night before, and popped them into the microwave. She hit the reheat button, got out a fork from the drawer, and sat at the bar. Then she opened Pinterest and started scrolling through outfits, searching for the perfect look for the party. She wanted to make an impression without looking like she was trying to.

When she was done with dinner, Imogene checked her phone, there were no messages. A nervous feeling welled up inside her and she sent a text to Gary.

"No one's home, and Mom isn't answering. Where are you guys?" She sent the text and flipped on the TV. When she next checked the clock, it read 9:15. It wasn't like her parents to stay out so late without telling her. Normally the two over-communicated, sending dozens of texts just to keep her up to date with their every movement.

Imogene stood and walked up the stairs to the master bedroom, opened the door, and flipped on the light. The room was empty. Scattered clothes lay about as if her adoptive parents had been in a hurry to leave that morning. Her dad had said that he had an important meeting in the valley.

Maybe Patrice went down with him, and they were having dinner there? That wouldn't be a big surprise, but something about it still left Imogene feeling unsettled. She sighed and went back to her room to get ready for bed. When she had changed, taken off her makeup and put on pajamas, she checked the clock, 10:15. She walked back down the stairs, her anxiety growing.

Where were they? Something was wrong. She went to the garage door and opened it. Both cars were inside. An icy shiver ran down her spine. "Mom," she called, then listened silently for a few moments. There was no response.

"Dad?" she shouted.

Silence.

She ran down the stairs to the gym and flipped on the light. A dark, wet, reddish gleam met her eyes. She stared in horror at the wrecked remains of her adoptive parents. A deep growl filled her ears. She turned. A huge shaggy shape stood in front of her. Imogene took an unconscious step backward as she took in the dark form.

The creature stood on its back feet and snarled at her, long sharp fangs protruding from an elongated muzzle matted with blood. Golden eyes stared out from the enormous head, and its shoulders were hunched to fit under the nine-foot ceiling. The creature took a step forward. Huge powerfully muscled front arms ended in human-like hands with long black claws held toward her.

Imogene stood frozen, unable to run or scream, her body rigid with terror. She heard a popping sound, and the wolf creature shrieked. There was a flurry of movement that Imogene couldn't follow, growls, the snap of jaws, the smell of burning fur. Her vision swam, and dark circles enclosed around the edges of her vision. She collapsed to the floor.

When Imogene woke a tiny man was gently wetting her forehead with a wet rag and cooing softly. "It all be right. Ol' Fen is here. No t'worries wit ol' Fen here. That nasty blighter be gone and deaded. It all be right."

Imogene stared blankly at the big green eyes. "Who are you?" she asked, perplexed. The little man grinned.

"I's Fen, I's here ta fetch ya."

CHAPTER 4
CHAOS

When Morgan strode into the grocery store three days after the moon impact, the power was out. There were camping lanterns set up at the ends of the aisles, and several customers held flashlights as they wandered through the store.

He frowned, taking in the empty shelves, then glanced over to the desk at the front of the store. The power had been out at the Steadman's place when he'd left, but it was rare for power to be out in town. A shiver made its way down his spine along with a sudden unexpected certainty. Something was wrong. He strode towards the desk.

"Hey, Steve," he said as he neared the counter. Normally well groomed, Steve's thin hair was mussed, his uniform rumpled, and his shirt stained with something dark. Steve looked up from where he was writing neat block letters on a square piece of cardboard with a sharpie. His red eyes met Morgan's with a distant, unrecognizing expression.

"Everything we have is on the shelf—" he began.

"Steve?" Morgan said cautiously.

The man shook himself, recognition coming into his eyes, and put on a forced half-smile. "Morgan," he said. "What are you doing here?" His voice was uncharacteristically rough, his tone accusing.

"I work tonight," Morgan said defensively. "I'm on the schedule."

"You should leave," Steve said firmly.

Morgan stared in surprise as he searched the man's face, finding no hint of the joking manner that was Steve's calling card.

"I have to work," he began. "If I go home now, Eric will be angry. I'll be in trouble."

"I can't let you work today," Steve said. "Things here," he paused gazing hauntedly down the nearest aisle, "they're getting bad."

"What do you mean?"

Steve bit his lip and looked around to where a small group of unhappy-looking customers milled by a check stand. When Morgan glanced at the group, a surly woman glared at him, and he turned away.

"I can't let you work today," Steve repeated. "I'm afraid that's all there is to it."

"I did nothing wrong," Morgan said.

"This isn't about you, Morgan," Steve said angrily, his eyes roving around the store.

Morgan noted the lines on Steve's face, they were deeper, his eyes sunken and morose.

"This is not your fault, Morgan. It's for your own good, for your safety."

Morgan blinked back at the manager. "Safety?" he said, shocked. "Bagging groceries isn't really dangerous or anything."

"Groceries aren't dangerous, but people are," Steve said,

lowering his voice to a barely audible whisper. "Go home, Morgan. I'll call you when things are better—when I know it's safe."

"I don't understand," Morgan said.

"When people are scared, they don't act right. They do things, things they wouldn't otherwise do, dangerous things." Steve shook his head. "Please go home. I promise I'll call you when all of this blows over."

Morgan searched the man's face a final time and finally nodded, feeling a sense of foreboding settle into his stomach. "When do you think things will get better?" he asked. His voice trembled as he said the words.

Steve looked back at him, his expression troubled. "I don't know," he breathed. "I'm not sure that they—" He paused, his voice sounding haunted. "Go home," he repeated. "I'll call you. Don't come back into town. When officials get things working again, you'll be the first to know, and you can come back to work."

Morgan looked around the dim interior of the building. He thought about Imogene and the cell phone. How would he be able to call her if he couldn't work?

"Alright," Morgan agreed dejectedly.

"Good," Steve said, nodding and looking over Morgan's shoulder. Morgan followed Steve's gaze. A big man with thick mutton chops wearing a plaid shirt was walking into the store. He had a large empty-looking backpack slung over his shoulder, and he looked angry. Morgan looked back to Steve. "Go now," Steve said.

Morgan turned and trudged toward the door.

"Morgan," Steve called after him. He stopped and glanced over his shoulder. Steve motioned him back.

"What's up?" Morgan asked as he returned to the counter, feeling even more confused by the man's behavior.

"How much do you have at home?"

Morgan just stared back at him, perplexed by the question. "How much of what?" he asked.

"Food."

Morgan shrugged. "I don't know, a few days' worth, I guess. I'm not sure when Eric last did the shopping, but he normally does it on weekends."

Steve frowned. "How'd you get here?" he asked.

"On my bike," Morgan said.

"Hmm," Steve grunted and seemed to consider. "OK, listen," he began, lowering his voice to a whisper so low that Morgan had to lean in to hear him. "Ignore what I'm about to say to you," he whispered. "Then go outside and bring your bike around to the back of the store. I'll meet you there in ten minutes."

"OK," Morgan stammered, nodding and taking a step back.

"I'm sorry, we just don't have anything," Steve said loudly enough for people nearby to hear him. "Hopefully, the truck will be here soon. We haven't gotten one in several days, so we're stuck until it arrives. Should be here tomorrow, I hear." He returned to his writing as though Morgan was a customer asking questions.

"Thanks," Morgan said, turned from the counter, and made his way out the door. He unlocked the rusted bike from the rack and pushed it into the parking lot, then made his way past a few dozen parked cars to the corner of the brick building. He turned, making his way to the back of the store where a long cement ramp ran up to the blue metal door that was labeled Emergency Exit Only. Morgan rolled his bike to the top of the ramp, laid it on the ground, and settled down to wait.

His mind returned to Steve's mad behavior, the unhappy looks of the customers, and then to the cell phone. He still didn't have enough for it. If he couldn't work, how would he get it? He wished he had brought his watch; he couldn't help but wonder how long it had been. The door creaked open a crack, and Steve's face appeared. His eyes darted furtively, taking in Morgan's surroundings and making sure that he was alone. He opened the door and motioned Morgan to enter.

Morgan jumped to his feet and slipped inside. Steve closed the door behind him. Morgan looked around the stockroom, it was tall with cement floors and an industrial feel. Dozens of empty pallets lined the walls. Only one of them had anything stacked on it, just a few boxes of food remained. He had never seen the storeroom emptier; usually there were several pallets with dozens of boxes stacked on top of them, waiting to refill shelves as they got low.

"Here," Steve said, holding out a small red backpack.

"Thanks," Morgan said hesitantly, taking the pack. "Steve, what is going on? I don't understand what all the theatrics are about."

Steve shook his head slowly and stared into Morgan's eyes. "Morgan, I'm sure you've noticed, but a lot of people's cars aren't starting, and the power's been out since the impact. There's something wrong, very wrong. I don't know what it is, but it's serious."

Morgan took in Steve's worried face and swallowed. "It's only been a day, surely—" he began, trying to push down the anxious feeling that was building in his stomach, but Steve interrupted him.

"Morgan," he said impatiently. "I think this thing, whatever it is, is a game changer. People around here are scared. They've been coming in all morning, buying everything they can get their hands on. No one is sure why things aren't working, it's almost like"—the man swallowed audibly— "like technology is falling apart. I don't think the power's coming back. I don't think cars are going to work again. Ever."

Morgan could only stare back at the man. He and the Steadman's lived on the edge of town, and from there things hadn't seemed as bad as Steve made them sound.

"I think the impact on the moon did something," Steve said, then nodded toward the backpack. "Open it."

Morgan unzipped it and held it out. Steve began picking items from the few remaining boxes and stuffing them into the bag.

"We stopped selling food about an hour ago," he said, grabbing and stuffing a can of peas into the backpack. Abruptly, he stopped and stared Morgan in the eye for several seconds. "We're keeping the rest," he said seriously, hefting a ten-pound sack of rice. "I'm about to close the store and ask everyone to leave until we start getting trucks again, assuming that ever happens. To tell you the truth, I'm only giving this to you because you're a good kid and I know you're probably going to need it. If it weren't for that, I'd keep it for myself."

Morgan searched the man's intense green eyes and felt a chill go down his spine from the fear that he saw there. He thanked the man, then turned and headed out the door, slinging the backpack over his shoulder and settling it onto his back before picking up his bike and lifting his leg over the bar.

He put a foot on the pedal and paused to look back at Steve. The older man waved once, then closed the door behind him.

Morgan took a deep breath and started around the corner of the store, pedaling slowly as he tried to take in all that Steve had said. Could things really be that bad? Steve had to be exaggerating or mistaken. He rounded the brick corner into the parking lot and froze as shouting erupted nearby.

"Hey! Stop!" The shout was a roar of anger. It emanated from the front door of the building as the man in the plaid shirt came sprinting outside and crossed the parking lot, his backpack bulging and it bounced awkwardly over his shoulder, slowing him. Behind, Todd came sprinting into the lot, his thick arms pumping as he pursued the man.

Morgan stared as the man in plaid jumped into an SUV and slammed the door. A crowd of people came out of the store, shouting and running in different directions, some holding food in their bare hands and others clinging to bags. Someone was shouting something that Morgan couldn't understand.

Todd approached the SUV and banged heavily on the window. After a few hard blows, the glass shattered. Todd abruptly backed away from the vehicle, his hands raised as a pistol jutted out pointed in his direction. There was a deafening roar. Todd dove to the ground, rolled to the side, and crawled behind a nearby car. He glanced up at Morgan, and his face was a mask of shock and terror.

The door of the SUV swung open, and the man in plaid stepped out. He pulled the trigger again, his pistol pointing toward Todd's hiding place. This time there was a feeble hiss, but the gun did not fire. Cursing, the man in plaid turned and dashed across the parking lot toward an old brown pickup. A blonde teenage boy sat in the driver's seat, and he stared in surprise as the man approached the truck and shoved the pistol into his face through the open window, screaming for the boy to get out of the car.

The boy looked terrified. He raised shaking hands in front of himself and stumbled out the door as the man threw his bag into the front seat, jumped in, and slammed his foot on the pedal. Nothing happened. The man cursed, got out of the truck and fled from the parking lot and into the adjacent street. The blonde boy stood dumbfounded.

"What is going on?" someone was shouting.

Morgan couldn't answer. His heart was thumping in his chest, and his body felt weak.

He glanced toward the front of the store. People were

fleeing from the open door in all directions like a flock of chickens chased by a fox. At the end of the group, a middle-aged woman shambled out of the store, she stumbled and fell on the sidewalk. She grunted and began pulling herself across the pavement arm over arm, her left leg dragging limply behind her.

Morgan didn't think. He heard his bike crashing to the ground as he sprinted toward the woman. His shoes thudded across the pavement, and he went down on one knee next to her. Blood was spreading down her white blouse, a red trail leading back toward the store's entrance.

"Ma'am," Morgan shouted frantically. "Ma'am! Are you OK?"

She shuddered and gasped, making a choking sound as her tear-filled eyes met his. Her head drooped, her body going limp. Gently, he rolled her to her side, her head lolled, eyes wide and unrecognizing. Morgan looked down at the red spot on her blouse. Blood was oozing from a large, ragged hole in her chest, coating the pavement below her. He put his fingers on her neck and then on her wrist.

There was no pulse.

Morgan's mind raced, he felt lightheaded and confused, he knew he was on the edge of panic. *Think!* He scolded himself as he gulped air into his burning lungs and forced himself to focus. Steeling himself, he leaned over and pressed his ear against her warm chest, ignoring the wetness. He listened, trying to hear a for breath over his own and rasping gasps.

Hearing nothing, Morgan laid her gently down, pushed aside a golden locket, and interlocked his fingers. He began pumping his hands down, counting a rhythm in time with the compressions.

One. Two. Three. Four. Five.

He leaned the woman's head back, put his lips to hers, and breathed a deep breath into her mouth.

One. Two. Three. Four. Five.

"Breathe!" he shouted.

He put an ear to her chest.

"Damn it!"

One. Two. Three. Four. Five.

"Breathe!"

One. Two. Three. Four. Five.

"Come on damn you, breathe!"

He went on for what seemed like an eternity, alternating between compressions and breathing into her mouth. Finally, exhausted, Morgan slumped to listen once more for the woman's heartbeat.

There was only silence.

He sat back numbly and glanced around the parking lot. It was now deserted. He glanced at where Todd had hidden behind the car. He was gone.

Morgan glanced down at the golden locket on the woman's chest. He lifted it, opened the frail metal, and looked inside at a photo. Two children, a little boy of about ten, and a little girl of perhaps three, peered out at him. He lifted his head and looked at the sky; warm fluid was sliding down his cheeks. He glanced to the corner of the parking lot where he'd dropped his bike. The bike and the backpack were gone.

CHAPTER 5
THE WOMAN IN WHITE

Morgan stared in disbelief at the empty spot of blacktop. The stretch of unbroken pavement seemed to stare back at him, mocking. At length, he shook himself and peered down the street in the direction of the Steadman's place. The street was nearly empty, a few cars sitting abandoned on the side of the road, obstructing his view. In the distance a single figure stood. Morgan watched as the figure shook a cell phone and cursed loudly before abruptly throwing it to the ground and stomping on it.

Morgan's mind felt thick, slow, and confused as he knelt beside the corpse. He glanced back to her slack face; her dark eyes were clouding and her face looked somehow less than human. He stood numbly and took one shaky step, then another. His hands were trembling, large wet patches stained his pants at the knees, and someone was crying loudly, weeping in heavy, shuddering sobs.

He scanned the area, searching for the source of the sound, but found himself alone. He sniffed loudly and wiped his face on the sleeve of his shirt, stifling the sobs. Slowly, he made his way to where he'd left the old bike and paused to take a deep calming breath before continuing onward, his shoes pacing forward mechanically, as if of their own accord.

How long was I in the parking lot? he wondered.

The sun was dropping in the western sky, darkness beginning to fall in the slow way of early summer, where each day was longer than the last. The warm western breeze brought the dry smells of sage, dust, and blood to his nostrils.

His arms ached, and his legs were unsteady, like he'd run a long way and done hundreds of push-ups. A long ghostly howl broke his reverie and sent violent shivers up his spine. His head snapped up, body tensing, a spike of adrenaline driving away the cobwebs in his mind. The howl had been distant, but he couldn't know how distant.

Morgan scanned the area; he was on the town's main street, a highway that ran from east to west from Heber City to Denver. A few dark shapes moved in the distance, bodies tense, heads casting around as they too looked for the source of the howl. The sun was sinking in front of him, casting red and orange plumes of color across the scattered clouds floating above the horizon. In the east, dark clouds roiled, bringing with them a threat that he could sense but not fully understand.

Coyotes? he wondered.

He'd heard a coyote's call before, on a camping trip years earlier, but these sounded different. It was lower, fuller, more powerful, and more sinister. The dead woman's face came to him unbidden, and he shook it away, trying to focus on the road before him. Numbness rose in his chest, a feeling of detachment that he'd last experienced that night in the hospital. The memory of his mother's eyes unseeing as life slipped away from her.

Think, he scolded himself. *What do you need to do? Pull yourself together.*

He looked around to get his bearings, and quickened his stride, falling into an easy ground eating jog toward the Steadman's house across town. There were still miles to go. He turned right and hurried three blocks south before swinging toward the east and rushing on as twilight fell into darkness.

The moon was low behind the horizon, the stars dark, making it difficult to see even the road at his feet as the darkness deepened. He glanced up at the darkened streetlights that normally guided his path.

He'd ridden this way in the dark dozens of times, perhaps hundreds, but lacking the streetlights to illuminate the way, the path felt unfamiliar and ominous. The miles dragged on; his legs wobbled like stretched taffy. His stomach growled loudly.

A thundering howl split the night.

This one was close. Morgan hesitated, listening intently for the sounds of softly padding of feet, or any indication that the thing that stalked the night approached. Finally, hearing nothing, he released the breath he'd been holding and strode on redoubling his pace.

He shivered, the thrill of a fear crawled up his spine as he proceeded. In the distance, he could just make out the shape of the small brick house on the outskirts of town where he lived with the Steadman's. A life full of thankless toil, a life he knew was not in accordance with the state's laws concerning foster children—not that he could do anything about the situation. Eric Steadman knew people. Well-placed people. People who made sure that the public would never hear about the things that happened behind the scenes in Vernal.

Almost there. Morgan stumbled over the curb and fell, catching himself with his hands. He stood and flexed a bruised palm as he shuffled across the gravel and dry grass toward the cracked porch. As he neared, there was a squelching sound, and the ground came up suddenly to meet him once more.

He cursed and kicked at the thing that had entangled his legs, knocking it to the side. A tree branch, he thought, though no trees stood nearby. But something felt wrong about it. It felt rotten and soft, with too much give to its surface.

Morgan stared at his feet, unable to see more than a vague outline. He shook his head and began to rise when something white fluttered nearby and he stopped. He got to his knees, crawled to the object, and picked it up. It felt wet in his hand, like morning dew had fallen on it. But it wasn't morning, and it was much too warm and dry for dew. He pulled it closer to his face, straining to see in the scant light provided by the few stars that now shone down on the desert.

The shape resolved into a tattered piece of fabric, torn and frayed at the edges. He turned it over. Three letters were decipherable on the fabric, QUE it read, a fourth letter that might have been an E was obscured by a jagged tear. The edge, by the rip, was wet. There was something familiar about the script. Morgan laid the scrap of fabric across his hand, and his finger traced the last letter. It had to be an E, he decided as he brushed across the damp surface. His finger came away sticky.

Something clicked into place in his head. QUEEN, he realized. It was a torn piece of the shirt Patrick had been wearing.

Morgan's stomach dropped to his toes as he stared at the torn piece of cloth. He dropped the fabric, wrenching his hand back as if bitten and wiping his fingers on his pants. Heart pounding, he turned and sprinted toward the door.

"Patrick?" he tried to shout, but the words came out as a croak. He looked at the house. In the dimness, he could now see that the door was open. Eric would never leave the door open. Morgan got to his feet and picked his way up the stairs and put his head through the doorway.

"Patrick?" he called again, this time managing a slightly louder croak. He waited for a reply. None came.

"Patrick, are you here?"

Silence.

Morgan cursed and took a hesitant step inside, his hands outstretched, feeling for the walls as he made his way inside the confines of the living room. A sickly smell like open sewer filled his nostrils, and Morgan choked and coughed before he could settle himself. He pulled the neck of his t-shirt up over his nose and mouth and took another step forward. He bumped into something with his foot as he slid it forward, and he nearly tripped. He glanced down. There was something large and misshapen on the floor.

Patrick's backpack, he decided. The boy was constantly leaving his things lying around, even in the middle of the hallway. Eric would never have let Morgan get away with something like that, but when Patrick did it, Eric simply stepped over the object without a word.

Morgan picked his way carefully over the bag and strewn contents, making his way toward the kitchen. His feet squelched wetly as he wound around the kitchen countertop and crossed the tile, his shoes sticking with every step. It felt like he was walking through wet paint. *Why would Eric paint the floor?*

His hands probed, finding the top kitchen drawer by the fridge and pulling it open. He rifled through the contents until his fingers found the hard, cold metal of a flashlight. He felt for the button, clicked it, and swept the beam across the room. It had been ransacked. Broken glass, papers, and red paint littered the floor. The couch lay overturned, and debris was scattered in all directions.

Were we robbed? Morgan wondered, his mind attempting to piece together the evidence.

"Patrick?" Morgan called again. "Eric?" Again, there was no answer.

He slipped around the cabinet and stopped, his eyes staring fixedly at the ground. Eric lay in a pool of blood on the ground, his body torn, long ragged slashes ran down his torso, his right arm was mangled, and his legs lay at unnatural angles.

Morgan screamed and recoiled, nearly tripping and crashing hard into the wall. He scrambled to his feet and vaulted out the door and across the yard toward the shed. Light from his flashlight swept across the large fleshy remains of Patrick's torso that lay torn like his father's.

A deep rumbling growl filled the air and Morgan froze, the hairs on his neck standing erect, his feet rooting in place. A deafening roar split the night, leaving his ears ringing and his body shaking.

He gulped, his head turning glacially, almost of its own accord, toward the sound. The light of the flashlight fell on a dark shape. The creature stood on two extremely hairy hind legs that bent backward, animal-like, at the knee. Its chest was equally hairy and covered in sinewy muscles that rippled with the creature's movements. It had broad shoulders and exaggeratedly long arms connected to enormous hands. The beast's thick fingers flexed, and blood dripped from the long claws. Its face was a monstrosity of fur and teeth, with a snout like a hyena and golden eyes that gleamed in the light of the flashlight like a demon's. It growled and took a step forward on massive dog-like paws.

I'm about to die, Morgan realized as he took an unconscious step backward, his eyes glued on the monster's hideous form.

A white blur flashed across his vision, and something struck him forcefully in the chest. He landed hard on his back, and the impact drove the wind from his chest. The flashlight spun through the air, its beam shining momentarily into his eyes, dazzling him before it hit the ground with a crunch and went out. The night became a black so deep that Morgan may as well have been thrust into a cave a thousand feet underground.

He gasped, trying to recover his breath as adrenaline coursed through his veins. His heart was pounding on his ribcage like a jackhammer.

Time stood still. Sounds that Morgan could not pinpoint nor interpret filled his ears. A cacophony of gasping, wailing, and grunting echoed in his ears.

Suddenly, a bright vector shone in the darkness. A golden blade appeared in the air before him, casting the shadows back and forcing him to turn away from its brilliance. He raised his hand as the sword weaved before him, whipping and slashing. Dark shapes leapt forward and back in counter-time to the light, moving too quickly for Morgan to track. His ears rang with a nightmarish symphony of growls, snapping jaws, and the slashing of a blade.

Morgan rolled, his hands frantically searching the ground for the flashlight. His fingers slid uselessly through the grass as a sudden yip was followed by a heavy thump. His fingers brushed something hard and cold. He picked up the flashlight and flicked the switch. Nothing happened.

He turned as the glowing blade moved slowly toward him. There was a distant howl, followed by a grave-like silence. Morgan gulped and stared up at the dark outline of a lithe form as it approached him. The golden light washed across feminine features; a faint smile adorned the thin mouth.

"It's OK," the woman said, her voice high, its tone soothing. "You are safe. I will not let them harm you."

Morgan swallowed and worked his jaw, but his voice failed to produce a sound as he stared at the woman and her long silver-blonde hair.

"You," he sputtered.

"Me," she agreed, striding to where Morgan lay and extending a hand. "You need not be afraid of me."

Morgan stared up at her, mesmerized, and blinked. She shook her hand impatiently in front of his face, and Morgan belatedly took it. She pulled, and Morgan was yanked from the ground and into the air. His feet landed awkwardly, and he nearly pitched back to the ground. A small, powerful hand grabbed his arm, steadying him. He looked up into the woman's face, his mind reeling. She was so strong!

"Sorry. I'm a bit keyed up just now." she said with a chagrined smile. "Let's go." She turned and strode across the yard.

Morgan stared after her uncertainly. "I need to get something, some things." He amended.

Aella stopped and glanced back at him over her shoulder. He waited as she looked at him, her gaze intense and unreadable. Finally, she nodded.

"If you must," she said. "But do so quickly, we have very little time. There are other skin walkers about, and they are certain to arrive here soon."

Morgan turned and scampered toward the house, stopping at the doorway. He cursed, took a deep steadying breath, and lifted his shirt over his nose before plunging inside. The light of the moon, crested the eastern hills and began to shine in through a window and the open door, lighting the room just enough to allow Morgan to make out the vague outlines of his former foster family. He averted his eyes and picked his way carefully across the floor, being sure not to step on any of the gruesome remains.

He moved to the hallway door and pushed it open. His room was remarkably intact, given the state of the rest of the house. Morgan grabbed a backpack from the small closet, unzipped the pocket, and dumped his schoolbooks on the ground. He gathered clothes from the wardrobe—a pair of shorts, a couple t-shirts, a thin waterproof jacket, and a few pairs of socks and underwear—and shoved them into the bag.

He went down the hall to the bathroom and grabbed some toiletries, then turned to leave. As he moved to pass his door, he paused and his eyes fell on the dresser. Biting his lip, he made his way there and opened the drawer. He pulled out the small box, removed the letter from inside, and slipped the folded page into his pocket before hurrying out into the night.

In the moonlight, Aella stood waiting, her body tense with watchful readiness, eyes scanning the area for any hints of a threat.

Who is this woman? he wondered. She had saved his life, that much he was sure of, but where had she come from?

"I'm ready," he said, stepping down the cement steps and nodding.

"I need you to put this on," Aella said, pulling out a small silvery medallion on a leather strap. She held it out to him.

Morgan hesitated. He recognized it. "Where did you get my medallion?" he said.

She stared back at him uncertainly. "Your medallion?" she began, then shook her head. "There's no time now. We can discuss it when we're a safe distance away. But we must go before more skin-walkers arrive."

Morgan stood looking at her. His fingers twitched as he stared at the medallion. "Skin-walkers? Are you from Skin-walker Ranch or something?"

"I don't know what that is," she said curtly, and nodded insistently at the necklace she held out before him.

He extended a shaky palm, and she dropped the medallion onto it. The metal of the pendant was hard and warm to the touch. He pulled it over his neck.

"Let's go." She turned, and the glowing sword disappeared from her hand. Morgan gasped but followed.

"Where are we going?"

"There is an old outpost north of town. We'll meet the others there."

"Others?"

"You didn't think you'd be the only one, did you?" she said, not bothering to slow down.

Morgan felt his cheeks flush.

"How is your cardio?" she called back to him. "Can you run?"

"I play soccer, so yeah, I can run."

"Excellent," she said, increasing her pace. "Keep up!"

Morgan hustled to follow as Aella ran at a near sprint down the road toward town. Morgan trailed and he quickly found himself becoming winded. When they approached an overgrown canal that ran east to west south of town, the woman leapt lithely over it, leaving Morgan frowning at the distance before making a running leap and failing to clear the edge. He cursed as he crashed into the embankment and his right foot sank to the ankle. He withdrew the appendage and continued, his right foot squelching wetly with every step.

By the time they arrive at the buildings on the outskirts of town, the moon had fully crested the horizon and Morgan was exhausted. His legs were heavy and weak after a long run at such a quick pace.

Aella stopped crouching and looked back at him. "Stay in

the shadows. We want to avoid being noticed," she said in hushed tones, and laid her index finger across her lips.

"By who?" Morgan asked, genuinely confused.

"Anyone," she said simply and began moving up the street still in a crouch, keeping to the shadows as she moved. Morgan frowned and started forward, doing his best to follow her lead but feeling certain that he was not succeeding.

A sudden howl split the night, and Aella cursed, pushing Morgan against a nearby brick wall. "Ouch," he said, wincing as pain lanced up his shoulder. Ahead, people milled in an open-air pavilion next to a sign with the inscription Cobble Rock Park. Aella pressed Morgan back against the wall as the people's heads swiveled, searching for the source of the sound.

The two waited silently, Morgan barely daring to breathe as Aella held him firmly against the brick and the figures in the park looked about and then began moving again. Morgan blinked, watching them, wondering what they were thinking.

There was something odd about them, something that seemed wrong. Morgan frowned trying to shake the feeling. Something about the way that they moved gave him the impression of someone who'd had more than a few beers. Then one of the figures walked face-first into a wall with a thud and collapsed to the ground before laying unmoving.

"Are they drunk?" Morgan whispered, his voice barely audible, even at close range.

"Moon sick," Aella said, watching the people intently.

"Moon sick?"

"The thing that hit the moon wasn't a meteor, Morgan."

"What else could it have been?"

Aella sighed. "I don't know that I can explain it, but a regular object, space debris or a meteor, wouldn't make the moon do that." She pointed up at the strongly lit moon with its crackling surface.

"The moon is what's causing people to act like that?" Morgan questioned, stunned.

Aella nodded. "They will be dead soon."

"Dead?" Morgan whispered intensely. "*All* of them will die?"

She met his eyes and peered into them, her gaze piercing him. Finally, she took a deep breath. "I'm sorry to be the one to tell you this Morgan. Some of them will undoubtedly live—but the rest," she shook her head somberly.

Morgan felt his head swim as he considered the statement. "But" he stuttered, "that can't be possible."

"Yesterday, there were more than eight billion people on the planet. In the next few weeks, that number will shrink to a few million, perhaps a few hundred thousand," she said.

"But how do you know?"

"It was foretold, many centuries ago." Aella's tone was grave, resigned.

Morgan frowned.

"Run!" Aella hissed suddenly and shoved Morgan into the street.

There was a sound of shouting behind them, and Morgan looked back over his shoulder as a huge dark shape bound into the crowd smashed a man to the ground. The man shrieked as the werewolf's sharp teeth crushed the bones in his shoulder.

"Run!" Aella repeated and sprinted towards the monster that was now shaking the man like a dog with a mouse in its jaws. The glowing sword appeared in her hand as she ran and then leaped impossibly high and swung the bright blade in a flashing arc. More dark shapes sped into the melee; the sounds of howls and snapping jaws split the night as Aella's bright sword flashed in wide arcs.

Morgan turned and ran. All weariness forgotten, he sprinted across the street, between two buildings, and leapt a barbed wire fence. He rolled as he hit the ground and came up running once more.

He sped into the night; the acrid smell of smoke met his nostrils, carried on a gentle breeze that blew into his face as he moved. A corner of his mind wondered what was burning. A house? A car? Something else? Nothing would surprise him on a night like tonight. He couldn't bring himself to look over his shoulder as he ran out of town and into a field to the north.

Vernal slipped further behind as he crossed an alfalfa field dotted with the rectangular silhouettes of hay bales. Headstones in some giant graveyard.

This will be my grave if I'm not careful, he thought, forcing himself onward. But after only a few moments, he slowed, his lungs burning, breath coming in deep, ragged gasps.

Morgan paused, peering into the night, back toward the town, flames rising from it. He stood silently looking for some sign of Aella, eyes straining into the dimness. In the distance, he picked out movement, a dark shape loping forward, its gait inhuman.

Cursing silently, he turned and hurried north, his body crouched low so the thing that pursued him would be less likely to see him. He reached the edge of the cultivated fields and ran across a small bridge that bisected a canal flowing with dark liquid toward the rocky desert terrain beyond.

Aella said there was an outpost, he reminded himself as he scrambled up the rocky hill. But how would he find it? A problem for later, he decided. He looked over his shoulder, and in the distance, he could make out the dark shape as it moved toward the edge of the fields, gaining on him rapidly.

Morgan stopped, heart pounding as he scanned the area. Where could he go? He cursed again and headed westward. Sweat was pouring down his face, his chest burning as he topped a rocky rise and looked down into a small valley thick with a mix of scrubby trees, desert grasses, and sagebrush.

He heard a loud noise, like tree limbs snapping from behind him. He turned to look back, but in the dimness, he could not make out the creature, or the trees that it was smashing through as it sped toward him, unconcerned with stealth.

I need to do something different, leave a false trail, he thought, his eyes searching the area. Near him, there was a large sandy area bordered by large slabs of sandstone. He stepped onto the sand and made his way across it. When he reached the other side, he circled and backtracked along the sandstone, then turned into the valley and hopped across a series of stones, avoiding touching the sand until he had put distance from his last steps.

He picked his way through the foliage, carefully avoiding breaking any twigs as the sounds of his pursuer got louder. He reached an area that was densely packed with scrub oak and aspen. He crawled inside, making his way into the center of the thicket and lay flat on his back.

A howl sounded from up the hill. Morgan's heart thumped, and his chest burned as he tried to control his breathing. Holding still, not daring to move, he stared up at the hilltop. A huge dark shape moved into the light, and Morgan stared at the werewolf. This one was larger than the others, it had a silver coat, with elongated arms and wicked claws that glinted in the eerie light of the moon. He swallowed unconsciously as the beast's head whipped from side to side. It raised its muzzle to the air, sniffing in several directions before gazing around again.

It doesn't know which way I went, he realized. A small particle of hope blossomed in his chest. He waited; time seemed to pass slowly as something sharp dug into his ribs. The discomfort went from troublesome to painful and finally to agony, but Morgan dared not move.

Finally, the creature turned, heading north and disappearing from view. Morgan let out a slow sigh and then adjusted, moving the rock from below his ribs. He positioned himself as comfortably as possible, using his arm as a pillow, and listened silently to the sounds of the breeze while the faint smell of burning filled his nostrils.

CHAPTER 6
THE OUTPOST

Morgan shifted, his senses coming suddenly to attention. He listened intently to the sound of soft footfalls on hard ground. They were punctuated with the soft crunch of a weight pressing down on desert foliage. His adrenaline spiked, eyes darting from side to side, as the sounds moved steadily toward him. Carefully he lifted his head, adjusting his perspective just enough to peek through the break between the brush.

Something silvery moved into view a dozen feet away, at the edge of a large round patch of sandstone. Morgan froze, holding his breath as a shape moved through the darkness making its way inexorably toward him. His mind raced, he couldn't outrun the creature, he was sure of that. His legs ached and his body felt sluggish, if he could manage to run at all, he was sure it wouldn't be far.

He braced himself, his hands searching the ground for a rock, anything he could use as a weapon, as the shape approached. A lithe, thin form came into view, pushing the trees apart and peering in at him. A breeze caught the long silver hair that hung at the shoulders and blew it away from pale skin.

"Aella," Morgan gasped, exhaling in relief. He sat up.

She hurried to him on silent feet. "Are you OK?" she whispered.

He nodded. "I thought you were that thing, the skin-walker. It followed me, it passed over there." He pointed toward the bluff on which the monster had stood.

"Which one? What did it look like?" she asked, scanning the area urgently for signs of the creature.

"A big grey one," Morgan answered.

Aella nodded. "I was afraid of that," she said. "He's the alpha, a real nasty piece of work."

Aella motioned Morgan out of his hiding place. He stood, and she nodded and pantomimed tiptoeing, giving him a shushing gesture with her finger.

He nodded as the woman set off, moving silently north through the short scraggly trees. Morgan followed trying to move both quickly and quietly, with less success than he would have liked. Aella kept turning, her face a mask of concern as a twig snapped below his feet. He grimaced but continued to follow the odd woman.

The pair made their way across a wide valley and into small rocky hills. Morgan struggled to keep up. They crossed a dry creek bed and crested a small hill where a depression in the land sunk away from them. Morgan looked down on the reflection of the moon on water. *Steinaker Reservoir*, he thought. He'd come further north and east than he'd realized.

He had covered at least a dozen miles since the time when he'd crouched next to the dying woman in the parking lot. Had it only been a few hours? It felt like another lifetime, separated by a gulf of misery and toil. Aella nodded and set off at a run. Morgan followed.

They crossed the valley, skirting the lake, and crossing a paved road before making their way across a wide field dotted with sage brush. Suddenly Morgan stumbled, his legs giving out and as he fell, his elbow hit hard on a patch of dense sand that kicked up into his face. He began to cough, the sound echoing off the rocks.

"SHHH!" Aella said urgently, her head darting from side to side as she scanned the area. They waited in silence for a long moment, Morgan straining his ears for the sounds of movement. Finally satisfied, Aella extended a hand. He took it and tried to get up, to keep going, but his knees buckled, and he dropped back to the dirt.

He was spent; he lay gasping, unable to make his legs bear his weight.

"I'm sorry," he gasped. "I can't," he began as he rolled to his back.

Aella sighed and grabbed his arm. Morgan grunted as this time she hefted him bodily over her shoulder and settled him into a fireman's carry. She shifted him once to settle his weight on her shoulders and began again to run.

Morgan bounced awkwardly with each step, his stomach and pride taking the brunt of the damage. Even burdened by his weight, Aella's strides were long and smooth.

Finally, they arrived at Moonshine Arch. Aella dropped Morgan unceremoniously, and he landed hard on a shoulder, causing it to ache from the impact.

He lay staring up into the sky. The moon had risen and slipped from behind the clouds. Its light kissed the tops of the cliffs and bathed the desert with a surprising amount of light.

"How are you feeling?" Aella asked, her tone light and friendly.

Morgan struggled to sit up. "Like I was hit by a truck, my

head is pounding," he said, his hand moving unconsciously to his forehead.

"Makes sense after the night that you've had," she replied. Morgan stared back at her trying to determine if she was being sincere. Aella motioned for him to join her as she moved towards a sandy hill. Morgan struggled to his feet, his head swimming as he rose and his legs still failing to work properly.

Aella produced a leather water skin and held it out to him. "Water will help with that headache, I'd wager. You're dehydrated."

He hesitated a moment before nodding and taking the skin. "Thank you," he said and unstopped the cap. He took a long pull, relishing the cool, almost sweet flavor of the liquid. He gulped it down greedily, paused briefly to gasp for breath, and took another long draw.

"Ahh," he gasped. "Where did you get this from? It's fantastic!" He lifted the bag to his lips and began to take another drink.

"From the lake," she said simply.

Morgan coughed and spluttered, spraying liquid into the air. Aella danced gracefully out of range of the spray, a wry grin spread across her thin lips.

"Are you insane?" he spat. "You can't drink water from the lake. I'm going to get giardia!"

She smiled wickedly back at him. "Oh, I wouldn't worry about that," she said, waving her hand dismissively. "Now come on, let's get inside." She motioned over her shoulder as she started up the hill.

"Wouldn't worry about it?" Morgan spluttered. "Giardia could *kill* me! Or you, both of us!" Morgan stared up at Aella as she ascended adjacent to the rocky curve of the arch.

"Nonsense, the Spring Queen wouldn't allow that," she said. "Well, what do you think?" she asked, gesturing toward the end of a flat sandstone wall that ran beside the path and ended abruptly at the top of the hill.

He stared at it for a moment, unsure of what she wanted him to comment on; it was just a stone slab like so many others in this part of Eastern Utah.

"I've been here before," he said simply. "Several times, as a matter of fact. It's not a secret or anything, lots of people come here." He wandered to the east of the stone pillar and sat down, eager to rest his aching legs.

"What about this?" Aella said, pointing at the unremarkable stone wall.

"I've been all around up there," he said, ignoring the strange way she was grinning at him. "There are dozens of formations just like that one." He looked out from the edge of the wall onto a bowl-shaped area of sandstone that reminded him of an amphitheater.

Aella put her hand out and pointed toward a small area on the wall. "Look," she pressed.

Morgan frowned but looked closer. In the face of the stone, there was a small indentation. It looked like someone had carved a small shape into the stone with something hard. It was shaped like the print of a deer's hoof, with two oblong indentations that met at the top.

Aella pressed her palm against the stone of the pillar over the indentation.

"What about this? Have you seen this before?" she said as she nodded toward the stone.

"Yea—" Morgan began to answer and then stopped cold. He stared at Aella's hand. Glowing, wispy tendrils streamed out of her palm and into the stone. The tendrils entered the stone at the indentation, where wriggling, glowing forms made their way outward onto the face of the stone.

Morgan stared as the forms wove themselves together and

brightened into five distinct patterns that appeared in a circular formation. He closed his mouth with a clunk and watched as Aella pulled her hand back from the pillar. The shapes had coalesced into the glowing symbols of a bear, a snake, a tiger, a bird, and a dragon.

"How did you—?" he began.

"I'm Valkryn Morgan, which is a kind of Ethermancer," Aella smiled brightly, flipping her hair in a falsely arrogant way, and winked at him.

He felt his face flush.

"What you see here," she said, in an instructional tone, like a schoolteacher settling into a lesson, "are the five Ethermancer orders, the five clans of Encartha."

She pointed to the symbols one by one. "Bear, Phoenix, Tiger, Snake, and Dragon Clans."

"Does everyone in—" He paused, unable to remember the name of the place.

"Encartha," she supplied, anticipating his question.

"Encartha," he repeated, "belong to a clan?"

"Not everyone in Encartha is a Valkryn, nor are they all Ethermancers. Only those that can gather can join a clan."

"Gather?"

"Do magic, you might say," she said and wiggled her fingers in an impression of a carnival fortune teller over a crystal ball.

Morgan knew she was trying to lighten the mood after the ordeal they had been through. He didn't feel ready to be cheered up but smiled despite himself.

"There are five clans of Valkryn," Aella went on, "each devoted to a Great Fae, what you might think of as a demigod, and each clan uses a symbol patterned after their patron."

Morgan frowned. Gods, monsters, and magic users. He felt like he was losing his mind. "Which clan do you belong to?"

"Tiger clan," she said. She leaned her head to the side and pulled her hair back. Just below and behind her ear, Morgan saw a small tattoo that matched the tiger symbol on the wall.

"What's the difference? I mean, why different clans? Aren't you all magicians?"

"None of us are magicians, not in the way you're thinking, but Ethermancers do use magic. Morgan, there is a lot to tell, but we really don't have time right now. The pack will be making its way this direction. Let's talk about it later. OK?"

He shrugged.

"Let's go in, shall we?" she said, once again pressing her hand to the pillar in the center of the symbols. There was a sound like rushing water, and the rock seemed to melt, flowing away to reveal a broad doorway where stone steps led downward into the darkness beyond.

"Hijole!" Morgan whispered, a feeling of awe settling over him as he stared at the opening.

"I thought you'd like it!" she said. "Let's go." She gestured for him to enter the opening.

Morgan hesitated, goggling at the space left behind.

"How did you—" he began, but Aella ignored him and simply motioned again for him to follow as she stepped inside.

It simply isn't possible. He'd been there before, leaned against the same stone wall, and felt its rough, solid surface. Now it was just *gone*. He reached his hand into the opening, and it passed through the space without resistance.

"It's safe," Aella said with a smirk pausing just inside the opening. "Come in. Let's get some rest. It's been a very long night."

Morgan hesitated and looked around. By the light of the moon, he could see distant pillars of smoke that rose from Vernal to the south.

How many people died today? How many more were driven mad by that thing that hit the moon? Where is Imogene?

"I have to find my sister," he said, a sudden panic growing in his chest. In all the confusion of the night, he hadn't even thought of her. *Where is she? Is she safe?* "I have to get to her."

"You're in no state to go anywhere tonight. You're exhausted and that werewolf is still out there," Aella said, but her tone was not unsympathetic. "Come get some rest. Let's talk in the morning."

He hesitated, standing in the doorway, his tired mind trying to conceive of some way that he could get to Imogene, to keep her safe in a world he no longer understood. In the distance, a wolf howled. A chill went up his spine, and he took a deep, calming breath.

"Tomorrow," he promised himself. A corner of his mind worried that Imogene might be dead by then. But Aella was right, he couldn't go on tonight. His shoulders slumped and he followed her into the outpost. The door sealed behind as they descended a flight of round stone stairs and into a long corridor. Decaying stone statues lined the walls, which were lit by glowing strands of light that coalesced into intricate murals depicting armored figures in heroic poses doing battle with a variety of monsters.

They arrived in a domed central room where thick pillars encircled the space, each one carved with reliefs of intricate vines, fantastical creatures, and men and women in armor. The smell of wet stone filled his nostrils.

At the center of the room stood a pedestal where the figure of a man stood proudly, a sword uplifted in one hand, a circular disk in the other.

Morgan stared in at the stone face. It was carved in a stoic frown, its muscles powerful, its bearing determined and noble. It was perhaps the greatest work of art he'd ever seen.

"This way to the boys' dorm," Aella said, indicating a path leading off from the main chamber.

Morgan nodded and made his way down the hallway and into a rectangular room lined with beds, several of which held sleeping boys that looked to be in their teens. Morgan stared for a moment, wondering who they were. He looked at them in fascination for a few moments wondering where they were from and how they'd gotten to the outpost. Finally, exhausted, he made his way to an open bed nearby and fell into it. He slept.

In the morning, Morgan woke stiff and aching from the previous day's adventures. He was alone in the dorm room. He got up and retraced his path toward the large, domed room.

He stopped and stared for a long moment at the statue, the columns, the glowing murals, and the variety of paths that led from the room. This was, he assumed, the center of the outpost, a sort of large gathering place where perhaps people had once stood and listened as another someone, an important someone, stood on the small dais positioned below the statue and addressed them.

"Morgan, you're up! Good, we have to get going as soon as possible," Aella's now familiar voice said from behind him. He turned, but the woman he'd met the night before was nowhere to be found. Instead, a woman he didn't recognize stood in the hallway staring at him, a friendly smile plastered on.

She had a coppery complexion, long dark hair, and sparkling dark eyes that rested above smooth, high cheekbones. She wore a strange form of clothing that Morgan didn't recognize. It had long sleeves, a pair of vertical fabric strips that ran from her shoulders to her waist where a wide belt was cinched. Below the belt she wore a pair of leather leggings and a breechclout embroidered with small symbols unlike any that Morgan had previously seen, along with a larger stylized tiger in the style of the tattoo that Aella wore by her ear.

He turned and glanced back at the statue. The figure wore a similar style of dress, except the embroidery on his breechclout depicted a phoenix in flight.

"I'm sorry," Morgan said, embarrassed. "I'm afraid"—he fidgeted— "You sounded like Aella" he finished, proffering a feeble smile.

"Ah, yes, my fault really," the woman said, lifting her left hand. On her wrist, she wore a metal bracelet with a group of small silvery charms, each of a different shape. She sorted through the charms, finally selecting one in the shape of a woman. She held it between her thumb and forefinger and squeezed.

In half a heartbeat her hair changed color, silvery locks replaced the black, her face morphed, her skin tone lightening, and her clothes transformed into a long-sleeved white t-shirt and a pair of blue jeans.

"Aella!" Morgan blurted, shocked by the transformation.

She nodded and gave a little curtsy. "I'm sorry for the deception, Morgan. This look"—she indicated her clothing—"is a disguise of sorts."

Morgan goggled as she pressed the charm again and the dark-haired, copper-complected girl reappeared. "This is what I actually look like. I use the disguise to make it easier for me to go unnoticed."

"Silver hair helps you go unnoticed?" he said doubtfully.

She shrugged. "Many people dye their hair these days in all kinds of colors, and I kinda like that detail," she said, smiling. "That was Fen's doing. Well really, the entire disguise was, but I asked for the rest of it. He changed the hair himself, and I thought it was a brilliant touch. Besides, it's not your people I'm trying to go unnoticed by. Are you ready to go?"

"But we just got here," he said. "I thought this place would be safe."

"It is safe, but Fen tells me there are several packs of werewolves headed this way. If they decide to camp out in the area, we could be pinned down here for weeks. We need to get out of here before our avenue of escape has been closed."

Morgan felt his temperature rise. "I'm not going anywhere," he said stubbornly. "Not until I find my sister."

Aella put her hands on her hips. "And where is this sister of yours?" she said, her voice rising.

"Imogene's in Park City."

She gave him an odd look and nodded impatiently. "OK, *where* in Park City?"

He frowned, suddenly aware of his own ignorance. "I don't actually know," he admitted. "Our caseworker only told me that the family that adopted her lived in Park City.

"So, you don't know where you're going. Do you know if she's still in Park City or where she *was* at the time of the event?"

His shoulders slumped further. "No, but it doesn't matter. I have to find her," he said, his voice sounding sullen, even to himself.

Aella moved closer to him and set a gentle hand on his shoulder. She was about his height, and she stared directly into his eyes with a look of concern and pity.

"Morgan," she began, and he stiffened, bracing himself for her next words. He felt sure he knew what she was about to say, and he didn't want to hear it. "Even if she is still alive, which I'm afraid to say is not certain, how can you possibly hope to find her if you don't know where she was at the time of the event?"

His stomach dropped, and he felt his anger rise, becoming volcanic. "I *have* to find her. I made a promise!" he shouted.

"Who do you have to find?" Morgan jerked in surprise and turned. The voice belonged to a short, thin teenage girl with an angular jaw, bright white teeth, and straight brown hair that hung to her shoulders. Her inquisitive green eyes bored into him.

Morgan bit his lip as she held his gaze, approaching from across the room to stand in front of him. He felt suddenly guilty for raising his voice.

The girl held out a hand. Morgan stared at it in confusion for a moment and then, belatedly, shook it.

"I'm Nayme," she said.

Morgan nodded to her. "My sister," he said. "I need to find my sister."

"Where is she?"

Morgan turned to see a short and somewhat pudgy boy with oddly matched clothes and mussed red hair.

"I—I don't know," he said.

"This is Aurelian," Aella said, indicating the boy. "He and Nayme are two of the other adepts that we've gathered. There are several more here. But, Morgan, I'm afraid I can't wait for you to figure out what to do about your sister," she continued. "I have to think about my charges here"—she nodded to the others— "and get them safely to Encartha. I sincerely hope you'll join us, but if you won't, we can't wait."

Morgan blinked, unsure of what to say. She'd been so insistent that he come with her. Why would she now be so cavalier about his reticence to go with her?

After a moment, Aella had pity on him and continued, "You hungry? We have time for a quick bite before we go. Everyone will need their strength. We all have a long way to go, and we have no transportation apart from our own feet."

"No transportation?" Aurelian repeated, his eyes wide.

"I'm afraid not," Aella said. "Cars seem to be affected by

the object that hit the moon. They began having trouble within hours of impact, and it would seem that most are no longer working at all. We certainly can't count on them at this point. We'll have to make our way to Encartha by another method."

Morgan frowned, considering the problem. Without a car, how would he get to Park City? Not that he knew how to drive—the Fosters had never let him take a driver's education course, despite the fact that his high school offered one for no additional charge.

"Where is Encartha anyway?" Nayme said.

"In the Grand Canyon."

"*Where* in the Grand Canyon?" Morgan said, matching the tone that she had used on him.

She looked down her nose at him. "Are you familiar with the canyon?" she asked. "Do you know where things are in it?"

"No," Morgan admitted.

"Then it doesn't really matter, does it? But for your knowledge, it's roughly in the middle, near Cape Royal."

Morgan didn't recognize the name, but he made a mental note of it.

"That's one of the busiest places in the whole canyon. I thought this place was supposed to be a secret!" Aurelian said, puzzled.

Aella nodded. "Well, it was a secret. Until that object hit the moon, Encartha existed—how should I put this? —in another plane of existence, on the other side of a barrier of sorts that separated the Fae world from yours. But now, the barrier is gone and both planes have come into union with each other. Now it's quite easy to find, assuming you know where to go."

"Now that the event we Encarthans long waited for has taken place, you will find many places formerly barren now have cities of various varieties. And I'm afraid that the reverse is also likely true."

Morgan looked at her intently, trying to understand the implications of her words. "Various varieties?"

"Well, of course, not all cities are *human* cities," Aella said.

"Ooh, ooh," Aurelian said, waving a hand in the air like he was in school, desperately trying to get the teacher's attention. "Are there orc cities?" he asked excitedly.

"I'm afraid orcs do not exist," Aella said. "But there are many other species that are very real and do have cities of their own. Fairies, elves, noblings, kappa, and elvenin all have cities of sorts, though Kappa cities are under water and I recommend avoiding elvenin cities if you can help it. The elvenin are quite touchy and very proud. Very proud indeed and slow to forgive."

Morgan's head spun. Fairies and what? He hadn't recognized half the words she'd rattled off, and he couldn't help but wonder what else about the world he now occupied he was likewise ignorant of.

"When you're ready, come get some food. The cafeteria is straight down that hall." Aella pointed to the corridor in the distance, then turned on her heel and left.

Morgan blinked at Aurelian and Nayme. They looked as startled as he felt.

"Breakfast?" Nayme said.

Morgan nodded, he would get some food at least, he would need strength for the journey. How far was it to Park City, he wondered. Several hours by car—and that was only if you drove at seventy miles an hour or more. His mind raced, would it even be safe to follow the highway? He doubted it. He could follow the river, but all the twists and turns would add distance.

Considering all of those factors, he guessed he would have to make his way nearly a hundred and fifty miles. His mind calculated, one hundred fifty miles divided by what? Twenty miles a day if he were on foot and moving at a good pace? It would take him a week to walk that far, longer if he followed the river. His heart sank as he trailed the other teens through the statue room, down a corridor, and into a room with a dozen tables in straight lines.

Three of the tables had other teens sitting looking at them. He stopped, staring back at them, there were ten of them, their heads turned towards him as Morgan entered the room.

"You're here?" He gasped.

CHAPTER 7
A CONVERSATION

Imogene stared into the looking glass, trying to straighten her hair with her fingers. Without a flat iron it was a lost cause. She sighed and put down the brush.

Beside her, Elina Pajarinen was laughing. "You think he's hot, don't you?" she said with a giggle.

"You have to admit that Zach *is* hot," Elina said. "Tall and dark, with those big shoulders, those eyes, and the way he carries himself." She fanned herself dramatically with her hands and laughed.

Imogene sighed. Less than a week had passed since her world had turned upside down, and the other girls at the outpost were already behaving as if nothing had happened.

"What about you, Sarah?"

"I like them taller and less bulky, like that Hugo boy that came in yesterday." She grinned wickedly.

Imogene turned and began putting her few remaining belongings in her bag. She glanced up at Nayme, who was quietly packing her own possessions, saying nothing to the others. Beside her, Alexa, a short pale girl, with striking blue eyes sat on her bed, her arms wrapped around her knees, staring into space and apparently unaware of the conversation. Of all the girls, Alexa had interacted with Imogene least since they'd arrived at the outpost. Imogene didn't think the girl was coping well with the changes. She wasn't sure she was either.

"Suits me fine," Kira, a curly haired girl with a round face, continued with a vixen grin. "Steve's more my flavor, a little less bulky than Zach but not as lanky as Hugo."

"Hey Nayme, who've you got your eye on?"

"She likes that little red-haired lump. What's his name? Autismian?" Elina purred.

Nayme turned on the others, her back rigid. "That's not funny! For your information, Aurelian is kind, something *some* people could use some instruction on."

Elina's eyes burned. "I guess if you like dough, he's your guy. He's as soft as butter in July. He'd probably melt if you touched him."

"I don't like him. He's just nice," Nayme said.

"Hey, Imogene, what about you? Who are you into? I'd hate to fight you all for my pick," Sarah said, giggling.

"What does it matter?" Imogene said. "We'll all be dead in a few days, anyway." She turned and headed toward the door.

"Wow, what a buzzkill," Elina said behind her as Imogene rounded the corner. She walked to the cafeteria and sat at the table. Alone, she placed her hand on the semi-circular marking positioned in the corner of the table. She waited as Aella had demonstrated, and a small opening in the center of the table slab melted away, leaving a rectangular hole. Inside sat a single dish filled with steaming eggs, sausages, utensils, a glass of orange juice, and a napkin. Imogene reached inside and retrieved the food. The opening silently sealed itself.

She grabbed the plate and pulled it close to her. She hadn't gotten used to the strange ways of the outpost. When she sat at the table at mealtimes, the table seemed to anticipate what she wanted and presented it to her in the perfect quantities. When she left her plate on the table after mealtime, it would simply sink back into the table.

"Genie!" Zach's voice said from across the room. She looked up, and he was striding over to her table, a wide grin on his face. Steve and Hugo were with him. She felt a twinge of nervousness as they approached.

"My name is Imogene," she said firmly and took another bite, trying to project confidence. They sat down, each placing their hand over the spot in turn.

"I like Genie though. Think of it as a pet name," Zach said.

"I'm not your pet," Imogene said fiercely, then turned and pretended to continue eating, feeling her temperature rise. Steve and Hugo laughed.

"Hear that, Zach. Sounds like you're not appreciated here," Hugo drawled.

"Oh, she'll come to appreciate my attention," Zach said. "In time."

Imogene's skin crawled, but she said nothing. More teens filtered into the cafeteria. Elina, Sarah, and Kira made their way over to the table and sat down. Behind them, Kenichi entered the room and sat alone at the other table. Imogene abruptly wished she had arrived after the others so she could choose who she sat next to. She could move, she knew, but she didn't want to make a scene. She wasn't sure how long she'd be with them, and getting off on the wrong foot seemed like a bad idea.

Alexa entered and gave Imogene a shy smile before sitting next to her. Imogene tried to tune out the conversation going on around her.

"You're here?"

Imogene looked up from her food and froze. She stared in disbelief at Morgan Foster de la Vega, her brother.

"What are you doing here?" he said, his voice full of surprise and relief. He strode to her table. Imogene bit her lip, her racing mind unable to form a response. She just stared back at him dumbly.

"I thought you were in Park City. I thought you were in danger or—"

She rolled her eyes. *And we're back to being parented by a know-it-all brother,* she thought. "Calm down, Morgan," she said, her voice filled with more disdain than she'd intended. "I'm fine." She folded her arms across her chest, and glared back at him, silently daring him to contradict her.

Morgan recoiled as if slapped.

"Immy—" he began.

She stared daggers at him.

"Well, isn't that fortunate," Aella said smugly. "I guess you don't need to make that trip to Park City after all." She grinned at Morgan.

"You *knew!*" he whispered, scowling back at her.

She shrugged. "I suspected. The spark often runs in families. After that—well, I'm not an idiot, and *Imogene* isn't really all that common a name these days. Why don't you sit down," she said, gesturing toward the tables.

Morgan glared at her before looking at Imogene and frowning. All the seats at her table were occupied.

Immy picked at her food as whispered conversations took place around her and teens snuck glances in her direction.

"Enjoy it while you can," Aella said, motioning toward the food. "Once we leave the outpost, things will be much more spartan."

"Do you mind if I sit here?" Morgan said to Alexa. Alexa

fidgeted, then began to rise. Imogene grabbed her hand and held her firmly in place.

"It's fine, Morgan. We can talk later," she said.

Zach grinned, apparently enjoying the scene.

Morgan stared at Imogene, his eyes intense.

She looked away. *Well, this is just great,* she thought. She could feel her brother's eyes boring into her.

"Alright," Aella said. "I've promised Morgan here some answers. So, you eat, and I'll talk." Imogene glanced up. Morgan hesitated, then made his way to the other table and sat next to Aurelian.

"First things first. Fen!" Aella called. There was the popping noise that Imogene had already learned to associate with the little gnome's comings and goings.

He was a strange creature, Imogene reflected, with powers that she couldn't understand. He could teleport after a fashion, covering long distances instantaneously. Beyond that, he had fought the werewolf that had come for her. He'd killed it somehow, but she couldn't imagine how a creature as small as he was could do that to a monster nearly ten feet tall.

"Mistress be's callings us?" the gnome asked, his characteristic long eyebrows wagging with the words.

Imogene watched Morgan while he took in the figure of the little gnome. Morgan's eyes goggled as he watched Fen. She almost chuckled. *Must be the first weird thing he's seen. It won't be the last.*

The other teens just kept eating. They, like Imogene, had gotten used to the gnome's appearances.

"Yes, if you please," Aella said, nodding toward Morgan.

"Mistress, they's be's a comin! We mus' be's goin!"

Aella nodded. "First, the disks," she said.

Fen pulled out a small leather bag, reached a hand inside,

and produced something small, round, and flat. He handed it to Aella.

"This is a touchstone," she said, lifting the disk. "For the gifted, it acts something like a key, unlocking and enhancing their powers. Keep it with you at all times and in contact with your skin as much as possible. When you're ready, your body will bond with it, absorb it, and in turn, it will strengthen you. Fen, if you would."

The gnome nodded and reached a hand into the bag and produced another disk. He held it out toward Morgan. Imogene stared at it as her brother accepted it. The little gnome then moved around the room, handing disks to each of the teens.

Imogene held out her hand. When Fen placed the palm-sized object in her hand, she nearly recoiled from the sensation that buzzed up her arm.

The disk was made of an odd substance that Imogene couldn't identify. Gray, light, and strong, she recognized the symbols of the Valkryn clans engraved on its surface.

"How can this make us stronger?" Imogene heard herself say aloud.

"It's complicated, and I'm not sure you'd understand the process," Aella began, sounding like a professor warming to her subject. "Let's focus on the effects instead of the process. It will make you physically stronger, faster, and more resistant to pain and fatigue. It will help you mentally as well, making you more focused and quicker in thought and action. Most importantly, it will magnify your ability to draw ether."

Imogene glanced over at Morgan. His eyebrows were knit together, face troubled. "What do you mean, draw ether?" he said.

"I didn't come for you by accident. That goes for each of you." Aella said, meeting each of the teens' gazes in turn. "The werewolves that came for you weren't there by accident, either. Fen, or I, came for each of you because of who you are—because of *what* you are."

"You," she said, pinning Morgan with a serious stare, "and your new acquaintances here are potentials, Ethermancers like me, though obviously untrained. You can draw ether, harness it, and in time, you'll learn to control it. To bend it to your will."

"That is awesome!" Aurelian said.

He looks like a kid at Christmas; Imogene mused at the boy's obvious excitement.

"How do we use it?" Nayme blurted. Imogene had met Nayme only briefly before Morgan had arrived, and she'd seemed shy and quiet. Not that Imogene blamed her, their lives had all changed so much in just a few days. She wondered what Nayme had left behind when Aella and Fen had come for her.

She watched as the small brunette glanced at Morgan and flushed. *Well, now,* Imogene thought.

"Well, there are a few branches of ethermancy," Aella continued, "depending on how you are attuned, you could become a Valkryn like me, a Weaver, an Imbuer, Alchemist, or an Ethermancer." She held her hand forward in a loose fist as a glowing, mist-like substance began pouring out of her hand. The mist clung together like writhing tentacles that twisted and grew, extending in a gentle arc and then hardening into the shape of a glowing sword.

"That is sick!" Aurelian said, amazed before looking around and reddening in embarrassment.

"How are you doing that?" Zach gasped.

"The intricacies of how it works are better left for later," Aella replied.

"What can they do? The eth-ethermancers, I mean?" Aurelian asked, interrupting Morgan, whose mouth was open to ask another question.

"It depends on what type of ethermancer they are. For instance, Imbuers. They can alter the state of matter and, as such, have the power to create permanent objects of great power; armor, and weapons, among other things." She gestured around the building. "Imbuers created much of what you see here in the outpost."

"Weavers can create projections with their power. Illusions so convincing that you would walk off a cliff fully confident that there was stone beneath your feet."

"Alchemists create concoctions filled with their power, like healing drafts, strength potions, things like that."

"Ethermancers can also project their power. This takes the form of light, heat, wind, and so on. They can also create energy shields that are extremely useful in battle."

"I've just shown you what Valkryn can do. We gather ether from all around into our bodies, then project it to form temporary physical objects."

"Any questions so far?" she asked.

"What kind of objects?" Hugo asked, his long face contemplative.

Imogene fidgeted nervously. She glanced at the other teens wondering what type of magic she might have. Would she actually even be able to do any of the things that Aella was describing? She doubted it. it just didn't seem possible. On the other hand, she wouldn't have believed that werewolves could be real either. Or, that something hitting the moon could destroy the world. She sighed loudly and Elina arched a thin eyebrow at her. Imogene bit her lip and turned her attention back to Aella who was going on about the types of projections Valkryn could form.

"Swords, shields, a solid wall, anything you can imagine.

But the primary difference is that imbuers make objects that are permanent. Valkryn's objects are temporary, ethereal. They disappear when the creators release them, or their concentration is broken."

"But you can form *anything*?" Aurelian's voice was full of skepticism. "There's always a catch, so what is it?"

Aella grinned and nodded. "Not a catch really, but ethermancy has costs, limitations."

"Like what? Do we have to sacrifice kittens under the full moon or something?" Zach said, chuckling at his own joke.

"Well, for instance, a Valkryn must understand what they are creating, understand it fully for their power to make it physical."

"Sounds easy enough," Hugo said through a mouth full of food.

Aella smirked. "You'd think that" she said. "But it's actually quite difficult. You must be able to imagine the object, picture it exactly, in every detail, and see it in your mind as clearly as if it were already present. Valkryn visualize what they manifest in three dimensions, hold it in their minds, and make the visualized objects real. It requires a significant amount of attention to detail, which people are not generally very good at."

"What happens if you can't visualize it in three dimensions?" Nayme asked.

"One of two things happens," Aella said. "Either you will fail to draw the ether at all, which is what usually happens to novices, or once you get to the point where your understanding and visualization is at a certain level, you may draw the ether, the object may form, but the object could be imperfect or incomplete."

"Incomplete how?" Morgan said.

"Imagine a badly rusted sword. It still looks like a sword, it has the general shape, but it's pockmarked and weak. The sword might be missing the hilt or the handle."

Morgan grunted in understanding, and Aurelian began fidgeting in his chair, his eyes roving among the other teams as though assessing them.

"What happens to people, Valkryn, that form things incorrectly or can't form them at all?" Nayme asked thoughtfully.

"Fortunately, the adage about practice making perfect applies." A grin formed on Aella's lips. "Normally a Valkryn refines their projections over time, making them more complete, more perfect as it were. It's very difficult to form something the first time, especially if the object is complex, so we start simple and add improvements and refinements over time."

"Take my sword, for example." The tangled web of mist and vines streamed from her hand and formed the shining shape of the elegantly curved weapon. "I've formed it thousands of times. Notice the smoothness of the blade, the intricate patterning around the hilt and blade," she said, indicating engraved symbols that ran up and down its flat edge. "When I first formed it, the blade was—rudimentary. Now the sword is nearly perfect, and I barely have to think about it."

"If it takes so much thought and understanding to create something simple like a sword, how do Valkryn create more complicated objects?" Nayme asked.

"Many don't," Aella replied. "Most Valkryn stick to a few objects, develop a repertoire over time, a few well-thought-out creations that they use over and over."

"How many?" Hugo asked, stroking his chin.

"That depends on the specific Valkryn. Some of the more talented and powerful Valkryn may have a dozen patterns they use with regularity and be able to create crude versions of others on the fly. Less powerful Valkryn may only have two or three items that they can muster."

Imogene stared at Aella's sword. It was long and thin with a slight curve to the blade. The handle looked like ivory, and the whole thing glowed with a golden hue.

"That's the most incredible thing I've ever seen," Aurelian said.

"How do we do it?" Nayme said, her tone eager.

Aella pointed to the disk in Imogene's hand. "You must bond with your touchstone. Without it, you'll be unlikely to draw more than a trickle of power, not enough to manifest anything bigger than the size of a walnut."

Imogene swallowed hard. An unexpected anxiety filled her. What would happen if she couldn't do it? Would Aella and the people of her city let Imogene stay if she couldn't.

The world had changed so much in just a few days, she couldn't guess what would happen to her without the safety that Encartha offered.

"Once you've bonded the touchstone," Aella went on, "your power will be amplified, and the process will be far simpler. You reach out, feel the surrounding energy, pull it in, and focus it here." She pointed to a spot just below her belly button. "Some know this as your don-tin, your internal furnace. You draw the power into your don-tin, focus on what you want to create, and then will the power into the projection."

"So that's why those things, those monsters, are chasing us? Because we can—or may eventually be able to—do that?" Morgan said. "Where do they come from, anyway?"

Aella nodded. "The skin-walkers are abominations, creations of Agartha, ruler of the inner kingdoms."

"Inner kingdoms?" Hugo said, his eyebrows drawn together in perplexity.

Imogene frowned. She was beginning to feel overwhelmed by the information. There was so much to this new version of the world that she didn't know. So many things she couldn't predict.

"We don't have time to go into detail, but, yes, Nayme, the Inner kingdoms are at the center of the earth. That is where Agartha rules and where the skin-walkers—the werewolves, as you might call them—originate. Agartha created skin-walkers from adepts like you. He twisted them into a hybrid amalgamation of adepts, animals, and the bound essence of a dark fae, trapping them in that form forever, bound to serve him for all time."

"That's awful," Nayme said.

"So, if those things catch us, they'll turn us into those—skin-walker things?" Aurelian asked. Imogene's heart was pounding inside her chest, and her skin felt cold and clammy as she considered the possibility of a lifetime of service, trapped in the twisted form of a monster. She shuddered.

"Most likely they'll just kill you," Aella said. "But it's possible."

The teens sat in silence, looking at each other nervously. "Here, in the outpost, you're safe, as this place is protected," Aella reassured them.

Imogene let out a breath she hadn't realized she was holding.

"But we have a problem. There are already at least a dozen wolves heading in our direction. We need to leave immediately before they pin us down here."

"Where are we going?" Hugo asked.

"Encartha. It's where I was born, it's a city in the Grand Canyon. Unfortunately, cars are no longer an option. So, we're going to have to use an alternate means of transportation."

"The Grand Canyon is *really* far from here," Imogene said.

"Hundreds of miles. If we can't drive, how do we get there? And, what about the wolves, if we leave won't they chase us?"

"We'll have to risk it, to find another way," Aella said firmly. "We can't stay here hoping the wolves decide to move on. The magic that sustains this place, that provides the food, water, and everything else that keeps it functioning is—damaged, its power fading."

"Can you fix it?" Nayme asked.

"That's not my area of expertise." Aella said. "There are some small areas of overlap between the branches of magic, but I have nowhere near enough skill or power of that type to make the required correction. If we had a trained imbuer who could repair the magic, we could wait them out for months or even years. Or if it were only one or two of us, we might be able to wait out the skin-walkers, but there are too many of us to hope for that." She shrugged.

Imogene's gaze flicked about the room taking in the somber expressions as each of the teens realized that they would once more be forced to risk being caught by the monsters.

"With that in mind, do any of you have any ideas?"

Imogene licked her lips and stared back at her, a knot forming in her stomach. The teens sat looking at each other, none offering any ideas. After a long moment, Morgan shifted in his seat.

"Well, there's always the river," he ventured hesitantly. "There are rafting companies in Vernal, so maybe we could take rafts?"

Aella thought for a moment. "That's not a bad idea," she said. "Where could we find some?"

"There's a place east of town," Morgan said. "It's a big shed not too far south of the highway, next to the river."

"Fen," Aella said, "see if you can find this shed."

"Mistress commands us," Fen said, bowing and then disappearing with a pop.

"Good, now in the meantime, let's try a little practical application, shall we? Everyone, hold your disk flat in the palm of both of your hands like this." She laid a disk in one hand and covered it with the other hand.

Imogene assumed the position, feeling self-conscious.

"Close your eyes," Aella said.

Imogene closed one eye, scanning the faces of the other teens with the open one.

"You too, Imogene," Aella said.

Imogene sighed and did as instructed.

"Now, take deep, slow breaths," Aella said, her voice taking on a flat, calming tone.

Imogene breathed in slow, even breaths. The exercise reminded her of the way her father would have her breathe while performing a kata when she was little. How long ago had that been? She pushed away the thought and tried to listen.

"Now, open your senses, reach out, feel the surrounding power. Don't attempt to draw it in, just be aware of it, experience it, open yourself to it."

Imogene tried to do as Aella described, trying to feel something, anything, outside of herself. She waited for what felt like a long time, extending herself as best she could.

"Do you feel it?" Aella said.

"No," a chorus of voices said simultaneously.

"Yes."

Imogene's eyes opened, and she stared at Morgan. He had said yes.

"Good," Aella said. "Now let's try again, this time—. "

There was a loud popping sound, and Fen reappeared on the table, standing on a plate full of hash browns. "Mistress!"

the tiny man shouted. "Fen is finding it!" he said excitedly. "Tis urgent, we's cannots be waiting."

Aella nodded. "Very well, will you all excuse me?" She stood and walked toward the door, the tiny man following her.

The teens sat in silence for a few moments, looking around and shrugging at each other.

"Hand me the eggs, would you, babe?" Zach said, indicating the plate in front of Imogene.

"I'm not your babe," Imogene snapped, her temper flaring. Zach leaned back and sucked his teeth. He grinned, looking her up and down. Imogene felt her face go hot as his gaze lingered on her body.

"Huh, looks like you got all the right parts to be." He winked suggestively at her, his grin turning to a leer.

"Leave her alone, asshole," Morgan said from across the room.

Hugo spun to look at him. "What are you going to do about it, sticks?" Hugo said, staring daggers back at him.

Morgan stood abruptly, his fists clenched in rage. "Teach you some manners," he shouted. "That's what I'm going to do."

"Bring it on, ribs," Hugo said, rising from his chair and puffing out his chest. Morgan started around the table.

"Leave it alone, Morgan. It's none of your business," Imogene spat.

"It's my business," Morgan retorted. "You're my sister!"

"Yeah, well, I'm not your daughter." She stood and strode away toward the hall. Morgan grabbed her by the arm.

"What's wrong with you?" he said.

"You're what's wrong with me," she spat, jerking her arm free. "You're always telling me what to do, treating me like a baby. That's why I left. I couldn't stand you telling me what to do. Not for another second!"

"Imogene—" he began.

"The worst thing is knowing that you're probably happy about all of this!" she screamed. "Admit it, you're glad my stepparents are dead!" He recoiled, eyes wide.

"I'm not glad they're dead, Imogene. What kind of monster do you think I am?" he whispered.

"But you're not sorry they're gone! You *wanted* them gone, wanted them out of the way!"

He furrowed his brow, his face tightening, but he didn't respond.

"I knew it," she said. Rage seethed within her. "You have to control everything!"

"I didn't want them gone, and I didn't want them hurt. I didn't even know them," he shouted. "I just wanted for us to be together. I've always just wanted us to be together."

"Yeah, well, I don't!" she shouted, her body shaking with rage. "I've never wanted it!"

The color drained from his face, and the room fell silent, so silent Imogene could hear her heart beating. She turned and ran down the hall toward the girls' dorm room.

CHAPTER 8
THE PATH

Imogene tramped southeast, leaving the outpost in the distance, her feet thudding loudly on the packed earth in a rhythmic pattern that reverberated all the way to her skull. The heavy pink backpack she carried weighed down her normally light footsteps. She adjusted the straps and quick-stepped to keep up with the teens in front of her.

She glanced back in the outpost's direction, feeling suddenly afraid. It had been her haven in a world gone mad, and now they were leaving it, heading south into the unknown. She shivered.

Focus, she told herself. *One step at a time, don't worry about what will happen, just keep going and the future will take of itself.* Easier said than done.

Imogene looked up at the others padding steadily ahead of her. How did they walk so quickly while carrying so much? Were their packs as heavy as hers?

Aella had made each of the teens add a significant amount of dried food and supplies to their individual packs before they'd left the outpost, despite Fen's assurances that there was food prepackaged in dry bags at the rafting shed. The owners must have been planning on a long trip themselves, Imogene reflected.

Morgan strode near the front of the group, a few feet behind Aella. He didn't appear to be having any trouble carrying his pack or keeping up the pace. She glared daggers at him; it was just like him to be unbothered. Imogene adjusted her pack and strode on.

The afternoon was lengthening, and the sun beat down on her from a clear blue sky. Imogene glanced toward Vernal. A plume of smoke rose in the distance where the town lay.

Strange how if you ignore the smoke, it looks like any other day, she thought.

"This way," Aella called and pointed to the southeast over a series of sandstone hills. "We aren't far now."

"Can't wait," Hugo said and winked at Imogene. She rolled her eyes and plodded on. They continued, weaving around the shifting, rocky hills, staying in ravines as much as possible to avoid being spotted from a distance. Finally, late in the afternoon, they rounded a bend, and Imogene spotted a large shed near the bank of a wide green river.

"There!" she blurted. The other turned to look at her. She flushed and pointed.

"We've made it," Aella said, pleased.

"We's mus' be's hurryin' ta go!" Fen said.

They double-timed to the shed door, and Aella opened the lock using tendrils of power.

They began pulling rafts from the shed and loading them with supplies. In short order, they had rafts, life preservers, and paddles positioned near the edge of the river.

When they had gathered, Aella took Fen aside, and they spoke briefly in hushed tones. Fen nodded abruptly, and then there was a popping sound, and the little gnome was gone.

"Alright," Aella began. "Let's get on the river as quickly as we can." She glanced back toward Vernal, where a new column of smoke rose from the town. "We'll be much better off not sticking around here. Fen will be in charge of that boat." She pointed toward the raft furthest upriver. "I'll take charge in this one." She indicated the raft furthest downstream. "Do any of you have rafting experience?"

Zach raised a hand. "I do," he said. "A bit."

"What kind of experience?"

"I spent a week rafting on the Salmon River a few years ago," he said.

Aella nodded thoughtfully. "Well, some experience is better than none. You'll be in charge of one of the middle rafts, so your job will be to keep this boat between Fen's and mine. Do you think you can do that?"

Zach nodded.

"Alright then, Zach. Take your place." Aella gestured toward a raft.

He walked to the raft and picked up a paddle. He was the most muscular boy in the group, with wide shoulders and strong cheekbones, and he stood with a competent air, hefting the paddle with one hand and grinning. He seemed confident enough.

Imogene didn't buy it. She would be terrified to be in his place and couldn't help but believe that he was too. She stared at him, searching for a crack in his armor. He looked up at her and winked. She felt her face flush.

Damn it, she thought. *Now he's going to think I like him.* She sighed and picked up a paddle. When she looked up another raft leader had been chosen, Oscar, a lean boy with a Hispanic accent that Imogene thought came from the Caribbean.

"The rest of you divide yourselves into the boats, no more than six in any raft. Make sure you get a paddle and a life jacket. You're going to need them," Aella finished. She followed her own advice, grabbing a paddle and buckling on a life preserver.

Imogene felt her stomach drop at the thought of the long journey. She'd always been afraid of the river; she hated not being able to see the bottom. She took a deep breath, swallowed down her fear, put on a life jacket, and turned toward the raft where Zach stood. She frowned and glanced at Morgan, who looked uncertain. She waited for him to make the first move.

He blinked at her for a moment before grabbing a paddle and a life jacket from two piles nearby. He moved toward the raft at the back of the group where Fen had reappeared, the little figure was picking something invisible from the billowing sleeve of his shirt.

Imogene started toward the first boat, but several of the other teens got there first, filling the spots that Aella had limited each boat to. Oscar's raft filled up quickly as well. She paused and looked at Morgan, then at Zach's raft. Steeling herself, she walked to the middle raft and stood near Zach and Hugo, carefully avoiding looking at either of them.

Several of the other teens gathered near Imogene. She caught movement from the back boat and saw that Morgan had started toward her.

"Hey!" she said to Alexa, who was staring uncertainly at the remaining life jackets. "Why don't you ride with us?"

Alexa nodded gratefully, grabbed a life jacket, and joined Imogene.

Morgan hesitated as Alexa took her place beside Imogene. He gritted his teeth, glaring at his sister, and she held back a grin. Her boat now had six. She knew Morgan would never try to push the limit to seven.

"Immy!" Morgan said, motioning for her to join him. "We

only have four." She stared back at him with eyes like ice picks. There was a tense silent moment, each of the siblings staring at the other, then Morgan finally blinked and returned to his original place.

"Take hold of the ropes, and let's get the boats into the water," Aella said.

Imogene took hold of the thick rope that lined the outer edge of the raft and began pulling it forward. The other teens did likewise, and the boat slid to the water's edge.

"Alright, lighter passengers first. The rest of you will help push the raft into the water," Aella said. The teens at the front began piling in as those in the back continued pushing the raft into the brown water.

The raft slid into the current, and Imogene jumped on. It bobbed momentarily from the weight of their bodies, which made Imogene feel shaky and unsettled. She'd never ridden in a boat, and she wasn't sure she liked the sensation. It felt unsteady, too precarious for her liking.

"Remember to follow directions!" Aella called over the gentle sounds of the river and the squeaking of the rafts. "Do what you're told, when you're told—that's how we'll all get safely to our destination. Am I clear?" Her voice was stern, commanding.

There was a murmur of assent from the teens.

* * *

Morgan watched as Imogene joined the others in her raft and they slid the craft into the cold water. He cursed inwardly at her stubbornness. Why did she have to be so damn difficult? He sighed as Kenichi tapped his arm and motioned towards the remaining raft. Aurelian and Nayme pushed from the front as they slid the boat into the river. Morgan and Kenichi pushed the boat from behind as the others crawled in. They slid from the bank and Morgan wobbled as he jumped onto the thwart, awkwardly pulling himself onboard.

* * *

Imogene glanced toward the back of the raft where Hugo and Zach sat, plunging their paddles into the river and driving forward, their shoulder muscles bulging. Hugo said something that Imogene couldn't make out, and the two hesitated. He nodded back toward the trailing raft.

Morgan sat at the back of his boat, driving his paddle into the water in rhythm with Kenichi, who sat beside him. Kenichi was a tall, thin boy with narrow eyes and long black hair. In front of them sat Nayme and Kira. Aurelian sat unstably on the thwart and was trying, unsuccessfully, to help with the rowing.

The freckled boy was making a mess of things. In his attempts to paddle, he kept sliding off the thwart and nearly falling into the center of the raft. Morgan was saying something to him that Imogene couldn't hear, and the boy gripped the raft more tightly with his legs. He steadied himself and knocked his paddle into Kira's, throwing off her timing.

"I'm sorry!" he called loud enough for Imogene to hear, despite his near proximity to Kira.

"Try not to drown on the first day!" Zach called and bellowed a laugh.

Morgan glared back at him, and Aurelian's face turned a bright shade of pink.

"Probably better if he does," Hugo said. "He's just going to make things harder for the rest of us. Better if he's left behind."

"That's a horrible thing to say!" Imogene said.

Hugo shrugged. "It's true though. We have a long way to go, and he will slow us down. This may seem like fun at first, but it's going to be dangerous."

"Dangerous how? The river isn't even running high, and people raft it all the time," Imogene said, her face hot.

"It's not the river I'm worried about," Hugo said, staring coldly back at her.

"Oh really? Then what does worry you?"

He paused, meeting Imogene's eyes cooly, then nodded thoughtfully and turned. "Look at her." He indicated where Aella sat in the lead east. "Watch her."

Imogene sat observing the woman for several minutes as the group progressed slowly southward.

"Do you see it?" Hugo continued.

"See what?"

"She keeps fidgeting, looking over her shoulder at us, scanning the area. If I'm any judge of character, she's afraid."

"So what?" Imogene said.

"Have you seen what she can do?" Hugo's blue eyes stared intensely back at her, and Imogene felt herself falling into them. "Superhuman speed and strength, and she makes a sword out of thin air."

"I'm aware," Imogene said. She had heard the other teens talking about Aella and her abilities, but Imogene had witnessed nothing extraordinary for herself, outside of the sword and felt that there was likely some exaggeration in the stories. Still, the sword was real enough and tracked with what the other teens had said. Just that was impressive, and she remembered how Fen had killed the skin-walker that had come for Imogene.

Hugo looked at her. "She's afraid. With all her skills, her speed, her strength, the powers she can use—she's *still* afraid."

Imogene looked back at the woman, watching more closely than she had before. Could Hugo be right? Then she saw it. The nervous expression, the darting looks.

"You see it, don't you?" Hugo said.

"Your point?" Imogene sighed, trying to play off the sickly feeling lodging in her chest.

"What could be so bad out there that someone like *her* would be afraid?" he half-whispered. "If I could do what she can, I wouldn't be afraid of anything. She's as nervous as a three-legged zebra staring down a pride of lions.

"If she's that afraid, this trip is going to be more dangerous than it seems. Some of us may not make it. For all we know, *none* of us may make it to this city of hers."

"So what? You just want to leave anyone behind that isn't as fast or as strong as you are?" Imogene probed.

The boy shrugged. "It's better if those who are unlikely to make it don't prevent the rest of us. It's the law of the jungle out here: who falls behind is left behind."

Imogene stared back at him, unable to frame a response. She looked away. His logic made a sick form of sense, but she couldn't bring herself to think about who else he might think was unlikely to make it.

She drove her paddle into the water and forced away the thought, losing herself in the slow rhythm, the soft sounds of the water, and the gentle curve of the river as it wound southward in sweeping undulations.

It was getting dark when Aella called out to the others and pointed to a small island in the middle of the current. The teens steered their rafts toward the island and pulled the boats ashore.

Imogene got out, stumbled on a rock, and nearly fell, her arms flailing wildly as she sought to reclaim her balance. A strong hand caught her arm, preventing her from falling.

She looked up into Kenichi's dark eyes.

"Thanks," she said, silently berating herself. She had to be more careful. She didn't want to get added to whatever list of *people unlikely to make it* that Hugo and his friends might be forming.

"No problem," the boy said, beaming. "I'm Kenichi." He held out a hand.

"Imogene," she said.

He nodded. "I know," he whispered, staring back into her eyes in a way that seemed to see into her soul. "You're Morgan's sister."

She fidgeted uncomfortably, unsure what to say next. She'd already made herself look like a klutz and she couldn't help but resent the tie to Morgan.

"We'll stay here tonight," Aella said, interrupting her thoughts.

"I guess I better help out," Kenichi said, nodding at the island. He gave Imogene a winning grin and turned from her.

Imogene looked around at the island, a large sand bar with some rocks and river plants at the center and lining the southern edge. It didn't look like a comfortable place to camp to Imogene. She longed for the plush queen-sized bed her stepparents had given her. She'd barely gotten used to sleeping in it, and she never would again. She might not sleep in any bed again.

A memory flashed before her eyes, a scream that hadn't sounded like her own, a trail of blood across the floor, a body so mangled it could hardly be recognized as human, a beast hunkering over it, its wet muzzle lapping at the red liquid.

She shook herself, forcing the intrusive thoughts away and stepped from the raft as it slid onto the beach. She couldn't think of that night; she *wouldn't*.

Focus on what's next, she told herself. *Finding somewhere to sleep*. She strode toward a spot near the center of the island where the ground looked flat and dry with a few tufty weeds sticking out in odd directions.

Good enough, she decided, beginning to kick rocks and branches aside, trying to make the spot as comfortable as possible. After a few minutes of work, she'd created a spot mostly free of the kind of rocks and sticks that would make sleeping on the ground impossible. It would have to do. She strode back to the raft. In its center was a large rectangular area where gear and dry bags were stowed. Imogene began opening bags until she found one with several tents inside of it. Imogene pulled one out and returned to her spot.

"Mind if I sleep in your tent?"

Imogene looked up to see Alexa smiling shyly back at her and holding out her hand. "I'm Alexa," she said. She was blonde and thin with the kind of naturally pretty face that women always envied: blue eyes, a doll face, and red, pouty lips.

Imogene took it. "I'm Imogene. We're all going to need to share these, anyway." She smiled again and began dragging the tent out. The two girls spread out the tent and readied the support poles.

"Do you think he's right?" Alexa asked suddenly.

Imogene looked back at her, confused.

"What do you mean?"

Alexa's face was drawn with fear and worry.

"What Hugo said, about leaving people behind, about some of us not making it."

Imogene took a deep breath and nodded. "He's right about the danger and about Aella. I think she's hiding something, I won't accept what he said about leaving people behind. But I don't know what Aella is afraid of out here." She paused in thought for a moment before continuing. "Maybe it's just the river. A lot of people are afraid of drowning, even strong, confident people are sometimes afraid of things like that."

Imogene tried to look confident so Alexa would think she

was talking about someone other than herself. "I doubt Aella has rafted all the way down the Green," she continued. "Maybe she's just nervous about that."

Alexa frowned and nodded; she looked slightly less afraid. Imogene glanced toward the north side of the island, where Morgan and the others who had ridden in his boat were setting up another tent. She opened her mouth and then hesitated. Whatever she had been about to say was interrupted by Aella calling to the group.

"Boys and girls in separate tents please," she said. "We don't need any additional passengers for our trip."

Some of the boys guffawed, and Zach made a rude gesture.

Imogene shook her head, and the girls finished setting up the tent.

CHAPTER 9
ON THE BANK

Morgan sat with his arms crossed, staring at the murky water as it flowed past in its unending bobbing course. Strange, he reflected, how the sound was becoming different over time. He'd been hearing it for so long that he no longer noticed. Days on the water were already starting to blend.

The sounds of footsteps in the sand brought his head up. Kenichi stood above him, holding out a steaming camp mug. Morgan took it and peered inside at the oatmeal. After a thorough inventory of the food they had, they'd been forced to reduce rations, eating only a small breakfast in the late morning and one larger meal in the early evening.

"Thanks," he said and took a sip. It needed brown sugar, but he didn't complain. He thought about the food and wondered how long they had before they'd run out. Not long enough, he was sure.

"You OK?" Kenichi asked, sitting next to him and taking a sip of his own stew. Morgan nodded. He could feel Kenichi's eyes boring into him.

"Are you sure about that?"

Morgan shrugged. Even if he wasn't, what could Kenichi do? Or Morgan for that matter? He'd tried on multiple occasions to talk to Imogene, and she'd ignored him each time, simply turning her back and walking away. He'd thought she'd soften over time, get over whatever it was that had made her so angry, but now he was beginning to wonder. What could he have possibly done?

"Why does she treat you the way she does?" Kenichi asked, suddenly seeming to decipher Morgan's thoughts.

"What do you mean?"

"She acts like she hates you."

Morgan shrugged again and took a mouthful of stew then glanced over to Kenichi. The boy shrugged his shoulders, making a sad face, bottom lip extended theatrically.

Morgan snorted. "I'm not really sure. I think," he began, uncertain of what he wanted to say, "I think it may have to do with our mom." He stared down at the darkening sand on the shoreline.

Kenichi nodded, encouraging him to go on.

Morgan took a deep breath. "The day she died I wouldn't let Imogene come into her hospital room. I just wanted to make sure everything was OK before she came in to say hi. But things didn't go how I thought they would. Our mom was very weak. I sat by her side, and she was—hallucinating, I think. She told me to take care of Immy and made me promise to not let anything happen to her. Made me swear to it."

Kenichi grunted. "Wow," he said and shook his head.

"They were her last—" Morgan struggled to complete the sentence as a lump welled up in his throat. "Those were her last words," he finished in a whisper.

"Dang," Kenichi said. "That's harsh. That's a hell of a thing to tell a kid." He leaned back, looking at the sky. "Hey, son, you just take care of this person who won't listen to you, will hate it when you tell her anything, and oh by the way, you have no actual authority over as far as the law is concerned. Make sure she's safe, happy, and well-adjusted."

Morgan chuffed. "Yeah, that's about the size of it."

"How long ago did she pass?" Kenichi probed.

Morgan blew out a long breath. "About two years ago, I guess," he said.

"Dang." Kenichi took a mouthful of stew and chewed contemplatively. "I hope you don't mind me asking this, but you two didn't live together, did you? Before all this I mean." He gestured to the canyon.

"No," Morgan said. "She was adopted by a family in Park City.

"How long ago did Imogene leave, to the other family I mean?"

"In September, so"—he did the math in his head— "about ten months ago." He paused, "Well, ten months before—" He pointed into the sky, where the moon was slowly making its way across the sky. It was clearly visible in the daylight and changed the color of the landscape subtly.

Kenichi nodded and took another bite of stew. He didn't seem to know what else to say about the situation. Morgan was glad that Kenichi was in the group. He was kind and the two of them got along. They were quickly becoming friends.

Morgan poured the last of his stew into his mouth and chewed. It felt good to talk about it, he realized. He felt lighter, like a part of the world had been lifted off of his shoulders. He took a deep breath, enjoying the smell of fresh air and sagebrush.

"What styles do you know?" he said suddenly.

Kenichi chewed slowly and raised a questioning eyebrow.

"Martial arts," Morgan said, grinning sheepishly. "I see the way that you move. You know what you're doing." He'd noticed Kenichi doing a stretch routine in the mornings as well as a kata in the evenings when there was enough room for it where they were camping.

"The kata's you do, seem strange to me. Almost like you're mixing more than one style. What did you study?"

Kenichi looked back at him for a long moment, considering.

"I study several," Kenichi said. "Studied," he amended with a wry grin. "At least I have over the years. Kung Fu, Shotokan, Aikido, Capoeira." He met Morgan's eyes. "But Capoeira didn't really suit me. Too much dancing about and not enough striking."

Morgan nodded. He could respect that. Capoeira was beautiful to watch, but he shared Kenichi's opinion. "Too much flash, and not enough substance," he said.

Kenichi nodded. "What about you? I've watched you too. I don't recognize the style." Morgan had done stretches and some forms when he thought no one was looking.

"I wish I could tell you, but I don't know what it's called," Morgan said sheepishly.

Kenichi smirked. "What do you mean?"

Morgan shrugged. "I just do the stuff my dad taught me when I was a kid. To tell you the truth, I'm not even sure I'm doing it completely right anymore. I've probably forgotten a good bit of it over time. He started teaching me when I was three. Before he—" Morgan paused, trying to decide how to phrase it. "He left the picture when I was ten, now I just do what I can remember."

Kenichi nodded thoughtfully.

"What do you mean left the picture? Did your parents get divorced?"

Morgan shrugged. "He's gone." he said and stared into the

distance for a few moments. "I like practicing, it makes me feel like he's with me. Like he's still part of my life."

Kenichi nodded. "Makes sense," he said. "Is he alive?" he asked.

Morgan winced internally. He sat for a long time looking out over the water. "I don't know," he said truthfully. "My mom picked me up from school one day. She had the van packed full of stuff. She told me we were going on a trip but wouldn't say where. We never went home, and I haven't seen him since."

"Dang," Kenichi said. "And I thought my home life was messed up."

Morgan grinned. "Yeah, it's not the best."

"Not the best? Boy, you need an award or something."

Morgan pretended to bow, as though accepting the praises of an imaginary crowd.

"Well, let's see what you've got," Kenichi said, standing and wiping the sand from his shorts.

"What I've got?" Morgan stared at him, dumbfounded.

Kenichi nodded, a toothy grin forming on his face. He raised his hands, making a fist in one hand, and covering it with the other. Then he bowed and took a fighting stance. He extended his hand and motioned Morgan toward him.

"Oh no," Morgan began, shaking his head vigorously. "I'm not fighting you, master of nine styles."

"Oh, come on," Kenichi said. "Just some light sparring. It will be fun. We've only done forms so far, and that's barely martial arts. Besides, I've just *studied* five styles, I'm not a master of them all. I'm only a master of three." He grinned widely and stepped closer, extending a hand to help Morgan up.

Morgan took a deep breath and took the proffered hand. Kenichi pulled him up, and Morgan looked around self-consciously. The other teens were sitting by the shore, eating their stew or milling about getting camp ready.

He turned and looked at Kenichi. "Ground rules?"

"Pull your punches and kicks, no full-out strikes."

"Alright," Morgan said hesitantly and started rolling his shoulders, trying to loosen them. Kenichi moved in, his fist jabbing out quick as a snake, and caught Morgan in the jaw. Morgan's head snapped back, and he stumbled into the dirt.

"You don't get to warm up for real fights," Kenichi said, his face a mask.

Morgan frowned, rubbing his jaw, and started to sit up. Kenichi moved to aim a kick at Morgan's face. Morgan dropped to the sand and rolled, finally staggering to his feet a few feet away.

Kenichi's next kick caught him in the side and knocked him sideways. He stumbled and pitched to the sand again, this time popping up quickly and spinning in time to block the next strike.

Kenichi poured the attack on, aiming strike after strike at Morgan, who backtracked and parried blows as best he could. He absorbed three more strikes in quick succession. Kenichi punched him in the ribs, kicked him in the thigh, and finished with an open-handed strike to the face that left Morgan's cheekbone burning.

Morgan felt his anger rising. This was supposed to be a sparring match. He blocked a strike and counter punched, aiming for Kenichi's face. He hit only air as Kenichi's head dipped sideways effortlessly as the boy stepped in, punching Morgan hard in the gut.

Morgan went down, coughing and clutching his side.

Kenichi stood and nodded to Morgan.

"Good," he said, smiling. "I can see the technique there below the surface. You know what you're doing, and your blocking is pretty good, but I'm guessing you haven't sparred in a while. You'll have to be faster, think faster, take advantage of your opponent's weaknesses, any moment of imbalance or hesitation."

Morgan nodded. Kenichi put out a hand and pulled him to his feet.

"Again," Kenichi said and raised his fists.

"I thought we were pulling our punches."

"I have been."

Morgan snorted. "Well, then I never want you to punch me full force."

Kenichi chuckled. "Ahh," he said mockingly, "is the little twig boy hurting you, big fella?"

Morgan shifted forward, trying to catch Kenichi distracted, and fired off a flurry of straight punches that the boy blocked. Kenichi spun, his back foot coming around in an arc and taking Morgan's feet out from under him. He hit with a hard thud and only had time to look up as a heel dropped toward his face. The heel stopped just above his nose.

Morgan sighed. "Got me again," he said.

Kenichi helped Morgan to his feet and patted him on the back.

Morgan looked to the side where the majority of the other teens were now watching him.

"Well, that was embarrassing," he said, feeling the color heating his cheeks.

"You fought well," Kenichi said.

Morgan gaped at him. "You annihilated me," he said, rubbing his jaw where Kenichi had punched him.

"Master of three, remember?" Kenichi said, grinning. "Compared to most, you did well."

"Hey, sticks," a voice called from near the campsite. "When you're done playing with the loser there, you should have a go against a real fighter." Hugo gesticulated toward Zach, who grinned broadly and cracked his knuckles.

"Yeah, try me on, sticks," Zach said, standing and stomping toward them.

Kenichi frowned. "No, thank you," he said and turned to walk away.

"Only fight amateurs?" Zach hissed. "I'm a cage fighter, a real pro."

"Fighting people twice your size is typically unwise if you can avoid it," Kenichi answered calmly.

Zach flexed his thick arms and nodded. "Fighting me is a bad idea no matter who you are. I don't blame you for being scared." Hugo and Zach snickered behind him.

"Ladies, come watch the contest," Hugo said, waving toward Sarah and Elina.

"Let's go, Morgan," Kenichi said and grasped his arm, pulling him away from the group that was beginning to gather nearby.

"You ain't going nowhere, boy," Zach said and moved past them, blocking Kenichi's path. Hugo moved to the other side, penning them in. "You're going to fight my man over here," he said, grinning wickedly. "It'll be fun."

Morgan looked around, wondering where Aella was. He was certain that she would not want the boys fighting each other. There was enough danger on the river without needless squabbles.

"I do not wish to fight him or anyone else," Kenichi said. "Morgan and I were simply sparring, getting in some practice."

"Well, he wants to fight you," Hugo said menacingly. "He thinks he can beat you."

Kenichi nodded. "I agree, you can beat me. Now, please let us pass."

"You hear that, Zach? He's given you permission to beat him."

"That's enough for me," Zach said, striding toward Kenichi with his fists clenched. He pulled back his arm and swung, leveling an arching punch.

Kenichi pushed hard on Morgan's arm. Caught off guard, Morgan stumbled to the ground. Kenichi dropped in a low crouch, his arm driving forward.

Zach crashed to the ground grabbing his genitals and crying out in pain.

"You cheated!" Hugo shrieked. "You punched him in the balls! You didn't fight fair!"

Kenichi looked down at Morgan, nodded, then turned and strode away into the darkening evening.

Morgan studied him for a moment as Hugo and Sarah tended to their friend. He looked up. Aella had arrived and was looking at him, her face an unreadable mask. He swallowed, stood, and followed Kenichi.

They walked along the shore for several minutes before Kenichi stopped and put his hands on his hips. He stood looking at the river, taking deep breaths for a long moment before looking at Morgan.

"You OK?' Morgan asked, seeing Kenichi's troubled face. The boy nodded and took another deep breath.

"You punched him in the balls," Morgan observed, chuckling. "I'd never have had the guts to do that."

Kenichi looked at him seriously for a long moment. "Morgan, if you ever find yourself in the position of having to defend yourself," he began, his voice steely. "Disable or kill your opponent without hesitation."

Morgan was taken aback. Kenichi had always seemed so calm, so kind. His words clashed with everything that Morgan had believed about the boy.

"But—" Morgan began hesitantly.

Kenichi cut him off. "Do not hesitate," he insisted. "When it comes to a fight, a real fight, when it's deadly serious and you're not sparring, hesitation will get you killed as surely as the sun rises in the east."

Morgan searched his face for a long time. "Do you think he would have hurt you?"

Kenichi nodded firmly. "If he could have, he would have without question. Those two have no good in them. They are not simple bullies, Morgan. They are killers."

Morgan frowned. "I seriously doubt that either of them has killed anyone."

Kenichi shrugged. "Perhaps not yet. But I have no doubt that they will eventually. One day—and I'd wager that the day will be sooner rather than later—they will do it. Let's just make sure it's not one of us."

Morgan thought about Imogene, Aurelian, and Nayme. They'd all been kind to him and somehow Morgan had gotten on Zach and Hugo's bad side. Would they be punished for being kind to Morgan? All the teens suddenly seemed vulnerable. He knew they faced dangers as they traveled toward Encartha, but what he hadn't considered was that danger could come from within their own party.

"Hey." Morgan turned to see Aurelian and Nayme standing on the beach nearby. He nodded. The two stood fidgeting and nudging each other for a few moments. Finally, Aurelian stepped forward.

"Could you guys teach us that? The way you were fighting?"

Morgan looked at Kenichi, who nodded back at him.

"Ok," he agreed. "We'll teach you what we can."

CHAPTER 10
THE INCIDENT

Imogene's eyes creaked open, and she groaned.

"Sleep well?" Alexa asked as Imogene rolled over mumbling to herself about a pain in her hip.

"Terrible," Imogene replied, "like sleeping on a warped board with a well-placed rock under my back for a bonus. I would have never thought sand would be so uncomfortable."

Alexa laughed. "It's really awful to sleep on. I learned that camping on the beach in Virginia when I was ten," she said. "I've avoided it since then, but I guess it's better than sleeping in the river."

Imogene grinned. "Is that where you're from?" she asked. "Virginia?"

"Yep, Virginia Beach," Alexa said.

Alexa was short with a ready smile. She'd sat next to Imogene the previous day as they continued their trek down the river and had remained mostly silent. But they'd spent some time talking as they'd tried to get ready to sleep the previous night, and Imogene had found herself liking Alexa more and more. She was upbeat and kind, and those seemed like important qualities, especially now that there were so many fewer people in the world.

"What did you think about what Hugo said a few days ago?" Alexa said tentatively, seeming to read Imogene's thoughts. "About Aella, I mean?"

Imogene sighed. "I've been thinking about that." She hesitated. "I think he's right about Aella being afraid. It's hard to know why she would be, given what she can do. But on the other hand, we do know there's a pack of werewolves hunting us. It's probably just that. It's a pretty good reason if you think about it."

Alexa nodded seriously.

"I just wish we knew more. I keep thinking I see things on the bank at night. I'm paranoid that the wolves will find us."

"Me too." Imogene said. "I know they can't sense us directly while we wear these," she held up her medallion," but if they're anything like dogs, they might be able to smell us."

"Gross," Alexa said, smelling herself and grimacing. "Yeah, I stink."

Imogene smirked.

"I can't shake the worry that Aella is scared of something else. But I don't know what it could be."

Imogene shrugged, sat up, opened her bag, and pulled out a shirt intending to change into it. "Word to the wise, change quickly," Sarah said from the corner of the tent. She'd joined the others in the tent late in the evening as they'd been nearly asleep. She was pretty with long red hair and a shapely form.

"Fen doesn't understand the concept of privacy," she finished.

"What do you mean?" Alexa asked.

"Let's just say that I was in the shower when he came for me. He just popped into the shower, right there in the tub while I was washing my hair! It was quite a shock."

Alexa began to laugh, and Sarah giggled in return. Imogene smirked, imagining the red-haired girl encountering the gnome.

"That's amazing!" Alexa said with a chuckle.

"And then he had the gall to be mad at me for taking too long!"

The three girls burst into laughter.

"I was just trying to get some clothes on!" Sarah finished.

Alexa sat up in her sleeping bag. "Aella came for me. Just wandered into my house, up my stairs, and into my room. She didn't even knock."

"What about you, Imogene?" Sarah said thoughtfully. "What happened when they came for you?"

Grisly images flashed before Imogene's eyes. "I'll change quickly," she said, changing the subject and pulling her dirty shirt over her head. There was a popping sound, and Fen appeared less than a foot away. Imogene scrambled to pull the new shirt up to her chest.

"Told you!" Sarah said, giggling. "He has an incredible sense of timing. I swear he has a thing for human girls!"

"Humans girls is nasty, with all dat"—he gestured vaguely toward Imogene's chest— "nonsense, you're be having. Tis time for eats!" he finished.

"Fen, you have to knock!" Imogene scolded him, her face flushing.

"There be's no doors for knockin'," Fen said, a puzzled look on his small face. "There can be no knockin' on tents," he finished.

"She means, you need to tell us before you just come in," Sarah said. "Especially if one of us is changing. Remember what we talked about before?"

"Fen remembers all ta things we's be talkin' bout," he said, "Aella's be's telling Fen ta same many of times, only Fen is thinking ta wearing of clothes is silly." He picked at his odd clothes indifferently. "Fens is only wearings them cause Aella is saying we's have to."

"Thank goodness for that," Alexa said, grinning at Imogene. The little man made a face and disappeared.

Sarah shrugged and started wiggling her way out of her sleeping bag. Imogene finished dressing, smirking at the others, and unzipped the tent.

A few minutes later Imogene sat on the sand with a bowl of oatmeal and spooned it mechanically into her mouth. She hated oatmeal. It wasn't so much the flavor that got to her—it was the texture, like a vaguely sweet sludge.

The sun was peeking over a stony ridge, flooding golden light over the thin valley where the river ran. She glanced upriver to the edge of the sandbar and rolled her eyes. Morgan and Kenichi stood together, the pair of them demonstrating something for Aurelian and Nayme. It looked like a martial arts form, similar to the one she and Morgan had learned as kids.

How long had it been since she had practiced? It felt like forever. Idly she wondered how much of it she could still do. She doubted she would be able to remember very much. In retrospect, it was probably a mistake. With the world how it was now, having a minimal amount of fighting prowess seemed like a good idea.

For a moment she considered walking over to where the group stood, but she shook her head, her natural stubbornness finding purchase, and took another bite of the sludge. Maybe she would practice later, alone when no one was watching. That would allow her to see how much she remembered before embarrassing herself in front of the others. She watched them as she ate.

Aurelian and Nayme stood awkwardly, trying unsuccessfully to put themselves into the pose that the boys were showing them.

"It's all about the breath," Kenichi said. "If you don't breathe, you can't fight."

"That's right," Morgan said. "That's the number one reason that inexperienced fighters lose. In the moment of stress, they hold their breath, which obviously deprives their muscles of oxygen, and the next thing they know they are panting and can't continue. So, you have to practice breathing, focus on it, make it as natural in a stressful situation as it is when you're at rest."

The movements were familiar to Imogene; Morgan was clearly using the same moves their father had taught them. But there was something unique and different in the way Kenichi moved. He was using a style unlike the one she had been taught. She bit her lip, watching Kenichi's lithe movements as he slipped through a few graceful poses.

"What are they doing?" Alexa asked, moving to sit next to her.

"Martial arts forms," Imogene said. "When we were little, my dad taught us."

"That's right," Alexa said, "I had forgotten about—" She paused, searching for the right words. "You two," she finished awkwardly.

Immy grimaced. "I guess we're not that similar when it comes to it. I took after my mom, and he's more like my dad."

She looked at Nayme. The girl was beaming at Morgan as he helped her adjust her stance.

I knew it. Imogene thought to herself, remembering the way she had looked at Morgan in the outpost.

"She's not being very subtle, is she?" Immy said.

Alexa giggled. "She's definitely into him. Are you looking for a sister-in-law?"

Imogene grinned. "There's no such thing anymore." Her words came out more melancholic than she'd intended.

She went back to her oatmeal, intent on ignoring the training session. When she finished, she sat her bowl down, feeling the hard outline of the disk in her pocket. The thing barely fit in the front pocket of her jeans. She pulled it out.

"Women's pockets are just too small," she mused. "So impractical. Looking hot is all well and good, but did we have to sacrifice practicality in search of beauty?"

Alexa agreed. "I hate them."

Sarah walked by wearing a red sports bra and a pair of tight leggings.

"Impracticality looks good on her though," Alexa said.

Imogene sighed. She glanced to the side where Zach stood, bare-chested and staring appreciatively at Sarah as she went by. There were certainly some benefits to looking good, practical or not.

She held up the disk. Her fingers traced over the strange symbols.

She thought about what Aella had said. "You have to reach out, feel the energy around you." She closed her eyes, trying to imagine the substance that Aella had talked about, the ether. She felt foolish sitting there with her eyes closed while the other teens were eating and talking. She opened her eyes, glancing again at where Zach stood grinning at Sarah. She was smiling back at him.

Imogene rolled her eyes. *This is stupid. I shouldn't care what they think.* She closed her eyes again, trying to block out everything but the disk. She took a deep breath, tuning out the sounds of Morgan's instruction, of the river running in the distance, of Hugo talking to Sarah.

Focus! she chided herself, trying to feel around her, expanding her senses in an attempt to locate something, anything out of the normal. Her fingers started to tingle. The sensation was slight at first, but it grew gradually stronger.

"Oh my gosh!" Kenichi's voice broke through Imogene's concentration, making her jump. The disk slipped from her hand and landed softly in the sand below her, her eyes snapped open.

"You were doing it!" he said excitedly. "Your disk, you were making it blur! I was watching you, and the disk, it—fuzzed. Like it was fading, becoming almost translucent! It was like looking at an out-of-focus piece of glass."

Imogene's heart raced, and she realized she was grinning. She looked up to where Morgan and his group stood staring back at her, then back up to Kenichi who was smiling broadly. She lifted the disk, inspecting it, turning it over. She stopped staring in surprise at the backside. Part of the disk was missing, leaving a slightly bumpy crater. It was like a drawing that someone had taken an eraser to.

"Amazing!" Kenichi exulted. "Come look at this, Morg," he said, waving his hand for Morgan to join them. Imogene locked eyes with Morgan, and he hesitated.

"In a minute," he said, turning his back to Imogene and starting to demonstrate another move to Nayme.

Imogene couldn't blame him for being hesitant, not after her previous outbursts. She felt a bit guilty about how she'd treated him. He was her brother after all. She frowned at his back. Along with the guilt, she couldn't help but feel somewhat betrayed by his unwillingness to see what she'd accomplished. It would have been nice for him to be proud of her achievement. So far as she knew, she was the first to make any progress with the disk at all, and he didn't even care.

Zach walked over and, looking down at the dissolved portion of the disk, congratulated her warmly. Imogene looked up at him, and he met her smile with a dazzling one of his own.

Imogene blushed as his gaze lingered on her, a broad grin on his face, for several moments. She bit her lip at a feeling that she couldn't quite identify. There was something wrong, but she wasn't sure what it was. She stood looking at him for several long moments before it occurred to her, "Where is your medallion?" she asked, their interlude forgotten. She has just noticed that he wasn't wearing a medallion around his neck. "You don't have it on. We're supposed to wear them at all times!" Imogene's voice was rising, and she could hear the near panic coloring her tone. "The wolves can sense you when you're not wearing it!"

"It's not a big deal," he said defensively.

"It is a big deal," Imogene insisted. "It's a huge deal; you're putting everyone here in jeopardy!"

"Mind your own business," Hugo said from a few feet away. "He's just taking a little break."

"You can't take breaks from something like this," Imogene said, exasperated. "Taking a break could be the difference between making it safely to Encartha and being killed by a pack of werewolves!"

"Listen, you little bitch, I'm not doing jack just because you say so," Zach said.

Kenichi stood quickly, interposing himself between Imogene and the two boys.

"Get out of my way, you little—" Zach began, cutting off to look up to where Aella had just turned in their direction.

He glared at Imogene and then at Kenichi. "This isn't over," he whispered. Turning his back to Aella, he pulled the medallion out of his pocket and slid the cord over his head as he walked toward Hugo, muttering and shaking his head, his fists flexing in anger.

Imogene felt sure that he had been on the cusp of hitting Kenichi.

"That one has a temper," Kenichi observed.

"That one is an asshole," Alexa said.

"Six one way, half a dozen the other," Kenichi said, grinning back at her.

Imogene snorted despite herself. She patted Kenichi's arm and whispered a soft thank you before pushing past as Aella called out to the group.

"Load up!" she said. "We've got a long way to go." The teens began loading supplies back into the raft, and Imogene joined in, placing cargo into the storage area of the nearest raft. The pile was growing. It seemed like more than they loaded on the raft for the previous leg of the journey. She looked up. The only person nearby was Aurelian.

"Hey," she said. "Is this too much stuff in one raft?"

He shrugged. "Theoretically it's a question of how much weight-bearing capacity the raft has and how many people are on board to row it. We just have to balance the amount of equipment with the number of rafters, making sure not to overload the boat."

Imogene stared at him. "So should we move some of this to another raft or—?"

Aurelian rubbed his chin with dirty fingers. "I don't know how much the rafts can carry or how many people are needed for the weight that it has. I could do the math if I knew how much each—" He glanced up at her, taking in her expression. "Maybe you should ask Aella," he said, his face reddening. He stood and quickly shuffled away.

Imogene sighed and began carrying items to the other rafts.

A few minutes later, the teens were gathered on the beach. Aella stood by impatiently. "Let's go," she said. "We're wasting daylight."

My bag! Imogene thought, just now realizing that she

hadn't seen it recently. She scanned the boats and couldn't find it with the other equipment. She glanced back toward the beach and noticed her pink backpack laying partially concealed in the scrubby brush. She hurried over and slung the bag over her shoulder before turning to hustle back to the boats.

By the time she made it back to the rafts, most of the group had taken their places. Only two spots remained, both of them on the boat where Hugo and Zach sat talking and giggling with Sarah and Elina.

Aurelian stood on the shore, looking hopelessly at the empty spots remaining. He glanced at Imogene. He shrugged and took his place near the back of the raft.

Imogene hesitated, not wanting to spend another day with Zach and Hugo. But the other boats were smaller and full of teens.

I'll move to a better spot next time we stop, she told herself and made her way to the raft, deposited her backpack, and climbed onto the thwart, paddle in hand.

The rafts launched, and the teens began paddling.

After an hour of intermittent paddling in calm areas of the river followed by rests in areas where the current was stronger, Hugo started to get restless. "Let's move to the front," he said.

Sarah and Emi agreed.

Imogene shrugged, not wanting to have another confrontation with the boys, particularly when Kenichi or Morgan, both of whom had stood up to them, were on another raft where they could not help her. The group paddled their way forward.

Aella lifted a sardonic eyebrow as they passed but ultimately did not attempt to stop them.

"Always lead from the front," Hugo concluded when they'd passed the other rafts.

Imogene didn't much care where they were in relation to the other boats, but if it would keep the boys from pestering her, she was happy to oblige.

As the morning rolled on, the group came to a section of river where the canyon narrowed, and the water poured through the narrowed channel with increased speed.

"Rapids coming up," Steve said, grinning.

Imogene glanced at Aurelian and gasped. The boy's eyes were closed, his face screwed up in concentration. His hands were glowing.

"Aurelian," she said. "Your hands! Look!" The boy opened his eyes and lifted them in front of his face. His palms were giving off a reddish-gold light that streamed from his fingertips in visible beams like a flashlight shining in a dusty room.

"What is happening?" Aurelian said, his voice rising in a panic. He held his hands out away from his body.

"Look out!" Hugo's cry brought Imogene out of her trance. The raft was rushing around a corner of the river where a group of rocks had created a diversion of the current that ran over a rough section of the riverbed resulting in a section of rolling white water. In the center of the was a large bent tree branch that had been broken off. Its endpoint was ragged and sharp, and it pointed upriver toward them. The raft was heading directly toward it.

"Row!" Hugo shouted, his oar plunging into the churning water.

Imogene drove her own paddle into the water and pulled hard. Aurelian fumbled with his paddle and cried out as the plastic melted in his hands. Imogene stared at the paddle as its shaft began to bend in the boy's grip like his hands were on fire. Liquid droplets of plastic began falling from his fingers into the boat.

"Row!" Hugo shouted again, and Imogene hesitated, torn

between the need to help with the rowing and her surprise about what was unfolding. Aurelian let go of the paddle, and it fell to the bottom of the raft. He was staring in horror at his hands again, his face a large O of surprise.

The raft, pulled by the power of the current, accelerated into the channel and bucked under Imogene, making her tip. She put her hands down to steady herself as the raft bounced over two more large waves. From the corner of her eye, she saw Aurelian trying to move to the edge of the raft using his elbows to hold himself up. He shifted, the raft bucked and he fell, reaching out a hand to brace himself.

"NO!" Imogene shouted too late. There was a loud pop, a rushing sound, and water rose up to meet Imogene, she plunged under its murky surface.

She kicked, her feet entangling in the deflating raft, she began to panic, trying to disentangle herself from the objects that now swirled around her in the depths.

Her lungs screamed for air as she floundered. Finally, she broke through the surface of the water and sucked in a breath.

She turned, kicking as the water swept her down the river.

Feet downriver, she told herself, remembering the short safety briefing they'd had before departing. She pointed her feet downstream, hearing the shouts of other teens around and behind her.

"Immy," Morgan's voice called from nearby. "Swim this way!"

She struggled in the churning water and lost track of where his voice had come from.

A strong hand grabbed her upper arm and dragged her from the water. She landed flopping like a landed fish on the bottom of a raft. She glanced up into Aella's worried face. Sarah sat dripping nearby.

"You OK?" Kenichi asked from beside Aella. "Any injuries?"

Imogene shook her head. "No, I think I'm OK."

"Paddle left," Aella said. "Fen and his group already have Hugo, Elina, and Zach. We just need to pick up Aurelian."

The others paddled the raft as Imogene gathered herself and sat up, finding an open spot on the thwart and taking a seat.

"What happened?" Nayme asked, her voice full of concern.

"Aurelian, he— Well, I'm not even sure what he did. He was sitting there with his eyes closed, and then his hands started glowing."

"We all stopped to look at it—it was just so amazing. We weren't watching, and then Hugo saw a tree branch sticking out into the river, we tried to maneuver away from it and we hit some rapids. Aurelian started to fall, the raft was bucking, and he tried to steady himself. When he put his hand on the raft, it popped."

"Guay! It popped? Just like that?" Nayme asked, her voice high with surprise.

Imogene nodded.

"That's not the strangest thing," Sarah said, her voice full of wonder. "The weirdest thing was when Hugo yelled for everyone to paddle away from that branch, Aurelian tried to help, and his paddle *melted!*"

Aella reached into the water and hauled a sputtering Aurelian into the raft. His eyes were wide, face red with exertion and fear.

"Sounds like we have an apprentice imbuer among us," Aella said. "You're beginning to find your powers, Aurelian. Congratulations."

A small shy grin worked at the corner of the boy's lips, and his eyes roved the group of teens who now sat so tightly together that they barely had room to row.

"Is that good or bad?" Imogene asked, searching Aella's face.

"Imbuers are very useful," Aella said. "Being an imbuer is not a problem at all. Unfortunately, we do have a problem. A couple of problems actually." She looked at Imogene, meeting her eyes, her gaze intense. "Two very large problems," she finished.

"What kind of problems?" Kenichi asked.

Aella sighed. "First, we now have too many passengers for these boats. Second, and perhaps more importantly, the boat that you were on," she said, nodding at Imogene, "had most of our food on board."

Imogene's stomach dropped, and she cursed.

CHAPTER 11
CHOICES

"We should go back for it." Nayme's voice was firm, insistent.

"It's way back there," Hugo sneered. "Bloody waste of time. You don't even know what it was."

"It looked like a dry bag. Just like the ones we have in our rafts, just a different color." Nayme folded her arms, putting her foot down firmly. "It's probably from another rafting trip. People come down here all the time."

"You an expert on rafting in Utah then?"

Her face fell. "I took a rafting trip with my aunt once," she said, addressing her feet, "before the moon."

"You're cracked," Hugo said, his face going bright red. "You don't know what you're talking about."

"We can find it," she insisted.

"We need to hunt!" Hugo's shout rebounded off the cliffs in echoing waves.

Morgan flinched and sat up. Hugo's face was blotchy and red, his hands clenched in frustration. It had been three days since one of the rafts had sunk, and their supplies had begun to run dangerously low.

"We will." Aella said in a calming tone and waved for the group to gather near the bank where they'd beached the remaining rafts for a break. Morgan looked for Imogene, but she'd already moved to the east and was standing with Kenichi and Alexa. He walked to where Aurelian and Nayme stood.

"What do you think we should do?" Aurelian asked.

Morgan looked at Nayme's intense face. "I believe Nayme," he said. She nodded to him gratefully.

"Thank you," she said.

"As you all know, we are short on supplies. We're going to have to do what we can to find things as we go," Aella said. Morgan caught the significant, deadly glare Nayme fixed on Hugo, and a small smile touched the corners of his lips.

"We're starving!" Hugo grated, his teeth gritted in fury.

"As it happens, I'm aware of our situation. But skipping the odd meal is hardly starving. People survived on less every day, even before the impact."

"We'll have to go to one meal a day soon," Aurelian said. "We'll be out of food in less than a week at this rate."

"How long is it going to take us to get to the Grand Canyon?" Nayme said.

Aurelian grunted. "I doubt we're even halfway," he responded. Nayme's eyes widened.

"You all know how dire our food situation has become," Aella said, garnering nods from all the teens. This much at least they all agreed upon.

She gestured toward the sheer cliffs that lined the river on both sides. "We're less than a half-day from the hunting grounds that Fen identified. On the east of the river the terrain is more fertile, and there are deer and elk that roam nearby.

Just be patient. We'll be there soon, hopefully before the day's end."

"That's too bloody long," Hugo said, his face still red and angry. "Just send Fen to one of the grocery stores, there's bound to be stuff left there. Pop, he's gone, pop, he's back with a bag full of goodies."

"Unfortunately, food does not travel well." Aella said. "It tends to become inedible."

"Well, he can at least find the stuff we lost. Why can't he do that?"

"He's tried Hugo. He's been up and down the riverbank looking and we're searching the shoreline as we go."

"Little fool really is good for nothing." Hugo sneered.

"What an ass," Nayme said as he continued to argue with Aella. "Does he think he's the only one who's hungry? Besides, it's only been a few days, and it's not like we're getting *nothing* to eat."

Morgan's stomach rumbled, and he glanced at Aurelian. The boy stood with hunched shoulders, kicking the sand with a toe.

Morgan patted him on the shoulder. "It's not your fault," he said. "None of us know what we're doing. It could have happened to any of us."

Regardless of whose fault it may have been, the loss was a big one; they had lost most of their food to the river and none of it had been recovered.

"Some of you want to hunt, and that's a good thing, but there are other options as well," Aella said. "First, some of you seem to have seen—or thought you saw—a couple of dry bags on the edge of their river a little way back."

She nodded to Nayme, who had pointed out the shapes on the shore.

"I don't know how we're going to hunt anything anyway. We don't have any weapons," Nayme said quietly.

Morgan nodded. "Better to go for the sure thing," he said.

"Well, we know Aella can manifest one," Aurelian observed. "You've seen it, haven't you?"

"I saw it," Morgan said. The sight of Aella standing above him with that burning blade in her hand was indelibly burned into his memory. "I'm not sure how helpful it will be hunting though."

"Why do you say that?" Aurelian asked excitedly.

Morgan chuckled. "Have you ever tried to get close to a deer?"

They shook their heads.

"Getting close enough to shoot one with a bow is hard enough. Guys at school in Vernal talk about it all the time." He looked at the others seriously. "Even experienced hunters fail to get a deer most of the time. Even when they manage it's usually after days of doing nothing but that."

"So, what are you saying? It's hopeless?"

He shrugged. "She's fast. I saw her run, and she was like a gazelle. Maybe she'll be quick enough to get one."

"I wonder if she can manifest something like a bow or arrow," Nayme wondered. "I mean does she have to be touching it?"

"I don't know," Morgan said contemplatively. "I've only ever seen the sword."

"That's quite enough, Hugo," Aella said loudly, her statement brought the three's attention back to where the woman was glaring daggers at the boy. Hugo clenched his fists but said nothing, temporarily cowed.

"We will pursue both options simultaneously. One group will head down to the hunting area, and a small group will stay here to search for the dry bags and any wild edibles that can be foraged. I will go with the hunting party, and Fen will stay here with the boat."

"Who wants to hunt, and who wants to search for dry bags?"

The teens stood for a long moment, looking at each other before anyone answered.

"I'll look for dry bags," Nayme said and looked at Morgan expectantly.

He took a deep breath, met her gaze, and said, "I'll go with her."

"I'll hunt," Imogene said.

Morgan gritted his teeth. Why did she have to make everything so hard? He turned his back on the group and walked, fists clenched, until he could no longer hear the conversation. He was joined a few minutes later by Nayme; Aurelian; two quiet boys; Steve and Gene, and, to Morgan's astonishment, Sarah. He looked at her quizzically.

She shrugged. "I'm not really the hunting type," she said.

"You're certainly welcome with us," Nayme said in a friendly voice.

They other teens slid their rafts into the current and began drifting downstream. Morgan and his group picked their way north over a rockslide that went down to the waterline that seemed recent. After a few difficult minutes, the ground flattened out, and the rock turned to sand, allowing the group to make much better time.

"How far back is it?" Morgan asked.

"I think it's about a mile or two," Nayme said. "Hopefully it won't take too long."

"Be sure to look for other edibles," Aurelian said. "Aella wants us to find edibles if we can. Sego lily, prickly pear, and dandelion are all edible and native to this area, so keep your eyes out for those."

"I don't know what those even are," Sarah said.

"Which one?" Aurelian said.

"Pick one," she said.

"Well, you know those cacti that have little flat round parts to them? Like a bunch of green prickly pancakes stuck together in strange ways?"

"Sure," she said.

"Those are prickly pears. You can slice off the skin and eat the insides. I hear they're not bad. Sego lilies are white and have three petals with a kind of purple-and-yellow center. You dig those up and eat the roots. Dandelions—"

"We all know what dandelions are," Sarah said.

"How do you know all this?" Nayme asked.

Aurelian grinned sheepishly. "I read a lot."

"What about the dandelions?" Morgan asked.

"OK, well you eat the leaves of those, but they can be a bit bitter, so the younger, smaller leaves are the best ones to get."

Morgan hadn't known about any of the wild edibles, but with Aurelian's descriptions, he thought he could recognize all of them. He scanned the area as he walked, and it didn't take long before he found some dandelions. He went over to them, picked some of the smaller leaves, and put them into his pockets.

They continued up the river, each of the youths spreading out, meandering slowly along the river and hillsides as they searched.

"Is this sego lily?" Sarah shouted. The others jogged over to look at the plant. It was a long thin flower with gray green somewhat pointed leaves.

"That's it!" Aurelian said excitedly. Sarah beamed.

Morgan knelt by the plant and grabbed a long flat rock from the ground and used it to dig up the root. It reminded him of garlic, but it was covered with a fibrous brown covering. He handed the root to Sarah, who held it up, a pretty grin adorning her face. She showed it to Steve who nodded. Morgan couldn't help but grin to see Sarah so pleased with herself.

She pocketed the small root. The group located several more in the area and dug the roots in turn. As the afternoon dragged on, they continued alongside the river, which wound around a large, pointed mesa before coming to a flat sandy area by the waterline where the remains of a fire pit lay. "I think it was around here," Nayme said. "It's going to be dark soon, so let's hurry and look for it."

The group fanned out, searching among the weeds and rocks on the shore.

Morgan paused when saw a dark lump on the shore that was partially obscured by the long grasses that grew on the shoreline. He padded forward and pulled the gray dry bag from the dirt by its handle.

"I found it!" he called, holding the bag exultantly above his head. Nayme came running over, her face flushed with triumph.

"Well," Nayme said, "open it."

Morgan stared, returning her radiant smile.

Aurelian nudged him, and he set the bag on the ground and began opening it. He reached inside and began pulling out the contents. There were seven gallon-sized clear plastic bags, each containing several individual packets of oatmeal, cream of wheat, and powdered milk. Two blue ponchos still in their packaging sat in the bottom of the bag with a lighter, two rolls of toilet paper, and a pink visor with a Nike symbol.

Morgan tossed the pink visor to Nayme. She grinned and made a show of putting it on.

"It's food!" Aurelian said excitedly.

"Glad we came," Morgan said, smiling at Nayme, who

beamed in return. "It could have just been a bag of someone's clothes."

"Let's get this packed back up and get back. It's getting late," Nayme said as Morgan began shoving the items back in the bag. He shouldered it, and the group headed back the way they'd come.

An ear-splitting howl sounded from Morgan's left, and his stomach clenched as fear surged up his spine. He recognized the sound immediately.

"Werewolf!" he shouted. "Back to the boat!"

His heart pounded in his ears as he ran. He spared a look for the others who were with him. Sarah, Steve, and Gene were ahead of him, picking their way through the boulder field. Nayme and Aurelian were falling behind him, even with the heavy bag that he carried. Aurelian stumbled and fell. Morgan turned back, grabbed his arm, and helped him to his feet.

"Are you OK?" he said. Aurelian nodded. "Good, let's go!" Morgan and Aurelian hurried toward the boat. Sarah was far in front of the others, exiting the craggy boulder field they'd passed on their way up the river.

A group of dark, predatory shapes hurtled down the side of the canyon wall, driving with inhuman speed toward the raft. They ran with a feral grace, heads bobbing in a hyena-like fashion. Morgan dug in and sprinted, his feet and arms pumping hard as he poured on the speed. He'd always been fast, as fast as nearly anyone he'd ever known, and he needed all of that speed now. He raced onward as more dark shapes came bounding toward the rafts.

Sarah pounded across the sand to the raft. Fen was gone.

"Mierda!" Morgan cursed as he pounded across the sand.

More inhuman shapes pounded down the canyon walls on his left. Behind him, he could hear Nayme gasping for air as she ran. Sarah reached the shoreline and heaved on the boat, trying to drive it into the river. It slipped forward and bobbed at the edge of the water. She leapt in with Steve just behind her.

The lead wolf, a huge beast with black fur leapt in a high graceful arc. Like a cougar pouncing on its prey, the monster came crashing onto Steve's back before he made the boat. It bore the boy down, teeth and claws flashing in the darkness, as Steve writhed and kicked, before becoming still.

Morgan couldn't remember when he'd stopped running. He just stood there panting and gaping as the creature's head came back up. In the low light Morgan couldn't see the color of the shapes that flew and dripped from its jaws, but he knew one thing with absolute certainty: Steve was dead. Gene went down as another wolf slashed at his legs and he tumbled to the ground.

Nayme's and Aurelian's heavy footfalls finally caught up with him. They looked on in horror as a huge shape came out of the darkness, clambering easily over the sharp twisting rocks in a direct line toward Sarah.

"Sarah, look out!" Morgan shouted as the dark shape sped toward her. She looked back at him, mouth open forming an O, terror filling her eyes as the creature careened through the air and bore her down into the raft. Her nascent scream cut off. There was a great pop, and the raft deflated, plunging Sarah and the wolf into the river. A huge spray of water erupted from the river, and a tendril shape grabbed the werewolf and dragged it under, kicking and thrashing. Sarah was nowhere to be seen.

More howling echoed in the canyon, Morgan grabbed Nayme's wrist and nearly dragged her from her feet as he sprinted toward the river.

"Into the water!" he shouted as they ran. Morgan, Nayme, and Aurelian catapulted into the cold water and kicked toward the center. Morgan looked back, finding more wolves lining the opposite bank.

"Stay in the middle," he hissed, trying not to swallow too much water. He floated, head turned toward the bank, where shapes were milling around, but he could no longer make them out.

He looked to Nayme, who was floating near him. He met her eyes; and raised one finger to his lips. "Try not to draw attention to yourself," he whispered, hoping it was loud enough for her to hear over the churning liquid.

"Just float. We're safe in the river, hopefully they'll lose us in the water." He wasn't sure if she'd understood him, but her scared face nodded and she leaned her head back so that only her face remained above water.

Morgan looked around. He couldn't tell where Aurelian was, but the boy had made it into the water, that much he was certain of.

He dipped his head back, looking up into the sky, which had now gone dark. The sun had gone down, and the moon had not yet risen. *How had the wolves known where we were?* he wondered, shock, anger, and fear still chasing each other around in his mind.

Morgan floated, remaining as still as he could, still holding Nayme's hand. He was afraid if he let go, they would drift apart in the darkness. Slowly the grunts, shouts, and howls from the bank faded into the distance as they drifted into the night.

Aella and some of the other teens had gone in search of prey. Instead, Morgan and his companions had nearly become it. Full darkness fell, leaving only the bobbing river, and the black spires of the mesas standing silently on the banks. A sliver of the evil moon crested through clouds that floated by like ghosts patrolling the dark skies. Paralyzed by fear, Morgan and Nayme slipped as still as corpses into the night.

CHAPTER 12
PURSUIT

"Come up with any great ideas?" Imogene said to Kenichi, who walked beside her.

"Maybe Aella can make a magic lasso, throw it around the deer's necks, and make them tell her all their secrets," Kenichi said.

Imogene snickered. "I doubt that deer have any juicy ones."

He grinned. "Oh, I don't know, the secret lives of deer might be spicier than you imagine. Aella could lasso a few, bring them under her power, make them tell her all their secrets, and maybe even make it into a TV show. Just imagine, *The Real House Deer of Zion Canyon*. It would be a hit."

Immy laughed. "Well, if you found a way for people to see it, it would be the only thing on."

"Sounds like a sure winner to me!" Kenichi said.

"Almost ready?" Aella called the group.

Imogene rose and stepped from the raft. They had beached the rafts on a section of river with a long sandy beach that extended for hundreds of yards below a large hill that, unlike much of the terrain, had a more gradual ascent. The days on the river had seemed fun at first, but now they dragged on. Imogene was exhausted and worn from long days in the sun, reduced rations, and the late-night watch duties that Aella had insisted they perform as a precautionary measure. She wondered how long she could go on like this.

"Alright," Aella said loudly. "I need someone to watch the boats. Who would like to do that?" There was silence until finally, Oscar raised his hand timidly. Aella nodded in approval, and the boy sat back down to wait.

Aella motioned the group forward, and the hunters began climbing from the river, between two jagged hills, and then ascending an incline where the path began switching back and forth in a series of steep inclines that rose sharply from the river valley. When they arrived at the top, Imogene was gasping for air.

The summit was wide and flat, covered with pine trees and green grasses, intermixed with quaking aspens. *Wouldn't have expected that,* Imogene thought. *It seemed so barren from the river.*

"Fen said he saw game here," Aella reminded the group in a hushed voice, noting the terrain. "We'll need to move quietly and carefully so that we don't spook any animals. Understand?"

Imogene's heart was pounding, but she nodded along with the others. Prior to her time under the evil moon, she'd never even thought about hunting at all, let alone putting herself in a position to participate in it. She felt totally out of her element, unsure of how she could even be of help, but determined to try.

"What do we do?" she whispered.

Aella gazed back at her and seemed to read her fearful expression, her face softened. "Not too far from here, there is a natural spring," she said pointing toward the trees. "Fen said there are deer and a herd of elk in the area that may be using it.

We'll have to wait, put ourselves where they'll be likely to pass, and hope that they'll come close enough. If they do, we'll strike."

Imogene met Kenichi's eyes. Of all the outlandish guesses they had come up with, none had been close.

"Strike?" Hugo said questioningly. "With what?"

"You'll need to manifest a spear, something long and sharp that you can use to stab one."

Fear coursed through Imogene's veins. She had yet to manage any type of manifestation. She felt the disk in her pocket. It was half gone. Aella had made them practice every morning and night since they'd left Vernal, and Imogene had met with some success in absorbing it.

"But" Kenichi began carefully, measuring his words, "none of us have ever succeeded in manifesting, and elk are huge. About the size of a horse."

Aella nodded, her face serious.

"Getting that close will be dangerous," Kenichi finished. Aella nodded again.

The teens looked at each other, their eyes wide.

"It will be," Aella agreed. "But little about this trip has been safe. I'm afraid that safety is a luxury that belongs to the world of before. That world is dead so you will just have to do your best."

"Why can't you just manifest an arrow and shoot one with it?" Hugo said.

"It doesn't work that way," Aella replied. "I'm a Valkryn, remember? Our manifestations have strict limits when it comes to distance."

"What kind of limits?" Kenichi asked after a significant glance at Imogene.

"I have to maintain contact with my manifestations. The moment they leave my hand, they dissipate. An ethermancer could direct a burst of energy at the deer, but aiming is difficult, and I can't use my power that way."

"What about the other ones?" Nayme asked. "Imbuers, was it? Would one of them be helpful? Should we have brought Aurelian along?"

Imogene thought again of Aurelian, who seemed destined to become an imbuer. She tried to imagine him being helpful and failed to see how the timid boy could fill that role.

"No," Aella said. "Of all different branches, imbuers have the shortest range of effective power. He's better off looking for our lost supplies. The other group will meet us at the shoreline at dusk, and we can set up camp."

Figures, Imogene thought and then felt guilty.

"Let's focus on the task at hand," Aella continued. "It's still fairly hot, so the game will be bedded down. They won't start to move until closer to dark. In the meantime, I want you to all practice manifesting. Concentrate on something long, like a spear. That will give you the range you'll need to have a chance at this method of hunting."

Imogene sat on a rock and considered how to begin. She tried to remember the instructions Aella had given them. Feeling awkward, she put a hand on her lower stomach and closed her eyes, trying to feel the area Aella had described. She focused, trying to sense her don tin, her internal furnace. Minutes slipped by. Her stomach growled and she repositioned. After what seemed a long time, she sighed and opened her eyes.

"I did it!" Hugo said suddenly, and Imogene looked up to see a purplish spear in his hand for a moment before it puffed away into mist.

"Damn!" he said disappointedly.

Imogene gritted her teeth and tried again. Closing her eyes, she focused on her stomach, trying to imagine it being filled with light and power. Nothing happened.

A few minutes later, Kenichi had a breakthrough, managing to make a short spike appear in his hand. It would be impractical to use against a large animal, but it was progress all the same.

"Keep trying," Aella encouraged. "You're almost there."

Kenichi patted Imogene on the back encouragingly.

Imogene focused again, trying to feel the power around her, beckoning it to fill her as Aella had described.

Nothing, she thought, frustrated. *Why can't I feel it?*

Imogene looked up to see Aella looking at her. "You'll get it," she said. Imogene nodded, trying to project a sense of confidence she didn't feel. By now she was certain that she would not be able to manifest anything. Still, she focused, trying and failing time after time.

Finally, she looked hopelessly back at Kenichi. He kept working, gradually adding length and definition to his spear. Each version was longer and displayed fewer pockmarks. Finally, Aella interrupted their attempts.

Imogene had failed to produce anything at all, not even the type of mist that several of the teens had produced before they were able to create a small object. Imogene looked up at Alexa. The girl was frowning, her face frustrated and angry.

Imogene consoled herself with the fact that she wasn't alone in her struggles.

"We need to get into position," Aella whispered, nodding in the direction where the water hole lay. The teens nervously stood and slipped through the trees, following the Valkryn in a loose line.

Imogene focused on her feet, trying with some difficulty to keep her steps silent. She'd done this type of thing when she was little before her father had gone. She tried to remember what he'd said, something about how she should place her feet. Was it toes first? She couldn't remember.

The water hole wasn't much more than a deep puddle a couple of dozen feet wide and bordered by a wide patch of mud that had been churned by countless hooves. A trickle of water ran from the pool, down a small depression, and toward the river. Nearby, several dozen large boulders and smaller stones of various sizes bordered the small clearing.

"I'll hide there, among the rocks, and wait for one to get close enough," Aella said, pointing to the formation. "The rest of you, conceal yourselves past the edges of the clearing." She indicated the ring of trees that bordered it. "Let me have the first attempt. If one of them gets close enough, I'll try to spear it. If I fail, you'll have to be ready. When the herd runs, hopefully, one of you will be close enough to make a second attempt."

"You'll have to move quickly, form your weapon, and stab them as they go by. Stay hidden until the very last moment. We're only going to have one chance at this."

Imogene glanced at Kenichi, her heart racing. He shrugged back at her.

This is insane, she thought.

The group took their places, Aella among the stones and the rest among the trees. They tried to spread out, covering as much of the area as they could. Imogene hid between a pair of jagged rocks and a tree that had fallen over, its trunk lying away from the trails where she imagined the animals would be likely to appear. She wiggled into position and prepared herself to wait.

Minutes passed like hours as the afternoon dragged on and the sunlight slowly began to fade. Imogene's back began to ache, wedged as it was between the two stones. She was just about to give up and stand to stretch when she heard a snapping sound on the far side of the clearing.

The elk appeared from between the trees in a small group. They paused, looking into the clearing alert, their heads standing tall on their shaggy necks, ears darting forward and back like satellite dishes intent on receiving a signal. Imogene forced herself to stay still. She knew Hugo and Zach were concealed not far from where the elk stood.

Get them, she thought, willing one of the boys to manage an attack. She forced herself to breathe in long, deep, slow breaths that would make no noise.

An elk proceeded into the clearing and lowered its muzzle to the water. Minutes passed as more elk emerged from the trees, a second group entering via a small path between the places where Imogene and Kenichi were hidden. The elk drank, paused to look around, and drank again.

With agonizing slowness, they began drifting closer to the rocks where the Aella lay concealed.

Closer. Closer, Imogene thought.

In a burst of movement, Aella appeared, a long, glowing spear in her hand. She jabbed at an elk, a cow, that had wandered close to the rocks. The herd bolted, turning as one and sprinting through the trees, angling away from Aella and toward Imogene's hiding place. Aella cursed loudly as her jab grazed the wheeling elk but failed to bring it down. It sprinted away from her, and like a blur she followed.

Crap.

Imogene gulped as the elk thundered across the open area in what seemed like a heartbeat. She froze as three careened past her. Then she saw it—the cow that Aella had attacked was running toward her. It wasn't running as well as the others. Blood oozed from its side, and its gait was labored.

As the beast crashed toward her, time seemed to compress. Without conscious thought, Imogene found herself standing, her feet braced, with a glowing spear in her hands. The cow banked, turning to angle away from where she stood. Imogene lunged, driving the point of the golden spear forward and toward the elk's flank. The impact jolted her to the side, flinging her forcefully to the ground as the weight of the animal ran down the length of the spear and tossed her aside like a rag doll.

She landed hard, white light exploded in front of her eyes, and the air in her lungs was expelled in a terrific rush, which left her gasping, desperately trying to draw a breath. The spear vanished in a puff of smoke. Panic filled her, her lungs burning as she tried to draw in oxygen that wouldn't come.

She coughed, and precious air rushed to fill her lungs. Her first breaths were ragged and painful, but they came. She knelt, struggling for air, and slowly her breathing began to normalize. A strong hand grabbed her by the arm and began helping her to her feet. Kenichi looked down at her, his handsome face grinning widely.

"You did it!" he effused and pointed to the ground a few feet away. Imogene turned. There, less than a dozen feet away lay the elk.

"Well done!" Aella said and slapped her hard on the back. "Well done indeed."

Imogene nodded, a wide grin sliding across her face, despite the pain that still radiated through her. Aella slipped past and moved to where the cow lay, a smaller version of her sword in her hand.

Aella processed the animal with a deft hand. In minutes she had quartered it, divided it into manageable chunks, and then sliced the meat from the bone in quick, efficient strokes.

She's done this before, Imogene realized. *Many times.*

Aella emptied her pack and produced several of the familiar dry bags, now empty of any contents. She filled the bags with large chunks of meat as Imogene watched, fascinated and horrified by the speed with which the woman butchered the animal.

When Aella was done, she handed out the bags, now bulging with the weight of the slaughtered elk. Imogene slung a heavy bag over her shoulder with surprising ease, and the hunters began retracing their steps to where the boat waited at the water's edge.

"That was so awesome," Kenichi said. He'd said it several times before, but it still filled Imogene with a trill of pleasure.

"He's right," Hugo said, for once sounding sincere. "That was amazing. Well done."

Imogene was taken aback. *Did he just compliment me?* She was astounded. She grinned to herself as the group filed back down the trail, talking and laughing about their adventure.

"That had to have hurt," Zach said, glancing over his shoulder at Imogene. "One second, I thought they'd all gotten away, and the next Imogene was standing there in the trail, spear in hand. Honestly, you just went flying when you stabbed it!"

"Why would that hurt?" Imogene said, her voice full of irony. "It was just a thousand pounds of elk sprinting full speed and knocking me flat. Are you implying that it should hurt?" The others laughed. Imogene grinned. It was nice to feel like a valued part of the group.

Her thoughts were interrupted by bellowing howls.

Imogene watched in horror as a huge werewolf catapulted from its hiding place among the rocks and bore Elina to the ground. The world erupted into screams and shouts that Imogene couldn't decipher. There was a growl to her right, and she turned. A gaping maw filled with rows of sharp teeth was barreling toward her with shocking speed.

Kenichi crashed into the creature's side and knocked it sideways. Its snapping jaws just missed Imogene's face, and she was knocked sprawling. She rolled, trying to find her feet as her head came up.

Kenichi was on the ground, trying to get a purchase, his feet slipping over loose gravely stones. A clawed hand swung in a brutal arc that caught him full in the face. Blood spurted into the air as he was flung sideways and collapsed to the ground in a heap.

There was a feral shriek, and Imogene saw red. Rage filling her, she yelled and sprang forward, her call distracting the monster's attention from where Kenichi lay prone and unmoving.

She sprinted toward the monster that snarled back at her, its large, malice-filled orange eyes staring into hers as she ran. She came to an abrupt stop and stood, her chest heaving as the wolf's jaw worked. It made a strange keening growl and then a whimper, a sound so delicate that it seemed out of character for a beast so deadly.

She looked down at the glowing spear in her hands. She'd skewered the creature, driving the point of the glowing spear through its chest so that the glowing end stood out behind the creature's grimacing face.

It whimpered, like a kicked puppy, and collapsed.

"Kenichi!" Imogene shouted, turning. The boy was on the ground, laying limp. Blood was pooling near his face. She rushed over to him and rolled him over. His face was a mess of torn tissue and blood. Four ragged gashes were torn through his cheek in a rough arc, leaving the bone exposed in several places. Imogene stared at the wound. She needed something, a bandage. She searched around and found only the dry bags full of meat. She looked down at her dirty t-shirt.

She pulled it off, turned it inside out, found the cleanest part she could, and pressed it to the wound, applying pressure in an attempt to stop the bleeding.

"Is he OK?" a voice said. Imogene looked up dumbly, only dimly aware that someone was standing near her. Hot tears were running down her face as she looked up into Alexa's terrified face, her normally tan complexion drained to the point of matching the color of the wispy clouds floating above.

"I, I don't—" Imogene cut off, her jaw working pointlessly.

"Let me see it, hurry, there are more wolves coming!" Aella said as she ran to them. Imogene released her bloody t-shirt, leaving it lying on Kenichi's still face. Aella knelt next to him and pulled back on the shirt. She cursed.

"Fen," she said loudly. There was a loud pop, and the little gnome stood next to her. She looked up at him. "I need your help," she said.

"Mistress knows, gnome healing, 'tis limited," he began.

"I know," she said impatiently, "but do what you can!" The little gnome nodded and moved over to the boy. He began chanting in a strange trilling language Imogene had never heard before. His hand drew in the air, making patterns in the sky that glowed with power as she watched. He put his little hands-on Kenichi's face.

The wounds began to knit themselves together, tissue regenerating, blood drying. The gnome bent over, panting and putting his small hands on his knees.

"'Tis all I can do," he said through deep breaths. "He too big for Fen."

Aella hugged the little gnome, burying his head in her chest. "You've done wonderfully," she said. "So very well!" She released the little gnome and looked around, assessing the conditions of the remaining teens.

Imogene stared down at the wound. The deeper parts had knit together over the bone, leaving gashes that, while still significant, no longer revealed the boy's skull.

"Twill be tough for him," Fen said sadly. "Fen can do's no more."

Imogene nodded, her stomach twisting within her.

"We'll have to carry him," Aella said and met Imogene's eyes, her gaze expectant.

"Elina?" Hugo said, his voice shaky.

"I'm sorry," Aella said regretfully.

"Dead?" Zach gasped. Hugo covered his mouth and looked like he might be sick.

Imogene looked up at them, meeting each of the boys' eyes in turn. Hugo's face looked stricken and hollow as tears formed in his eyes and ran down his face. His mouth worked, and he turned, dazed, and he began making his way down the trail toward the raft. Zach just stared past Imogene dully, not seeing her.

"Hugo," Imogene said. He kept walking, not acknowledging her or even seeming to hear her.

"He's in shock," Aella said. "Let him go." She slung the bag from her shoulders and held it out to Imogene, who took it in one hand. "You take the meat. I'll carry Kenichi. Hurry, we can't wait for the others. We have to get him to the rafts before more wolves arrive."

Imogene nodded and slung the bags of meat over her shoulder. Aella hefted Kenichi over her shoulder and nodded at Imogene.

Imogene glanced around, seeing another discarded bag, the one Kenichi had been carrying. She picked it up and slung it over her shoulder as well. When she'd turned, Aella had already begun walking down the trail, Kenichi draped over her left shoulder.

She's so strong, she thought vaguely as she followed, roughly a hundred and fifty pounds of meat draped over her own slight shoulders. They marched down the switchbacks toward the river.

They rounded a corner and looked to the area where they had beached the boats. As they did, dark shapes appeared on the sand from both ends of the beach, sprinting toward the rafts and a shocked Oscar.

"Into the rafts!" Aella shouted. "Move to the center of the river, we'll be safe there, the wolves won't enter," she finished and sprinted with inhuman speed to the rafts, gently laying Kenichi inside one.

It was a trap, Imogene realized. The skin-walkers had waited for them, hidden out of sight until they returned, when they would be disorganized and vulnerable. They were intelligent, not the rabid beasts she had imagined at first. How had the monsters known where to find them?

"Let's go!" Hugo cried, bracing himself against the side of the raft and pushing it with all his strength toward the relative safety of the water as another group of dark, predatory shapes careened toward the raft.

Aella was suddenly there. She met the wolves, a dervish with a brightly flashing blade, spinning and slicing in an elegant flowing dance of death. Two of the shapes went down, and another recoiled, howling in pain.

More wolves pounded across the sand as the first raft slid into the flow. Aella was making frantic waving motions toward the boats as more teenagers sprinted across the sand.

Aella formed a tall glowing shield that a large wolf promptly collided with, stopping instantaneously and making a sickening crunching noise before falling limply to the ground.

Aella's sword arm lashed out again, slashing at an onrushing wolf and severing its forepaw. The beast fell to the ground, yelping loudly. She stabbed it in the back, and it convulsed and lay still.

Imogene sprinted. Summoning all her remaining speed, she headed across the sand to where Alexa, Kira, and Hugo pushed frantically trying to shift a raft into the current. Four teens had a raft at the edge of the water and Zach and Oscar jumped aboard. Just behind them, Imogene swung her bags with all her strength, tossing them into the boat with Alexa, Kira, Hugo, and the injured Kenichi and dove onto the back of the raft.

"Row!" someone was shouting.

"Look out!" another voice yelled. A huge figure landed in the boat and long fangs bit into Oscar's shoulder. He screamed as the wolf shook him violently. Oscar's foot spasmed outward and knocked Zach into the current. The boy disappeared into the rushing water. A second wolf leapt aboard and began slashing at the remaining teens with its long claws.

A sickening smell, like blood and rotting meat, filled Imogene's nostrils as she struggled to pull herself aboard. Accompanying the smell was a deep growl that made the hair on her neck rise. A corner of her mind braced for sharp fangs to bite into her exposed flesh. But she dragged herself gasping into the boat.

She glanced back, a wolf was shaking Oscar's body like a dog with a chew toy and the second wolf was dragging a teen down as the raft bucked, there was a popping and the raft started to list. The raft disappeared into the water. Imogene dragged her eyes away from the sight and gazed into Aella's haunted face.

The woman was covered in blood that wasn't her own. Imogene couldn't help but wonder how many of the monsters the Valkryn had killed. Not enough to save them all. She forced herself not to look back to the monsters still snarling and baying on beach.

There was a soft pop, and Fen stood on the thwart.

"Mistress! They's gone! Ta others, there be wolves! I come to help mistress and when I's goings back, ta others is gone!"

CHAPTER 13
DECISIONS

Morgan woke damp and shivering on a small sandy island that lay situated between two divergent flows of current. He lifted his head from the numbness of his left arm and looked around. The morning was gray, dark, and threatening. Large rock formations rose like giant teeth to rend the sky above him. A stiff hopeless wind swept the alien landscape. He clenched his jaw to stop his teeth from chattering.

He looked to his side. Nayme lay curled into a ball next to him. Aurelian was flat on his stomach beyond her. Another breeze blew across the island, making Morgan's shivering more intense. Nayme stirred, moaned softly, and struggled to a seated position. She pulled her legs up tight against her chest and wrapped her thin arms around them.

"I'm freezing," she said dispiritedly and yawned.

"Me too." Morgan blew on his hands and then rubbed them together. His clothes, still wet from the river, had pulled all of the heat out of him. Nayme combed her fingers through the snarled and gritty locks of her hair and pulled it into a rough bun. She picked up a stick lying nearby and shoved it into the bun, pinning it in place.

"Any sign of them?" she asked.

"Who?" Morgan said, trying not to focus too hard on his memories of the night before. "Aella and the others, or those things?" His voice sounded hollow and afraid.

She snorted, a small unintentional smile forming at the corners of her mouth. "I'm trying to convince myself that everything that happened last night was some sort of hallucination."

He shook his head disconsolately. "It wasn't a hallucination. That's the second time they've nearly killed me. As for our companions, I think they're long gone."

Aurelian rolled over, balled fists rubbing at his eyes. He sat up and pulled his arms in close, shivering as he looked to the others.

Morgan caught Nayme's gaze and smirked. She followed his eyes to Aurelian, and he snickered.

"What?" Aurelian asked, confused.

Nayme reached over and brushed some sand and a six-inch twig from his face. Aurelian grinned, shrugging.

"Not exactly the Hilton," he said gamely.

Morgan stood and began looking around the island. It was a small and roughly triangular stretch of ground covered with sand, rocks, and a few small plants positioned in the center of the river.

"Anyone else hungry?" Aurelian said, his stomach growling loudly, emphasizing the point.

"Yeah," Nayme admitted in a soft voice. "But we're going to need to be careful. We don't have a lot of food."

"We wouldn't have any if you hadn't seen that bag," Morgan said appreciatively.

Nayme's expression dropped abruptly.

"If I hadn't insisted that we go back for it, we would be with the others."

Morgan shrugged. "Maybe. But we don't know what happened during the hunt. Wolves could have—" he left the comment hanging.

She shrugged a hesitant acceptance.

"What do we do for water?" Morgan asked. His gaze landed briefly on Nayme and then returned to Aurelian.

"We can get water from the river, but obviously it's not safe to drink without filtering," Nayme said.

"We can use the old hole-digging trick. That will at least make it a bit more likely to be free of the nasty little things that make you sick," Aurelian said.

"The hole-digging trick?" Nayme asked.

"You dig a hole a few feet away from a river or some other water source"—he motioned to the river on both sides of them— "and let the water seep into it. By the time the water seeps through the dirt and stuff, the bad stuff gets filtered out."

Morgan's and Nayme's eyes met, and she looked as skeptical as he felt.

"I saw a survivalist do it loads of times on TV," Aurelian said.

Nayme nodded.

"Let's get some breakfast," Morgan said decisively. "I suspect we're going to need our strength, and we won't have any if we don't eat. Particularly after such a long cold night." He met Nayme's eyes and held them as if waiting for her approval. She nodded her consent.

"How are we going to cook it?" Aurelian asked.

"We don't have anything we can burn," Morgan said, scanning the island, "at least not here. We'll have to cross and see if we can find something lying around." Nayme looked to the shore, her face unreadable.

They couldn't stay on the island for long, but Morgan dreaded the thought of leaving its safety for the uncertainty of the shoreline.

Aurelian met Morgan's eyes, the expression on his face mirrored Morgan's thoughts.

"What's the plan?" Aurelian said, looking at Morgan. "Long term I mean—after breakfast?"

Morgan started and looked back at him, meeting his questioning eyes. He turned to Nayme, and she tilted her head expectantly.

"How should I know?" he said.

"Come on, Morgan," Nayme said. "Where do we go from here? You live in Utah, and we're from other states"

Morgan grunted. "I've only lived here for a couple of years, and that was way north of here. I don't even know where we are, so why am I suddenly in charge?"

Nayme stared back at him, hand on her hips frowning at him expectantly. Morgan crossed his arms and stared back at her.

"Everyone else is gone," Nayme said finally.

"I'm not going to tell you what to do. Go wherever you want," Morgan said.

"We're going to the Grand Canyon," Nayme said. "That's obvious."

"Really?" Morgan said, feeling his temper rising. "Obvious, is it?"

"It's literally the only place that is safe," she said.

"How do you know? Because a woman we barely know anything about, said so?" he said. "How do we even know that we can trust Aella?"

"Morgan—" she began.

"Did either of you ever see a werewolf before Aella showed up?" he said, staring them down. "Because I certainly never had. How do we know that she's not the reason they came for us in the first place? She could have been the cause of our problems, not the solution."

"That's ridiculous," Nayme said, folding her arms in front of her chest, a stubborn look on her face.

"Ridiculous is assuming that she has good intentions without actually knowing her. None of us had ever had anything so—bizarre happen to us before—and we probably wouldn't have had she not shown up out of the blue with her baubles and gnomes and hoodoo."

"Technically," Aurelian said, interjecting into the conversation and cutting off a retort from Nayme before it could form, "none of us had seen a meteor that could destroy technology either. But—" He pointed up to where the moon was shining in iridescent splendor between the scattered clouds.

"I trust her," Nayme snapped.

"Well, I don't," Morgan said, clenching his fists and digging in, unwilling to be swayed.

"She may not have trusted you either," Aurelian said.

This statement appeared to take Nayme by surprise, and her mouth hung open, some unspoken response dying on her lips.

"What do you mean?" Morgan said, cocking his head inquisitively.

"At the outpost, I heard something Fen said," Aurelian said hesitantly.

Nayme nodded for him to continue. "What did you hear?"

"It was just after you arrived. I was heading to the cafeteria, and I heard Fen whisper something to Aella. He said the new boy can't be trusted."

Morgan felt his heart lurch within him. The feeling

surprised him. He had harbored a distrust toward Aella but somehow hearing that she distrusted him still hurt.

"What did she say?" Nayme probed.

Aurelian shrugged. "She just told Fen to keep an eye on him, that's it."

"You don't actually know it was Morgan then? Did they say his name?"

Aurelian shook his head. "No, but who else would they have been talking about?"

"Never mind," Morgan said, turning to stride away.

"Morgan, come back," Nayme called from behind him. "We need to stick together."

"You may need to stick together," he said heatedly. "I only need—" He cut himself off, unsure how to finish the sentence. Instead, he kicked a nearby rock. Aella and Fen hadn't trusted him? What cause did they have?

"You're not going to the Grand Canyon then?" Nayme asked.

Morgan stopped. "Why should I?" he said, rounding on her.

"Because—" she said, glaring into his eyes. He stared back at her, holding her gaze, jaw fixed. She wilted under the pressure of his gaze and looked down, her voice softening. "Fine," she said finally. "If we're not going to the Grand Canyon, then where are we going?"

Morgan frowned, shaking his head. "I'm not in charge. I'm not going to tell you what to do."

"Why not?" Nayme said. "Tell me that you wouldn't have told Imogene what to do if she were here." She stared at him, her gaze penetrating.

He hesitated.

She lifted her eyebrows questioningly. "Well?"

Imogene was still going to the Grand Canyon if she was

still alive. "That's different," he began.

"How?" she said, cutting him off.

"I promised I'd take care of her."

"And did Imogene want you to make that promise? Did she ask you to make it? It seemed to me that Imogene didn't want your help at the outpost or on the river. We *do* want your help! We have no idea where we are, and we have hardly any supplies. We have to stick together to have any chance of surviving! And on top of that, we only know of one place in the world that *might* be safe, and you don't want to go there!"

The words stung. She was right, but how could he possibly hope to get them all the way to the Grand Canyon? It was hundreds of miles away, and he had no idea how to get there. Even if they did manage to arrive at the canyon, it was vast. How would they find a hidden city there?

"Morgan, we need to stick together, and we have to make some hard choices." Nayme's voice was soft, entreating.

"Morgan," Aurelian said softly, "I'm afraid."

Morgan turned to the boy, who stood with his arms folded. He looked small and frightened. Morgan exhaled loudly. "I am too," he admitted. "I don't know what to do. I'm not a leader. I'm just a kid."

Nayme took a step toward him and laid her hand on his arm. "But you're the oldest kid here," she said, nodding at him. "And you're—good. You have good intentions. If you make mistakes, fine. With you in charge, at least I know that you're making the best choices you can for all of us."

Morgan stared at his feet, clenching his fists in frustration. "Fine," he said and locked gazes with Nayme.

His father's voice seemed to reach out to him over the stretch of time: *Think, Morgan. What things do you need first? What are the highest priorities?*

"I'll go, for Imogene's sake, in case she makes it to Encartha. What do we need?" he said.

"To get to the Grand Canyon?" Nayme asked.

"That's the end goal," Morgan replied. "What do we need to achieve that goal?"

"We'll need the basic stuff to start with: food, water, shelter," Aurelian said and then looked down at his sopping clothes, "dry clothes, packs," he continued, "some way of protecting ourselves."

"Good," Morgan said. "Hopefully we'll be able to find some of that stuff in a town downriver."

"We need to stay away from the wolves," Nayme said thoughtfully. "Do you still have your medallions?"

Morgan reached to his neck and found the medallion resting safely against his chest. He pulled it out. Aurelian nodded and produced his. "I still have my disk too," he said. Morgan slipped his hand into his pocket, touching the cool metal of his own.

"OK, good," Morgan said, his mind racing. "It would be great if we could find or manifest some weapons. Have either of you had any success with that?"

Nayme shook her head, and Aurelian looked at his feet.

"Me neither," he said. "We'll need to practice since we'll need protection from the wolves for sure." He paused, looking toward the darkness of the town beyond. "And from whatever else we might run into."

"Alright," Nayme said. "What do we do first?"

"I guess we go down river," Morgan said hesitantly. "But we should be careful. There could be wolves out there."

Nayme nodded, and they stood looking across the water for a long time before Morgan sighed and headed into the slow current. They forged the river and, shivering and soaked, headed downstream.

They followed the river south for the next two days, sleeping on an island one night, and hiding under the shelf of rock on the bank the next.

The sun was fully up, beating brutally down on them when they finally looked down from the top of a hill to where a small town lay in the distance.

"You were right," the boy said.

Morgan grunted. "Had to be one eventually, I'm just glad it was this close."

Nayme nodded, and they headed toward the distant buildings.

They followed the river for a half hour before it broadened and became marshier. When swarms of mosquitos began hovering around them, they moved away from the river to the east and found a gravel road headed in the correct direction.

They walked for hours, passing rocky, yellow stone mesas; dry unkempt fields; and finally arrived at two small, shabby, and deserted-looking houses that were nothing more than mobile homes secured on a permanent foundation.

"Should we look inside?" Aurelian asked, staring at the ramshackle buildings.

"I think we'll have to," Nayme said hesitantly. "There could be food."

Morgan nodded. "I'll take a look."

He approached the door and knocked. With no answer he pulled on the door handle and opened it. The place was empty and covered with dust. It looked as though no one had lived there for a very long time.

"I guess we keep going," Nayme said. Morgan nodded and they continued down the gravel road.

"Where are you from?" Morgan asked Aurelian. If he was going to be with these two for a while, something that seemed very likely, he thought he should try to get to know them better.

"I'm a Bender," Aurelian replied.

Morgan stared back at him, confused.

"From Bend, Oregon," Bender finished sheepishly.

"Is that what they call people from Bend?" Morgan asked.

Bender snorted. "I think only I say that."

"Bender, huh? I think that's what I'm going to call you," he said, testing the sound. "Bender."

The boy grinned back at him.

"What about you, Nayme?"

"Spain," she said through labored breaths.

"Spain? Why are you in Utah then? Did Aella find you in Europe?"

Nayme shook her head tiredly. "I came to the States for a cousin's wedding, but the wolves attacked." She walked silently for a few moments before gulping and whispering, "They killed her, her fiancé, and the aunt I was staying with. They nearly killed me too. Aella stopped them."

Morgan grunted, unable to find the words for a response. The three trudged onward.

A large, thin-looking yellow dog barked halfheartedly at them as they passed a particularly rundown house. Morgan stared back at it, but the dog didn't even stand. He wondered if it was strong enough to get up. How long had it been stuck behind the chain link fence that kept it bound? *It would likely be dead soon, like the rest of the world,* he thought.

Morgan stopped, staring at the animal. The dog growled at him menacingly.

"What is it?" Nayme asked.

He didn't answer. Instead, he walked slowly to the gate. "You like dogs?" Bender asked.

"Not really," Morgan said. He slid open the latch, pulled the gate open, and stepped away, leaving the door agape. He met the dog's eyes and nodded.

He felt Nayme's gaze on him and finally turned. A grin tugged at the corner of her lips, and she nodded.

"Should we go in?" Bender asked hesitantly.

Morgan looked at him, towards town, then back at the dog. Finally, he shook his head. "Let's keep going. I think we'll have better luck in town. I want to get there before we stop."

Bender nodded, and the group turned toward the town. As they walked Morgan turned and looked back. The dog was now standing where they had left him. He looked up at Morgan and then walked slowly toward the gate. Morgan hesitated, wondering if the dog would follow them. Instead, it padded away in the direction of the river.

Nayme stared at Morgan for a long moment. He looked back at her and shrugged before continuing onward.

In the distance, the road rose up a small hill and was intersected by a much wider road that ran from east to west. At the junction, a weathered gas station sat looking bereft and deserted. Morgan glanced over his shoulders to the others and pointed at the station. "Let's see what we can find in there," he said.

Bender nodded enthusiastically, and the group made their way to the corner of the intersecting paths. In the distance beyond the station, Morgan could now see I-70.

Good to know, he thought, trying to drudge up any facts about where the freeway went and failing.

He motioned to the others to stay where they were, and he made his way carefully toward the building, keeping his eyes peeled for movement.

The front of the building was glass that looked like it hadn't been washed in a decade. Tan dust covered it from floor to ceiling making it impossible for him to see inside from where he stood, a short distance away. Cautiously, he slid toward the door keeping his eyes shifting, trying to detect any indication of life.

Arriving at the door, he gave the handle an experimental tug. It slid open easily. A thin layer of dust kicked up from the ground with the movement of the door. A rancid smell wafted out of the opening.

Morgan coughed as the stench assailed his senses. He turned toward the others. "Someone's dead in there," he said, meeting first Nayme's and then Bender's eyes. Of the two, the small boy looked to be the more afraid. His eyes were wide, and his mouth hung open.

Morgan took a deep breath, pulled his shirt up over his nose, and slipped inside. He walked into the store and looked around. Behind the front counter, there was a pool of something that may have once been liquid, an unpleasantly bloated-looking hand peeked out from behind it. It must have been the source of the smell, he reasoned.

Morgan carefully averted his eyes and made a mental note to avoid looking behind the counter at all costs. On the front counter, he noticed a blue backpack and moved to pick it up.

He glanced inside, then dumped the contents onto the glass surface; two school books and a spiral-bound notebook. He hefted the pack and made his way up and down the small aisles, gathering water bottles, sealed food items, and a couple of hats. He stuffed everything except the hats into the bag, zipped it up, and slung the now heavy bag over his shoulder.

He glanced at the shelves, taking in the bags of food and wished he had another pack to fill. A sudden cry from outside of the store made the hair on Morgan's neck stand up. He slipped to the door and peeked out.

Nayme and Bender were no longer standing where he'd left them. "Nayme?" he called, sticking his head out the door and looking in both directions. Seeing no one, Morgan slipped out the gas station door and flattened himself against the building. He started for the nearest corner.

"Well, lookie here," a rasping voice said. Morgan spun to see a dirty man running directly toward him. The figure was only a few feet away, and his large fist took a swing at Morgan's head.

Morgan whipped his head back in a practiced move that caused the fist to swing past, missing his face. Barely. He had dropped into a fighting stance automatically, and a corner of his mind began sizing up the opponent. The man was tall and broad, his muscles flexing as he reset his feet and growled.

"Just hold still now," the dirty man sneered. "The captain will want to have a chat."

Morgan's mind raced, his father's voice echoing through memory.

"He's bigger than you, Morgan, stronger. What do you do?" the voice seemed to ask.

Morgan backed away. He had to stay out of the man's grasp. If the big man got a hold of him, the fight would be over. Morgan shifted into a ready position, waiting just out of reach for the big man to make his move. The man bared his teeth and started forward.

Morgan fired a quick front kick, hitting his assailant's left knee just as the man's weight landed on it. He grunted in pain as his knee bowed backward. Morgan spun, his leg extending in an arc that brought it swinging at the back of the man's remaining foot. It connected, and Morgan felt it stop cold. He stumbled as the big man's weight and low center of gravity prevented the sweep from knocking him from his feet.

Wrong move, he realized and cursed.

A thick hand grasped Morgan's neck in an excruciating

grip, and he grimaced in pain as he felt himself being wrenched into the air, his feet scrambling for purchase.

"You little shit," the man said, furious. "I ought to break your pencil neck." Morgan's hand whipped out, forming a wedge shape.

The strike caught the man in the throat just above the Adam's apple. He made a choking sound, and Morgan slipped from his grasp, falling hard on his side on the hard pavement. He groaned and tried to pick himself up as he heard the man's gasping cough.

Morgan tried to scramble away, his eyes focused over his shoulder to where the big man was doubled over, both hands held to his injured throat. Morgan tried to rise and swung his head around. He ran directly into another figure, and he stumbled to his knees. His hand shot out and struck the man in the groin. Stars exploded before his eyes as a boot crashed into the side of his head, and Morgan hit the ground.

Dazed, he tried to rise, but his legs didn't seem to be working correctly.

"Little bastard tried to cheap shot me!" The speaker was tall and lanky with curly brown hair and a scraggly beard. He had tan skin and wore filthy black jeans and a pair of worn leather boots.

There was deep laughter nearby, "What are you worried about Baud, you ain't using it anyway." There were several guffaws and more deep laughter. "That'll be enough now, lad," the laughing man said. Morgan lifted his head, trying to clear his vision. "Fighting a man twice your size takes guts, and I like that. But let's not be foolish."

"Well, I'll be. What's this?" Baud grabbed Morgan's medallion and lifted it into the light.

"Leave it!"

Baud let go of the medallion.

The shorter man looked like a mad cross between Jack Sparrow and John Wayne. His long greasy hair was braided in several places and fell in matted, curly strings. He wore a long brown-leather duster over a billowing linen shirt. He had on a blue waistcoat that looked like it may have been made from an old woman's fancy drapes, and it was buttoned nearly to his neck with intricate brass buttons.

The man had a serviceable-looking samurai sword slung over his shoulder on a baldric that buckled to a belt at the waist of his modern jeans. They clung to his thick thighs and tucked into knee-high bucket boots. The two inches that he gained from the high heels of the boots brought the man's height up to perhaps five foot six. At his waist, he wore a large golden belt buckle with a five-pointed star book-ended by a pair of engraved revolvers. On the star were the words "Mud, Blood, Guts, and Glory."

The man stood staring at Morgan and stroked his thin black beard, which was braided in three places: at the center under his chin and at each corner of his jaw. Suddenly he grinned broadly.

"Well, little fighter," he said enthusiastically. "Welcome to our little crew!" He gestured with open arms. "I'm delighted that the three of you've chosen to join us. Oh, where are my manners? I'm Captain Majesty Capnell, but my men just call me The Captain or Majesty for short."

Morgan quirked an eyebrow and wiped the blood from his nose as the man bowed with a flourish.

Majesty began walking toward the corner of the building. "Let's go," he called as he strode away.

Half a dozen dirty men emerged from behind the store along with Nayme and Bender, who were bound and gagged, two men holding each of them by the arms. Next to them stood a grinning Zach.

"Your little fighter friend here has convinced me not to kill you—yet, you're very lucky." Majesty said, grinning broadly at the other teens. He looked at Zach, then at Morgan, and began to laugh. "Put them on the ship," he said in a commanding tone.

The thin man's leg kicked out, and Morgan saw black.

CHAPTER 14
MAJESTY

Morgan awoke, his body aching, face pressed uncomfortably onto a hard wooden surface where he'd lain for a day and a half. Something sticky and wet was running down his face and into his left eye, which felt swollen and sore. His right eye cracked open. A thin sliver of light shone into the dark wooden box where he was crammed.

The box rattled and bounced jarringly; the soft sound of a breeze and a hum he couldn't identify were the only sounds that reached him. It was hot inside the confined space and sweat ran down his face in rivulets. He lifted his head, and his stomach lurched, a wave of nausea threatening to overtake him. He rested back against his arm, taking deep slow breaths for several minutes before he could raise it without feeling faint.

Uncomfortable, he struggled to roll his body off of his aching shoulder, but the space was too cramped for him to reposition effectively, particularly with his hands and feet bound as they were at the wrists and ankles. He wiggled and shifted until he could angle his body to take advantage of the longest section of the floor and straighten his aching back.

"Hello?" he croaked, his voice coming out gravely and almost unintelligible. He swallowed and tried again. "Anyone?" he rasped louder. There was no response. He looked around the box and through a small crack in the floor he could see black pavement passing by.

"Hello?" he called. A loud thumping knock on the top of the wood above his head served as an answer. He shifted, trying to breathe, anything to distract his mind from the growing swell of panic that was rising in his chest. He closed his eyes, trying to picture himself in a large opening, curled into a ball instead of wedged into an area smaller than a coffin.

Morgan's agony grew as time crept slowly by. Finally, a jarring motion signaled a stop. Morgan's heartbeat faster as he heard distant voices calling to each other. A metallic click sounded next to his ear, and the lid of the box creaked open. Morgan blinked as the bright light of an evening sun shone into his face and the dark outline of a man leered down at him.

"Have a nice ride?" he said and cackled a maniacal laugh that exposed a mouth full of crooked, yellowing teeth. He grabbed Morgan by the hair and yanked, dragging him roughly onto the ground, where he landed painfully on the hard blacktop. He kicked Morgan hard in the stomach, earning a gasp as the air was expelled from his lungs.

A heavy boot stepped roughly on Morgan's face, pressing it into the pavement so hard that Morgan thought his jaw would break. When the boot lifted, Morgan was left moaning in pain.

"Try to punch me in the junk, will ya?" the wiry man whispered in Morgan's ear in an angry voice. The smell of unbrushed teeth and a body unwashed for far too long filled Morgan's nostrils, and he gagged.

"Ought to gut you, you lil' bastard." Baud spat. "Cap'n says I can't do it just yet, but never you mind about that, Baud is patient. I'll gut you yet." He pulled a long, curved knife, the type Morgan had seen fishermen use, from a battered leather sheath on his hip and held it up, licking his lips in anticipation. Morgan gulped, staring at the point of the blade, painfully aware of the exposed skin of his stomach.

"Baud!" The captain's voice boomed from behind him. "Put him in the brig with the others."

Baud looked up, clenching his teeth together, then said in an obsequious voice, "Aye, cap'n." He pulled Morgan roughly up and began dragging him across the pavement. Morgan's feet flailed for purchase as they made their way toward a dilapidated single-story house with faded and chipped paint that may once have been white.

They rounded the old house into an area that was more horse field than a yard. He dragged Morgan to a cinder block building that was dug into the red dirt. Two scruffy-looking men with curved swords stood next to a weathered door. One of the two, recognizing Baud, nodded and unlocked the door with a key retrieved from his pocket.

Baud dragged Morgan to the doorway, where wooden stairs descended to a gloomy darkness lined with spider webs. The guard shoved Morgan through the door, and he crashed face down onto the stairs. Unable to catch himself, he thumped heavily and bounced down several stairs before stopping halfway down, his ribs screaming in pain from the impact.

He tried to turn, sliding further down the stairs as he tried to point his feet downwards.

"Enjoy your stay, young master," Baud intoned with false civility and cackled. The heavy wooden door slammed shut, plunging the area into darkness, a heavy clicking sound accompanying the door's lock. Morgan blinked in the darkness, the few slivers of light penetrating through holes in the ceiling providing scant visibility.

"Morgan? Is that you?" Bender's voice echoed off the walls of the cellar from a dark corner. The boy sounded terrified.

"It's me," Morgan said, his voice coming out in a horse rasp. "But I wish it was someone else." He grimaced and was rewarded with pain from a split in his lower lip from where Baud had punched him. Bender rose and walked over to where Morgan lay. He wore no bonds and set to work untying the ropes at Morgan's wrists.

In a few moments, Morgan was free, and he rubbed his painful wrists, which were now raw and sore from his bonds, in relief. "I guess we should have been more careful," he said.

"Guess so." Bender's voice was glum and despairing "But what I don't understand is, how did we not notice them?"

Morgan shrugged. The thought hadn't occurred to him. "Where's Nayme?" he asked, suddenly seeing only Bender's small frame where he sat in the corner, arms wrapped around his knees.

"I'm here," Nayme said from the other side of a wooden divider. She walked to the corner and looked down at him. She was chained to the wall by the ankle, but Bender had already untied her hands.

"Where are we?" Morgan asked. The details were still fuzzy in his brain, and he was having trouble remembering everything that had happened since he'd entered the gas station.

"A shed of some sort," Bender said. "But for all practical purposes, it's a prison. The pirates locked us in here when they pulled us off the landship."

"Pirates?" Morgan asked, surprised.

"That's what they call themselves, land pirates, and their

leader calls himself the captain. The weird truck things with sails that they ride, they call them landships."

Morgan stared back at the boy incredulously. "Are they insane?" he asked.

Bender shrugged. "Probably. We shouldn't be surprised if people go a bit nuts after all that's happened, with the world ending and all."

There was a click and a rattle, and light rushed into the cellar. A pair of bucket boots thumped down the wooden stairs, and the captain strolled over to where Morgan lay.

"What's your name, fighter?" he asked, peering down at him with a crooked grin.

Morgan didn't answer.

The captain's face quirked. "Boy, it's polite to answer questions directed to one's person," he said, adopting an ironic tone.

Morgan swallowed. "My name is Morgan," he said.

The captain waved his hand dismissively. "I already knew that" he said and stood, looking down at his fingernails. "Your scrumptious little friend over there called out to you, but niceties must be maintained." He leaned against the wall, crossed his arms, and stared down at Morgan in a way that made him feel as though he were on trial.

"Let's get right to it, shall we, Morgan," the captain continued, pausing to look up as he turned the name over, testing the sound of it. "Morgan, Morg, Gan, Gandry, Marty, Marion?" He looked questioningly at the other pirates and shrugged. "Morgan is certainly too cumbersome, sort of formal-like, and Marion is too feminine. I think Morg will have to do," he concluded with a nod.

"Yes, Morg. It has a nice deathly ring to it," he said, waving thick dirty fingers in the air. His face became suddenly hard, and he leaned forward. "Morg, you may be wondering what I want from you, yes?" His eyebrow quirked up questioningly.

Morgan shrugged.

"Yes, of course," the captain continued. "Well, you see, today you have an extraordinary opportunity." The captain stood, making a sweeping gesture and clenching his fist. He grinned broadly and looked down at Morgan with a haughty expression. "Today," he said. "You will have the enviable opportunity of joining our fine crew!" He spread his arms wide. "Congratulations!" he finished jovially.

"You see, I need people, Morg," he said, "and you three are just the kind I'm looking for. Oh, you're untrained all right, but with a little—coaxing, you three will be part of the core of my new army."

"But we're not soldiers," Nayme said.

"True, but you may have noticed that teensy-weensy event"—he raised a hand pointing into the sky— "we have to take what we can get these days." He began to pace. "You see, when that devil of an asteroid plowed into the moon, it destroyed the world as we knew it. What you see now, is just the bones. There's no getting it back now, can't be helped. And of course, all the governments of the world died that day as well. It's chaos, anarchy!" The captain's grin turned wicked. "A perfect place for pirates."

"So, you're going to"—Morgan hesitated, his mind working— "what, steal from people?"

Majesty guffawed. "Boy, the world you knew died under the light of the evil moon. Now anything goes. We're all just picking a living off the bones of the old world, like a bunch of great, bloody vultures."

"But pirates, they get rich off of hurting people," Morgan said.

"I like to think of it as another form of government.

Governments have always hurt people, Morg," the captain said. "Laws, taxes, enforcement"—he counted them off on thick fingers— "they are all just used to control the people, forcing them to live and act a certain way. Now that all of that rubbish is gone, we get to live under our own standards, as it were. The way I look at it, my crew and I here provide a valuable service. Take the little corpse of a town we found you in. It's dead, floor to ceiling dead, no survivors. Nothing to do there but take what you can. Think of what we do in places like that as recycling."

"Recycling?" Nayme blurted, wrenching her head away from the pirate that held her. "That's nonsense."

"Waste not," Majesty said.

"And what about in other towns?" Morgan said. "Towns that are still alive?"

"We love living towns!" Majesty said. "Why, we set up shop in one just a few days ago, a kind of satellite location if you will. Now the people there are protected, safe from all the dangers in the wide world. It's a much bigger world than it once was, you know. Just a month ago you could get on a plane and fly to Europe. Now Europe might as well be on another planet!"

"Take this place, the people here were just hiding out, hoping against hope that they would be safe. That couldn't last forever!" He gestured toward the town. "But fortunately for them, we come along, and now they're," he paused, seeming to consider his words, "under our protection."

"Your protection? They just have to, what?" Morgan asked skeptically, "provide you shelter food, and anything else you want in exchange for your," he made quotations with his fingers, "protection?"

"Exactly! Now you're getting it!"

"But what gives you the right—?"

"Morgan, Morgan, Morgan. There is no such thing as *right*—right is an illusion; there is only might. There have always been people who want nothing more than to tell everyone else how to act, how to live, and when to breathe. Bureaucrats, politicians, or oligarchs"—he waved his hand dismissively—"whatever they choose to call themselves, these pocket Napoleons take it upon themselves to dictate the actions of others with no more inherent authority on the subject than you or I have." He rounded on Morgan and moved close enough to whisper in his ear. "I'm *just* that sort of person, and I've already begun to make my own kingdom."

Morgan stared back at him, horrified by his words.

"Given the time people would create new governments, some towns are likely well on their way to doing just that. But they aren't thinking correctly, they'll go with something like a council or some such nonsense. Those kinds of governments always fail. I'm just making it all simpler for them by skipping that part and going straight to the end of the road, dictatorship." Capnell opened his arms. "And as things go, my oppression is quite minimal. We'll pop into town a few times a year, the people give us a token offering of food, clothing, amiable company, that sort of thing, and then we leave. As long as they don't resist, no one is harmed."

"But you're forcing them—"

"Government *is* force, Morgan. Choosing a government is an exercise in deciding how much oppression you are willing to tolerate. Every government forces, every government dictates what people can or cannot do. I just do my dictating at the end of a cutlass." He drew the sword with a ring. "Well, Samurai sword really, but who's keeping track?"

"Well Morgan, what will it be?" Majesty said.

Morgan spat in his face.

Majesty backhanded him, leaving Morgan's head ringing,

and then wiped Morgan's spit from his face with a handkerchief.

"I can see you need some time to think about my generous offer," Majesty grated then turned. He called back over his shoulder as he headed toward the door, "In the meantime, I'll give you a taste of what will happen should you fail to accept my generosity." He nodded to Baud. "Ten lashes," he said as he sauntered out.

Two burly pirates grabbed Morgan and dragged him from the cellar and into the evening air. Morgan tried to resist, but it was pointless. The pirates dragged him bodily to a nearby telephone pole that stood next to a small stream, shackled his hands to a bolt set above his head, and ripped the stained shirt from his body.

Baud strode over to Morgan and grinned broadly. "I'm going to enjoy this," he said and licked his lips.

"Baud!" Majesty called. "He's got something in his pocket. Bring it to me."

Morgan tried to wrench away as Baud dug the disk from his pocket and carried it to the captain, placing it in his hand. Majesty looked at it and arched an eyebrow as Baud stared back at him.

"What are you waiting for?" he snapped, and Baud shuffled back to where Morgan hung. He produced a long whip and held it where Morgan could see it. He grinned widely and winked before stepping into position, drawing back his arm and swinging.

Crack! The blow landed between his shoulder blades, and Morgan screamed as liquid fire raced across his bare skin. Crack, crack, crack, crack. Morgan collapsed from the pain, his body hanging from the shackles, tears spilling down his face as the remaining lashes fell.

When it was over, the pirates unlocked Morgan's hands,

dragged him a few feet, and let him drop. He tumbled to the ground, where he lay still gasping and sobbing, his body partially submerged in the dirty water of the stream. His arm began to tingle.

"Good, now let's make sure he's ready," the captain said. "Bring the others."

The captain knelt next to Morgan. "Now I can see you're the heroic type," he said. "That's something you're going to have to get over. But in the meantime, I'll make this decision easy for you. You join my little operation here, or your friends will get the same treatment you just had."

The pirates dragged Nayme and Bender to the pole and bound their hands.

"Morgan!" Nayme sobbed as two pirates dragged her to the post. "What did you do to him?"

Baud laughed.

"Come on now, boys. We haven't got all night," Majesty said impatiently. "Final warning, Morg."

Baud walked to the bound teens and tore their shirts from their backs, leaving Nayme in her bra and Bender bare backed. A rough hand grabbed Morgan by the hair and dragged him to his knees. He looked up at his friends' fearful faces as Baud and another burly pirate held whips at the ready.

"S-stop," Morgan gasped. "I'll do it, just don't hurt them."

The captain laughed. "I knew you'd see it my way." He nodded to Baud, who frowned in disappointment.

"But Cap'n—" Baud began.

"Who's the captain here, Baud?" Majesty growled.

Baud swallowed. "You are."

Majesty nodded. "That's right, I am!" He glanced at the bound teens and then to Morgan. "Still, probably best they know what waits for betrayers." He lifted a single finger, and

Baud grinned triumphantly. The whips cracked, and both teens screamed.

The pirate holding Morgan's head pushed it forward, and he fell into the stream. The captain stepped beside him and placed the disk on the ragged agony of the whip marks. There was a tingle on his skin where the disk lay, and through the haze of pain Morgan heard a voice say softly, "Welcome to the crew."

CHAPTER 15
KENICHI

Imogene slid over the side of the raft and splashed into cool water up to her knees. She set her feet and gave the rope a strong tug.

More teens slipped into the water beside her, splashing their way onto the shore as the raft slid across the sand with a scuffing sound, remarkably like a zipper. *Strange,* Imogene reflected, looking up from the raft to the red and gold cliffs that rose on both sides of the river. *Zippers are so two weeks ago.*

It had been less than a month since the object had hit the moon and destroyed, if not the entire world, the portion of it that Imogene had always known. Just a few days since they had found the raft that Morgan and his group had been on, shredded and torn.

She swallowed the lump in her throat as she recalled the stricken look on Fen's face as he'd told Aella about the bodies he'd seen near the torn raft when he returned to the group of teens that had been left to search for missing dry bags. Imogene blinked away the tears that were forming at the corners of her eyes and forced away the unwelcome thoughts of her dead brother. Why had she been so awful to him? He'd been wrong all those years ago, but he was just a child, he couldn't have known that she'd never have another chance to say goodbye to her mother. She took a deep breath and glanced over her shoulder to the far side of the island.

It was a rough spit of land bordered by sandy beaches, small trees, and short grasses. *Scrubby, small, and wind-swept. Like everything in this wasteland.*

Kenichi lay nearby; Imogene's bloody tank top still pressed to the ruin of his face. He grimaced in pain, despite the poultice that Aella had made of local plants she said had medicinal properties.

Names of plants, their uses, and so on had seemed so useless to Imogene prior to the event, but now she wished she knew them. It was the type of knowledge that could mean the difference between eating and going hungry, being healed or dying of infection or disease. Aella, it seemed, knew them all. She was a virtual encyclopedia of survival knowledge.

Encyclopedia. Imogene turned the word over in her mind. She knew what it meant, but she couldn't remember using one in real life.

I bet they'd be useful again. Isolated in the wilderness as they were, the group was entirely dependent on Aella to show them which plants were useful, which were edible, and which would heal a wound—or poison you if you ate it. Imogene sighed and watched as Aella strode toward the middle of the island and began instructing teens where to set up the tents.

We're dependent on her for our lives. For the lives of those that are left, she corrected herself.

They'd lost so many of the group that had embarked on the trek down the river. Imogene considered Aella's strange robes, her long embroidered half-skirt, and her long black hair.

She was beautiful, with high cheekbones, smooth skin, and

shapely lips. But Imogene couldn't banish the image of the woman as she slid among the werewolves dancing with graceful arcs, her glowing sword spraying black blood as it tore through their flesh.

Beautiful and terrible.

If it hadn't been such a large pack, Imogene had no doubt that Aella would have prevailed. But the wolves' timing had been impeccable. They'd attacked when Aella and her charges were at their most vulnerable, strung out, separated into two groups, and distracted. It was almost too perfect, with no sign of them for days and then a highly coordinated attack across multiple locations.

Imogene frowned. If the wolves were this clever, this strategic, did the group have any realistic chance of getting to Encartha? They'd lost three quarters of the group, and they hadn't even made it halfway to the Grand Canyon.

She turned to see Alexa staring back at her, her gaze inscrutable. Imogene forced a half smile, but Alexa just turned and began sliding tent supports into place. Alexa hadn't said a word to her since the attack.

"Hey," Hugo grated. Kira turned her head as she hammered a tent stake into the ground with a rock.

Kira lifted an eyebrow questioningly.

Hugo looked back at her, a single eyebrow arched. "No way," she said.

"I'm telling you, she did," Hugo said, plastering a self-congratulatory grin onto his face.

"Listen," Kira said, shaking her head, "there's no way Aella knew that those wolves were coming."

"How could she not?" Hugo insisted. "Think about it, she has that little imp, who she keeps sending out to look for things. He can come and go as he pleases, here and gone from moment to moment. With him"—he snapped his fingers to indicate the way that gnome would pop into the group and then disappear in a flash— "she had to know what was coming, what was out there."

"He's not an imp!" Imogene said, surprising herself with her sudden anger.

Hugo glared at her. "Ignore the Muppet," he said, sending her a frigid glare. "I'm not saying she set it up. I'm only saying maybe she—you know—*let* it happen. She had to know we couldn't make it, burdened as we were. She just turned her back a bit to get rid of the excess mouths."

Kira shook her head.

"I'm serious," Hugo continued. "I mean think about it, we had too many people, and we were running out of food. She had to lighten the load, make sure the more important ones made it."

Imogene's blood boiled at the insinuation.

"Lightened the load?" Kira said dubiously.

"Yeah, you know, cull some of the herd in order to save the rest. Farmers do it all the time," Hugo continued. "Although she may have done better to get rid of scar face over there!" he said, nodding toward Kenichi.

"We're not cattle," Imogene growled.

"You're not?" Hugo intoned in false shock. "Well, you certainly look like part of a heifer. Now shut up, no one is interested in the opinions of the livestock."

Imogene stood, her fists clenching, face flushed in anger.

"Her head's going to pop," Hugo said, laughing and pointing at her. Imogene gritted her teeth as Hugo walked away laughing.

"He's trying to goad you," Kenichi said calmly and waved her closer. "Ignore him."

"You heard what he just said! He said we should get rid of you, said we were—"

"They're just words, Imogene, and words spoken by a fool should never be heeded. Japanese granite."

Imogene stared back at him in confusion. "What are you talking about?"

"It's a martial principle I learned from my sensei," Kenichi said.

"I don't understand," she said.

"It means, be like a piece of granite. Stone does not get angry when it's insulted."

"Of course not. It's stone," she said dumbfounded.

"Exactly!" Kenichi said. He started to smile, but the pain brought a grimace.

"That doesn't make any sense," she said.

"Yes, it does, what does a stone do if you threaten it?" Kenichi said, looking back at her with his exposed eye.

"Nothing."

"And if you yell at it?"

"Nothing," she said.

"When you insult it?"

Imogene cocked her head to the side, folding her arms over her chest. "How long are we going to go on like this?" she asked, sitting down next to him and pouting.

Kenichi raised a calming hand. "Eventually, the antagonizer gets bored and leaves the stone alone. Be like the stone, Imogene. Do not react to Hugo or his games, and eventually, he will get bored and leave you alone."

Imogene frowned and turned away. "I can't let him get away with being such a jerk."

"It's not your job to make that tool into a good person," Kenichi said sagely. "And you can't prevent his behavior. We just have to put up with him until we make it to Encartha."

"He is a tool," Imogene said sullenly.

Kenichi grinned. "He is not a nice person. But he targets

you to get a reaction." He met her eyes, his face compassionate. "I think it makes him feel powerful, makes him feel better about himself and the situation. The reaction is what he wants from you. Do not play his game."

Imogene nodded thoughtfully. She wasn't sure that she could ignore Hugo's jibes, but Kenichi was right.

"You don't think he's right, do you?" she asked, meeting Kenichi's eye with her own intense gaze. "About Aella, I mean. You don't think—"

"No." Kenichi interrupted, his tone firm. "I don't believe that she knew the wolves were there." His liquid gaze was firm, committed.

"But what about Fen? I mean Hugo is right about him being able to come and go."

Kenichi nodded thoughtfully and looked around the area at the tall, cliff-lined mesas in every direction. "There's a lot of country out here—too much for any one person to watch. Too much even for him." Kenichi pinned her with a stare. "Besides," he continued, "Fen was with us in the rafts the entire time before the attack. Then Aella had him watching the other boat. When exactly was he supposed to be scouting for the wolves?"

Imogene considered this, eventually nodding reluctantly. "What about the food? We don't have much, and we still have a long way to go."

Kenichi nodded. "True," he admitted, "but Aella doesn't strike me as the kind that wouldn't have a plan." Imogene shrugged and sat on a small log near the water's edge.

"But she didn't plan to come this way. She told us that before," she said mulishly.

"When?" Kenichi asked, sounding skeptical.

"At the outpost, remember? She had planned to take us by

bus. But—" She pointed up at the glowing strangeness of the moon that was beginning to crest the eastern horizon.

Kenichi grunted in reply, his brow furrowed.

"How far do you think we've come?" Imogene asked.

He took a deep, considering breath before answering. "It seems like a long way," he said slowly, "but it's hard to tell with the way the river twists and turns." He looked at Imogene and gave a little shrug. "Even if I could say how far we've come with perfect accuracy, I have no idea how far we had to go in the first place."

"True," Imogene conceded. "But I'd feel better knowing we had traveled hundreds of miles and not fifty."

Kenichi grinned. "I see your point," he said. "Let's just assume we've traveled a great distance. It will make us both feel better."

She cocked her head, her eyebrow rising. He just grinned back at her with the uninjured side of his face. She shook her head, unable to resist the grin that tugged at the corners of her own mouth. She pressed her lips together and looked out over the passing water. The pair remained in silence for several minutes while growing affection for the boy and doubt warred for control of Imogene's emotions.

"I don't even remember how long we've been doing this," she said, distantly looking back into Kenichi's dark eyes.

He frowned.

"We get up, we float, we stop for the night, and then we repeat it. Day after day, it's the same."

Kenichi nodded and sat back, his eyes wandering over the landscape as the light in the canyon gradually dimmed. He grimaced in pain.

"Are you OK?" she asked.

"It hurts, but I'll be fine," he said.

"I resented him," Imogene blurted suddenly. "I wanted him gone."

"Who?"

"Morgan."

Kenichi frowned, his thick eyebrows furrowed as she met his gaze.

"We were in a home," she began, a small quaver in her voice betraying her feelings as she continued. "A foster home. It was terrible. No one wants to adopt teenagers," she went on, "especially older boys."

Kenichi nodded knowingly. "I'm aware of the challenge."

"I thought if he was gone," she said, tears stinging her cheeks, "maybe someone would adopt me."

"Wait," Kenichi said, sounding confused. "I thought you had parents. Adoptive ones."

"I did," she said, her voice hollow, "but that was after our mom died and Morgan and I went into the system. We shuffled around from foster home to foster home for two years. Morgan always talked about someday being together, just the two of us. Finding jobs, an apartment, and living on our own. But time passed, and nothing happened. It wore on me, never knowing when we would be moved again. I hated it. Finally, I told my caseworker that Morgan was mean to me and that I wanted to be separated. She agreed to help me find a different place to live. Within a month, they had moved me to another foster home, and I was adopted shortly thereafter." She looked guiltily at Kenichi, willing him to understand.

He swallowed slowly, his uncovered eye a dark impenetrable pool. Hours seemed to pass as her heart pounded uncontrollably in her chest.

"I understand," he said finally.

"You do?" she said hopefully.

He nodded. "I know how I felt when my parents died.

Alone, desperate, aching for someone to come along and make it all better. I think I can see how it might feel if you believed that someone was holding you back from ever having a family again." He paused for a long moment, as though searching for the right words. "It would be hard not to resent that person."

Imogene nodded. "I know it was wrong," she said, her voice starting to steady. "But when I was adopted, I was so happy. I didn't want to think about my old life. About where Morgan—" She paused, swallowing the lump in her throat. "The couple that adopted me was wealthy, kind—" She shook her head fondly. "They gave me the kind of life I had always dreamt of. A big house, an allowance, friends, parties, I was happy." She looked back at the dark water passing silently by. "Then the wolves came, and they killed my foster parents because they were looking for me. I am the reason they're dead too."

Kenichi reached a trembling hand out and laid it gently on her arm, patting it weakly.

"I came home and found them—" She stopped talking, the lump in her throat preventing further words.

For a long time, they sat there, Kenichi's hand lying gently on Imogene's arm as tears ran down her face and dropped silently to the sand.

"I think he forgave you," Kenichi whispered as Imogene looked at the boy's kind face. "I didn't know Morgan well, but you can just tell some people can't hold a proper grudge." He turned a half grin at her. "They just seem to forget it and go on with life. Morgan struck me as that kind of person, the forgiving kind. A genuinely good person. You don't meet people like that very often."

Imogene sat silently, considering the statement. He was right, she knew. She'd said awful things to him, done awful things. He just kept forgiving her, kept trying to be a part of her life.

Imogene was not that kind of person. Morgan had been better than her, no wonder she had resented him. Imogene pictured his face in her mind. If Morgan was really gone, she needed to find a way to remember him, to do justice to his memory.

"Have you had any luck yet?" she asked, trying to sound casual. He glanced back at her.

"With what?"

"You know," she said and waved her hand as if swinging a sword.

He shook his head. "Not since the elk. Only you and that douche bag have had any luck manifesting anything since then." He motioned toward where Hugo and his thugs were sitting in a circle, laughing to themselves.

"I only did it once," Imogene said defensively. "I haven't been able to do it again."

"Still better than me," Kenichi responded.

"True," she agreed. "But still not amazing." She watched the flowing water pass, considering. "I wouldn't know what to do with a sword if I could manifest it anyway," she said glumly. Kenichi cocked an eyebrow.

"Wouldn't you?" he asked skeptically.

"No. Not any idea at all."

"Huh, I thought that maybe you'd taken martial arts before, when you still lived with your brother. He definitely did, and he was very talented."

Imogene frowned. "Really?" she asked.

"Yeah," he said. "His technique was—unique, different from anything I've ever seen—but well-practiced and effective. If I were Hugo, I would have left him alone."

Imogene remembered all the times she'd seen him practicing. "Our father started teaching us when we were very young, but when he was gone, I stopped. I haven't practiced in years. I don't remember much. I was too young. "

"I could teach you," Kenichi offered gently. "What I do is different from what you learned before, but with your past experience you'd take to it quickly."

She looked at him, considering. "Kenichi, I don't think you're in any shape—"

"I'll be giving verbal instructions for now," he said. "When I get a little better, we can practice together. I can also give you some weapons training if you want."

"What kind of weapons training?"

"That depends on the type of weapon you want to use."

She thought for a moment. "Well, I used a spear for hunting, and it worked alright."

He nodded. "True, but I'm not sure you'll be able to find something around here to work for that purpose. We need a stick or something solid for you to practice with."

She frowned, then stood and searched the island, finally returning with a mostly straight stick about three feet long. "Will this work?"

"It will do for a sword, but it's too short for spear work."

"OK, we'll do the sword for now then. Maybe we'll find something better later."

Kenichi nodded and gestured to a flat spot of sand.

"So what do I do?"

"First," he began, "let's start with breathing."

Imogene frowned. "Breathing?"

"That's right. Fighting is as much about breath as it is about muscle, speed, and technique."

Imogene stared at him skeptically.

"Think about it, when you fight, your body produces a lot of adrenaline. Remember when the wolves came?"

"Do I have to?" she said, groaning.

"Not about what happened, but about what your body did."

"I have no idea what my body did. I was too afraid to care."

"There are several things that happen when your adrenaline levels rise," he explained, beginning to tick things off on his fingers. "Your heart starts beating faster, your blood pressure increases, you begin to breathe more heavily, oxygen rushes to your brain, and your pupils dilate. All of this is to help you be able to react more quickly and more powerfully. When these changes occur, your body consumes more oxygen than normal. You must learn to breathe as well as move so you don't get too tired too fast. Understand?"

She nodded.

"Ok, so as we work, pay careful attention to your breathing. We want deep steady breaths as much as possible. Now," he continued, "hold your stick in both hands like this." He mimed using both hands to grip the stick at the base.

She assumed the position.

"Now. Place one foot slightly forward, stand on the balls of your feet, and hold the stick so that it's at roughly eye height of your opponent. Your grip should be looser toward the bottom of your hand, tighter toward the top."

She adjusted her grip.

"Good," he said. "This is position one."

He continued with his explanation, moving slowly through position after position, instructing her on how to stand, how to hold her sword, and naming each new position. After a few minutes, she stopped him.

"What's the point of all these positions?" she asked, her breath coming in deep gasps.

"Breathe deeply," he said.

She rolled her eyes but adjusted her breathing to take in longer, deeper breaths.

"Happy?" she said tartly.

"Yes," he said, satisfied. "You're a natural."

Imogene nodded. "Thanks." She felt a rush of exhilaration build in her. It felt good to move her body, to have something productive to do. Something she could do for the future that didn't involve sitting on a raft as it floated slowly downstream.

"Positions are bases, like in baseball. They give us a safe place to land before moving on. We'll practice each day together when we stop," Kenichi said, "if that's OK with you?"

"Absolutely," she said and took a final swing, envisioning a werewolf in the path of a shining sword as she did so.

"I have to rest," he said.

"OK," Imogene said, frowning.

Kenichi did not look good, he was pale, and his face was sweatier than hers despite his lack of activity. Frowning, she stood and strode over to Aella.

"Aella," she said, "I'm worried about Kenichi."

Aella nodded, glancing over at the boy. "How's his color?" she asked.

"Not good, and he's sweating heavily. I think he's running a fever."

"I was afraid of that," she said, frowning as she took a deep breath. Finally, she sighed, "I was really hoping to avoid this."

"Avoid what?"

"There is an elvenin outpost on an island in Lake Powell. We'll have to take him there."

"Elvenin?"

"They are like a kind of half-elf, half-cat creature. I'm afraid they don't like me much."

Imogene cocked her head. "Why not?"

"It's a long story, but it doesn't matter, we're going to have to go there. It will be dangerous, but if, as I suspect, Kenichi's wounds are becoming infected. We have no choice."

CHAPTER 16
ESCALANTE

"Well, now, you my friend, have a gift for healing." Morgan didn't answer. "Two days after a whipping like that, and already the wounds are closed. You three must be on something good. Your friends healed even faster than you did. Where can I get some?" Stig laughed at his own joke and began applying the salve to Morgan's wounds.

"I swear, ol' Baud had it out for ya. I never saw him whip someone so gleeful like. What did you do? Tell him he reeks?" He chuckled again and leaned down close to where Morgan's head lay on the cot. "He smells like a three-day-old case of ex-human," Stig whispered. "He was a dirty blighter even before the event, he never learned to bathe an appropriate amount. But the bastard is handy in a fight and a genius with a whip, so he has his uses."

Morgan's ears got hot, his blood boiling in anger as he thought of Baud and his whip.

"He's a psychopath," he grated.

Stig laughed heartily. "That he is!" He slapped his leg as he guffawed, tears forming in the corner of his eyes. "Ah, well, it's the world we live in after all. I reckon ya had to be a bit nuts to survive that monstrosity of a planet-killin' meteor."

Stig replaced the bandages on Morgan's back, motioned for him to turn over, and reached his hand out.

"It didn't hit the planet."

"And I'm right happy about that!" Stig stood up, straightened, and saluted the sky. "Time ya got outta that bloody cot now, boy!" Morgan shifted gingerly to a seated position and took Stig's hand. He gritted his teeth in pain as Stig helped him to his feet. "Cap'n's bloody right, Morg. You're a bastard of a tough'n, no doubt. You'll be sittin' at the cap's side in no time at all. Probably why Baud doesn't like ya none. He figures that's his rightful spot."

"He's welcome to it," Morgan said.

"That's no way to see things Morg. Not many outfits to choose from these days."

Morgan gritted his teeth and wobbled as he got to his feet. He nodded at Stig's questioning look to indicate he was OK. Stig had been assigned to care for Morgan and had been tending to his wounds twice a day. The man was handsome with long blonde hair that he kept in a ponytail, a medium build, green eyes, and a faint accent that Morgan thought might be South African.

"Let's get going." Stig said.

"Where?" Morgan asked apprehensively. The pirates had traveled to a new city each morning, stopping in Loa, Bicknell, and Boulder consecutively to search for supplies and survivors.

"Home," the pirate said.

Stig led Morgan out of the old house. The pirates had spent the last two days in abandoned houses along the road that they seemed to have used on more than one occasion.

In the streets were three of what the pirates called landships, a contraption that had many of the characteristics of a boat, including several sets of sails, a wooden deck, a hold, and a bow-shaped front, all of which were supported on a diesel frame.

Three land-ships were parked outside, and pirates were loading them. Bender and Nayme each sat on a different ship. Morgan met Nayme's eyes. She returned Morgan's look, and he thought he could see fear in her eyes. He wondered if she knew where they were headed.

Stig motioned Morgan toward the middle ship, so he walked up the lowered gangplank. He made his way to the front and sat cross-legged on the deck, his head leaning forward as they pulled out of town, pushed by a sudden breeze that rose up behind them at almost the exact instant that the captain settled himself in his chair.

Morgan glared at Zach, who was on the lead ship talking and laughing with Baud, the pirate that had laid open Morgan's back with the whip.

They headed south on the highway and wound through the desert town lined by rocky red plateaus and then into a desert wasteland characterized by scrubby trees and sparse yellow grasses.

In the afternoon Morgan sat forward on the bow trying to see the small town as the ships rolled forward toward Escalante, Utah.

"You're gonna love it here," Stig said. Morgan glanced around and saw Nayme sitting with Marcus, a black-haired pirate about twenty years old. She laughed at something he said, and her hand landed on his arm. Morgan stared at her thin fingers resting on the pirate's muscled appendage.

The ships rolled into the small town with its spread-out buildings. "I know it's not much today, at least as far as the old world went," Stig continued, "but we're gonna make it the wonder of the new world!"

"How are you going to do that?" Morgan asked skeptically. "Looks like just a crappy small desert town."

"Well it is a crappy small desert town," Stig said, grinning. "You gotta have vision, my boy. Just imagine a water tower, a couple of hotels, a few bars—" He glanced back at Morgan. "I mean, how grand does it really need to be when every other city is in ruins?"

Morgan smirked. He had to admit that he liked Stig. The man was friendly, funny, and outwardly kind. It was odd that he had become a pirate, though it seemed that *pirate* was perhaps the wrong word for the group. They were more like scavengers and scoundrels than pirates.

Morgan's gaze was drawn back to where Nayme talked with Marcus. She was looking up at him, biting the corner of her lip while he said something.

"What's it like?" Morgan asked, wrenching his attention away from Nayme and focusing it forcefully on Stig. "I mean you've been a pirate for longer than us"

Stig looked around at the small town and shrugged. "A lot like things were before," he said. "Some of the pirates lived here before the moon. I'm one of the few new faces like you, but I've known Everett and Marcus most of my life. According to the others, Baud and the captain showed up here a couple of months before the event. Eckerd and his friends from town here took a liking to them, and next thing you know, this is the site for the capital of whatever we end up calling ourselves."

"The interesting thing," he said, whispering conspiratorially. "Is this: how did the captain know about the event beforehand?"

Morgan frowned. "What do you mean?" he said.

"Well, according to Eckerd, when the captain showed up

here before everything with the moon went down, he told them it was going to happen. Started talking about an event happening and told them about these ships of his. He'd already built one of them. I would have thought Majesty was nuts."

Morgan grinned at him. "I wouldn't have blamed you."

Stig nodded. "I'm sure," he said. "The thing was, he was right. Somehow, he knew what was coming. It sounds crazy, but I'll be damned if he wasn't right. By the time it happened, he and his guys had already built two more ships. We're working on more, of course. We'll need them eventually, as we get new members, but we had a huge jump on things compared to other places."

Morgan searched the man's affable face and shrugged. "I suppose you did," he said.

Stig patted him on the back again. "You and your friends are going to love it here."

"What about Zach?" Morgan asked.

Stig shrugged. "I mean, even a douche like him is going to like it here, and if he don't, we'll just send him packing."

Morgan laughed, glancing back at the ship Zach was riding with Baud and a few of the other pirates. Zach seemed to be fitting in very well with the pirates—too well for Morgan's taste.

The ships pulled off the road into the parking lot of a brick elementary school, and the wind abruptly stopped blowing. Morgan wondered again about the wind—it didn't make any sense. The pirates had attributed it to the captain's luck, which was famous among them, but there had to be a better explanation.

"Right this way," Stig said. "I'll show you to your quarters."

Morgan climbed down the gangplank, and they strode to the boat where Nayme and Bender stood. Stig bowed dramatically to Nayme, who bit her lip. He held out his hand, and she took it, using it for support as she climbed down the plank. The group set off toward the school, passing the captain who was talking to an overweight woman who had scurried out of the school as soon as they had arrived.

"Morg, I don't remember where you said you were from," Stig said.

"Philly originally, but I lived in Vernal before the event," he said.

"Ahh, so you're used to crappy desert towns!" Stig said.

"You have a point," Morgan said and patted Bender on the back. "Not like Bender here. He's from Oregon. Bend, Oregon, which is why we call him Bender."

"Well, Bender, I'm afraid you're going to have to get used to crappy desert towns like Morgan and I are," Stig said.

"I like desert towns fine!" Bender exulted. "I never did like humidity."

"Well, wait till it's a hundred and twenty and see what you think then!" Stig said.

Bender stopped and blinked at him. "Does it really— I mean, is it that hot here?" he stuttered.

"Yes sir!" Stig said. "That fair skin of yours is gonna be redder than yonder cliffs." He pointed to a bright red section of cliffs in the distance.

Bender gulped audibly, and Morgan repressed a grin as they entered the school. Stig held the door for Nayme and then led them down a hall, showing them dorm rooms that had been set up in the classrooms—several for the men and only three for the women, who were the minority among the pirates.

"Nayme, this is Haley," Stig said, motioning to a blond woman who was folding a pair of shorts.

She nodded to Nayme. "Nice to meet you."

Nayme grinned and looked back to Morgan, her eyes wide.

"Don't worry," Stig said, laughing. "I'll bring them back to you."

Nayme bit her lip, her face turning red. "Am I that obvious?" she asked.

"It's alright," Stig said. "I get it. You don't know us well, and the world is crazy these days." He shrugged. "But trust me, you're safe here, and so are your friends."

Morgan gave her an approving nod. "We won't be far," he said, hoping to reassure her. She turned slowly and headed into the dorm room.

Stig motioned for Morgan and Bender to follow, turned on his heel, and strode down the hallway passing by a group of metal lockers. "We're in here," he said, indicating a room on the right not far from where they'd left Nayme. "You can pick any bunk ya like, leastwise any that don't have stuff on em. That one's mine," he said, pointing to a bunk near the back corner of the room where sunlight shone in through the window.

The boys selected two bunks near Stig's and set their packs down on them.

"So, how do you keep busy all day when you're not out pillaging?" Morgan said, feeling a bit sarcastic.

"Oh you know, the usual," Stig said. "Compete in drinking and arm-wrestling contests, eat raw meat off the bone, deprive virgins of their virtue— Just what you'd expect from a horde of bloodthirsty near savages. Obviously."

Bender snickered, and Morgan couldn't help but grin. "Obviously," he said.

"I'm afraid we do chores mostly," Stig said seriously. "I wouldn't have thought about it before, but this place requires a fair amount of upkeep. We're doing a lot of gathering of supplies and food right now."

"That's what we were doing when we ran into you actually.

Some of the smaller towns have very few people, if any, left in them. Others have had very few casualties. The toll seems to vary greatly from place to place."

"Why is that?" Bender asked. "I mean why would one town be hit very hard while others are not? Presumably, everyone was exposed to the same thing."

"Don't know," Stig said. "Seems random. Green River was more or less a complete loss while other towns were nearly untouched."

Bender frowned, considering.

"What I don't understand is what caused people to die in the first place?" Morgan wondered aloud.

"Don't know that either," Stig said. "Captain seems to think it was something to do with some type of energy that was released by the impact."

"Energy?" Bender asked. "What kind of energy?"

Stig shrugged. "Whatever kind of energy that makes the moon crackle and glow like there's a giant lightning storm on its surface, I guess. Honestly, you're asking the wrong guy. I just work here." He winked at the boy. "As I said, Captain seems to know more about this stuff than I do. You can ask him if you want, but I don't think anyone knows for sure."

Bender nodded thoughtfully.

"In any case," Stig continued, "right now we're just trying to build enough of a supply of the things we'll need to get through the winter, spring, and summer. We're going to have to figure out how to make a living in the desert, now that the modern world isn't around to provide things like food and medicine. We can't count on a weekly shipment of stuff anymore."

Morgan frowned. He'd thought about the problem of food a lot on their trip down the river—but only in the context of getting to Encartha. He hadn't considered how survivors in the wider world would feed and clothe themselves, living in the husk of the old world."

"Surviving in this new world is going to be tough," Stig said. "At the end of the day it's going to require unified communities in order to make it happen. That's why I stick with the pirates."

Morgan quirked an eyebrow at the odd statement. "You're talking about stable, unified communities, and *that's* your basis for staying with the pirates?"

"Captain may seem nuts with his little pirate fascination, but he's smart. He has all kinds of plans for how to make sure as many people as possible survive, and he's good at bringing people together. He talks a big game alright, but he's been bringing in most of the people we find, adding them to our numbers, working to build a community—more than a community actually—a network of communities, all supporting each other. I've said it before, but this is probably the safest place to be these days."

Heard that before, Morgan thought to himself. How many places out there would be making that same claim in the coming months and years? With so many fewer people in the world, people had gone from being a commodity to a very valuable asset. And on top of that, they were likely scared. Safety would be a huge selling point for those looking to find some stability in their lives.

"Getting near time for grub," Stig said. "What say we go get some food?"

Bender nodded vigorously. The boy had slimmed down considerably during their trek south.

They retraced their path toward the girls' dorm, arriving just as Nayme strode out the door.

"Perfect timing," Stig said. "We were going to grab some food, you interested?"

"Sure," Nayme said and fell into line as they walked down a series of hallways until they arrived at the school's cafeteria.

"How much of the population of the town lives here in the school?" Bender asked as they filled their plates from a series of warming trays that had been set up.

Stig served himself a helping of potatoes. "About fifty," he said. "There are others in town, probably two or three hundred in total. But then this wasn't a big town even before the event."

"Stig!" a deep voice called from behind. Morgan turned to see Marcus standing in the doorway. The man beckoned to Stig with a gesture. Stig stood.

"Be back in a jiffy," he said and started across the room. After a whispered conversation that Morgan couldn't make out, Stig returned and raised a single finger. "Before I go, I should tell you."

"Yeah?" Bender said.

"I've got you all jobs."

"What kind of jobs?" Morgan said.

"The scouting kind," Stig said, grinning. "Well, for you at least, Morg. Got a couple of ideas for the others."

"Like Boy Scouts?" Morgan said, confused.

"Like lookout scout," Stig said.

Morgan frowned. "I don't know much about scouting," he admitted.

"That's alright. I'll show you the ropes. Right now, I gotta run so we'll have to talk later." The pirate stood and walked away, leaving the three teens sitting alone at a table.

"Well?" Morgan said.

Nayme shook her head. "Everyone seems so friendly," she said. "The women in the dorms were nice. Everything seemed great."

"Same here," Bender said, taking a large bite of fried

chicken. "I think we could actually be OK here," he finished through a mouth full of food.

"They whipped us, Bender." Nayme said incredulously.

"That was an initiation. I don't think they'll do it again. Unless we do something drastic, that is."

Morgan looked at the boy, considering. *Imogene may still be out there.* He looked at Nayme. *Could Nayme and Bender be safe here?*

"There's something wrong, Morgan," Nayme whispered suddenly, leaning in conspiratorially.

"What do you mean?" he said.

"When I was in the women's dorm, I heard something. Something I wasn't supposed to hear."

"Like what?" Bender said, taking another bite.

"It was small, just a fragment of a conversation really," she said.

"Go on," Bender said.

Morgan nodded encouragingly.

"Well," she began, glancing around to make sure no one was listening. The cafeteria was empty except for the cook, a huge, muscular man with a large belly, who was in the kitchen area washing a large pot. "Haley, the pirate woman, walked away for a few moments, and I had chosen a bed near the door. You know, in case I needed to get out quickly."

Morgan frowned. He hadn't thought of that.

"Well, I was pulling a few things out of my pack since they have a little set of drawers there. The kind that they use for files, you know the ones I'm talking about?"

"What did you hear, Nayme?" Morgan said, feeling impatient.

"I'm getting to it," she said. "Now where was I?"

"The drawers," Bender put in.

"Ah yes," I was putting my things into the drawers, not that

I have much, just a few things really. I've never had less, to tell you the truth. My family's never been wealthy, but we always—"

"Nayme," Morgan said, "stay on topic."

"I am on the topic," she said, glaring at him.

"No, you're not, you keep veering off onto tangents."

"You're not helping, Morgan," Bender said. "Just let her tell it her way."

"Thank you, Bender," Nayme said, giving Morgan a triumphant look down her nose. "There was someone outside talking in a loud whisper. That's why I noticed. If they'd been talking normally, I probably wouldn't have paid any attention, but they were trying to talk softly, and for whatever reason, the sound was carrying, you know like a stage whisper would—"

"Nayme," Morgan said, exasperated.

She lifted a bony finger in warning. "Someone is missing," she blurted, then glanced around, her face turning red.

Morgan glanced at the cook. He was still washing the pot and didn't turn. Morgan released the breath he hadn't realized he'd been holding.

"It sounded like whoever it was is important," Nayme continued. "And there's more."

Morgan looked at her expectantly, waiting for her to go on while Bender masticated, attention riveted on Nayme.

"It sounded to me like there were others. Several people have gone missing in just the last little while. I think there could be trouble." She looked from Morgan to Bender and then back.

Morgan frowned. "There are plenty of reasons that someone could go missing," he said carefully.

"For instance?" she said.

"Maybe they got lost, or maybe they just didn't like it here."

"Maybe they lost a bet and didn't want to pay up," Bender added. Morgan looked at the boy quizzically.

She frowned. "Maybe," she said doubtfully.

"You're right about one thing," Morgan said. "We should be careful. We don't know these people. They seem nice, but they also call themselves pirates. We should be sure they're worthy of our trust before we give it to them."

"How do we do that?" Bender said.

"I don't know," Morgan said. "I guess we just try to be cautious and reserved and take nothing for granted until they prove to us that they're worthy of our trust. We'll keep our eyes open and look for signs of trouble. If we see something that doesn't seem right, we'll get our stuff and get out of here." He looked from Bender to Nayme. "Agreed?"

"Agreed," they said in unison.

CHAPTER 17
LOOKOUT

"How's the library?" Morgan asked, taking a bite of breakfast. Nayme sat across from him picking at her own breakfast with an air of disinterest. Bender was chewing happily on a combination of toast and eggs, his cheeks bulging exaggeratedly.

"Great," Bender said. "I've always enjoyed books, and the pirates are bringing them in by the dozens from libraries all around the area. It feels good to be doing something useful, something more normal."

"I think it's perfect for you," Nayme said. "Wish I could say the same."

"What's wrong with what you're doing?" Bender said.

"I'm learning how to sew," Nayme said, her eyes narrowed dangerously. "I hate it. Next thing you know they'll have us wearing corsets."

"Why would they have you wear corsets?" Bender asked.

Nayme glared at him. "Why are they making the women do the sewing, the cleaning—"

"Cook's a man," Bender said, "so you don't have to do that."

"That's for our safety," Morgan said, grinning.

Nayme rolled her eyes. "You should be so lucky for me to cook for you."

"Lucky to be alive?" Bender said.

Morgan laughed and extended his fist, Bender bumped it.

"You're the worst," Nayme said.

Morgan winked playfully at her, grinning impishly. She shook her head ruefully, an involuntary smile quirking the corner of her lips.

"What about the other thing?" Morgan asked. "Anything?" He took a bite of eggs.

"I habmt herb anbythmg," Bender said around cheeks full of food.

"Don't choke, Bender," Morgan said. "What about you, Nayme?"

She frowned and shook her head. "I shouldn't be upset about this. It's good that I haven't noticed anything and everything they've told us seems to check out. But I can't help but feel—not disappointed but"—she paused, thinking— "like we're missing something. Something important."

Morgan looked at Nayme, trying to read her expression. "Do you think that there is something we're missing, or do you only wish there was?" he asked.

She exhaled deeply and moved the food around her plate with her fork for a long moment before answering. "I guess I wish there was," she admitted.

"Why do you wish there was?" he asked. "I mean, this is the safest we've been since the event."

She shook her head and frowned. "I'm not sure."

"Do you feel safe here?" Morgan pressed.

She thought about the question in silence. "Yes," she said at last. "I think I do, as safe as I can be. But I'm not sure that I'll ever really feel safe again, at least not for a very long time. Those wolves, they took something from me that I'm not sure I'll ever get back."

"What did they take?" Bender asked, concerned.

She frowned, thinking deeply and trying to formulate her thoughts. "I never used to wonder if I was safe. I just knew I was. It probably wasn't true even back then, but the point is that I believed it, I felt like I was invulnerable. Before, when bad things happened, they happened to someone else. There was always a distance—it happened to a friend, to a relative, or to someone other than me. That may sound silly, but I'd never actually considered the fact that I could be injured or killed."

She paused; her green eyes locked with his. "But when that wolf cut off our path to the raft, I realized I could die, really die. I could *smell* it. The stink of it. It was one of the worst things I'd ever smelled."

Her eyes drifted, looking into another time and place. "Those claws slashing, teeth snapping." She fixed Morgan with a steady gaze. "I thought I was going to die."

Morgan nodded, understanding. He remembered that moment. He'd frozen, staring in wonder as the wolf ran at Sarah.

"I saw that wolf bite down on Sarah's neck." Nayme shook her head as tears formed in the corner of her eyes.

"I'm sorry," Morgan said.

"It's not your fault," she said, sniffling. "I need to stop being such a baby." She wiped at her eye with the knuckle of her left hand.

Morgan sat feeling pain in his chest, unsure what to say.

"We all feel that way," Bender said, taking hold of one of

her hands. "This life, this world we're all in; it's a hard world full of violence and uncertainty. It's hard for all of us."

Nayme nodded. "Thank you," she said. "It's good to know —" She paused. "It's just good to have friends." She reached out her hand toward Morgan, and he took it, feeling the warmth of her soft skin.

"I think that we're safe here," Bender said, his face taking on an almost determined set. "As safe as we can be. We have our medallions, so the wolves won't be able to track us. After the ride on the ships, they won't have a clue where to find us."

"Neither will the Encarthans," Nayme said thoughtfully.

Morgan frowned. *Neither will Imogene, if she's still alive.*

His mind drifted to the group that had gone with Aella. Imogene had been with them when Morgan's group had been attacked. She would be safe.

"How far do you think they've gotten?" Morgan blurted suddenly. "The others, I mean. Assuming they're still alive, how far do you think they've travelled?"

Bender frowned, and Nayme looked thoughtful.

"I'm not super familiar with the geography, but I do know that when John Wesley Powell made the journey it took him about four months to get to the bottom of the Grand Canyon. He was exploring though—not being chased by werewolves. They probably stopped frequently and explored some of the side canyons and things. But if I were to guess, I'd say that it would probably take at least a month to get to Encartha, depending on where in the canyon the city is located. Assuming that there actually is an Encartha in the first place!"

"We were on the river for what? A week and a half, two weeks or so?" Morgan asked, beginning to feel excited.

"Yeah, about that," Nayme said cautiously.

"And we've been here for a week," he continued, "plus the two days that we were on the ships and the days walking to

Green River." He paused, rubbing his chin. "I need a map." He met Nayme's eyes. "I'll be right back," he said, rising and jogging out of the cafeteria.

"Where are you going?" Nayme called out to him as he ran.

"I'll be right back," he called back and burst out a side door and onto the pavement. He jogged across the street to a convenience store the pirates had turned into a kind of hub for goods. Everything that was brought into the town via the ships would be brought there first, cataloged, and distributed to the various members of the crew or to a longer-term storage facility.

Morgan burst through the front door to see Marcus sitting on a chair behind the counter.

"Hey Morg," Marcus said. "What's up?"

Morgan nodded, and he looked around. The store was full of boxes of goods, which were stacked high in each of the aisles. He turned back to the front of the store, his eyes searching. Finally, he located a stand where some paper maps sat. He strode over to the rack. "Can I take one of these?" he asked.

"Sure," Marcus said. "Are you planning on doing some sightseeing?"

Morgan chuckled. "Just curious about this place. Thanks," he said, pulling out a map of Utah and opening it on the counter. He smoothed it flat and began searching the middle part of the state, his fingers roving until he found the small town of Escalante. Then he found Green River and Vernal. He compared the distance. He looked at the distance between the two and compared it to the distance from Green River to Escalante and from there to Lake Powell.

His mind raced. The others could have already reached Lake Powell. It was hard to tell with all the winding the river did. But the current would be slower once Aella's group got to the lake. They would go slower, and they'd probably have to row their way. He stared at the size of the lake and the distance from Escalante to the northern shore. He bit his lip. *Could I make it?* He wondered. Would it be possible to make it to the short of the lake by the time the others arrived there?

"Are you finding what you need?" Marcus asked in a friendly tone.

Morgan looked up. "I think so. Thank you, Marcus!" he said and folded up the map. He jogged out of the store and back to the cafeteria. His mind was racing as he returned to his seat.

"Well?" Nayme said expectantly.

Morgan paused. "Nothing," he said.

She leaned back in her chair, crossing her arms. Morgan looked away and took a bite of food.

"Really?" she said. "Nothing? Nothing at all? I thought we were friends."

"We are friends," he said between bites.

"Friends who hide things?"

He looked back at her, trying not to show the guilt that his deception had settled into his chest. "I was just wondering about something."

"What?"

He looked from Nayme to Bender, who shrugged.

"I just wanted to know how far the Grand Canyon was," he said.

She shook her head slowly. "And?"

"Far," he said.

"How far?"

"Far enough."

"For what?" she insisted.

"For it to take a long time to get there from here."

"Is that what you wanted to know?"

Gathering himself he set his expression. "Yeah," he said coolly. Her gaze burned into him but he held his ground.

"Fine," she said. "Don't tell me."

Morgan shrugged.

"Whatever you're planning, we'd help you know?"

He nodded. "We're good, Nay," he said.

"Save the pet names for people you're honest with," she said and stood, grabbing her tray and striding away. Morgan stared at her back as she emptied the tray and left the cafeteria through the nearest door.

"What's up with her?" Bender asked, staring back at where she'd disappeared.

"You can never tell with girls," Morgan said. The two returned to their breakfasts, eating alone with their thoughts as Morgan's eyes kept finding their way to the door that Nayme had left through.

"Ready, Morg?" Stig said from behind him. Morgan turned to take in the blond pirate's smiling face.

"Yeah," Morgan said, standing and nodding goodbye to Bender. "Later, Bend."

Bender nodded as Morgan slid from the chair and followed Stig toward the door. Stig led him across the street to the gas station. Morgan nodded to Marcus as the two entered.

"Got your stuff right there," Marcus supplied, pointing toward two heavily packed overnight camp bags.

"Thanks, Marcus," Stig said as he and Morgan hefted the bags and strode back into the sunlight.

The two headed out from town following the pattern that Stig had used the first day the scouted, first to both of the two outlook stations on the north side of town to deliver supplies to the lookouts that watched the comings and goings of the towns. It was nearly dark when the two approached the third, southern lookout post.

"What do they do in the dark?" Morgan wondered aloud as the two hiked up a steep rise toward the small, hastily constructed, wooden building that sat overlooking the city. They had been up to the lookout point a few times during the day but tonight would be his first night on duty.

"Who?" Stig asked, pausing to look back at Morgan.

"The lookouts. What do they do when it gets dark? I mean, they can't really look out for, well, whatever they look out for in the dark, can they?"

Stig smiled. "It's a real problem," he said, agreeing. "We're trying to get a hold of night vision goggles. We have a couple pairs—they have them back at the north tower—but they are unreliable. Sometimes they work, other times they don't. Anyways we need some for down here. Luckily there's just desert south of here. It is unlikely that anyone will come from that way."

Morgan grunted, looking out over a road that ran south from the town and into the distance. "What about the road?" he said, nodding in its direction.

Stig glanced over and nodded. "Runs a while and jogs east then south where it turns to dirt. Not a lot of traffic comes that way, not even before the event. We watch it best we can, just on principle, but like I say, mostly just desert that way for miles and miles. The closest thing is Lake Powell, and it's about fifty miles that way." He pointed off the southeast.

Morgan stared. *Fifty miles. That's a long way alone on foot through the desert.* He sighed.

"Any water out that way? Short of the lake I mean?"

Stig shrugged. "Doubt it," he said. "I've never explored much farther than the ridge line here. But with names like Death Ridge and Carcass Canyon doesn't inspire a lot of optimism." He chuckled to himself and began moving toward the lookout position.

Morgan frowned and pulled the water hose attached to the shoulder of his pack to his mouth and took a sip. The water, stored inside the pack and sheltered close to his body, was still cool, despite their long march across the valley. *How far could I get with the water in the bag?* he wondered. *Fifty miles on foot, in the heat of the desert. I need at least one more, probably two or three.*

"Where the hell is Eckerd?" Stig said, looking around as the two neared a small tower. Built of timbers and plywood, the tower was fifteen feet tall with a small room on the ground floor and a ladder that led to a loft for looking out over the valley. It looked abandoned. Morgan walked to the structure and looked around. The door hung open, and the scattered contents of a backpack lay strewn as though someone had hastily unpacked it by throwing things in every direction.

Stig looked at Morgan. His normally calm face was troubled.

"Where could he have gone?" Morgan said.

Stig looked around, rubbing his chin. Finally, he sighed. "Probably three sheets to it down in Basher's Pub," he said. "Damn drunk."

Morgan nodded. "What do we do?" he said.

Stig frowned. "Hate to ask this, Morg," he said. "But can I trust you to cover the watch alone? I'll head down and talk to the captain, find out where Eckerd went, and send someone up to take over for you at first light."

Morgan swallowed and looked around. "I've never done a watch," he began. "I don't even know the signals."

"Night signals are easy," Stig said, handing Morgan a flashlight. "Signal every hour, north tower goes first, followed by the west, south is last. Just watch for the other towers to signal and then follow their lead. Two quick flashes for trouble, three long flashes for all clear. Can you remember that?"

Morgan nodded.

"Then you'll do it?" Stig asked.

"Yeah," Morgan said hesitantly. "I'll do it."

Stig sighed in relief and patted Morgan on the shoulder. "Thank you!" he said. "You're the best! I'll make sure you get your duty off tomorrow."

Morgan nodded, his mind racing. "Stig," he said, "can I ask you a question?"

Stig frowned and cocked his head. "Sure, Morg, anything."

Morgan swallowed. "The others, Nayme and Bender—they're safe here, aren't they?"

Stig smiled. "Safe as a pig in California," he said.

Morgan looked back at him frowning.

"Lots of vegans in California, vegetarians too," Stig said, grinning. "If I were a pig, that's where I'd want to be."

"I'm serious, Stig," Morgan said firmly.

"So am I, Morgan," Stig said, his tone serious. "Nowhere is safe, not like it was before the event. But this is as safe as anywhere—."

"But if something happened to me, if I were killed or gone, would they be safe here with your crew?" Morgan blurted, interrupting.

Stig looked taken back, blinking back at Morgan in silence for a long while. "Nothing's going to happen to you up here, Morg, but even if it did, your friends would be safe with us. They're part of the crew. We need all types here, and to tell you the truth, they're both great. Bender doesn't talk much, but he's smart, smart as anyone I've ever known. A bit booky maybe, but smart. And Nayme—she genuinely cares about people, even pirates. You're lucky to have such good friends."

Morgan nodded thoughtfully. "Thanks, Stig," he said.

"It's just one night Morgan, and almost nothing ever happens up here. You'll see." Stig patted him on the shoulder then turned to leave. "We'll see you safe in the morning," he called back over his shoulder.

"Thanks, Stig," Morgan called as the older man tramped

down the trail toward the valley. When he was out of sight, Morgan sat his pack down and looked around. He wandered over to the small room and sticking his head inside. After a few moments, he retrieved an object and exited. He wandered over to the discarded pack that lay nearby and began pulling things out of it. He rummaged a few moments before finding what he was looking for and pulling it free. He held up the two jugs of water. He smiled and carried them over to his own pack and slipped them inside.

Three jugs of water should be enough. At least he hoped it would be.

CHAPTER 18
THE CITY IN THE LAKE

Imogene felt Kenichi's head for the fifth time in an hour. In the five days since the attack, his condition had continued to deteriorate, culminating in the early hours of the previous evening when the boy had collapsed and nearly fallen into the river. Now his fever was spiking and he'd begun to moan and speak in gibberish.

"How far is it?" Imogene repeated. She could hear the tension in her own voice, but she couldn't help it.

"You've asked five times in the last hour," Hugo said in irritation.

"I'm not asking *you*," Imogene said. "I'm asking her." She pointed toward where Aella sat in the back of the boat.

"In a boat this size, you're asking everyone," he said, "especially if the person you're talking to is in the *front* of the boat."

"Leave her alone," Alexa said. "She's got just as much right to speak as you do."

Hugo started to stand, making the boat begin to rock.

"All is be's sitting in ta raft!" Fen called from behind them where he sat steering the small craft.

Hugo sneered and sat back down.

Alexa met Imogene's eyes and made a face, her eyes crossing, her tongue sticking out. Imogene couldn't help but grin a little. The smile faded as she looked down at Kenichi, who slept silently at the bottom of the raft. The wounds on the left side of his face were angry and red with large scabbing sections that wept a greenish puss and had to be cleaned frequently. Imogene carefully dabbed the side of a gash with a piece of her sacrificed tank top.

"How's he doing?" Kira asked hesitantly as she gazed down at the livid stripes across the boy's face.

"I don't know," Imogene said. "The wounds are hardly weeping at all now, and his fever has come down some, but the red areas around the wounds are getting worse, more streaked. I don't know what it means."

"Good," Kira said, obviously trying to sound upbeat. "He looks—" She hesitated, searching for the right word and unable to find it.

"He's a fighter," Imogene said. "Whatever Fen did, it helped." She pointed at a long wide wound that began near the corner of his jaw and ended on his nose directly between both eyes. "This one was the worst," she said. "It nearly took his eye, see." She pointed to where the skin-walker's claw had sliced through his cheek, scoring the bone and passing through the upper section of his nose just below the eyebrow. "He's lucky."

Kira nodded and patted her on the back. "How are you holding up?" she asked, her concern evident.

"I'm OK," Imogene said.

"Well, let me know if you need anything," Kira continued. "I mean that." A touch of a smile met the corner of Imogene's mouth as Kira patted her hand.

"Thank you, Kira. I really appreciate it."

Kira nodded, and silence fell between them.

"I guess we should start rowing?" Alexa said, picking up a paddle from the bottom of the raft. "We've run out of current."

"It would take us weeks to row the length of the lake," Aella said. "Fen, if you would."

"Aye, mistress. Fen is happies to be's helping," he said, nodding so vigorously that both his eyebrows and ears flopped up and down like a pair of birds trying to take off. The little gnome picked up a stick he'd gathered from the edge of the river the previous day and set it carefully in front of him. The little gnome closed his eyes.

"Are we praying to sticks now?" Hugo said.

Aella shushed him angrily from the back of the boat, and he rolled his eyes.

Fen's eyes opened, and he raised his hands and began to gesture over the piece of wood, his hands moving in a complicated pattern that reminded Imogene of a conductor bending over a stack of sheet music. When he'd finished, one end of the stick had begun to glow with a greenish-yellow light. He sat back against the rear of the raft, braced himself, and stuck the stick into the water. Around the submerged portion, the glow began to spread, forming first around the stick and then extending to the raft. From there it spread out to form a rough circle surrounding the craft.

Imogene felt a hum in the air, and the water started to move. The boat jerked, propelled by a sudden current in the water that pushed the raft forward.

"How did you do that?" Kira asked, her mouth gaping.

"Fen is not the doings," the imp said. "Fen is only doin' ta askin'. Is Spring Queen who is the doing," he finished.

Kira looked at Imogene and shrugged.

The Spring Queen again, is it?

They sped across the lake at an unnatural pace, bouncing

over the water like a small flexible speedboat, propelled by the current of glowing water. Fen was steering, his little arms turning the stick at different angles as they cruised between the red rock canyons.

"Why didn't we do this before?" Kira asked.

"Ciegos is never be's understanding," Fen said, his frown forming a deep, upside-down U.

"They're learning," Aella said gently. "What we're doing is a request. The fae can be fickle and hard to understand. It's best to only ask them for favors when one is in real need. The Spring Queen has already intervened on our behalf on more than one occasion. I think a bit of gratitude is warranted."

Kira frowned. "I didn't mean—"

"It's OK," Aella said. "You are new to this world. The fae are challenging, even for those of us who have always been a part of their world. But they are powerful and can be capricious, so they deserve our respect. As for Fen, he's just grumpy." The little man's frown deepened, and Aella winked at the girls.

"Mistress would be's grumpy if she was the failing," Fen complained.

"You didn't fail, Fen," Aella said, placing a gentle hand on his shoulder. "Things just went—unfortunately. It's no one's fault but the wolves."

They traveled quickly, winding through canyons of orange and red rock. Imogene couldn't help but stare at the natural wonder as they passed.

"We'll stay on the raft tonight," Aella said as darkness began to fall. "Fen will get us to our destination."

Fen looked disgruntled but did not complain as the teens settled into the bottom of the raft as best they could, crowding next to each other in the cramped spaces between the thwarts.

Imogene pulled Kenichi to the side and leaned him against

the edge of the raft, using their backpacks to give him some padding. Then she settled close against him and laid her head on his chest. She lay there as the stars began coming out, listening to the combined rhythms of his breathing, heartbeat, and the breeze.

She lay awake long into the night. After the wolf attack, aspects of her had changed. Imogene had first noticed it the day afterward. When they'd stopped for the night and had been unloading, Alexa had tried to pick up one of the bags of meat that Imogene had carried. She could barely lift it, yet Imogene had carried several such bags for a mile or more without trouble.

There were other things as well: she felt less tired and had taken to sleeping only five hours at night while feeling more energetic than she had before. Perhaps the strangest change was to her vision. Her night vision, even when the ever-bright moon was not up, now allowed her to see almost as well as she could during the daytime. Finally, Imogene drifted and slept.

"What are those things?" Kira said loudly.

Imogene stirred and sat up as the raft sped toward an island. The island itself was small with ramshackle buildings built one on top of one another in apparently random order. On its outskirts, pillars had been driven into the stone below the surface of the water. Beyond the pier-supported structures, hundreds of boats had been tied, nailed, and secured with every form of connection imaginable.

"Elvenin," Aella supplied. "They're pretty rare, though it may not seem that way here. This is something of a refuge for them, their capital city."

The raft sped around the southern end of the island and approached an opening in the jumbled mess of attached craft. Fen directed them toward a large wooden ramp that ran from a courtyard that was surrounded by buildings of all shapes and sizes.

In the courtyard, dozens of small creatures were going about their business. They were bipedal with long triangular ears and short blue fur. They wore brightly colored wraps around their waists and ankles and had bare feet, which, like their hands, had four digits with long curving claws. Their faces had a pronounced feline shape with a large pair of teeth that protruded from their mouths, even when closed.

One of the creatures sauntered down the ramp toward them as they made their approach. It was about three feet tall and wore an additional robe over its shoulder that reminded Imogene of a frat party.

"They are so cute," Kira said, grinning as she watched the elvenins tail wave back and forth in the air as she walked. Aella hushed her and waved for the group to remain silent.

"Purpose of your visit?" the little elvenin said in a high-pitched, wispy, and feminine voice. She opened a large book and began to scribble inside with a quill that was nearly half as tall as she was.

"We have an injured member. We seek help for him and a place to sleep for a few days while he heals," Aella said, climbing to the front of the boat and bowing low. She rummaged inside of her robe and produced a silver coin, which she tossed to the elvenin. The little creature caught it out of the air with two fingers without even bothering to look up.

"Thank you," she said. "Human and human-sized quarters are located in the Northwest corner of the Ilendrin, past the fairy zone and the nobbling rooting areas. "That way!" The little creature pointed over her shoulder with her small thumb then she looked up, finally seeing Aella's face. She gasped then shrieked a high yowling wail that brought several of her kind running from nearby. "I recognize you, Aella of Encartha. You are forbidden entrance. Depart at once!"

"We seek asylum. This one has been grievously wounded by the abominations." Aella gestured toward Kenichi. "Look at him. Without help, he'll die. By your people's laws, injured creatures may seek refuge."

"All except criminals may seek refuge," the elvenin hissed.

"Criminals?" Imogene gasped, unable to keep quiet any longer. "We're not criminals," she said.

"She is Aella of Encartha, breaker of truces," the elvenin said, pointing with a clawed finger.

"I was defending myself. The hag attacked me. I only protected myself and my companions," Aella asserted, glaring indignantly at the small figure.

"Then why did you flee?" the little elvenin snapped.

"I had to get my wards to Encartha. They were in danger, so I left to *protect* them."

The little elvenin frowned and stared back at Aella as though deciding something. "Even if that is true, the law clearly states that you must resolve such matters through a tribunal before you can once again enter Ilendrin. You cannot enter."

"Your people's laws—" Aella began angrily.

"I know my people's laws, Aella. I'll thank you for not lecturing me on them. I was among those that wrote the laws we now follow." She lifted her head and straightened her body, adopting a lofty pose that seemed odd to Imogene, given the creature's small size.

Aella stared defiantly at the little creature, her face set in a frown. "We have an injured member of our party. He will *die* without aid! He has done nothing wrong. He has not violated your laws and must therefore be given asylum."

"And we shall give it to him," the little creature said firmly, a grin slipping across her face. "He may enter Aella, breaker of the peace, but you may not."

"But you just said—" Aella began.

"Two of your number may enter with him and bear him to the healers," the elvenin woman continued interrupting her. "The rest of your party must remain here."

"They do not know the city. They are unfamiliar with your ways or those of the other creatures that inhabit your city. They will be—"

"I will show them to the healers. That is the purpose of your visit, as is the asylum you seek. Therefore, I shall make that option available by conveying them myself. Two of your number, along with the injured. No more than that will be allowed inside," the elvenin said with finality.

Aella glared back at her in silence for a moment, anger and frustration warring on her face. Finally, she took a deep breath to regain her patience and nodded. "Very well," she said through gritted teeth. "Imogene, Alexa," she said, turning to look at them, "you will take Kenichi to the healers."

Imogene gasped. "Why m—" she began. Aella silenced her with a gesture, and she sat back.

"I will speak with my companions before they leave us," she said to the elvenin woman who nodded and turned, walking back up the plank and seating herself on a small chair.

Aella turned to them. "Be very careful what you say and do while you are here," she said seriously. "Imagine if you could combine the deadliest characteristics of all the cats, you're familiar with. Speed, agility, power, ferocity, feral grace. Now imagine pairing that with fur that is nearly impenetrable, even by Valkryn weapons, and razor-sharp extendable claws three inches long, then you'd begin to understand the type of creature you'd be facing in an elvenin.

"They are among the most dangerous creatures in the

world, more deadly than werewolves, dryads, or even snow hags. You must tread lightly. The Elvenin are easily offended. Avoid their ire, and most importantly, get Kenichi help. If you fail to do that, he will be dead in a matter of days."

Imogene stared back into Aella's dark eyes, a shiver of fear sliding up her spine as she contemplated the task ahead of her.

"I'm trusting you two, Kenichi is counting on you. One more thing: we need information. I've never had so many wolves pursuing me, not in all the years I've brought adepts back to Encartha, and I've been doing it twice as long as any of you have been alive. We need to know why they are pursuing us like this."

"But how can we—," Alexa said.

"I'm not without friends here," Aella interrupted. "Seek out the Watcher in the Woods, a yarkin named Ecthillian. I understand he makes his residence here these days. Tell him I sent you. He knows much, and he may have an idea why the pursuit has become so—aggressive." She met Imogene's eyes. "Can you do that?"

Imogene took a deep breath and took in Alexa's face. The blond girl looked terrified. Imogene was sure she must look the same. She nodded.

"Why do they get to go?" Hugo blurted. "They can't even carry him."

"They can carry him," Aella said. "Imogene is stronger than either of you."

Hugo guffawed. "I bet she is," he said.

Aella smiled and nodded to Imogene. "Pick him up," she said, nodding to Kenichi. Imogene fidgeted, biting her lip in an attempt to dissipate some of her nervous energy. She leaned down and gently lifted the boy's arms and wrapped them around her neck. She slid her arms under his neck and knees and stood, lifting him easily from the bottom of the boat.

Hugo's eyes bulged in surprise at how simple it had been, like she was lifting a small child.

Aella turned to look at Hugo. "Any questions," she said. He looked shocked, staring with wide eyes as Imogene stepped nimbly out of the raft and onto the ramp before turning.

"When she takes you to the healers," Aella said, nodding toward the small elvenin woman, "Tell them what happened. You'll need to pay with this." She took several silvery coins from her robe and handed them to Alexa. "Three coins should be enough. The rest you can use for food and a place to stay while you wait. You won't be allowed to remain with Kenichi during the healing, so when you've dropped him off, go to the Silkie's Pleasure—it's an inn in the southern part of town. Tell the person at the desk that I sent you. I am friends with the owner, so you can stay there."

"What are you going to do?" Alexa asked, sounding scared.

Aella frowned and took a deep breath. "Well, we can't stay here," she said, rubbing at her chin with long thin fingers. "We'll have to find a beach, somewhere safe where we can wait until Kenichi gets stronger. Any ideas, Fen?"

"Fen is knowing a place," the gnome said. "Is not being far."

Aella nodded. "I'll send Fen to meet you here each morning to check in."

Imogene nodded.

"Be careful, you two!" Aella said. "We're counting on you. We cannot afford any mistakes!"

"No pressure," Alexa said.

"We will," Imogene said and motioned Alexa toward the top of the walkway. The two strode up the plank to where the elvenin woman waited, arms crossed and tapping a toed claw rhythmically on a wooden plank. Aella and the others watched as they did, and Imogene couldn't help but feel a spike of fear as Fen dipped his stick into the water and the raft began pulling away. They were alone, in a strange place among strange creatures they couldn't even name.

"Follow," the small elvenin said as the girls approached. She turned and sauntered off with the girls trailing behind. Imogene followed, holding Kenichi in her arms.

"How are you doing that?" Alexa asked.

"I don't know," Imogene said honestly. "He just doesn't feel heavy."

"He looks heavy," Alexa said. "He's bigger than you. You look sort of ridiculous carrying him like that."

"Not much I can do about that unless you want to carry him," Imogene said, raising a questioning eyebrow. Alexa shook her head in adamant refusal.

"Better you than me," Alexa said with a grin. "I wouldn't be able to pick him up, let alone carry him across town."

"Well then I guess we're both lucky that I can manage," Imogene said.

They followed the elvenin through a warren of thin streets. Imogene found herself gawking around, mouth open as she stared at a small building that looked like a birdhouse. A tiny, winged woman stepped out of the door and closed it behind her. She was about six inches tall, with pale white skin, and long black hair, and wore a tiny purple dress. She winked at Imogene and laughed before flitting off into the sky on gossamer wings singing to herself in a sing-song voice.

"Are those fairies?" Alexa asked. Imogene shook her head in wonder.

"There are many races here in Ilendrin," the elvenin woman said in an impatient tone. She strode quickly, and the girls had to hurry to keep up, despite the elvenins short legs.

The three continued through the thin streets of Ilendrin, while Imogene and Alexa gawked in amazement as strange creatures of every conceivable size and variety milled past, pressing close to them. Imogene struggled to slide between all the strange creatures while carrying Kenichi.

"Excuse us, human." A tall, lizard-like creature with a long neck and goggling eyes said, its face suddenly pressing within inches of Imogene's. She yelped and recoiled, nearly dropping Kenichi in the process. He groaned.

"Can you point us to a Lemurian apothecary? I've heard there is a great one about these parts. We've come all the way from our people's enclave in Mount Shasta, and we've run out of the cream that keeps our skin damp. This dry climate is murder on the skin, you know."

"I—don't know," Imogene said hesitantly. "I'm not from here."

"Oh, I quite understand. Everything here looks the same, don't you know."

Imogene looked around, and the buildings of all different shapes and sizes, from her perspective nothing looked like anything else.

"Yeah," she said, trying to sound confident. "Well, good luck." She slipped past them and hustled down the path, trying to catch up with the elvenin woman who had ignored the interchange with the Lemurians.

"The healers," the elvenin said, holding an arm outstretched to indicate the wooden building that lay at the end of a thin street, then turned and strode away without looking back. The building had a sign that hung above a crooked door. The sign had a geometric background with swishes and hard lines behind a plant that Imogene didn't recognize.

"Guess we're on our own," Alexa said and strode toward the door, opening it wide as Imogene struggled to fit Kenichi's limp form through the door without smacking his head on the jam.

Inside, a tall creature stood behind a wooden desk scribbling something in a large ancient-looking book. It was tall with a small torso and long extremities. It reminded Imogene forcefully of a plant with mottled green and brown skin. The creature looked up from the book it was writing in, its face expressionless.

"Can I help you?" it asked in a grinding, heavily accented voice that Imogene struggled to understand. Alexa quickly explained the situation, showing the creature Kenichi's wounds. It leaned over, looking down at the boy with golden eyes.

"Bring him in," the creature said, walking to the door and showing them to a room down the hallway. "Set him on the bed."

Imogene sat him gently on the mattress and stepped back to make room for the creature as it swayed into place and began examining Kenichi's injuries. It hummed to itself as it bent over the boy.

"His injuries are grave. He has an infection of the blood. Without intervention, he will die very soon."

Imogene swallowed. "Can you help him?

"I believe so, but it will take time, several days," the creature said, "and it will not be cheap."

"Ooh," Alexa squeaked, pulling a couple of the coins that Alexa had given them from her pocket. "Will this be enough?" The creature selected two of the coins and nodded.

"He must remain here. We will care for him. You may return to visit." The creature leaned over the boy and began murmuring to itself in a strange language.

When the girls remained standing nearby, the creature turned. "Was there something else?" It asked.

"No, I guess not," Imogene said, feeling awkward.

The creature nodded. "Then I'll leave you to find your own way out," it said, motioning with a long-fingered hand toward the doorway. Imogene nodded hesitantly, and the two girls walked slowly from the building into the daylight of Ilendrin.

"Well, what now?" Alexa asked.

CHAPTER 19
ILENDRIN

Imogene and Alexa leaned against a wooden rail on the pier, looking out at the opening of the small bay. The bay was natural, a small horseshoe-shaped opening that had been expanded by the addition of many docks that extended at odd angles into the lake beyond. Connected to all of the docks were hundreds of ramshackle crafts, ranging from modern houseboats to small wooden dinghies that looked so old that Imogene would have never considered putting a foot into them for fear of them sinking.

She stared for a moment at one of the crafts, an old schooner, at least she thought that was the name. It was an old wooden ship complete with multiple masts and extensive rigging. A pirate's flag hung from the top of the central mast. She shook her head. Ilendrin, the elvenin city, made no sense to her. It wasn't just the odd buildings and ships but the inhabitants as well. A compilation of dozens of creatures she'd never imagined or even had a name for.

There was a loud crack, and Imogene turned to see Fen standing on a nearby pier blinking his large eyes at her.

Imogene righted herself and strode quickly toward him. After their night in the strange town, she was happy to see the little man. Gnomes at least she was becoming more used to.

"You is being survived Fen is seeing," he said happily and plopped himself down on top of the wooden pillar, his legs dangling beneath him a good couple of feet above the pier's deck.

"We got a room at the inn Aella told us about," Imogene said, standing next to him and looking down at the little man, feeling a small measure of warmth for him.

"Tis good at the Silkies' Pleasure. Is Fen's favorite," he said. "How is Kenichi feeling?"

Imogene shrugged. "The healers wouldn't let us see him this morning, said he's too weak, that we'd have to wait a few more days."

Fen nodded knowingly. "Aella is having for yous other tasks."

Alexa folded her arms, and Imogene felt her shoulders tense. The previous day had proven to be quite stressful, and she didn't fancy another episode.

"What other tasks? Alexa said.

"We's be's seeing too many's ta wolves around da lake. We's needing to know why. We needs asking ta Watcher."

Alexa sighed audibly. "Cook a skunk," she said.

Imogene looked at her in confusion.

"Doesn't sound tasty, does it?" she said in explanation.

Imogene frowned. "We're going to need a little more to go on. We don't even know who the Watcher is"—she looked around at the variety of odd creatures going about their business at the harbor— "or *what* he is," she amended.

"Ta Watcher is beings a Yarkin. He is being big and hairy, like a bear but walksing on two feets and is having a big belly,"

Fen concluded, pasting on a self-satisfied grin. "He beings easy ta find!"

Imogene glanced up to where Alexa stood, arms crossed and staring at the small gnome, her lips quirked in frustration.

"For you, perhaps, but we don't know anything about the kinds of creatures that live here, and besides, you can do that sensing thing."

"Fen is not bes sensing *everyone*," he said, sounding aggrieved and pulling on one of his long ears. "Fen is only sensing latent *talent*. The rest of the things is being just as hard for Fen to find as is for yous twos."

"Where do we look?" Imogene said, interrupting the response that Alexa was preparing. If Fen could only sense talent that hadn't emerged, did she even need to keep wearing her medallion? Her abilities had *begun* to manifest themselves, after all. She affected a chilly stare, directing it at Fen. She'd seen Aella do this, and it had always seemed effective.

Fen waved away her look, turning his head so that he wouldn't have to look at her. "There is being only so many places in this town big enough for a yarkin. This town is not being so large as yous twos be thinking. Looks in ta bigs places."

"We were not the ones who asked for this, I may remind you," Imogene said, feeling her patience begin to wane. She was growing fond of the little gnome, but she needed a direct answer. An *informative* answer. "We were told to do it. The least you can do is give us a little direction."

"Fen is being giving you directions," he said. "Looks for yarkin, he is sayin. Yarkins is bigs, is looking like bears, he is saying. Looks in the big places," he concluded, crossing his little arms in front of his chest with finality.

Imogene ground her teeth. "Anything else?" she said. "Perhaps you have a needle and an extremely large haystack we can help you with?"

"Mistress bes telling you to be sure ta bes quickly," Fen said, a grin returning to his face. "This is the alls." The little gnome seemed unfazed by her sarcasm. Imogene wondered if he understood sarcasm at all.

"Fine," she said. "Then we better get going. Come on, Alexa. We'll just have to search the *whole* city. Thank you *so much* for all your help, Fen."

"Fen is being sure that the bigs places are nots on the outs of ta city," the gnome concluded before a loud crack announced his departure.

"That gnome is really beginning to annoy me," Imogene said and strode back toward the city. Alexa nodded as she joined her, and together they headed into the warren of thin streets.

"What's our plan of attack?" Alexa asked while dodging to the side to avoid a large stick-like creature that was at least twelve feet tall.

"We're just going to have to search the area in as systematic a way as we can," Imogene said. "We'll walk this way until we hit a street on the left, then follow it to its end. When we've finished that, we'll follow the road back this way and keep going until we find something. Whenever we see a building, we think is large enough to house the Watcher, we'll knock."

"Left, left, left," Alexa said, affecting a drill sergeant's tone. "Sounds like a colossal waste of time if you ask me."

Imogene nodded. "Not my favorite way to spend the day, but we don't have anything else to do—or much choice."

They spent the morning wandering up and down the small alleys that constituted the streets of Ilendrin, meandering in and out of the small curving offshoots. On more than one occasion, Imogene had begun to feel lost or turned around and had to look up at the sun to figure out which direction was north.

As the morning progressed, they found several buildings large enough to conceivably house something like the Watcher, but time after time the occupants of the buildings had professed not to know where he was. Imogene rather doubted they were telling her the truth.

Finally, at noon Imogene called a halt to the search, and the two girls bought some street food, a wrap of some kind that smelled good, but with ingredients Imogene couldn't name, from a vendor that looked nearly human. Only its blue-green skin, yellow eyes, and a small, pointed ridge on its forehead differentiate it. All in all, those differences seemed quite small when compared with some of the other creatures they'd seen.

They ate while sitting on the edge of a cement planter that lined one of the nearby stone buildings. The structures in this section of town were built from a coarse variety of gray stone blocks.

"This is not going well," Alexa said, frowning and taking a bite of her sandwich. "Mm!" she said in surprise, her mouth full. "I'm glad we picked that cart instead of the one before." That cart had been operated by a creature that had looked suspiciously like a warthog. It had *smelled* like a warthog too, and the girls hadn't even managed to determine what the creature was selling before the stench got the best of them and they opted to find their lunch elsewhere.

Imogene chewed, barely hearing her companion as she stared at the mass of strange creatures. She never would have dreamed just a few weeks earlier that all of these different types of creatures had even existed, let alone imagined herself wandering around a strange city surrounded by them.

She couldn't help but think about Morgan. The nagging feeling that he might still be alive kept coming back to her. She couldn't accept that her big brother was dead. Perhaps it was because she hadn't seen his body and hadn't had the opportunity to verify the fact and gain some closure. It had been different when her mother had died, Imogene had known her death was coming. Night after night she'd awoken in a cold sweat, feeling sure that she would be gone. Then finally it happened.

She shook her head, trying to clear her scattered thoughts.

"There," Alexa said, suddenly pointing down the street. "I think that's him! Look!"

Imogene looked up, surprised, her eyes searching the crowd and landing on a large and furry form lumbering through the masses, its head towering above the crowd.

He was tall and a bit ape-like with elongated hairy arms that arced to match his long striding steps. A massive bear-like head grinned as he made his way through the crowd like he was enjoying some private joke.

Alexa jumped up, shoved her half-eaten sandwich into Imogene's surprised hands, and bolted toward the large figure. Imogene stared as the girl forged through the crowd, stopped in front of the creature, and began talking loudly, her arms gesticulating animatedly. She turned and pointed back toward Imogene, who belatedly began to stand, feeling foolish for her hesitation. The creature nodded to Alexa and began to cross the distance toward where Imogene stood, awkwardly holding the two half-eaten sandwiches.

Imogene nodded as the yarkin approached her.

"Imogene, this is the Watcher," Alexa said, grinning.

The creature nodded its huge head toward her. "My name is Ecthillian, but some know me by that name," he said in a deep rumbling voice. "What can I do for you two?"

"We are friends of Aella," Imogene said, hardly believing that they'd found him. "We need your help."

Ecthillian's expression turned serious. He looked around the crowd, trying to see if anyone had overheard what Imogene had said, before he put a huge finger to his massive lips and nodded toward a large building down a thin alley from the street where they stood.

"We'll talk there," he said. "Come on." He motioned for the two to follow as he trudged toward the building. Imogene handed Alexa her sandwich and glared at the girl as they crossed a small courtyard and approached the large stone building that stood at its end. Ecthillian swung open the heavy wooden door and motioned the girls inside.

Imogene entered and looked around. The room was like an average American sitting room, only the proportions were wrong. It had two extremely large chairs facing a fireplace that was taller than Imogene. A huge oval rug sat on the rough wooden floorboards.

"Have a seat," the yarkin said, motioning toward one of the chairs. Imogene frowned and walked over to it. The seat was at chest level, and she glanced back at the yarkin for confirmation. He nodded encouragingly. She put her arms on the edge and leapt, scrabbling into the seat like a toddler.

Alexa tried the same maneuver, hopping and flopping on her chest on the cushion. She got stuck, kicking her legs ineffectually. Imogene grabbed the girl's arm and hauled her up. Alexa's face turned red, embarrassed after the climb as the two sat next to each other in the large seat, their legs dangling in the air like a couple of overgrown children.

The yarkin settled into his seat. "To what do I owe the pleasure?" he said. "How is my old friend Aella?"

Imogene glanced at Alexa, hoping the girl would respond. When she looked patiently back at her silently, Imogene frowned and took a deep breath. "Aella is fine, I suppose. She's outside of the city, staying on another island in the lake."

"Aella is here?" the Watcher said excitedly. "You must tell her to come to see me. It's been too long since we had a chance to chat."

"She can't," Imogene said. "The cat thingies won't let her in. They call her—" She paused, trying to remember what they had called themselves.

"Breaker of the peace," Alexa supplied.

"Thanks, yes, breaker of the peace," Imogene said.

Ecthillian sat back and pulled on the long hairs protruding beneath his snout like a man unconsciously toying with his beard. "That is not good. The elvenins hearts are in the right place, but they're—touchy, you might say. Easily offended."

Imogene nodded. "We've noticed," she said. "Aella told us to find you. She thought you might be able to help us. We have a friend who is with the healers here. He was hurt by a werewolf. She thought you might know why there are so many of them pursuing us."

"It's not uncommon for them to hunt potentials. They've done it since they first began slipping through the barrier hundreds of years ago," he said.

"Aella thought it was strange."

Ecthillian tipped his head to the side, furrowing his eyebrows. "Aella would know better than I what is normal for such things. How many of them are pursuing you?"

"I don't know exactly. A couple dozen at least," Imogene said.

The big creature's eyes widened impressively. "A *couple* dozen? That's a lot of skin-walkers," Ecthillian said, his gaze becoming far off. "Where did you come from precisely? Which direction?"

"We came down the Green River, from Vernal."

"From the north then," Ecthillian said. "Then those are not the ones that I've heard about."

Imogene glanced at Alexa, who was biting her lips nervously, eyes flitting back and forth between Imogene and Ecthillian.

"What ones have you heard about?" Imogene prompted.

"The streets of Ilendrin are abuzz with tidings of a large group of wolves at the far end of the lake, by the dam. They are preventing anyone from going that way. The elvenin are very displeased by it," he said, meeting Imogene's gaze with his large dark eyes.

"Are there more downriver?"

"Down lake actually. But yes. No one's heading that way right now, not even the elvenin."

"Why are they there?" Alexa said.

Imogene frowned. "They're waiting for *us*," she said, feeling the truth of the statement, even as she said it.

The yarkin shrugged. "That is, perhaps, the simplest answer, especially with the changes the moon has wrought. The barrier will be weakening much faster now. Before the moon incident, the barrier was decaying, its power draining slowly away. After the incident, it began to decay in earnest. Its power once drained in a slow trickle. Now it is like the rushing of a great river."

"What does that mean?" Imogene said, feeling her frustration rising.

"It means Agartha will escape soon. He'll be free of the prison Isshii put him in all those millennia ago, as will his armies. When that happens, only Encartha will stand in his way."

"From what?" Alexa said.

"World domination, the enslavement of all species not loyal to him. Perhaps the destruction of the world as we know it." Ecthillian shrugged. "It's hard to say what his intentions are. Agartha is not precisely sane. He's an abomination, a hybrid like his skin-walkers."

"Hybrid?" Imogene pressed.

Ecthillian nodded. "Part adept, part demon."

"I don't believe in demons," Alexa said.

"I doubt they care whether you believe in them," he said, shrugging. "Either way, I must warn you that the situation is grave. If what you say is true, there are wolves behind you and wolves in front. If Aella is not allowed entrance into Ilendrin, your situation will be dire indeed."

"We have to get to Encartha," Imogene said.

"We'll just have to get the wolves off of the dam," Alexa said.

"If only it were that simple," Ecthillian said.

"There is so much land out here," Imogene said. "Surely there is a way to get past them, even if there are that many."

Ecthillian leaned back, tilting his head up in thought. "The problem is that the terrain that is passable is very open. With the moon as it is, the task is more difficult, as you will not be able to move under cover of darkness. Perhaps impossible—for humans, at least."

"Couldn't we just do it on a cloudy night?" Alexa said.

Ecthillian nodded. "Sure, how much time have you got?"

"What do you mean?" Alexa said.

"This is southern Utah, girl," he said. "It's sunny here about two hundred and fifty days a year. It usually gets cloudier in the late fall and winter, so if you can wait that long —" He shrugged.

"Maybe the wolves will give up," Alexa said. "If we wait for a week or two, maybe they'll—."

Ecthillian shook his head. "I wish that were true, but I'm afraid there's no hope that they'll lose interest. Skin-walkers are relentless and single-minded. They won't give up until either they are dead or their quarry is."

Imogene exhaled, her mind racing. "He's right," she said. "The other pack has been following us since Vernal. Those wolves have travelled hundreds of miles through difficult terrain. They certainly won't give up when all they have to do is sit and wait."

"Then what do we do?" Alexa said, her voice rising in frustration.

"We need a distraction," Imogene said, "something to pull the wolves away from the area while we make our escape. Make them think we're going in a different direction."

Ecthillian sat back, a slow grin beginning to cross his face. "I have an idea," he said. "It'll take some convincing, but it could work."

"Convincing? Who would we need to convince?" Imogene said.

CHAPTER 20
THE DRYAD

Morgan hefted the pack, walking quickly south, following a fold in the terrain where it would be difficult to see him from the wooden structure atop the rise. Bright red clouds littered the sky as the sun crested over the horizon. A warm wind blew across his face. He was already beginning to sweat. It was going to be a long hot day. He paused and looked back at the small town situated at the foot of the small hills and felt an unexpected pang of regret.

I should have said something to them, he thought. But what could he have said? He wasn't sure. What do you say to friends that you're abandoning?

Imogene was the priority. He had to get to her and make sure she was safe. He couldn't do that with Nayme and Bender. He felt certain of that. Still, leaving them behind without a word seemed a betrayal. The pirates had been kind to them, and he truly counted Nayme and Bender as friends. But he could not abandon Imogene.

They will be fine, he told himself. *Safe. The captain has it all under control. This is as safe a place as any.*

As safe as Encartha? he wondered. Probably not, and yet getting to Encartha would be difficult, perhaps impossible. After all, they'd only made it this far because of other people. First Aella and then the captain and his pirate subordinates.

He shook his head and strode south along the fold in the earth until he passed out of sight of the lookout stand. From there he moved closer to the ridge line in irregular zigzags until he reached the top. This part of the ridge line ran almost due south over gently rolling hills dotted with juniper trees, sparse grasses, and the ever-present sagebrush.

The ridge line ran south and east in a long gentle arc. From his map he had discovered that he could follow it almost the entire way to Lake Powell. By the time he ran out of ridge line, he should be in visual distance of the lake. It was a perfect way to keep his bearings.

The sun rose, driving the temperature up as he moved along the ridge. At noon he stopped under the cover of a small tree and ate while looking down a ravine toward a thin valley in the west where a dirt road passed. His mind kept drifting back to Escalante and his friends there. How could he feel so torn? He'd known them only a short time.

He turned and looked toward the ravine and its dirt path. Movement caught his eye, and he watched as a figure moved along the road heading southward.

Strange, Morgan thought. *It's probably too far south for scouts.* He stared at the figure, trying to determine who it was and where they were going. He frowned. The whole thing felt somehow wrong. He opened his pack and searched inside, finally retrieving the pair of binoculars he'd gotten from Eckerd's pack the night he'd kept watch two days before. The man had eventually turned up, red-eyed and confused. *Drunk,* Morgan thought harshly.

He put the binoculars to his eyes and peered down to at the figure which had stopped and was standing on the trail. The figure turned and took a few steps north before jerking to a stop again and wobbling before turning south and shambling forward.

What is he doing? he wondered. *Is it one of the pirates? Maybe he is dehydrated and confused.*

Morgan had heard of things like that. He stood as the figure continued moving south away from Escalante. He grabbed his pack and set off, trailing after the figure, moving quickly downhill, and trying to get close enough to see the figure better, without the aid of the binoculars. He crested a rise, looked down into the thin canyon, and saw the figure leave the road and head up a rocky hillside with a strange shuffling gait. The figure came to a shambling stop and began to turn.

Morgan ducked low as the figure's gaze turned toward him. Concealed by a few rocks and some scrubby plants, Morgan saw with a shock that the figure was Zach. The boy's face was red and blotchy, his eyes unfocused and milky.

What is wrong with him? Morgan wondered as he watched the boy. Zach's face spasmed and shook, his features contorting and his arms twitching awkwardly. The boy turned and moved away, his gait even more ungainly than before. Morgan stowed his pack behind a bush and slipped from his cover, staying low, moving as quickly and quietly as he could manage.

Zach weaved back and forth toward the dark rim of a natural stone cave. Morgan followed, keeping himself hidden behind the tall sagebrush, rocks, and the occasional juniper tree. He watched as Zach approached a group of men that was gathered in a semi-circle around the dark entrance of the small cave. The figures stood silently unmoving as Zach approached. None of them turned to look as the boy took his place in the semi-circle.

Time passed as Morgan waited, watching from cover as the men stood motionless, facing the opening. First ten minutes, then fifteen, then thirty. Morgan wiggled uncomfortably, the hard ground digging into his side. He shifted, trying to relieve the pain.

What am I doing? I need to get moving. This is a waste of time. I need to get to Lake Powell to meet Imogene. If she passes by before I get there, I'll never know. Why am I wasting my time with this?

He considered his options for several minutes before deciding. Crawling on his hands and feet, he started toward the larger sagebrush for some cover. Just then, one of the men in the clearing began keening, an eerie sound that made Morgan pause in his tracks. He slowly turned his head to look at the mouth of the cave. There were loud shuffling and scraping sounds punctuated by a rhythmic thumping emanating from inside the depression. His heart raced as the hair on the back of his neck stood up.

Two men emerged from the cave entrance with another in tow, their captive struggling to get away. Morgan's eyes widened as he recognized Marcus, a black haired pirate with a long beard who ran their local gas station, being held between them. At the same moment, he saw Eckerd alongside an associate who Morgan couldn't quite name. They dragged Marcus to the front of the semicircle.

Morgan shuddered as he stared at Eckerd. The pirate's face was pale and lined with purple veins that stood out from his skin in a waving pattern that radiated out from his milky eyes. A strange mound protruded from his forehead, standing on a stalk, like a mushroom growing on a forest floor. A woman appeared behind them, striding into the circle of men.

She was tall and thin with bright red hair and a beautiful face. She looked over the men, a greedy gleam in her eye. She glanced over to Marcus, and the boy looked back at her defiantly.

"One more for my army," she hissed in a voice that began to change until it no longer sounded human. "Hold him down. Be sure he cannot escape."

As Morgan watched, her body began to ripple, swell, and distend. Her hands distorted, bloated, and remolded into hooked pincers that extended from scaly, segmented arms. Her face elongated, her jaw widening. Sharp fangs descended from between her teeth, dribbling with a dark liquid. Legs sprouted from her torso and grew, lengthening crab-like until they reached the ground. The monstrous thing that had been the red-haired woman crept toward Marcus as a long scorpion-like tail rose from behind her. Marcus screamed, his face a mask of horror as the creature moved toward him. He bucked and writhed, trying to tear himself free from the men who held him.

The monster lurched forward, its claws catching Marcus' arms and driving him backward onto the ground. He screamed again, kicking frantically, trying to strike the monster and free his pinned arms. The monster crouched over him, its face dipping venom, its tail rose high and darted down in a vicious sting that drove into Marcus's forehead.

He shrieked in animalistic pain, and his body convulsed, trying to free itself from the stinging barb. His feet kicked, twitched, and then lay still. His body sagged as the barb withdrew, dripping a viscous black fluid. Morgan covered his mouth, gritting his teeth to keep from crying out in horror.

The creature backed up, and Marcus began to twitch, his movements jerky and unnatural. He writhed on the ground, then folded over, put his hands on the stones, and stood. The whites of his eyes were red, his pupils turning a filmy white, the hole in his forehead from the barb already closing.

"Master, command me," he gurgled in a grating voice unlike his own.

"It is time, my pets. My precious drones," the creature hissed. "We are strong enough now. The town and its people will be ours tonight," it said, a note of triumph in its tone.

Morgan slid himself backward, shuffling away from the nightmare by the cave. He crawled until he could slip around the ridge line and away from sight. He stood and began to run back toward Escalante, finally falling into a long-distance jog.

His mouth went dry, and a corner of his mind cursed his stupidity for leaving his pack and the water bottles inside it behind. After more than an hour of jogging and walking in turns, he reached the outskirts of the small town. He found a bike lying in a yard and jumped into the seat and began to pedal toward the school.

As he rounded a corner, he saw the captain and Stig standing outside. There were pirates running in all directions as he approached.

"Morgan!" Stig called to him. "Where have you been? I was afraid you'd gone missing like the others."

"Stig, Captain!" Morgan gasped as he neared. "I found the missing men. They've been taken by, well, a monster south of town."

"A monster?" Captain said dubiously. "What kind of monster?"

"I don't know, a kind of scorpion woman monster thing," he said lamely.

Stig looked at him skeptically, frowning as you might when speaking to someone who was not entirely sane.

"A scorpion monster?" Captain said, sounding worried. "Morg, describe it to me," he said.

Morgan nodded. "At first it looked like a woman, but then it sort of transformed into this scorpion thing, and it stung Marcus."

"Where?"

"South of town."

"Where did it sting him?" The captain spat.

"In the forehead."

"What about the others, the men that were with them. What did they look like?"

"There was something wrong with them. They were pale with red lines like veins on their faces."

"Their foreheads, did they have growths on them?" Majesty said urgently.

"Y-yes," Morgan stammered. "How did you know?"

Majesty cursed. "How many men?"

Morgan just stood looking back at him, dumbfounded.

"Morgan, how many men? How many men were there?"

"Ten or twelve, I think," Morgan said.

"That's all of them then," Majesty said, nodding to Stig. "Stig, send the word to the lookouts. We need to abandon the town and get everyone out of here!"

"But, Captain, it's just a few men, we have dozens more. This is our home," Stig said.

"It's a dryad, Stig. I know you don't understand," the captain laid a hand on the man's shoulder. "Several of the crew have been taken, and more are on patrol, we have fewer than two dozen men here. We'll find another place, but we must get out of here now. Sound the alarm, run!"

Stig nodded and turned, running for the school.

"Morg," the captain said, "get your friends and meet me at the ship there." He nodded towards one of the ships parked at the gas station.

A shiver of fear ran down Morgan's back as he ran toward

the school. He burst inside, heading to the dorms as the school fire alarm began to blare.

"Bender, Nayme!" Morgan shouted as he rounded the corner and slid to a stop in front of Nayme's dorm room. It was empty. He turned and sprinted toward the boys' dorm. "Bender!" he called. Bender's bed was made, and his possessions were in his locker. Morgan cursed. *Where are they?* His mind raced. The cafeteria? He ran down the hall and into the cafeteria, where Cook stood with a look of determination on his face.

"Have you seen Bender or Nayme?" Morgan shouted.

"Afraid not," the cook said. "What the blazes are the bloody bells about?"

"We're under attack," Morgan said. "We have to leave town, Captain's orders."

The big man harrumphed and hurried toward the back of the kitchen.

"Where are you going?" Morgan called.

"Can't leave without my good knives!" The big man called and ran.

Morgan turned and ran down the hall heading toward the library, hoping his friends would be there. He rounded a corner and came to a crashing halt as he collided with Baud.

"Morgan! There you are," Nayme said, hurrying over from beside Baud and helping to pull him to his feet. Bender stood nearby, looking nervous. "Where have you been?" she nearly shouted. "We've been looking everywhere for you!"

Morgan grinned. "Just discovering an attack on the city is all," he said as he stood and nodded to Bender. "Good to see you two!" he said.

"Blasted fool!" Baud said, collecting himself from the ground and picking up the object he had dropped. It was a curved cavalry sword in a brass sheath. He slid the sheath through his belt loop and nodded to a nearby door. "Head to the front. That's where Cap'n will be. Take this." He held out a hunting knife in a sheath. Morgan took it and slid it into his belt, then nodded and motioned to the others to follow. They dashed to the door and burst outside into a courtyard where Stig and the captain stood surrounded by drones.

Nayme gasped as they looked out at the gathered crowd of people standing in the darkness outside of the school. Townspeople and pirates alike stared back at them. They were in various stages of infection, some having eyes with little enough red that they just looked tired, and others had mushroom-like protrusions from their foreheads and veined skin.

The drones parted, and the dryad slipped through the mass of them, grinning wickedly with her sharp teeth.

"So, my little captain," she hissed malevolently. "I think we'll be taking control of your little city," she cackled.

Morgan took an involuntary step backward as the long spike of her tail lashed above her head, her sharp claws clacking loudly as she tapped them against each other.

The ring of drones began to draw in around them, hemming them in. The door behind them opened, and Cookie came striding out, wearing his dirty apron and carrying several long kitchen knives.

"Looks like a bad one, cap," he said sardonically, taking in the group in front of him.

Capnell nodded. "Have any more of those knives by any chance?" he asked.

"Course I do," Cookie said, pulling a cleaver from the pocket of his apron and handing it to the captain.

A howl split the night.

The heads of the drones spun, searching for the sound.

"Captain!" Baud yelled. "I told you this place were buggered," he said, looking at the captain with a strange expression filling his eyes.

"Baud," Capnell said, reaching his hand out to the man. "Stay there."

Baud shook his head. "Not this time, captain." He bowed in a jerky way to the captain, drew the cavalry sword, and screamed, "RUN!" Charging toward the dryad, he hacked and slashed, taking out one of the creatures with a powerful swing that made a sickening crunching sound. The other drones quickly moved in to block him from reaching their master.

Morgan leaped into action, taking three big steps before springing himself at the nearest drone. He leaped, bringing up his left knee to give him altitude. He flew and kicked out with his right foot, his heel smashing into an infected pirate's face. There was an audible crunch as its bones broke, and the drone crumpled to the ground.

Morgan landed near two drones and spun, swinging his heel in an arc that connected with the face of the second, smaller drone that had once been a woman. The drone's head whipped sideways, and it collapsed in a heap. The third drone attacked, aiming a broad arching punch at Morgan's head. He dropped to one knee, and the punch flew harmlessly by. Morgan exploded from the crouch and jumped with all his strength, bringing his elbow up and driving it into the underside of the creature's jaw. Its head snapped backward, and it fell, tripping over the body of the first drone.

A hand grabbed Morgan from behind, he drew the knife from the sheath at his belt and spun. He sunk it into the drone's chest, and the milky eyes went wide as it toppled over, the body wrenching the knife from Morgan's hand.

The captain screamed, "NO!" and started forward. Morgan's head whipped around, and he saw Nayme grab the man's arm and tug him toward Morgan.

"If you go, you'll both die," she insisted. "Honor his sacrifice and escape."

A loud howl echoed from somewhere nearby.

The group of humans turned and fled toward the opening in the perimeter of the creatures that Morgan had created. The captain slashed at a muscular male drone with his samurai sword as he passed, scoring a deep slice in the former crewman's chest.

Another drone lurched forward, catching hold of Nayme's arm above the elbow. She screamed. Bender took a frightened step back as Morgan launched himself at the drone, driving his right knee into its back just above the hip. It snarled, its head and torso turning toward him. His left fist shot forward, knuckles driving into the throat. It reeled backward, and its hand slipped off of Nayme as it tumbled to the ground.

Morgan grabbed Nayme by the hand and pulled her free of the closing circle of drones. He pulled her, and Bender followed as together they sprinted westward to where a single land-ship stood, tall sails visible in a sky that was beginning to lighten as the malevolent moon made its way towards the top of the mountains to the east.

Morgan glanced back over his shoulder as he ran just in time to see the dryad spear Baud in the chest with her long tail. Baud slumped to the ground, and the dryad's malevolent stare turned on Morgan. Cookie was surrounded by a group of drones that were closing in from all sides. He slashed wildly around him as the drones attacked, heedless of his blows.

Why didn't he run?

The drones Morgan had knocked down were impossibly on their feet again, walking with awkward gaits and limbs that stuck out in unnatural ways.

Morgan stumbled, his hand ripped from Nayme's as he hit the ground. The curse that ripped from his lips was swallowed by a chorus of howls that bounced off the rolling hills to the north. A look of terror spread across Nayme's face as she craned her neck to try and pinpoint the source of the sound. Morgan tried to count them—three, five, ten? But it felt like hundreds of howls filled the air.

Suddenly, dark creatures burst from behind the school and into the open. They sprinted toward the melee with long inhuman strides. The dryad leaped forward, her tail plunging through the throat of one wolf as it launched itself into the fray. The wolf fell to the dirt, quivering in pain and struggling for life. The drones and wolves surged into each other, limbs and teeth flailing and slashing in a confusion of sprayed blood, bodies, and snapping jaws.

Nayme pulled Morgan up by the arm, and they ran into the night, pounding down the pavement toward the waiting land-ship. The others, not noticing Morgan's fall, were far ahead of them, piling into the ships as a sudden breeze began to build. As Morgan and Nayme ran, the captain leaped into the driver's seat of a ship and began throwing levers. Morgan watched in horror as the ship lurched and began to roll forward. Bender jumped on and turned, his frightened face searching for Morgan and Nayme.

The captain was going to leave them; Morgan was sure of it. The land-ship was picking up speed, heading onto the street facing away from where Morgan and Nayme trailed, now running in a full sprint toward the back of the ship.

The captain looked back and motioned for them to come. The ship slowed slightly, and the two dove, grabbing the back rail and hauling themselves onboard. The wind picked up, and the ship lurched forward again, picking up more speed. Gasping for breath, Morgan put a hand on Nayme's arm. She patted his elbow and nodded.

The ship headed down the street, heading south and turned onto the highway, the cacophony of the drones and werewolves fighting echoing in Morgan's ears as they went. A dark shape landed on the road in front of them. A snarling wolf with bared teeth blocked their path.

The ship careened into it, knocking the wolf flat. The ship bucked but continued forward as it drove over the top of the big wolf with the sound of screeching metal and a crunching sound that added to the discord of the battle.

Morgan looked up at the captain and found the man's face was a mask of concentration as the land-ship rolled past the edge of town down the highway to the south.

"We aren't going to get far like this," the captain said gravely. "That front wheel is mangled, and the struts are shot. We'll be lucky to make it more than a few miles before we're stuck." He met Morgan's eyes, his expression grim.

"Every mile we travel is one we won't have to do on foot," Morgan said, and the captain nodded. They rolled on into the night, the wheel wobbling and making a metallic grating sound as it rolled.

CHAPTER 21
CAPTAIN

Morgan sat in the small hollow under the shelter of a large pine tree that stood on a ridge above the road. Nayme and Bender snored gently as he stared transfixed at the small flames. He glanced at Nayme. Her pretty face was smooth and still, and her chest rose and fell slowly as she slumbered. He reached over and gently pulled a lock of her hair and tucked it behind her small ear.

He had nearly left them behind, nearly abandoned his friends along with the pirates. What would have happened to them if he hadn't seen Zach, hadn't followed him to the cave? He examined the curve of her lips. He might be almost to Lake Powell by now, on his way to try to meet up with Imogene. Would Bender and Nayme be dead? Guilt stabbed at him for his near betrayal, his *intended* betrayal.

There was nothing for it. They had only one choice now: they had to get to Encartha. Morgan wondered how far they'd traveled. How many hours had they driven? They'd begun as night fell and had driven long into the night as the moon slid slowly up into the sky. He reached out and gently caressed Nayme's cheek.

A soft crunching sound brought Morgan's head snapping upwards. Majesty strode into the light of the fire and nodded to Morgan as he crossed the open area, a stoic expression on his face. With great care, he unslung a large black backpack from his shoulders and laid it down gently next to him before lowering himself.

Majesty sighed. "Well, that's it for the ship," he said. "The axle's done. We won't be able to get it moving again."

Morgan nodded gravely. "What's next?" he asked.

Majesty arched an eyebrow at him and stared silently. "For who?" he asked.

"For us," Morgan said.

Majesty inhaled deeply, pausing to collect his thoughts. "So, it's *we* now?" he asked Morgan, arching an eyebrow in slight surprise.

Morgan averted his gaze, embarrassed by the remark. He stared at the flickering flames for a moment before raising his eyes to meet Majesty's intense stare, awaiting a response.

Clearing his throat, Majesty spoke sternly. "*We* keep going," he said as he looked away and ran a hand through his beard, gently tugging on the end of the braid. His intense gaze returned to Morgan. "But I cannot join you in the *we*," he said firmly, locking eyes with Morgan.

"What do you mean?" Morgan said hesitantly.

"Don't kid with me, boy. It's unbecoming." The captain settled himself heavily to the ground and leaned against a large rock. He stared through the tree into the light of the moon as it passed through the scattered clouds. "I said I can't come with ya," he repeated.

"Come with us where?" Morgan said.

"To Encartha."

Morgan gasped in surprise. "Encar—," he spluttered. "How did you—?"

A broad grin slid across Majesty's face, and he winked, his pointer finger tapping at the side of his head. "Majesty's no fool. He always knows."

"I've never said anything about Encartha, and neither have the others. At least, not as far as I know." He glanced unintentionally down at his friends.

Majesty chuckled. "You can stop giving them the stink eye, boy," he said. "They didn't rat you out."

Morgan frowned up at him.

Majesty winked and pointed at Morgan's chest. "That there is the culprit, it's a dead giveaway," he said.

Morgan looked down at his chest.

"My shirt?" he said, confused.

"The medallion," Majesty said. "Only one place to get one of those."

Morgan reached down and palmed the medallion under his shirt. He looked up at the captain, eyes narrowing. "It's just a necklace," he said.

"Aye, I bet it is!" Majesty said, stifling a laugh. "And I'm just your average inland boat owner!"

Morgan frowned in silence, unsure what to say.

"Let me guess, your finder gave it to you?" Majesty said.

Morgan nodded.

"What was he?" he said.

"She was a woman, *is* a woman," he amended.

"Not that. Aye, great she was a woman, but what was she?"

"I don't know what you mean."

"Valkryn, Ethermancer, what? The other sorts don't normally become finders." the captain said.

Morgan stared blankly back at him. A cool breeze caressed his face, and he shivered. The temperature was dropping.

"Boy, did she teach you anything? What type of magic did she do?"

"Oh, um, she manifested things. A sword mostly, from what I saw."

"Valkryn then. Did she survive, when you were separated?"

"Last I saw her," Morgan said.

Majesty looked at him contemplatively. "What happened? Was this before we picked you up by Green River?"

Morgan nodded and stared back into the fire. He took a deep breath before proceeding. "Wolves, they found us by the river."

"Did someone take off their medallion?" Captain asked, his voice full of surprise.

Morgan shrugged. "I don't know. It all happened so fast."

Majesty grunted. "Not unlike what just happened in Escalante. What clan?"

Morgan looked up at the man. "Clan?"

"Aye, boy. Which Encarthan clan was she a member of?"

"How would I know?"

"She didn't say?"

"Not that I remember."

"You can tell which clan an Encarthan is devoted to by their secha—or their mark. She'd have had a mark behind her left ear. Here," he said, pointing to a spot on his own neck just behind and below the ear.

"It was a tiger—or maybe a bear, I think," Morgan said, trying to think back to when had first noticed it outside of the outpost.

Majesty grunted, rubbing his chin. "What about her secha, was she wearing one of those?"

"I don't—" Morgan began.

"It's a sort of half-skirt thing," Majesty said. "It hangs from a belt in front and behind your legs. It would have had a symbol on it."

"Yeah," Morgan admitted.

"What was on it?"

Morgan shook his head. "I don't remember," he said.

"Well, I guess we can't puzzle out her clan then."

"How do you know all of this?" Morgan said. "You know a heck of a lot more about Encartha than I do."

The captain laughed, shook his head, and sighed. "I ought to. I'd know more about it than just about anyone, especially outside of the city itself."

Morgan stared back at him expectantly.

Majesty looked into the fire silently as Morgan waited. Finally, Majesty sighed dramatically and bit his lip. "I'm *from* Encartha," he whispered.

Morgan's eyes goggled. "What?" he nearly shouted.

"Sshhhh!" Majesty hissed. "We don't know what's out there!"

"Sorry," Morgan said, abashed. "But how could you be from—" He stopped, staring at the captain as something clunked into place in his head. "You're a Valkryn!" he said.

Majesty laughed. "Afraid not, lad," he said. "Valkryn are all," he mimed swinging a sword, his face contorting mockingly. "That's not me."

Morgan frowned thoughtfully. "The wind," he began slowly, "It always blows when you want it to. It's not luck like the pirates say, you *make* it blow. You are a Valkryn!"

The captain winked at him. "Caught on, have you? Ah well, I guess my secret is out. strictly speaking though, that's not a Valkryn power," he said.

Morgan stared at him.

"It's an ethermancer power, a weaver power," Majesty said.

"Is that what you are? An ethermancer?" Morgan said.

"HA!" Majesty said, "I flunked out of ethermancer school. That's why I'm living it up out in the wide world instead of sitting in some tower practicing how to be a blowhard."

"You certainly don't need any additional practice with that," Morgan said wryly.

Majesty grinned. "Is that right?" he said.

"How do you flunk out of ethermancer school?"

"It's easy really," Majesty said. "In my case, it came down to a matter of diversity. I can't do any magic that's not wind related. No temperature manipulation, no energy shields, no vibration, not even light projection."

"Ethermancers can do all that?" Morgan asked.

Majesty nodded. "Decent ones can."

"Is that why you left?"

"After a manner of speaking, technically I left by accident. I failed my test, and I was going to be released from my clan. I was only a devout, but my family had a history, and I couldn't stomach the thought of joining one of the crafting guilds. So I started looking for the distortions, the tears in space-time that allowed passage in and out of Encartha. Most of them weren't known by the majority of Encarthans in those days. One day I found one, and I couldn't believe it. I was so curious and figured, what was the worst that could happen? So, I decided to take a peek outside. Damn thing closed behind me. I almost died! If Baud hadn't found me, I would have starved to death."

"Baud saved you?" Morgan said in surprise. "He doesn't seem like the type to, well, be all that helpful."

"He doesn't look it, does he?" Majesty laughed. "But he'll surprise you, he looks a mess, but he's shockingly capable, a natural survivor that one."

Morgan frowned. He hadn't gotten to know the man. He'd always been put off by the way he'd talked, the way he'd behaved, the violence he espoused, and the whipping he'd given Morgan. He hadn't seemed like the type of person that Morgan would want to be around.

"That's the other reason I can't go to Encartha. I'll need to be meeting up with my boys, Baud especially."

Morgan stared at the man. "But he's dead," he said.

"Baud? Dead?" The captain laughed. "From that little scrape? No way, he'll have found a way out of that mess, believe you me."

"But he was surrounded," Morgan said. "I saw that thing stab him."

"Your finder sure didn't teach you much, did she? Never count out a man until you see him dead at your feet. No, Baud will be at the rendezvous point, I promise you that," Majesty said and nodded to himself.

It seemed a long shot to Morgan. Even if he'd avoided the dryad's sting, the man had been totally surrounded, fighting with that cavalry sword against multiple enemies.

"How long were you with her, your finder?" Majesty said, interrupting his thoughts.

"Less than two weeks before—" Morgan said, trailing off and shrugging.

Majesty nodded. "Were there others? More adepts?"

"There were about twenty of us originally, including those two"—he indicated his friends—" and myself. My sister was with them," he said, trying not to let his voice crack.

"Ahh," Majesty said with interest. "Well, that explains things, why you were leaving us and all."

Morgan gulped and stared uncertainly at the man.

"Don't get me wrong, lad. I'm right grateful you warned us about the dryad, nasty devils they are, like to have killed us all without that warning. I'm right grateful to you for that." He pinned Morgan with a stare. "But I know the look of a man deserting."

Morgan hung his head, a sick feeling settling in his gut. "I'm sorry," he said.

"Don't gotta say sorry to me. Those two, however— They were worried, thought you were hurt or killed or some such."

Morgan stared down for a long moment, thinking about his friends, then took a deep breath and looked up, meeting the captain's eyes.

"They look up to you, depend on you. They look to you to lead them," Majesty said seriously.

"I didn't ask them to," Morgan said, defiant. "I don't want them to."

"If you have to ask for people to follow you, then you're not suited for it," Majesty said. "Real leaders are born to it."

Morgan shook his head. "I don't want to be a leader."

"Well, want it or not, you've got it," he said, grinning wickedly.

"I can't get them to Encartha," Morgan insisted. "I don't know how to get there, and you just said you won't go."

"Aye, I said that. Didn't say I wouldn't tell you how to find it though, did I? The fact of the matter is that it's right simple. Follow the road signs heading to the north rim of the Grand Canyon. Encartha will be there, you can't miss it."

Morgan thought about it. He wasn't sure how far they'd come or how far there was to go to the north rim. On top of that, they kept being surprised by werewolves. How would they survive if the wolves found them again? His brain hurt from thinking about it. There was just no way he could do it.

"We won't make it," he said morosely. "We'll never get there. If you leave and go to your rendezvous point, we'll die."

"You never know what you're capable of until you are faced with your limits," Majesty said. "You'll make it. I have a sense about these things. You're like Baud, a survivor. You'll find a way to get yourself and your friends there. If things go bad, just manifest yourself a weapon and get to fighting. You seem to have a knack for that too."

"I can't manifest," Morgan said. "I can't even gather. I've practiced almost every night since Aella found me, and I can't do it."

"Did you absorb your disk?" the captain asked.

Morgan pulled it from his pocket, the piece of it that remained was smaller than a quarter.

"Good. Gathering's the easy part, if you don't mind my saying," Majesty said. "It's a lot like breathing."

"Breathing?"

"That's what I said. Boy, you've got to get out of the habit of repeating what people say."

Morgan scowled.

"This Aella told you about your don-tin, did she?"

"Yeah," Morgan said, unconsciously placing a hand on the spot she'd described.

"That's it," Majesty said. "As I said, drawing is just like breathing. When you breathe, all you do is open up your lungs and the air rushes in to fill them. Open up your don-tin, and Ether will rush in to fill it."

Morgan frowned, considering, wondering how on earth you opened a part of your body that you couldn't even feel, let alone know how to operate.

Majesty stood and stretched. "Well," he said. "It's time I get going. I've taken you as far as I can. It's up to you now, Morgan. Get yourself and your friends to Encartha, become Valkryn or whatever damn thing you're going to be. I'm sure our paths will cross again."

"Just like that, you're leaving?" Morgan said. "How are you even going to get to your rendezvous point?"

Majesty grinned and pointed to the large bag. "With that."

"Looks like a heavy pack. Long journey ahead of you

carrying a pack that big." Morgan said assessing the size. "Maybe you'd be better off coming with us to Encartha. We'll help you with it. Each of us can take a turn carrying it. It will be easier that way."

Majesty laughed. "Oh, I'm not going to need help carrying it," he said. "It's going to carry me. That's a paraglider in there. Having sway over the wind does have its advantages." He gestured in the air like a plane floating on the wind.

"You're going to fly?" Morgan said, amazed.

Majesty pointed at his forehead. "I'm a boy scout, don't you know," he said. "I'm always prepared." He picked up the pack and slung it over his shoulder. "Tell your friends I'll be seeing them. They always have a place in my crew if they want it. The same goes for you." The captain nodded at Morgan, stood, and turned to stride out of the small clearing.

"Oh," he said, pausing. "If you run into an unhappy fellow by the name of Telleran in Encartha, tell him Michael Capnell says hello." Majesty turned and strode from the clearing. Morgan stared after him in silence, a sickly lost feeling filling him.

CHAPTER 22
GLEN CANYON

Imogene breathed in deeply and glanced at Kenichi. His face was pale and drawn. "How are you feeling?" she asked. "Is your knee still hurting?"

He looked back at her and nodded. "I'll be OK," he said. "I might be a little slow, but I think I can do it." Imogene nodded, careful not to betray the dread that crept silently within her at the thought of what he'd have to do. He started to rise, and she stood, pulling on his arm to help him to his feet. He moved with a pronounced limp, and he was still quite weak. Even so, his coloring had improved, and he was awake! The scars on his face had softened further, becoming a bright pink compared to the livid red they'd been when she and Alexa had brought him to the healers. His scars would never fully heal, she was sure. Still, he was alive, and Imogene was glad to have him up and talking.

She nodded at the tall nobbling as Alexa took Kenichi's other arm, and they led him toward the door. The nobbling bowed, its face still impassive. A part of her mind wondered idly whether the creature was capable of other facial expressions.

They made their slow way to the dock, weaving through the crowds. Imogene's stomach fluttered as she considered leaving Ilendrin. It was strange, full of odd creatures that she'd never imagined, but since her arrival nearly a week before, she'd had three meals a day and a daily bath. Most importantly, nothing had tried to kill her. A vast contrast to her other experiences since leaving the outpost.

When they arrived at the dock, Fen was waiting for them, sitting impatiently in the back of the raft. She nodded to the little gnome and helped Kenichi into the craft.

"The supplies were delivered then?" she said, noting the long ropes and harnesses fabricated by a local merchant, as well as a two-week supply of food. If they didn't make it to Encartha in that amount of time, they wouldn't be making it at all.

Fen nodded impatiently and picked up the nearby stick. He thrust its glowing end into the water at the back of the raft, and they began to accelerate until they bounced over the small waves like a speedboat.

They sped between the canyons, finally arriving at a small island where several small tents had been set around a fire pit. It seemed that Aella had managed to upgrade their equipment in other ways while she and Alexa were in the city.

Aella stood and strode toward them.

Imogene smiled and waved to her as they neared the beach, then turned as Kenichi did the same, a broad smile splitting his scared face.

"Good to see you up and moving," Aella said as she grabbed the front of the raft and pulled it up on shore. She nodded to Imogene. "Well done," she said.

Imogene grinned and put a hand on Alexa's shoulder. "We did it together," she said, smiling.

"So," Aella continued, "we have a plan?"

Imogene nodded. "We do," she said, and then she began to explain.

"You want to jump off the dam?" Kira said, eyes wide.

"The Glen Canyon dam? You want to jump off of it?" Hugo asked hesitantly.

"I'm not jumping off a dam," Kira said as the group sat around the campfire discussing the Watcher's escape plan.

"You know, well, that would kill us, right?" Hugo said. "I mean, it's hundreds of feet tall, and we're not like you—" He looked around at the other teens. "I mean, we're comparatively fragile. Aella may survive a fall like that, but the rest of us are screwed."

"We're not intended to be falling," Imogene said. "We're rappelling."

"That's a big dam," Kira said, frowning. "We're talking about hundreds of feet here."

Imogene nodded. "Seven hundred feet," she confirmed.

"Son of a—" Kira said and stood and stomped away, shaking her head.

"That's too far," Hugo said. "We'll never find ropes that long."

"We already have them," Imogene said, nodding toward the boat where the coils of rope lay. "The Watcher had a friend of his make them. They're thin and light, but he assures me they are long enough and strong enough for us to safely make it down."

"The bigger challenge is the wolves," Aella said.

"We're getting some help with that as well," Imogene said. "The Watcher has some friends that he's convinced to help us out. I think this plan can work, but we'll need all of you to get ready to go, pack your things, and get some rest. The moon has been coming up a couple of hours after the sun has already set, so if we can get there at the right time, it will be dark enough for us to slip by. We'll use that to help cover our movements."

"What will these friends of Ecthillian's be doing?" Aella asked.

"I'm told that elvenin mystics are very good with glamours," Imogene said. "If they choose, they can make it appear as though something else was standing where they are. A dog, a horse"—he glanced at Aella meaningfully—"another person."

"They're going to pretend to be us," Aella said, piecing the plan together.

"That's right," Imogene said. "They'll act like us, heading overland as if we were trying to slip past the blockade the wolves have created. They'll get close enough for the wolves to see them and start to pursue them. When the skin-walkers are far enough away, we'll slip onto the dam, set the ropes, and rappel down."

"What if the wolves come back?" Hugo asked.

"Ecthillian has a plan for that too. The mystics will notify us in the event that the wolves turn back."

"How?" Hugo's voice was skeptical.

"They're bringing what amounts to a set of fireworks," Imogene said. "They'll shoot them off if the wolves abandon the chase and head back toward the dam."

"What about the boat?" Hugo asked after a brief silence. "How do we get it down?"

"Fen will handle that for us," Imogene said. "He can teleport, you know."

"I thought you said that he can't teleport things larger than him. He has to be able to carry it in order to take it with him?" Hugo said.

"That's correct, but he's not going to teleport the boat down, we're going to throw it off the edge."

Hugo gaped. "But it will pop!"

"Fen has some tricks up his sleeves. He is going to steer it as it falls, give the falling raft some small course corrections, and keep it from falling too fast."

"That sounds risky," Hugo said.

"It is," Imogene agreed. "It's the part of the plan that most worries me."

"What happens if he makes a mistake?" Kira asked in a small voice, her dark eyes wide with trepidation.

"Then, I'd say we're going to have a hard time staying ahead of the wolves on foot," Aella said seriously.

Imogene nodded and pushed down the fear that was rising within her. This was their only way. They'd racked their brains for another possibility and failed to produce a plausible alternative. If they were going to make it to Encartha, this would have to work.

When the time came, they loaded the boat and set off. The sun had set by the time they rounded a bend and saw the dam in the distance. Fen steered the craft toward the western bank of the lake, where the stone lowered in a gradual curve to the waterline. Five small figures stood on the bank next to one very large one. Aella stood waving and hopped from the raft to the shore. She bowed low to the group.

"It's good to see you, my friends!" she said to the small creatures. She strode quickly over to Ecthillian and gave him a big hug.

"These are my friends, Avanir, Neldeira, Rolung, Todelin, and Varien," she said, introducing a group of elvenin. "They'll need to have a look at you so that they can cast a glamour that looks like you," she said. The little mystics walked forward, each approaching a teen and carefully studying them for several minutes.

Imogene felt strange as the mystic named Neldeira stared at her carefully from a distance of less than a foot. After a thorough inspection, the mystics stepped back, each making a series of gestures in the air. The air seemed to ripple, and the mystics were replaced by five teens, each a replica of their chosen doppelgänger.

"Amazing," Imogene said in awe, staring back at the mystic who was now indistinguishable from herself.

"Thank you, my friends," Aella said to the elvenin as they walked up the embankment, heading toward the bridge.

Fen steered the raft away from the shore as Ecthillian and the mystics disappeared into the gathering darkness in the direction of the dam.

"What will happen to them?" Imogene asked, nodding toward the elvenin mystics. "Won't they be in danger? What will happen if the wolves catch them?" In the excitement, she hadn't even considered the possibility.

Aella nodded. "Some," she said. "But I wouldn't worry too much about them. Elvenin are much faster than skin-walkers. Besides, I feel sorry for the wolf that manages to catch up with one of them. Elvenin have incredibly thick hides and fight like honey badgers. And Ecthillian is just as deadly."

The teens returned to the boat. Imogene's heart pounded inside her chest as she took in the paleness of Kenichi's face.

"Fen, is it working?" Aella whispered in a voice just barely audible. Imogene sat next to her and doubted the others heard the exchange. There was a small pop, and Fen was gone. The boat began to slow as the glow faded. There was a second pop, and once Fen was back in place, the boat picked up speed.

"Tis working, mistress. Ta wolves be's going."

Aella nodded, and they set off, heading across the channel

toward the far side. The raft moved silently through the darkness toward the dam. It touched down on stone, and the teens shuffled out, moving as quietly as they could as they dragged the raft onto the shore.

"On the count of three," Aella whispered. Only Kenichi stood to the side as they lifted the raft onto their shoulders and walked up the stone ramp, moving quickly on silent feet until they reached the pavement at the pinnacle of the structure.

"There," Aella said, indicating a large metal structure that rose up on both sides of the flat top of the concrete. The group scrambled to the spot, sat the raft down, and began hurriedly pulling the coils of rope from inside. There was a popping sound, and Fen stood on top of the metal structure. Hugo tossed him one end of the rope, and the little gnome caught it on the first attempt. Imogene sighed in relief, and the others frantically began strapping on harnesses and their packs.

A howl sounded in the distance, and Imogene's head snapped up, facing to the west, the direction that the elvenin had headed. A large bright light shot into the air and exploded, a red glow filling the night sky with light. In the distance Imogene could see the shapes of wolves running in their direction.

Aella cursed. "They've discovered the ruse. We have to go! Now!" There was a popping sound, and Fen stood next to the raft while two long ropes hung down from each side of the metal structure.

"Fen, how long do we have?" Aella asked, her voice tense. Two quick pops, and the gnome had returned.

"They's less than two miles. They know we's here," he said. "You's muss be sending ta raft!" Fen hissed.

"Do it!" Aella shouted. Imogene and the others grabbed their corners of the raft and dragged it to the edge.

"On the count of three," Aella hissed. "One, two, three."

The teens shoved, and the raft and its cargo, tied tightly inside slipped over the edge, and fell toward the water below. There was a series of popping noises, so quick that they sounded like a popcorn popper. Imogene stared in wonder as the raft flattened out and seemed to float away from the dam and down toward the darkness below like a feather on the wind.

"Go!" Aella hissed as the teens took their places. Kenichi and Kira went first, attaching their harnesses to the ropes and stepping over the edge. Kira jumped backward and arced several dozen feet before her feet thudded against the dam and she shoved off again. Kenichi stumbled on his first jump. Imogene stared in fear as he spun in the air then righted himself and jumped again, continuing his descent. His jumps were smaller and less controlled than Kira's, his face looking pained as he moved down the dam at an agonizingly slow pace.

"Go!" Aella said to Alexa, and the girl clipped onto the rope Kira had used. She began descending in a series of long arcs. She had nearly reached the halfway point when Kenichi finally set foot on the cement at the bottom. Hugo clipped into the rope and headed toward the bottom of the dam.

Imogene looked up as the light from a second red explosion in the sky revealed the wolves sprinting forwards. They had nearly reached the corner of the dam; their howls reminded Imogene of a pack of hunting dogs baying at prey they'd spotted. Imogene was the prey.

Aella cursed again. "Go!" she shouted as Alexa neared the bottom. "They're almost here!" Aella said in a warning tone to Imogene. "They're less than a half mile away now and closing fast. We have to get down as quickly as possible!"

"I'll be right behind you," Imogene said. Aella nodded and clipped into the rope as Alexa unclipped at the bottom. She slipped over the edge, and Imogene looked up as a third red explosion cast light over the area. The wolves were almost on top of her, howling as they careened around the curved top of the dam toward where she stood alone. She looked down. Hugo had just reached the bottom.

She clipped in and swung her feet out over the edge of the dam, placing them firmly against the cement. She braced herself, her hand holding the rope firmly next to her harness, her heart thumping heavily in her chest as she kicked hard, letting the rope slide through the leather glove on her right hand in a controlled arc that brought her back to the wall a few dozen feet below. She repeated the move as the baying at the top of the dam intensified. She tried to tune out the sound as she focused on her descent. The wall swung toward her, and she kicked out again, wind streaming past her as she hurtled toward the platform that sat at the bottom next to the huge gates that controlled water flow out of the reservoir.

Two hundred feet to go, one hundred feet. Imogene raced toward the bottom, moving as quickly as she dared. Assuming she was nearing the bottom, she glanced down. Fifty feet below her the other teens stood at the base of the dam looking upwards as she and Aella sped toward them. Imogene kicked, driving herself away from the surface of the dam in a broad arc. There was a sickening lurch, and Imogene spun into empty air, the severed end of the rope trailing after her as she cartwheeled, arms flailing, plummeting towards the ground below.

She heard a scream that was not her own as she tumbled in darkness.

Out of nowhere, a wrenching pull on her harness jerked her out of her free fall.

"Gotcha!" Aella shouted. Imogene crashed against the woman as Aella's feet pounded into the cement. The impact dazed Imogene, and bright lights appeared momentarily in front of her eyes as they spun out into the air once more.

Aella's powerful grip hauled on the rope, slowing their descent as they made a final arc and landed hard on the metal of the walkway at the base of the dam.

Imogene clattered to the ground, her breath coming in quick terrified gasps. She looked up at Aella's face. The woman was looking down at her, concern written across her fine features.

"Are you OK?" she asked. "Can you get up?"

Imogene ran her hands down her legs and over her arms and torso. "I think, I think I'm OK," she said. "A little beat up, but I don't think anything is broken."

"Good," Aella said, taking her hand and helping her to her feet. "We don't have time for that." Aella and Imogene quickly unharnessed and ran down a plank toward a series of structures that lined the river on both sides. Aella cut a neat hole in the side of the building with her glowing sword, and the group passed through its dark insides, illuminated by only the light of the weapons glow. She repeated the move on the far side of the building and Imogene looked out over the Colorado River. Fen sat in the raft a few dozen feet below, the water surrounding it glowing gently.

Imogene jumped, landing in the water with a splash and swimming quickly to the raft. Fen grinned at her as she pulled herself over the side and landed in the bottom. She sat up and reached over the side, helping to haul the other teens into the boat.

Imogene pulled Kenichi into the boat and leaned him against its side. His pale, scarred face looked back at her. She started to laugh, looking up at the tiny figures at the top of the dam. They had made it!

CHAPTER 23
NORTH RIM

"Morgan!"

He groaned as someone shook his arm.

"Morgan, wake up!"

His eyes cracked open, and he winced as sunlight stung them. He blinked, trying to rouse himself, and looked up into Nayme's troubled face. Even with a smudge of dirt and some twigs in her hair, she was pretty.

"I'm up," he said.

"Where's the captain? I heard howling. We haven't left the wolves behind." she said as Morgan twisted and sat up to look around the clearing where they'd spent the night.

He frowned. "Gone, flew the coop, almost literally."

Her eyebrows drew down in confusion. "He flew away?" she said skeptically. "What, is he a bird now?"

Morgan nodded. "Almost. He's an ethermancer. He was the one making the wind that powered the ships. He kept a paraglider in the hold. After you two were asleep, we had a little chat, and then he packed it up and flew away."

Nayme stared at Morgan as if he'd grown a second head. "He just left us?" she said.

Morgan nodded. "He was nice enough about it, considering he was leaving us here to die," he said.

"You hear that?" she said, shaking her head and glancing over to where Bender stood with his hands in his pockets.

Bender nodded, frowning. "I wish I were surprised," he said. "Let's face it, he wasn't exactly reliable."

Morgan grunted and stood. "There are some supplies on the ship. Let's grab what we can and get going. We have a long walk ahead of us. If any of those wolves survived that fight they'll be hot on our tails."

They gathered supplies and two packs from the ship, loaded them, and headed south, moving at a steady ground-eating pace. At noon they reached a weathered wooden sign that said Grand Canyon, North Rim. They followed the road.

On their second day of walking down the cracked and broken asphalt, they passed out of flat sagebrush-covered terrain and into more rugged, ponderosa pine and quaking aspen-covered land.

"Do you think he was telling the truth?" Bender asked as the three huddled around a small tepee fire that evening.

Morgan just looked at him, an eyebrow quirked.

"About how to get to Encartha? About him being from there, all of it?"

Morgan glanced back at the smaller boy, who looked worried, scared, and exhausted. "He sounded sincere, but—" He shrugged.

"Hard to tell with that guy," Bender concluded.

"Exactly," Nayme agreed, a sad smile turning up the corner of her lips. She had begun to look wan and pale, almost fragile as they traveled. Morgan didn't like it.

"Are you OK?" he asked, unable to contain his curiosity.

She nodded.

"Are you sure?" The corner of Nayme's lip turned up and she nodded, but Morgan was unconvinced.

He sighed and looked out over the small valley. In the distance, a deer ate placidly at the edges of the meadow. He cursed inwardly. If any of them had been able to use their powers, perhaps they could have found a way to hunt.

Without the ability, they were left to forage. His stomach growled. He'd eaten all of his share of the pine nuts that Bender had found as they made their way south. They'd also consumed everything the captain had left in the ship when he took his glider and flew away. If they didn't make it to Encartha soon, they were going to be in trouble.

Morgan glanced at Bender. "We should probably get some sleep."

Bender nodded and forced himself to his feet. He walked across the small distance and crept into a thicket that they found there.

Nayme gave Morgan a supportive smile and slipped into the thicket as well.

They're surprisingly resilient, Morgan thought as he watched the two crawling into the thick brush. *I was wrong about them.* Morgan looked out over the valley and thought of Imogene and the others on the boat. Had they made it to Encartha already? How long had it been since they had been separated? He had no idea. It felt like another lifetime.

He sighed and stood, took one more long look out over the valley, and then crept into the thicket. He lay down next to Nayme, on the opposite side of Bender, his back pressed close to her, hoping the proximity would provide them each some warmth in the cool of the night. He closed his eyes.

The following morning Nayme didn't rise. Bender shook her gently, calling her name. She moaned, and her eyelids fluttered in response. Morgan put his hand on her forehead and found it covered in sweat.

"What's wrong with her?" Bender asked as Morgan shook her gently.

"I don't know. I don't see anything wrong with—" He cut himself off as he noticed an angry red scratch on her arm. He cursed. "Look at this," he said, lifting her limp arm and showing Bender the spot.

"That looks infected," Bender said, staring at the scratch where a thick yellow liquid oozed from the wound.

"What happened? I didn't even know that she was hurt." Morgan thought for a moment. "She looked pale last night," he said.

"I saw her rubbing her arm a few times, but she didn't say anything about it to me. What about you?"

"Nothing," Morgan said. "I even asked her if she was OK."

"What do we do?" Bender asked.

Morgan contemplated the problem. He didn't know how far they were from Encartha, but he knew they couldn't carry her, not more than a very short distance. "We'll have to make her a litter," he decided.

"Will we be able to pull it?" Bender asked, looking skeptical. A distant howl brought Morgan's head up.

"We'll have to," he said nervously. "They're getting closer."

Bender swallowed and nodded. The boys exited the thicket and searched the area, finally finding some long branches that were thick enough to support Nayme's weight. Morgan took his extra shirt out of his bag and tore it into long strips. Bender gave up his as well, and Morgan began lashing the boughs together to form a large triangular shape with remnants of clothing and supple branches across the middle portion.

Morgan looked at it critically. He doubted it would be very

comfortable or that it would last all that long. But it would have to do for now.

They slipped back into the thicket and Morgan gently slid his arms under Nayme's neck and legs. He picked her up and found that she was lighter than he'd expected. He slipped out of the thicket and laid her gently onto the litter, grabbing a thin green bough from a nearby tree and lashing it on the side. Then pulled the bough across Nayme's torso, lashing it on the other side, and repeated the process until she was tied securely in place.

It was difficult work, so Morgan's hands were aching by the time he finished. He pulled experimentally on the branches, and they held. Nodding, he turned to Bender.

"Let's get out of here. We'll each grab a side." He pointed to the poles. "Well, you get the idea."

Nayme's eyes flickered open. "Morgan," she said softly, her voice barely a whisper. He met her green eyes with his own dark brown gaze. "I'm sorry." She gulped trying weakly to raise her head.

"Stay there," he said. "You're too weak to get up. We'll get you the rest of the way."

"I'm sorry about everything," she said, a tear rolling down her face as she looked at him. Gently he reached up and wiped the tear away.

"You'll be OK," he lied. Her condition had deteriorated so quickly that he doubted she had more than a day or two to live if they couldn't get her help.

She snorted. "You're a terrible liar."

"*You're* a terrible quitter," he retorted. She grinned weakly in response, and he gently pulled a stray lock of hair out of her face. Her hand lifted weakly and reached toward him. She laid it against his cheek, and the corners of her mouth lifted.

"You're pretty great," she said.

"I won't let it go to my head."

She closed her eyes, her breaths becoming deep and steady. He took her hand, held it, then placed it gently in her lap.

"Let's go," he said, and the boys double-checked the bindings before hefting the litter to their shoulders. Morgan repositioned, trying to find a place where the rough bark of the litter didn't dig into his shoulder, and they set out.

Dragging the litter over the rough ground was harder work than Morgan had thought it would be. After only a few minutes, his legs burned, and his breaths came in ragged gasps. He looked at Bender. The boy's face was red, his small muscles straining. Morgan felt a warmth in his heart for the boy who faced each challenge without complaint.

They continued forward, step after relentless step as they wound further up the road into a clear mountain valley. A second howl sounded in the distance behind them, much closer than the previous one had been. Morgan cursed and looked back at the deep drag marks the litter left in the soil. He signaled for a stop, and Bender nodded. Gently they laid the litter down. Bender bent down, hands on his knees. His arms and legs were shaking with exertion.

"We can't go on like this," Morgan said between deep breaths. Bender nodded, still bracing himself.

"I'm sorry," Bender said. Tears welled in his eyes as he looked hopelessly back at Morgan.

"It's not your fault," Morgan said. "Take a rest, save your strength. He looked down at Nayme's still form. Her face was serene, but red streaks extended from the wound all the way to her fingers and below her shirt sleeves. She was in trouble. He wondered if the scratch was infected, or if it was poisoned.

If she is poisoned, how long does she have before— Morgan shook the thought away.

"We really need something with wheels," Bender said, frowning. "What I wouldn't give for a working four-wheeler right about now." Morgan tried to smile.

"Why stop there? I vote we get a helicopter!" he said, trying to lighten the mood and earning a small chuckle from Bender.

"What are we going to do?" Bender said, his voice turning somber. Morgan looked at him, reading the exhaustion and fear that hid behind his eyes.

"We're going to have to carry her," Morgan said glumly. "At least try. We know that the medallions interfere with the wolves' ability to track us, but those"—he nodded back toward their tracks left by the litter—"will lead them right to us."

Bender sighed deeply and nodded.

"Even if we don't get too far, we may be able to find somewhere to hide and wait for them to pass."

A long howl, even closer than before, sounded from down the mountain. "They're close, within a few miles," Bender said in a small voice.

"We'd better get going," Morgan said. He moved to the litter and began loosening the branches that held their friend in place. In a few minutes, she was free. "Help me get her on my back," he said.

He knelt next to Nayme and grabbed her arm, using it to pull her to where he could wrap it over his shoulder. He tried to set his feet, and Nayme lolled to the side, nearly falling before he caught her. He looked at Bender, who was trying to help Morgan get her into position.

"I think we're going to need to tie her hands together so that she doesn't slip off," Morgan said. Bender nodded and began untying sections of the litter, adding the pieces of the torn shirts to a pile.

Carefully Morgan selected the broadest sections of fabric and began looping them around Nayme's wrists. He bound them gently but firmly and slid her arms around his neck. Morgan counted to three, and both boys lifted. Morgan gritted his teeth as Nayme slid up onto his shoulders in a fireman's carry.

"Let's go," he said.

They proceeded up the road, walking as far as Morgan could manage, and then stopping to rest. Their progress slowed to a seeming crawl.

"Morgan," Bender said, pointing to a small game trail that ran from the road and into the trees.

Morgan nodded for Bender to follow it, and the boy dashed forward, checking back over his shoulder every few minutes as they wound through the trees toward the south. The trail moved through the trees and away from the road. In the distance, Morgan saw a small building that lay in the clearing next to a sign. He bit his lip aching to read it, were these the outskirts of the park? Another howl echoed in the distance.

"How are they still following us?" Morgan cursed in frustration.

"I don't know," Bender said, defeated.

"Should we hide in there?" Bender said.

Morgan shook his head. "The walls wouldn't stop them. We have to make it to Encartha."

He stared down the trail that wound past the building and over a small hill, then split into two divergent paths. If only they could make the wolves go down one trail while they went down the other. He was tired, too tired. He wouldn't be able to carry Nayme much further. The howl sounded again.

"Morgan," a soft voice said near his ear. He slid Nayme gently to the ground, looking into her eyes as she lay in the path. Her eyes fluttered as he looked at her.

"It's OK," he said gently.

"Leave me," she rasped. "Leave me and save yourselves."

"I'm not going to do that," Morgan said firmly.

"Please," she said, and a tear slid down her cheek. "I don't want to be the reason you're both dead."

Morgan shook his head defiantly. "No," he said firmly. "I'm not leaving you, Nayme."

"Please," she said again. "You're my friends, both of you, and I want you to live." She waved him closer. He moved his face down close to hers. She lifted her head weakly and kissed him gently on the corner of his jaw. Then her eyes fluttered and rolled back, her head slumping to the ground, breaths coming in uneven gasps.

Morgan gulped. The two boys sat in silence, looking at each other, neither able to speak.

"I'm sorry," Bender said, his voice breaking. "She's too heavy for me to—" His voice broke off as he began to sob.

Morgan looked at Bender and saw it, the guilt and shame that the boy felt were written on his face. "It's OK, Bender. Some things are outside of our power to change." He reached out a hand and laid it on the smaller boy's shoulder.

He glanced back at the trail. Two paths, but in the end, it didn't matter. The wolves had pursued them for months across rivers, deserts, and mountains. Even with the medallions meant to mask them from the wolves, the wolves still pursued them, still found them. A sense of certainty filled him, he could not escape the wolves, would not escape them. The monsters were going to kill them all.

His hand found the medallion at his throat. It simply wasn't enough, its masking power was not enough to hide them. Idly he wondered how much it masked from the wolves, how much easier it would be for the wolves to find them without it on. Maybe it would be easier to just take it off and let the wolves find them. Maybe—he gasped.

"I have an idea," he said, pinning Bender with a grin. "It might get rid of the wolves."

The boy blinked at him in confusion, a hesitant smile playing at the corners of his mouth. "How?" he asked.

"For this to work I need you to do something for me."

"What?"

"Just promise me you'll do something for me. I swear it won't cause you any harm."

Bender looked at him suspiciously, furrowing his eyebrows as though he expected a trick.

"Trust me."

"Fine," Bender said hesitantly. "What do I need to do?"

"Good," Morgan said, trying not to let his face betray the sudden pang of regret that had settled into his stomach. "I'll tell you when it's time. Let's keep going."

Bender nodded and helped him to his feet. Together they made their way down the trail crossing through the trees, past a small creek, and over a rise until they got to a fork in the path.

"This way," Morgan said, indicating the path that continued south. The other path diverted to the west, curving slightly as it moved into the distance.

Bender turned and walked down the path taking the fork toward the south. He stopped and helped Morgan as they made their way down a declining section of the trail. Across the path Morgan saw a thick stand of trees with smaller brush grouped around the bottom, creating a natural barrier.

"In there," Morgan said, pointing toward the grouping. Bender nodded, and the two climbed the rise and entered the thicket. Morgan nodded to the center of the small stand of trees, a place where thick grass grew.

"Can you pull out the sticks? I want to lay her there," Morgan said, pointing with extended lips at the area that appeared most comfortable. Bender nodded and began pulling fallen branches out of the way.

When Bender had cleared the area, Morgan slid Nayme from his back and onto the grass. It felt cool and soft under Morgan's hands as he laid her head gently down. When he was done, he sat back breathing deeply and stared at Nayme's limp form.

"What am I supposed to do?" Bender asked.

"Nayme was right, Bender," Morgan said firmly. "We can't escape with her."

"So you just want to leave her here?" Bender said, sounding horrified.

"No," Morgan said gently. "I want you to stay with her. When the wolves have gone, keep going until you get to Encartha. Get help and bring them back for her."

"I don't understand," Bender said in frustration, tears sliding down his cheeks. "What are you going to do?"

"I'm going to lead the wolves away," Morgan said, reaching back and unclasping the necklace that held his medallion. Slowly he curled the chain into his hand and held it out to Bender. The boy took it with shaking fingers.

"They'll kill you!"

"Better one of us than all of us," Morgan said. "Besides alone I may be able to hide, double back, or find a way to get past them."

Bender frowned doubtfully.

"Take care, Bender," he said with an air of finality. "Get Nayme to safety, and if you can't do that, at least get yourself there."

Forcing himself to his feet, Morgan turned and began to run back down the path, leaving his friends huddled in the brush. The wolves had to still be nearly a mile away, based on the volume of the baying noises. He had maybe five minutes to put some distance between himself and his friends before the wolves caught up to him.

He was helping his friends. The thought lifted his spirits, and he ran a bit faster, his head held high. He arrived at the fork and turned down the opposite path from where his friends had turned. How long had he known them now? Two months? Three? It didn't matter. There was no one in the world he felt closer to now than the two friends he'd just left in the trees.

He sprinted into the forest, arms and legs pumping rhythmically, his body doing the work unconsciously. Scattered thoughts swam through his mind; Imogene's shape floating away on a raft in the darkness, the day his father didn't come home, his mother's cancer, Imogene. Nayme's pretty face drifted into his mind, her smile in the moonlight by the river, her fear as she met his eyes on that gray morning after the attack, her face calm and relaxed as she slept under the shadow of a small tree in the desert. He couldn't stop seeing that face.

I'm going to die, and all I can picture is Nayme.

A bugling howl rang out behind him, and he knew the wolves had caught up.

Pushing even the thoughts of Nayme aside, Morgan ran with everything his exhausted body had left. His flight had turned into a purely panic-fueled headlong rush. Neither knowing nor caring where he was going, he drove forward, leaping over a downed tree, and careening down a steep decline, only vaguely aware that if he were to stumble, he would likely break his neck.

Might be preferable to what the wolves will do to me.

A crashing thumping rhythm was growing louder behind him. He glanced over his shoulder. Three dark shapes were momentarily visible at the top of the ridge, bounding after him with supernatural speed. Legs burning, sweat dripping into his eyes, he hurtled forward through thick trees and up a small rise then skidded to a stop just in time to prevent himself from running off the cliff and into open air.

He looked over the cliff edge. It dropped hundreds of feet into the rocky red depths of the Grand Canyon below. Somewhere, perhaps nearby, Encartha stood. There was no time to consider that now. He turned and ran along the edge until a huge hairy form crashed to a stop in front of him, snarling with razor-sharp teeth and cutting off his path.

Morgan's head whipped around as a second dark shape burst from the undergrowth. Red eyes met his dark ones, and his blood chilled. He turned and ran back the way he'd come, snapping jaws sounding behind him. A third figure crashed through the brush in front of him. Morgan was surrounded. He reached for the knife at his belt.

The beast bellowed a half howl, half roar, and charged. It leaped forward, its maw of razor-sharp teeth snapping shut on air as Morgan threw himself to the side and rolled to his feet, trying to create distance between himself and the abomination. The creature bounded after him, raking the air with its claws. He wrenched himself backward, tripping over a stone as the claws swept across the front of his chest. He landed hard on his back, the impact driving out his breath. He forced his rebelling body to roll. There was a loud, dull thump next to his head. Stars exploded before his eyes and he blinked, trying to clear his vision.

Not stars, teeth! His hand came up, driving the knife into the hairy throat just below the monster's jawline. Red eyes bulged, and the creature landed hard on him, pinning him to the ground. It spasmed weakly and lay still.

Morgan tried to move, but the creature's bulk held him firm. Dimly, he was aware of more crashing sounds and a bugling roar. The wolves would have him in a moment. He was going to die. The knowledge of that reality didn't fill him with the panic he would have expected. His mind wandered again, and he saw his mother's face and heard the words she'd spoken moments before succumbing to the cancer that had ravaged her body.

"Morgan," she said, her eyes becoming momentarily lucid after days of a kind of swimming, pain-induced delirium. "I need you to do something for me. Can you do something for me?" He nodded, holding tight to her fingers, not trusting his voice to say the words around the large lump that had formed in his throat.

"You have to—" she cut off, coughing and grimacing in pain.

Tears formed at the corners of Morgan's eyes as he looked down at her.

"Morgan, take care of your sister," her voice rattled as she spoke, making it difficult for him to understand her. He inched closer trying to catch every word. "Take care of your sister. You're all she has. Take care of your sister. Make sure—she's my baby, my little girl."

His mother's hands gripped his and shook violently as she sucked in a pain-ridden breath. "Promise me, Morgan. Promise me," she gasped.

Morgan nodded, tears sliding down his face.

"It's dark, Morgan. I can't see. Promise me."

"I—promise," he choked out. His mother's face seemed to relax, a peaceful expression settling over her.

"Thank you, Morgan," she whispered in a voice so low he could barely hear her. "Thank you, I love bo—."

A sudden shame filled him as he remembered the way his mother had fought for two long years, much longer than the six months her diagnosis had given her. She had been so brave.

Even in her final moments, she had tried to take care of her children. Anger filled him. He heaved against the corpse with all the strength he could muster, and slowly he slipped from under the monster's body. He scrambled to his feet just as another beast hurled itself at him.

Unarmed and gasping, he rolled to the side and came up running, no longer sure which direction was which. Something wrenched his leg to the side, and he fell. Pain exploded from the rent flesh where the wolf's claws had slashed him. A maw full of teeth snapped beside his face, and he fell and rolled. The monster bounded forward. Morgan grabbed a large rock and smashed it into the beast's head with a crunch. It fell, unbalanced by the blow, its feet scrambling over the rock and slashing a rent in the muscle of Morgan's chest. Then it plummeted from the edge toward the canyon below.

He gasped in pain as he rolled to his knees. His anger exploded, an intense rage born of desperation and pain. He breathed in a deep breath all the way to his belly. Fire filled him, settling below his navel as strength surged in his muscles. He reached out with his mind, calling to the sudden force streaming into him, begging for it to fill him, to be part of him. He felt swirling patterns of matter around him, it was everywhere, in the air, in the ground, in the trees, inside of him.

He focused, holding the image of a sword in his mind, willing the power to embrace the thought that filled him, willing the sword to form in his hands. He saw the details in his mind, its handle of wood, ivory, and metal, the gentle curve of the blade, the fine edge, the sharp point. He shoved, driving the power from his gut, down his arm, and into his outstretched hand.

Morgan stared down in wonder as he felt the weight of the sword settle into his hand. It was pocked and imperfect but still strong, sharp, and glowing brilliantly. He met the blood-red eyes of the nightmare charging toward him.

Die bravely. Like Mom did, he thought, steeling himself.

The wolf rushed forward, swinging a clawed arm in a vicious slice. Morgan stepped back with his uninjured foot, whipping his sword upward as he did so.

The wolf let out a bellowing roar of pain and anger as Morgan's sword sheared through the flesh of the arm just below the elbow. A spray of blood splattered Morgan and the rocky ground nearby. The creature swung with the other arm, too fast for Morgan to react, and knocked him sprawling to the ground.

Pain exploded from Morgan's face where it had smashed against the stone. His head swam, and darkness gathered at the edge of his vision. The creature sprung at him, maw gaping wide toward him in an attempt to finish him off.

Morgan rolled to the side, his right arm extending in an arc above him as the roll took him out of the path of the monster's pounce.

The wolf crashed wetly to the ground, its head shorn into two unequal halves that fell wetly to the stone. Morgan groaned and turned over, staring around himself in shock. The wolves were dead.

CHAPTER 24
RACE TO ENCARTHA

Chapter 24: Race to Encartha

Imogene held on tightly as the raft bucked and tossed in the violent currents that passed over and around large boulders submerged in the Grand Canyon's depths. The bluish light of the moon reflected off the walls of the deep canyon and cascaded over the broken stone cliffs. The effect changed the normally red stones into an alien ghost world of purple and violet.

Howls sounded from high cliffs above. At the rim of the canyon, the pack continued their dogged pursuit of the small band of survivors that huddled in the scant protection of the rubber raft as it careened through the canyon.

The skin-walkers were getting closer, gaining on the teens despite the speed of the rushing water beneath their floating salvation. How long had the chase gone on? Imogene could no longer track the time since they had first boarded the rafts on the shore of the Green River in early summer. The pack had pursued them with vigor down the length of the Green and Colorado rivers, never far behind, never relenting, hounding them and their Valkryn guide across hundreds of miles and two states.

But as the chase continued something had changed, the pack's pursuit had become frantic, a feverish pursuit of seemingly impossible energy. Earlier in the chase, the wolves had fallen behind at times or disappeared from view, giving the group hope that they had given up. Now, the chase was almost over. One way or another it would end today.

From the corner of her eye, Imogene could see Aella's silhouetted form bracing herself against the raft. She shifted her own grip on the rope she held. It would not do to fall out of the raft now, not when they were so close to their destination.

The raft reached the edge of another set of rapids.

"Row," Fen's high cracking voice insisted over the rushing roar of the river. "Row, row, row."

Imogene focused, picturing an oar, and the power moved through her to coalesce in the shape of a glowing oar. In the time following the hunt, Imogene had improved her skills at manifesting and could now form an oar with a high degree of consistency.

She drove the oar into the water, moving in time to match the cadence the little gnome shouted. Each successive stroke, she drove the oar deep and pulled with all her strength. Stroke after stroke, the time stretched on, her shoulders and arms burning with effort.

From the corner of her eye, she caught movement near the top of one of the cliffs to the north and west. Another pack of wolves appeared at the edge of the cliff, tiny with distance. There were now wolves on every side of them.

Imogene cursed, pointing and shouting at the others. "They're above us." She pointed to the cliff. "In front and above."

Kenichi's scarred face looked up, his mouth a great 'o.'

Imogene gritted her teeth, seeing the fear on the boy's face. She glared at the wolves, anger and frustration burning in her chest.

Isn't it enough? Haven't we given enough, fought enough, lost enough?

She drove her oar deep into the churning water, pulling hard despite her fatigue toward the rapids straight ahead in a desperate bid to put distance between the raft and the wolves.

The raft tossed and pitched as they careened over the edge of a large drop-off propelled by the force of tens of thousands of cubic feet of water rushing through the gorge. They splashed down, water doused Imogene's face, and she spluttered, wiping the liquid from her eyes with her wrist.

The raft rounded a corner. Ahead Imogene could see the walls of the canyon widening, the path of the river becoming straighter, and the current slowing.

"There," Aella shouted, her hand pointing ahead to where the river widened, becoming a large dark pool. To the north of the river was a small flat, sandy area. Beyond it, a series of steep rises were interspersed between sections of vertical cliffs that rose thousands of feet.

"Pull up there!" Aella shouted. The teens responded without hesitation this time, driving oars into the water in strong synchronized bursts of forward momentum.

Aella was first one out of the boat as it scraped over the small stones and onto the shore. She grabbed the guide rope and hauled the craft further up the gravel. Teens began jumping out of the raft and running up the beach. More howls echoed through the canyon.

"Leave everything! Just run!" Aella roared.

Imogene's eyes darted unconsciously upward, scanning the area for signs of danger even as her feet hit the gravel. She turned and grabbed Kenichi's arm, pulling him stumbling from the raft.

Aella streaked toward the cliff-side, shouting over her shoulder for the teens to follow. Hugo, Kira, and Alexa followed closely behind her, bent over as they ran. Imogene pulled Kenichi's arm around her shoulder, and the two surged forward, matching their strides so that Imogene could bear a portion of Kenichi's weight.

They moved up the embankment, crossing over jagged rocks and weaving up a small path. Kenichi's face was pale; his teeth gritted in concentration. "Keep going," Imogene said, trying to sound calm. "You can do it."

Kenichi didn't respond. He just plowed forward in a limping half-run. Great beads of sweat began running down his face as they climbed the canyon. Imogene did not like how he looked, like a man on his last legs.

It was too much, she realized—the injuries, the lack of time for healing. He needed to rest.

Imogene looked up to where Aella bounded sure-footed as a goat, winding back and forth, following a trail that Imogene could only decipher at very close range. Kenichi winced and stumbled. Imogene caught him, pulling him back up.

"Are you ok?" she said.

He was gasping with effort. "I'm just so tired," he said.

"I know, but we have to keep going. We are so close to Encartha. We can make it." Imogene said it as steadily as she could, hoping that her statement was true.

Trumpeting howls sounded from all around the two teens. Imogene's head swiveled to the side, searching for the source of the sounds, her heart pounding in her chest like a jackhammer. She was carrying a significant portion of Kenichi's weight and her own, and she felt herself tiring. Imogene was stronger now than she had ever been in her life, stronger than anyone she had ever known, but it wasn't enough. She wasn't sure how much longer she could keep this up. She looked up and saw the cliffs towering hundreds of feet above her.

Ahead, a narrow trail materialized seemingly from nowhere as they topped a first rise. She pulled Kenichi beside her onto the thin trail that continued through a narrow gap in the steep, rocky faces until they arrived at a cliff that rose hundreds of feet above them, sheer and jagged. Imogene looked around. Where had the others gone?

"Where are they?" she said, her voice nearing panic. She glanced at Kenichi. His sodden face hung down, and he looked drawn, great drops of sweat dripping from his face. Imogene cursed and looked for any sign of the others, the path, anything that would tell her where to go.

"There it is!"

The trail led steeply upward between two boulders and then switched back up the side of the cliffs in a fashion that had been invisible to Imogene until she was right on top of it.

"Let's go!" she said as she pushed Kenichi between the boulders in front of her. "I'm here if you need me."

Kenichi winced. In too much pain to talk, he limped forward, leaning against the stone wall, bracing himself against it with every step of his injured leg. He stopped. "I can't," he said. "I can't put my weight on it."

Imogene gritted her teeth. The wolves were nearby. She couldn't see them, but she knew they were near. She slipped past him.

"Put your arms around me," she ordered. His arms were shaking as he wrapped them around her. She grabbed a leg in each hand and hoisted him onto her back. She climbed. Imogene did not like the sound of Kenichi's ragged, pain-filled breaths in her ear. She had to get him to Encartha where he could rest and finish his recovery.

They continued their climb up the canyon, coming to a ledge thinner than Imogene's body width. She gulped as she tiptoed toward the ledge, her inside shoulder pressing into the stone. With both arms holding Kenichi, she had no available she could not hold onto the rock. She looked down from the edge of the cliff to the river now far below, a distance of several hundred feet at least. It was a mistake. The sickening feeling of the rope going slack, her body pitching into the void filled her, fear chilling her to the bone. If she slipped, it would mean both of their deaths.

She took a deep, steadying breath. *Don't look down. Don't look down*, she told herself. *Just focus on the path and take one step at a time.*

Imogene slid a trembling foot onto the ledge, her shoulder against the wall. She couldn't shake the feeling that the stone was pushing back against her, driving her away from safety and toward the open air, waiting for her just inches beyond the edge of her shoe. Agonizingly, she shuffled forward, sliding first her left foot a few inches, and then repeating the move with her right. Seconds passed like hours. A slight gust of wind brushed across her. It felt like a tornado bent on pulling them from their perch and into the gorge below.

Finally, her foot landed on a wider section of the path, and she stepped onto a broad flat area where several large, mostly flat stones leaned against the vertical surface of the cliff. It was like a stone city bus stop, complete with a bench stuck to the side of the mountain.

Breathing hard, Imogene sat Kenichi down and slumped next to him, her face dripping with a cold sweat born of fear, and her muscles trembled with fatigue. She looked toward the river. It seemed like hours had passed since they had beached the rafts. The canyon had gone eerily silent but for a stiff breeze that whistled through the rocks of the canyon.

"Imogene," Kenichi said, his voice serious. She looked at the boy. His face was pale and drawn, his voice stoic and regretful. "You have to leave me here. You can't do it anymore." He met her eyes, his gaze firm. "I can go no further."

"It's OK. We can take a rest. We have a few minutes. I know that part was hard."

"No," he said firmly, "I'm done Imogene, I have nothing left, and you won't make it carrying me. It's just too far. I've come as far as I can—I don't say this lightly. I've been a martial artist for years, I know my body's limits, and I can recognize those same limits in others. You can spend no more energy on me, not if you are to make it to the top."

"Don't—" Imogene began, but Kenichi cut in again, this time more forcefully.

"Immy, I'm out of gas." He said wistfully as a tear glided over his dirty cheek. He reached up with a trembling hand to wipe it. "I want you to go," he continued, his voice firming.

"I can't just leave you here. What about the skin-walkers? They could be just behind us."

He put his hand gently on her shoulder and squeezed it softly. "Yes, you can. You can, and you must. I can't go on, but you can still make it. If the werewolves come, I'll make sure they're not what takes me." His face was grim, and the image of him leaping from the cliff side popped unbidden into her mind. She pushed the thought away.

Imogene stared into his sad eyes, her mind racing frantically. She knew he was right—she couldn't carry him all the way to the top despite her increased strength. He was bigger than her, and she was exhausted.

"Thanks, Immy," he said weakly as he grabbed her hand. "You're a good person, and so was your brother." His voice broke with emotion as he said the words. Imogene's throat constricted at the mention of Morgan. "I wish I could have spent more time with you. With both of you," he finished and squeezed her hand.

"You will," she said firmly. "I'm not leaving you, Kenichi! We're going to make it. Both of us!"

"Im—" he began, but she cut him off.

"And if we don't," she said, "then we'll fail together. Either way we'll face it as a team."

"Immy—." He shook his head and leaned it back against the stone, closing his eyes as more tears ran down his face. Imogene pulled firmly on the hand that she held, and Kenichi stumbled to his feet. She drew his arm over her shoulder, holding him against her body to provide him with support.

"We can do this, Kenichi! Let's go!"

They pressed on, moving up the mountain slowly but determinedly. Their fates would depend on whether they could reach safety before the skin-walkers overtook them.

They crested a rise and entered an area of loose rocks and dirt that rose several hundred more feet before ending in another layer of sheer stone. At the top of the cliff, Imogene could make out man-made formations: a vertical wall of stone blocks with rooflines, parapets, and towers rising above it. Another section of cliff rose above the wall where a checkerboard pattern of windows and balconies carved from solid rock looked out on the canyon below.

"Look!" She nudged Kenichi, who stood with slumped shoulders, head hanging down with fatigue. Slowly, he raised his head to look where she pointed, and his eyes widened.

"Wow!" he said. "It's bigger than I realized." The city covered the entire mesa. Imogene looked to her right and saw a second mesa. It was likewise covered with a host of tight, oddly arranged structures.

A small dirt trail wound before them, and they picked their

way forward around the sharp rocks, moving as quickly as they could manage.

Imogene rounded the edge of an incline and there, in the distance across from her, she could see the others toiling, crossing through a boulder field, with Aella in the lead. Relief washed over her at the sight of the others. They weren't as far behind as she had feared.

Sweating, and exhausted, they clambered over a large rock near the top of the rise. Aella, Alexa, Kira, and Hugo had reached the edge of the sheer red cliffs and were moving toward a spot where the cliff sides came together in a deep v.

Deafening howls sounded from both sides of her, and Imogene's eyes caught movement at the edge of her vision. Dozens of wolves came bounding from behind boulders, charging with inhuman grace and violence toward Aella and her remaining charges.

Imogene screamed involuntarily as the wolves darted between Imogene and Kenichi on one side of the area, and Aella's group on the other.

Time slowed into a slow-motion horror scene as the wolves moved to cut them off. In a flash, Imogene knew it was hopeless. The wolves were too close, and she and Kenichi were too tired to outrun them.

She stared in despair.

In the distance, Aella spun into action, her familiar glowing sword sweeping out in violent arcs that drove the wolves back. She was shouting something Imogene couldn't understand while Hugo and the others got behind her and began climbing up the cliff. On some unseen path, they seemed to float upwards as Aella stood at the mouth of the small chasm, acting as a human shield while the teens ascended.

How long can she hold them off? Imogene wondered, standing still, her heartbeats pounding in her skull as she waited for the wolves to discover her. A huge, muzzled face turned and looked directly at Imogene. She took an unconscious step back. The beast growled and turned to charge her.

Frantically she pushed Kenichi behind her and drew, pulling in the power around her and manifesting the spear she'd used on the elk. A small part of her mind noticed that its form was better, with fewer seams and less pitting. She held it out in front of herself, putting the point between her body and the onrushing wolves, setting her feet in a defensive stance. More wolves peeled off from the fight with Aella and turned on Imogene — soon one had become six.

What chance do we have against them? She knew the answer: none. The wolves would kill them both, but maybe, just maybe, she could take some of them with her. At least she could die fighting and not whimpering like some child. *You can do that much*, she told herself.

She bent her knees in preparation, focused, calculating her attack, knowing she'd likely get only one.

One. I can kill one if I time the blow properly.

Time seemed to creep as she waited, the monsters speeding across the distance. Imogene's ears took on a strange humming ring. Fifty feet, thirty feet, twenty, ten, a wolf leapt for her. She crouched and sprung forward and upward with all her strength. Her spear whistled through the air in a sweeping vertical arc that drove the tipped blade through the beast's open lower jaw, between its yellow eyes, and out the top of its head.

Imogene's leap carried her clear of the falling body, her hand wrenching the spear free of the corpse. Her eyes caught more dark shapes swarming in from behind and to the side of her as she crashed towards the ground. She had no time to look and see if Kenichi still stood.

Her eyes focused on the next wolf as it approached from

her left. She spun and swung her spear, and its sharp tip caught the wolf full in the face. The wolf's momentum crashed against the spear shaft, spinning her, and she fell. She landed hard, and her concentration was broken. The spear turned to mist.

Imogene rolled and came up on one knee, her mind half expecting the bite that would end her to snap down. Instead, she froze as she took in a scene that her mind couldn't process. Dozens of dark shapes were moving around her, where before there had been a handful. There were werewolves, tall and furred with sharp snapping teeth, but intermingled with them were other shapes, lighter and angular, like giant knights clad in a style of armor that she didn't recognize.

She stared as the groups swarmed each other, tooth and claw meeting metal-covered fists, swords, and maces.

Hope bloomed in her chest, and she gathered herself, reforming her spear and diving to avoid a slashing, clawed arm. Imogene grunted as pain exploded in a burning arc across her back. She rolled and came to her feet, spear whipping out and taking a wolf in the thigh, then reversing across the chest of the monster. Blood sprayed onto her face, and the monster toppled backward.

Imogene spun, leveling her spear as another monster bounded forward to swing a heavy, clawed arm at her face. She tried to get her spear up in front of her to block, but it was too late, the beast's heavy limb smashed into her face, knocking her sprawling.

She landed with a heavy thump, and the breath exploded out of her, leaving her gasping and aching on the stones. The spear puffed and disappeared in a cloud of smoke once again. A dark shape rose above her, but she could not make it out. Her vision was dark, cloudy, and unfocused. A clawed hand drew back and slashed toward her. Blackness filled her vision, and all went still.

EPILOGUE - ENCARTHA

Morgan breathed deeply, smelling the scents of pine and his own sweat.

"How far do you think it is?" Bender said, looking up at him as they traipsed through the trees.

"I don't even know if it's here for sure," Morgan said, pausing momentarily to adjust Nayme's weight. He'd been carrying her for the last couple of miles, and yet he felt less tired than he had before the fight with the wolves.

"It has to be somewhere around here." Bender gestured widely. "I mean, this is the Grand Canyon, right?"

"The canyon is huge, Bender. The size of some of the eastern states I bet. We're going to be lucky if we find it at all."

The canyon lay before them, a sweeping vista of towering cliffs and plunging canyons of red rock. They followed the cliff edge westward. They'd agreed that it was the most likely direction since the signs had pointed that way when they'd been fleeing the wolves.

They rounded a bend, and on a mesa separated from the north side of the canyon by a wide open area stood a city of thin spires, rock walls, and flapping pennants. A thin, golden, shimmering bridge spanned from a narrow protrusion of rock at the north rim to the northernmost point of the mesa.

"Stop right there," a deep voice commanded in an accent that Morgan didn't recognize.

Morgan looked up to see a row of men emerging from the trees nearby. The leader was tall, with a lean, muscular build. He wore a light gray long-sleeved shirt that clung to his muscular physique and had a loose hood that obscured his face and draped over his shoulders to hang halfway down his chest. A thick leather belt circled his waist above loose leggings and knee-high boots. A thin rectangle of rich green fabric hung from the belt, set with an intricate group of patterns, and depicted an elaborate bear embroidered in silvery thread.

Morgan stared at the man and his companions, who wore a similar pattern of dress. They carried no weapons.

"What do you want in the canyon?" The tall leader asked, pulling back his hood to reveal a chiseled face and long black hair pulled back into several braids. His green eyes stared fiercely at Morgan and his companions.

Morgan cleared his throat. "I uh," he looked at Bender for support, but the boy just shrugged.

"We are heading to a place called Encartha," he said.

The stern man nodded. "What business do you have in our city?" he said.

"One of your finders came for us," Morgan continued.

The man's eyebrows came together, his expression skeptical. "Who?"

"Her name was Aella," Morgan said.

"Aella Massika?"

"I don't know her full name. She just said her name was Aella. She traveled with a gnome named Fen."

The man's posture relaxed, and he nodded. "That's her," he said. "What are your names?"

"I'm Morgan. This is Bender," he said, nodding at the boy, "The one on my back is called Nayme."

The man nodded. "Well, Morgan, welcome to Encartha."

* * *

A hulking figure strode up beside Imogene where she stood looking out over the twin bright blues of the sky above and the ocean below. A salty breeze flung her hair back, whipping it out momentarily like the flag of one of the dead nations.

"How are you feeling?" Exzel said in his deep rumbling voice. He put a meaty hand on the railing and glanced down at her from where he towered like a full-grown man beside a child. Even without his segmented black armor, he was a Titan, huge and muscular, his movements lithe and dangerous, like a panther ready to pounce on unsuspecting prey.

Imogene shrugged.

"Kenichi is looking much better. You were right—he just needed time to heal."

Imogene kept her face forward, staring into the distance as the water rushed below her. She said nothing.

"I know you're upset," the big man said, "but I promise that you will be safe."

"I don't want to be safe!" she screamed, her temper breaking as she turned on the big man, her fists clenching. "I want to be let go! I'm sick of being told where to go and what to do!"

The big man held up his thick arms in a conciliatory gesture. "I know," he said, his voice calm, appeasing. "I wish I could let you, but as I've told you, I'm under orders."

"From a country, hell a continent, that doesn't even exist!" Imogene railed, unable to control her outbursts after two weeks confined to the small space of the ship, on a journey she didn't want, to a place she'd never heard of.

"Atlantea exists," the big man said, his tone kind. "In fact, we should be there soon." He stared out over the water as they continued eastward into the morning sun.

"Well, that's not what my geography teacher would have said," Imogene insisted. "Atlantea wasn't on Google Maps or any satellite imaging that I ever saw."

The big man grinned, his white teeth standing out in stark contrast to his dark skin. "We had an arrangement with the government."

"Which government?"

"Pick one. We had agreements with all of them."

"And just what did that agreement consist of?" Imogene said, crossing her arms and kicking a leg out to the side.

"It was simple: they didn't reveal our existence, and we didn't kill them," Exzel laughed.

Imogene shook her head and turned to look out over the bow, she'd never been on a ship at sea before. So far as she knew, no one had been on a ship like this, however. It floated over the water, suspended in the air on a water foil of a type she'd never seen. But that wasn't what really made it strange.

"Take a seat," Exzel said. "It's your turn."

Imogene grimaced. "I hate how it makes me feel."

"You'll get used to it. Anyway, we all take our turn," Exzel said, nodding to the row of large captain chairs that lined the stern edge of the deck. They were black and made of a substance that Exzel called Artionium. It felt like leather, but according to Exzel, was resistant to heat, sun, or rain. The chair had comfortable armrests that were cupped on both sides, allowing the sitter to slip their arms inside it. In the end, the person sat their hands on glittering metallic balls. Imogene glared at them.

"Come on now," Exzel said. "We all pull our weight."

Imogene glared at him and took a deep breath before walking over to the seat and settling into it. She flexed her hands, hesitating before resting her hands on the spheres. She shivered as the gossamer fibers slid out of the metallic sphere and began burrowing into her skin. The process wasn't painful, but it made Imogene's skin crawl.

She sat in silence, trying to keep her focus from what was happening to her in the chair. On the horizon, a silvery white point appeared in the distance. She watched in fascination as it grew larger, turning into an island with pale sandy beaches and strange trees she didn't recognize. A glimmering white city sat on top of it, blood-red banners flapping from ancient battlements. She gasped. It was beautiful.

"Told you you'd like it," Exzel said, grinning widely. "Welcome to Atlantea."

Under an Evil Moon

Copyright © 2026 by Twisted Vale, LLC

All rights reserved.

No part of this book may be reproduced, distributed, or transmitted in any form or by any means—electronic, mechanical, photocopying, recording, or otherwise—without prior written permission of the publisher, except for brief quotations used in reviews or critical articles.

This is a work of fiction. While certain real locations, landmarks, and geographic details are used to provide atmosphere and realism, the events, characters, and interpretations presented are entirely the author's imagination. Any resemblance to actual persons, living or dead, is purely coincidental.

The world of *Under an Evil Moon* exists beyond the light of reason—where truth, myth, and madness often share the same shadow.

For information or permissions, contact:

Twisted Vale, LLC

Email: josh@twistedvale.co

Printed in the United States of America

ISBN: 979-8-9938983-1-5

 Formatted with Vellum

www.ingramcontent.com/pod-product-compliance
Lightning Source LLC
LaVergne TN
LVHW091710070526
838199LV00050B/2340